Praise for The

The Fa

"Charles Stross's *The Family Trade* is an inventive, irreverent, and delightful romp into an alternate world where business is simultaneously low- and high-tech, and where romance, murder, marriage, and business are hopelessly intertwined—and deadly."
—L. E. Modesitt, Jr.

"Quirky, original, and entertaining. *The Family Trade* could be *The Godfather* of all fantasy novels."
—Kevin J. Anderson, *New York Times* bestselling author

"*The Family Trade* is one of those rare delights—a book that is fun, intelligently written, and which leaves a reader breathlessly wondering what will happen next. Readers beware: Stross weaves a tale that continually builds to an engrossing climax. Once you get into this, you'll find yourself hooked."
—David Farland

"Stross not only creates an alternate world that is fascinating and original, he even does the unheard of, for a fantasist: His depiction of our world is deep and real. His characters behave in ways that make sense. They know all the things they should know, and don't know the things they shouldn't. The result is that we readers can trust this author completely, dive into this story, and let it carry us wherever the current flows.

"Not to mention the fact that it's simply a great adventure, full of danger, of plots within plots, of forbidden love and political murder."
—Orson Scott Card

The Hidden Family

"*The Hidden Family* is a festival of ideas in action, fast moving and often very funny, but underpinned by a rigorous logical strategy. . . . Stross's breezy, almost-Heinleinian mode of narration is on fine display."
—*Locus*

"Miriam Beckstein, aka Countess Helge Thorold-Hjorth of the Clan, finds her own world to conquer in this fast-moving sequel to *The Family Trade*. . . . Stross continues to mix high- and low-tech in amusing and surprising ways. . . . [He] weaves a tale worthy of Robert Ludlum or Dan Brown."
—*Publishers Weekly*

"Writer Charles Stross, whose books burst with pop-science ideas, intrigue, strong characters, and even romance, continues his Merchant Princes series. . . . Stross is an energetic writer who creates page-turning reads. . . . Readers will be relieved to learn that there is a lot to look forward to in *The Hidden Family*, including a finale that is all Gothic romance: regrets, a ball, and a happy reunion." —*BookPage*

"These days, finding a science fiction or fantasy novel that *doesn't* feature a kick-ass babe who is either cybernetically enhanced, a martial arts master, or a trained ninja killer (or all three) can be hard work. The genres don't lack for Buffyesque role models. But there's something different about Miriam, the heroine of Charles Stross's fantasy series The Merchant Princes. . . . It is a tribute to the budding powers of Stross, who works successfully in both the science fiction and fantasy genres, that he pulls off this feat in a fashion both amusing and gripping. . . . Miriam is a terrific character, turning the tables on all who would attempt to manipulate her, and setting in motion events that promise to transform the evolution of no less than three separate worlds. For those of us who actually are journalists working on deadline, Stross gives us an escape fantasy that is most seductive, indeed." —*Salon*

"Stross effectively keeps all the plates spinning that he launched into motion in the first volume of this series. . . . Stross is having great fun with these books, and it's contagious." —*SciFi.com*

The Clan Corporate

"Stross and his feisty heroine are currently about the best practitioner and heroine the old motif boasts, and many are and will be the readers hoping for more than the three volumes they've given us so far." —*Booklist*

"Stross is a cunning writer." —*Locus* on *The Clan Corporate*

"*The Clan Corporate* offers more proof, if any were needed, why Charles Stross has become universally acknowledged as one of science fiction's major new talents." —Mike Resnick

THE CLAN
CORPORATE

TOR BOOKS BY CHARLES STROSS

*Forthcoming

THE CLAN CORPORATE

BOOK THREE OF THE MERCHANT PRINCES

CHARLES STROSS

TOR®
fantasy

A TOM DOHERTY ASSOCIATES BOOK
NEW YORK

This is a work of fiction. All the characters, organizations, and events portrayed in this novel are either products of the author's imagination or are used fictitiously.

THE CLAN CORPORATE: BOOK THREE OF THE MERCHANT PRINCES

Copyright © 2006 by Charles Stross

All rights reserved.

Edited by David G. Hartwell

A Tor Book
Published by Tom Doherty Associates, LLC
175 Fifth Avenue
New York, NY 10010

www.tor-forge.com

Tor® is a registered trademark of Tom Doherty Associates, LLC.

ISBN 978-0-7653-4822-7

First Edition: May 2006
First Mass Market Edition: September 2007

Printed in the United States of America

0 9 8 7 6 5 4 3 2

For Andrew, Lorna, and James

acknowledgments

Thanks are due James Nicoll, Robert "Nojay" Sneddon, Cory Doctorow, Andrew Wilson, Caitlin Blasdell, Tom Doherty, and my editors, David Hartwell and Moshe Feder.

1

TIED DOWN

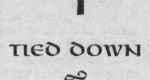

Nail lacquer, the woman called Helge reflected as she paused in the antechamber, always did two things to her: it reminded her of her mother, and it made her feel like a rebellious little girl. She examined the fingertips of her left hand, turning them this way and that in search of minute imperfections in the early afternoon sunlight slanting through the huge window behind her. There weren't any. The maidservant who had painted them for her had poor nails, cracked and brittle from hard work: her own, in contrast, were pearlescent and glossy, and about a quarter-inch longer than she was comfortable with. There seemed to be a lot of things that she was uncomfortable with these days. She sighed quietly and glanced at the door.

The door opened at that moment. Was it coincidence, or was she being watched? Liveried footmen inclined their heads as another spoke. "Milady, the duchess bids you enter. She is waiting in the day room."

Helge swept past them with a brief nod—more ac-

knowledgment of their presence than most of her rank
would bother with—and paused to glance back down the
hallway as her servants (a lady-in-waiting, a court butler,
and two hard-faced, impassive bodyguards) followed her.
"Wait in the hall," she told the guards. "*You* can accompany
me, but wait at the far end of the room," she told her attendant ingénue. Lady Kara nodded meekly. She'd been slow to
learn that Helge bore an uncommon dislike for having her
conversations eavesdropped on: there had been an unfortunate incident some weeks ago, and the lady-in-waiting had
not yet recovered her self-esteem.

The hall was perhaps sixty feet long and wide enough for
a royal entourage. The walls, paneled in imported oak, were
occupied by window bays interspersed with oil paintings
and a few more-recent daguerreotypes of noble ancestors,
the scoundrels and skeletons cluttering up the family tree.
Uniformed servants waited beside each door. Helge paced
across the rough marble tiles, her spine rigid and her shoulders set defensively. At the end of the hall an equerry wearing the polished half-armor and crimson breeches of his
calling bowed, then pulled the tasseled bell-pull beside the
double doors. "The Countess Helge voh Thorold d'Hjorth!"

The doors opened, ushering Countess Helge inside, leaving servants and guards to cool their heels at the threshold.

The day room was built to classical proportions—but
built large, in every dimension. Four windows, each twelve
feet high, dominated the south wall, overlooking the regi-
mented lushness of the gardens that surrounded the palace.
The ornate plasterwork of the ceiling must have occupied a
master and his journeymen for a year. The scale of the architecture dwarfed the merely human furniture, so that the
chaise longue the duchess reclined on, and the spindly ro-
coco chair beside it, seemed like the discarded toy furniture
of a baby giantess. The duchess herself looked improbably
fragile: gray hair growing out in intricately coiffed coils,
face powdered to the complexion of a china doll, her body
lost in a court gown of black lace over burgundy velvet. But
her eyes were bright and alert—and knowing.

Helge paused before the duchess. With a little moue of

concentration she essayed a curtsey. "Your grace, I are—am—happy to see you," she said haltingly in hochsprache. "I—I—oh *damn*." The latter words slipped out in her native tongue. She straightened her knees and sighed. "Well? How am I doing?"

"Hmm." The duchess examined her minutely from head to foot, then nodded slightly. "You're getting better. Well enough to pass tonight. Have a seat." She gestured at the chair beside her.

Miriam sat down. "As long as nobody asks me to dance," she said ruefully. "I've got two left feet, it seems." She plucked at her lap. "And as long as I don't end up being cornered by a drunken backwoods peer who thinks not being fluent in his language is a sign of an imbecile. And as long as I don't accidentally mistake some long-lost third cousin seven times removed for the hat-check clerk and resurrect a two-hundred-year-old blood feud. And as long as—"

"Dear," the duchess said quietly, "do please shut up."

The countess, who had grown up as Miriam but whom everyone around her but the duchess habitually called Helge, stopped in mid-flow. "Yes, Mother," she said meekly. Folding her hands in her lap she breathed out. Then she raised one eyebrow.

The duchess looked at her for almost a minute, then nodded minutely. "You'll pass," she said. "With the jewelry, of course. And the posh frock. As long as you don't let your mouth run away with you." Her cheek twitched. "As long as you remember to be Helge, not Miriam."

"I feel like I'm acting all the time!" Miriam protested.

"Of course you do." The duchess finally smiled. "Imposter syndrome goes with the territory." The smile faded. "And I didn't do you any favors in the long run by hiding you from all this." She gestured around the room. "It becomes harder to adapt, the older you get."

"Oh, I don't know." Miriam frowned momentarily. "I can deal with disguises and a new name and background; I can even cope with trying to learn a new language, it's the sense of permanence that's disconcerting. *I* grew up an only child, but *Helge* has all these—relatives—I didn't grow up with, and they're real. That's hard to cope with. And *you're* here, and part of it!" Her frown returned. "And now this evening's junket. If I thought I could avoid it, I'd be in my rooms having a stomach cramp all afternoon."

"That would be a Bad Idea." The duchess still had the habit of capitalizing her speech when she was waxing sarcastic, Miriam noted.

"Yes, I know that. I'm just—there are things I should be doing that are more important than attending a royal garden party. It's all deeply tedious."

"With an attitude like that you'll go far." Her mother paused. "All the way to the scaffold if you don't watch your lip, at least in public. Do I need to explain how sensitive to social niceties your position here is? This is not America—"

"Yes, well, more's the pity." Miriam shrugged minutely.

"Well, we're stuck with the way things are," the duchess said sharply, then subsided slightly. "I'm sorry, dear, I don't mean to snap. I'm just worried for you. The sooner you learn how to mind yourself without mortally offending anyone by accident the happier I'll be."

"Um." Miriam chewed on the idea for a while. *She's stressed*, she decided. *Is that all it is, or is there something more?* "Well, I'll *try*. But I came here to see how you are, not to have a moan on your shoulder. So, how are you?"

"Well, now that you ask . . ." Her mother smiled and waved vaguely at a table behind her chaise longue. Miriam followed her gesture: two aluminium crutches, starkly functional, lay atop a cloisonné stand next to a pill case. "The doctor says I'm to reduce the prednisone again next week. The Copaxone seems to be helping a lot, and that's just one injection a day. As long as nobody accidentally forgets to bring me next week's prescription I'll be fine."

"But surely nobody would—" Miriam's whole body quivered with anger.

"Really?" The duchess glanced back at her daughter, her expression unreadable. "You seem to have forgotten what kind of a place this is. The meds aren't simply costly in dollars and cents: someone has to bring them across from the other world. And courier time is priceless. Nobody gives me a neatly itemized bill, but if I want to keep on receiving them I have to pay. And the first rule of business around here is, Don't piss off the blackmailers."

Miriam's reluctant nod seemed to satisfy the duchess, because she nodded: "Remember, a lady never unintentionally gives offense—especially to people she depends on to keep her alive. If you can hang on to just one rule to help you survive in the Clan, make it that one. But I'm losing the plot. How are *you* doing? Have there been any aftereffects?"

"Aftereffects?" Miriam caught her hand at her chin and forced herself to stop fidgeting. She flushed, pulse jerking with an adrenaline surge of remembered fear and anger. "I—" She lowered her hand. "Oh, nothing *physical*," she said bitterly. "Nothing . . ."

"I've been thinking about him a lot lately, Miriam. He wouldn't have been good for you, you know."

"I know." The younger woman—youth being relative: she wouldn't be seeing thirty again—dropped her gaze. "The political entanglements made it a messy prospect at best," she said, frowning. "Even if you discounted his weaknesses." The duchess didn't reply. Eventually Miriam looked up, her eyes burning with emotions she'd experienced only since learning to be Helge. "I haven't forgiven him, you know."

"Forgiven *Roland*?" The duchess's tone sharpened.

"No. Your goddamn half-brother. He's meant to be in charge of security! But he—" Her voice began to break.

"Yes, yes, I know. And do you think he has been sleeping well lately? I'm led to believe he's frantically busy right now. Losing Roland was the least of our problems, if you'll permit me to be blunt, and Angbard has a major crisis to deal with. Your affair with him can be ignored, if it comes to it, by the Council. It's not as if you're a teenage virgin to be despoiled, damaging some aristocratic alliance by losing your honor—and you'd better think about that some more in future, because honor is *the* currency in the circles you move in, a currency that once spent is very hard to regain—but the deeper damage to the Clan that Matthias inflicted—"

"Tell me about it," Miriam said bitterly. "As soon as I was

back on my feet they told me I could only run courier assignments to and from a safe house. And I'm not allowed to go home!"

"Matthias knows you," her mother pointed out. "If he mentioned you to his new employers—"

"I understand." Miriam subsided in a sullen silence, arms crossed before her and back set defensively. After a moment she started tapping her toes.

"Stop that!" Moderating her tone, the duchess added, "If you do that in public it sends entirely the wrong message. Appearances are everything, you've *got* to learn that."

"Yes, Mother."

After a couple of minutes, the duchess spoke. "You're not happy."

"No."

"And it's not just—him."

"Correct." Her hem twitched once more before Helge managed to control the urge to tap.

The duchess sighed. "Do I have to drag it out of you?"

"No, Iris."

"You shouldn't call me that here. Bad habits of thought and behavior, you know."

"Bad? Or just inappropriate? Liable to *send the wrong message*?"

The duchess chuckled. "I should know better than to argue with you, dear!" She looked serious. "The wrong message in a nutshell. *Miriam can't go home, Helge.* Not now, maybe not ever. Thanks to that scum-sucking rat-bastard defector the entire Clan network in Massachusetts is blown wide open and if you even *think* about going—"

"Yeah, yeah, I know, there'll be an FBI SWAT team staking out my backyard and I'll vanish into a supermax prison so fast my feet don't touch the ground. If I'm lucky," she added bitterly. "So everything's locked down like a code-red terrorist alert; the only way I'm allowed to go back to our world is on a closely supervised courier run to an underground railway station buried so deep I don't even see daylight; if I want anything—even a box of tampons—I have to *requisition* it and someone in the Security Directorate has to fill out a risk assessment to see if it's safe to obtain; and, and . . ." Her shoulders heaved with indignation.

"This is what it was like the whole time, during the civil war," the duchess pointed out.

"So people keep telling me, as if I'm supposed to be grateful! But it's not as if this is my *only* option. I've got another identity over in world three and—"

"Do they have tampons there?"

"Ah." Helge paused for a moment. "No, I don't think so," she said slowly. "But they've got cotton wool." She fumbled for a moment, then pulled out a pen-sized voice recorder. "Memo: business plans. Investigate early patent filings covering tampons and applicators. Also sterilization methods— dry heat?" She clicked the recorder off and replaced it. "Thanks." A lightning smile that was purely Miriam flashed across her face and was gone. "I should be over there," she added earnestly. "World three is my project. I set up the company and I ought to be managing it."

"Firstly, our dear long-lost relatives are over there," the duchess pointed out. "Truce or not, if they haven't got the message yet, you could show your nose over there and get it chopped off. And secondly . . ."

"Ah, yes. Secondly."

"You know what I'm going to say," the duchess said quietly. "So please don't shoot the messenger."

"Okay." Helge turned her head to stare moodily out of the nearest window. "You're going to tell me that the political situation is messy. That if I go over there right now some of the more jumpy first citizens of the Clan will get the idea that I'm abandoning the sinking ship, aided and abetted by my *delightful* grandmother's whispering campaign—"

"Leave the rudeness to me. She's my cross to bear."

"Yes, but." Helge stopped.

Her mother took a deep breath. "The Clan, for all its failings, is a very democratic organization. *Democratic* in the original sense of the word. If enough of the elite voters agree, they can depose the leadership, indict a member of the Clan for trial by a jury of their peers—anything. Which is why appearances, manners, and social standing are so important. Hypocrisy is the grease that lubricates the Clan's machinery." Her cheek twitched. "Oh yes. While I remember, love, if you are accused of anything never, *ever*, insist on your right to a trial by jury. Over here, that word does not mean what you think it means. Like the word *secretary*. Pah, but I'm woolgathering! Anyway. My mother, your grandmother, has a constituency, Miri—Helge. Tarnation. Swear at me if I slip again, will you, dear? We need to break each other of this habit."

Helge nodded. "Yes, Iris."

The duchess reached over and swatted her lightly on the arm. "Patricia! Say my full name."

"Ah." Helge met her gaze. "All right. Your grace is the honorable Duchess Patricia voh Hjorth d'Wu ab Thorold." With mild rebellion: "Also known as Iris Beckstein, of 34 Coffin Street—"

"That's enough!" Her mother nodded sharply. "Put the rest behind you for the time being. Until—unless—we can ever go back, the memories can do nothing but hurt you. You've got to live in the present. And the present means living among the Clan and deporting yourself as a, a countess. Because if you don't do that, all the alternatives on offer are drastically worse. This isn't a rich world, like America. Most women only have one thing to trade: as a lady of the Clan you're lucky enough to have two, even three if you count the contents of your head. But if you throw away the money and the power that goes with being of the Clan, you'll rapidly find out just what's under the surface—if you survive long enough."

"But there's no limit to the amount of shit!" the younger woman burst out, then clapped a hand to her face as if to recall the unladylike expostulation.

"Don't chew your nails, dear," her mother said automatically.

It had started in mid-morning. Miriam (who still found it an effort of will to think of herself as Helge, outside of social situations where other people expected her to *be* Helge) was tired and irritable, dosed up on ibuprofen and propranolol to deal with the effects of a series of courier runs the day before when, wearing jeans and a lined waterproof jacket heavy enough to survive a northeast passage, she'd wheezed under the weight of a backpack and a walking frame. They'd had her ferrying fifty-kilogram loads between a gloomy cellar of undressed stone and an equally gloomy subbasement of an underground car park in Manhattan. There were armed guards in New York to protect her while she recovered from the vicious migraine that world-walking brought on, and there were servants and maids in the palace quarters back home to pamper her and feed her sweetmeats from a cold buffet and apply a cool compress for her head. But the whole objective of all this attention was to soften her up until she could be cozened into making another run. *Two* return trips in eighteen hours. Drugs or no drugs, it was brutal: without guards and flunkies and servants to prod her along she might have refused to do her duty.

She'd carried a hundred kilograms in each direction across the space between two worlds, a gap narrower than atoms and colder than light-years. Lightning Child only knew what had been in those packages. The Clan's mercantilist operations in the United States emphasized high-value, low-weight commodities. Like it or not, there was more money in smuggling contraband than works of art or intellectual property. It was a perpetual sore on Miriam's conscience, one that only stopped chafing when for a few hours she managed to stop being Miriam Beckstein, journalist, and to be instead Helge of Thorold by Hjorth, Countess. What made it even worse for Miriam was that she was acutely aware that such a business model was stupid and unsustainable. Once, mere weeks ago, she'd had plans to upset the metaphorical applecart, designs to replace it with a fleet of milk tankers. But then Matthias, secretary to the Duke Angbard, captain-general of the Clan's Security Directorate, had upset the applecart first, and set fire to it into the bargain. He'd defected to the Drug Enforcement Agency of the United States of America. And whether or not he'd held his peace about the real nature of the Clan, a dynasty of world-

walking spooks from a place where the river of history had
run a radically different course, he had sure as hell shut
down their eastern seaboard operations.

Matthias had blown more safe houses and shipping networks in one month than the Clan had lost in all the previous
thirty years. His psycho bagman had shot and killed
Miriam's lover during an attempt to cover up the defection
by destroying a major Clan fortress. Then, a month later,
Clan security had ordered Miriam back to Niejwein from
New Britain, warning that Matthias's allies in that timeline
made it too unsafe for her to stay there. Miriam thought this
was bullshit: but bullshit delivered by men with automatic
weapons was bullshit best nodded along with, at least until
their backs were turned.

Mid-morning loomed. Miriam wasn't needed today. She
had the next three days off, her corvée paid. Miriam would
sleep in, and then Helge would occupy her time with education. Miriam Beckstein had two college degrees, but
Countess Helge was woefully uneducated in even the basics of her new life. Just learning how to live among her recently rediscovered extended family was a full-time job.
First, language lessons in the hochsprache vernacular with
a most attentive tutor, her lady-in-waiting Kara d'Praha.
Then an appointment for a fitting with her dressmaker,
whose ongoing fabrication of a suitable wardrobe had
something of the quality of a Sisyphean task. Perhaps if
the weather was good there'd be a discreet lesson in horse-
manship (growing up in suburban Boston, she'd never
learned to ride): otherwise, one in dancing, deportment, or
court etiquette.

Miriam was bored and anxious, itching to get back to her
start-up venture in the old capital of New Britain where
she'd established a company to build disk brakes and pio-
neer automotive technology transfer. New Britain was about
fifty years behind the world she'd grown up in, a land of opportunity for a sometime tech journalist turned entrepreneur.
Helge, however, was strangely fascinated by the minutiae of
her new life. Going from middle-class middle-American life
to the rarefied upper reaches of a barely postfeudal aristoc-

racy meant learning skills she'd never imagined needing before. She was confronting a divide of five hundred years, not
fifty, and it was challenging.

She'd taken the early part of the morning off to be
Miriam, sitting in her bedroom in jeans and sweater, her seat
a folding aluminum camp chair, a laptop balanced on her
knees and a mug of coffee cooling on the floor by her feet. *If
I can't do I can at least* plan, she told herself wryly. She had
a lot of plans, more than she knew what to do with. The
whole idea of turning the Clan's business model around,
from primitive mercantilism to making money off technology transfer between worlds, seemed impossibly utopian—
especially considering how few of the Clan elders had any
sort of modern education. But without plans, written studies,
and costings and risk analyses, she wasn't going to convince
anyone. So she'd ground out a couple more pages of propos-
als before realizing someone was watching her.

"Yes?"

"Milady." Kara bent a knee prettily, a picture of instinc-
tive teenage grace that Miriam couldn't imagine matching.
"You bade me remind you last week that this eve is the first
of summer twelvenight. There's to be a garden party at the
Östhalle tonight, and a ball afterward beside, and a card
from her grace your mother bidding you to attend her this afternoon beforehand." Her face the picture of innocence she
added, "Shall I attend to your party?"

If Kara organized Helge's carriage and guards then Kara
would be coming along too. The memories of what had happened the last time Helge let Kara accompany her to a court
event made her want to wince, but she managed to keep a
straight face: "Yes, you do that," she said evenly. "Get Mistress Tanzig in to dress me before lunch, and my compli-
ments to her grace my mother and I shall be with her by the
second hour of the afternoon." Mistress Tanzig, the dressmaker, would know what Helge should wear in public and,
more important, would be able to alter it to fit if there were
any last-minute problems. Miriam hit the save button on her
spreadsheet and sighed. "Is that the time? Tell somebody to
run me a bath; I'll be out in a minute."

So much for the day off, thought Miriam as she packed the laptop away. *I suppose I'd better go and be Helge . . .*

"Have you thought about marriage?" asked the duchess.

"Mother! As if!" Helge snorted indignantly and her eyes narrowed. "It's been about, what, ten weeks? Twelve? If you think I'm about to shack up with some golden boy so soon after losing Roland—"

"That wasn't what I meant, dear."

Helge drew breath. "What do you mean?"

"I meant . . ." The duchess Patricia glanced at her sharply, taking stock: "The, ah, noble institution. Have you thought about what it *means* here? And if so, what did you think?"

"I thought"—a slight expression of puzzlement wrinkled Helge's forehead—"when I first arrived, Angbard tried to convince me I ought to make an alliance of fortunes, as he put it. Crudely speaking, to tie myself to a powerful man who could protect me." The wrinkles turned into a full-blown frown. "I nearly told him he could put his alliance right where the sun doesn't shine."

"It's a good thing you didn't," her mother said diplomatically.

"Oh, I know that! Now. But the whole deal here creeps me out. And then." Helge took a deep breath and looked at the duchess: "There's you, your experience. I really don't know how you can stand to be in the same room as her grace your mother, the bitch! How she could—"

"Connive at ending a civil war?" the duchess asked sharply.

"Sell off her daughter to a wife-beating scumbag is more the phrase I had in mind." Helge paused. "Against her wishes," she added. A longer pause. "Well?"

"Well," the duchess said quietly. "Well, well. And well again. Would you like to know how she did it?"

"I'm not sure." A grimace.

"Well, whether you want to or not, I think you need to know," Iris—Patricia, the duchess Patricia—said. "Forewarned is forearmed, and no, when I was your age—and younger—*I* didn't want to know about it, either. But nobody's offering to trade you on the block like a piece of horseflesh. I should think the worst they'll do is drop broad hints your way and make the consequences of noncooperation irritatingly obvious in the hope you'll give in just to make them go away. You've probably got enough clout to ignore them if you want to push it—if it matters to you enough. But whether it would be *wise* to ignore them is another question entirely."

"Who are 'they'?"

"Aha! The right question, at last!" Iris laboriously levered herself upright on her chaise, beaming. "I told you the Clan is democratic, in the classical sense of the word. The marriage market is democracy in action, Helge, and as we all know, Democracy Is Always Right. Yes? Now, can you tell me who, within the family, provides the bride's dowry?"

"Why, the—" Helge thought for a moment. "Well, it's the head of the household's wealth, but doesn't the woman's mother have something to do with determining how much goes into it?"

"Exactly." The duchess nodded. "Braids cross three families, alternating every couple of generations so that issues of consanguinity don't arise but the Clan gift—the recessive gene—is preserved. To organize a braid takes some kind of continuity across at least three generations. A burden which naturally falls on the eldest women of the Clan. Men don't count: men tend to go and get themselves killed fighting silly duels. Or in wars. Or blood feuds. Or they sire bastards who then become part of the outer families and a tiresome burden. They—the bastards—can't world-walk, but some of their issue might, or their grandchildren. So we must keep track of them and find something useful for them to do—unlike the rest of the nobility here we have an incentive to look after our by-blows. I think we're lucky, in that respect, to have a matrilineal succession—other tribal societies I studied in my youth, patrilineal ones, were not nice places to be born female. Whichever and whatever, the lineage is preserved largely by the old women acting in concert. A conspiracy of matchmakers, if you like. The 'old bitches,' as everyone under sixty tends to call them." The duchess frowned. "It doesn't seem quite as funny now I'm sixty-two."

"Um." Helge leaned toward her mother. "You're telling me Hildegarde wasn't acting alone? Or she was being pressured by *her* mother? Or what?"

"Oh, she's an evil bitch in her own right," Patricia waved off the question dismissively. "But yes, she was pressured. She and the other ladies of a certain age don't have the two things that a young and eligible Clan lady can bargain with: they can't bear world-walkers, and they can no longer carry heavy loads for the family trade. So they must rely on other, more subtle tools to maintain their position. Like their ability to plait the braids, and to do each other favors, by way of their grandchildren. And when my mother was in her thirties—little older than you are now—she was subjected to much pressure."

"So there's this conspiracy of old women"—Helge was grasping after the concept—"who can make everyone's life a misery?"

"Don't underestimate them," warned the duchess. "They always win in the end, and you'll need to make your peace with them sooner or later. I'm unusual, I managed to evade them for more than three decades. But that almost never happens, and even when it does you can't actually win, because whether you fight them or no, you end up becoming one yourself." She raised one finger in warning. "You're relatively safe, kid. You're too old, too educated, and you've got your own power base. As far as I can see they've got no reason to meddle with you *unless* you threaten their honor. Honor is survival here. Don't *ever* do that, Miriam—Helge. If you do, they'll find a way to bring you down. All it takes is leverage, and leverage is the one thing they've got." She smiled thinly. "Think of them as Darwin's revenge on us, and remember to smile and curtsey when you pass them because until you've given them grandchildren they will regard you as an expendable piece to move around the game board. And if you *have* given them a child, they have a hostage to hold against you."

Mid-afternoon, Helge returned to her rooms to check briefly on the arrangements for her travel to the Östhalle—it being high summer, with the sun setting well after ten o'clock, she need not depart until close to seven—then turned to Lady Kara. "I would like to see Lady Olga, if she's available. Will you investigate? I haven't seen her around lately."

"Lady Olga is in town today. She is down at the battery range," Kara said without blinking. "She told me this morning that you'd be welcome to join her."

Most welcome to—then why didn't you tell *me?* Helge bit her tongue. Kara probably had some reason for withholding the invitation that had seemed valid at the time. Berating her for not passing on trivial messages would only cause Kara to start dropping every piece of trivia to which she was privy on her mistress's shoulders, rather than risk rebuke. "Then let's go and see her!" Helge said brightly. "It's not far, is it?"

The battery range was near the outer wall of the palace grounds—the summer palace, owned and occupied by those of the Clan elders who needed accommodation in the capital, Niejwein—and separated from those grounds by its own high stone wall. Miriam strolled slowly behind her guards, taking in the warm air and the scent of the ornamental shrubs planted to either side of the path. Her butler held a silk parasol above her to keep the sunlight off her skin. It still felt strange, the whole noble lady shtick, but there were some aspects of it she could live with. She paused at the gate in the wall. From the other side, she heard a muffled tapping sound. "Announce us," she told Kara.

"Yes, milady." A moment later, the doors opened onto bedlam.

Lady Olga Thorold Arnesen—of Thorold, by Arnesen—was blond, pretty, and on first acquaintance a complete ditz. Her enthusiasms included playing the viola, dancing, and making a good marriage. But first acquaintances could be extremely misleading when dealing with children of the Clan, as Miriam had discovered. Right now the ditz was lying in the grass on the other side of the door, practicing her other great enthusiasm with the aid of a Steyr AUG carbine chambered for 9mm ammunition. The more delicately inclined Helge winced and covered her ears as Olga sent a final three-round burst downrange, then safed the gun and bounced to her feet.

"Helge!" Olga beamed widely but refrained from hugging her, settling instead for brushing her cheek. "How charming to see you! A new creation, I see you're working your seamstress's fingers to the ivory. I suppose you didn't come to join me on the range?"

"If only." Helge sniffed. "It's business, I'm afraid." She took in Olga's camo jacket and trousers. "Are you coming to tonight's circus?"

"There's enough time to prepare later," Olga said dismissively. "I say, Master of Arms! You there! I'm going now, clean this up." She handed the gun over, then turned back to her visitor. "It's an excellent device, you really must try it one of these days," she said, gesturing at the rifle. The range master and his apprentice were fussing with it, unloading the magazine and stripping out the barrel and receiver. "There's a short version too, police forces use them a lot. I'm going to get them for my bodyguards."

"Really." Helge found it impossible not to smile at Olga's enthusiasm—except when it was pointed right at her, so to speak, a situation that had only happened once, due to an unfortunate misunderstanding she was not keen to repeat. "Let's walk. Somewhere quiet?" She glanced round, taking in the plethora of servants, from the range master and armorer and their assistants to her own bodyguard and butler and lady-in-waiting and Olga's two impassive-faced mercenaries from the Kiowa nation.

Olga chuckled. "I'm hardly dressed for polite company."

"So let's avoid it. The water garden?"

Olga cocked her head on one side: "Yes, I do believe it will be nearly empty at this time of year."

"So let's go. Leave the escort at the edge, I want to talk."

The water garden began near the far end of the firing range, where a carefully diverted stream ran underground through a steel-barred tunnel in the walls of the grounds and then through sinuous loops around cunningly landscaped mounds and hollows. Trees shaded it, and small conservato-

ries and rustic lodges provided a retreat for visitors tired of
the bustle and business of the great estate. However, it was
designed for the lush spring or the fiery autumn, not the heat
of summer. At this time of year the stream ran sluggish,
yielding barely more than a trickle of water to damp down
the mud, and most of the plants were either past their peak or
not yet come to it.

Helge and Olga walked alongside the dry streambed on a
brick path encrusted in yellow and brown lichen, Olga in her
grass-stained camouflage fatigues, Helge in a silk gown fit
for a royal garden party. Presently, when they passed the second turn in the path, Olga slowed her pace. "All right, be you
out with it."

"I'm—" Helge stopped, an expression of mild puzzlement on her face. "Let me be Miriam for a bit. Please?"

"My dear, you already are!"

"Huh." Miriam frowned. "Well, that's the problem in a
nutshell, I suppose. Have you been over to the workshop
lately?"

"Have I?" Olga rolled her eyes. "Your uncle's been running me ragged lately! Me and Brilliana—and everyone
else. I think he sent in Morgan du Hjalmar to do the day-to-
day stuff in your workshop, and a couple of Henryk's people
to audit the organization for security, but honestly, I haven't
had time to keep an eye on it. It's been a rat race! I'm lucky
to have the time to attend the midsummer season, he's working me like a servant!"

"I see." Miriam's tone was dry.

Olga looked at her sharply. "What is it?"

"Oh, nothing much: every time I ask if it's safe for me to
go over there and look in on my company I get some excuse
from security like, 'We can't go there, the hidden family
gangsters may not honor the ceasefire' or 'We think
Matthias's little friends may be looking for you there' or 'It
isn't safe.'" Miriam took a deep breath. "It feels like I'm being cut out, Olga, and they're not even trying very hard to
hide it. It's insultingly obvious. I get to sit here in Thorold
Palace practicing dance steps and hochsprache and court etiquette, and every time I try to make myself useful something

comes up to divert me. From my own company! The one I
set up in New Britain that's showing a higher rate of profit
growth than anything else the Clan's seen in thirty years!"

"Profit growth from a very low baseline," Olga pointed
out, a little tactlessly.

"That's not the *point*!" Miriam managed to keep her temper under control. "While they're keeping me on the shelf
under glass I can't actually meet people and make deals and
keep things moving! I'm isolated. I don't know what's going
on. Hell, do *you* know what's going on? Is Roger messing
around with epoxides again or is he working on the process
quality issue? Did Jeremiah sort out the delivery schedules?
Who's handling payroll? If it's that man of Bates's it's cost-
ing us an arm and a leg. Well? Who's minding the shop?"

Olga shook her head. "I'm sure Morgan was taking care
of all that," she said slowly, not meeting Miriam's eyes.
"Things are very busy."

"Well, you're actually going on-site," Miriam pointed out.
"If you don't know what to look for, how should Morgan
know? I'm the only person in the Clan who really knows
what the company is good for or where everything goes, and
if they're keeping me away from it, there's a good chance
that—" She stopped.

Olga busied herself looking around the lower branches of
the trees for the mockingbird that had been serenading them
only a minute before.

"*Why* am I being frozen out?" asked Miriam.

"I couldn't possibly comment," Olga sang, almost tone-
lessly, an odd affectation she sometimes used when forced to
deliver bad news, "because were I to repeat anything I heard
from his excellency in the Security Directorate that would
be an act of petty treason, not to say a betrayal of his trust in
me—but has anything else happened to you lately?"

"Oh, lots." Miriam's voice sharpened. "Deportment lessons. Dancing lessons. A daily dossier of relatives and their
family trees to memorize. How to ride a horse sidesaddle.
How to address a prince, a pauper, or a priest of Sky Father.
The use of reflexive verbs in hochsprache. More clothing
than I've ever needed before, all in styles I wouldn't have

been seen dead in—or expected to see outside a museum or a movie theater. I've been getting a crash course." She grimaced, then glanced sidelong at Olga. "I went to see Ma—Iris, I mean, her grace the duchess Patricia—this afternoon. She's turned almost as stone-faced and Machiavellian as that dear grandmother of mine."

"Really?" Olga chirped, just a little too brightly. "Did she have anything interesting to say?"

"Yes, as a matter of fact she did." Miriam tapped one foot impatiently. "She asked me what I thought about *marriage*, Olga. She knows damn well what I think about marriage; she was there when I married Ben, and she was still there when the divorce came through, and *that* was over ten years ago. She knows about Roland." Her voice wobbled slightly as she named him, and for a moment Miriam looked a decade older than her thirty-three years. "Ma's frightening me, Olga, it's as if something's broken inside her and she's decided it was all a mistake, running away, and she needs to conform to expectations."

"Well, maybe—" Olga paused. She glanced around. "Look, Miriam. I *think* it's safe to tell you this, all right? But don't talk about it in front of anybody else." She took a deep breath. "You *are* being kept away from your operation in New Britain. It's a security thing, but not, not Matthias. I think her grace was finding out what you think about marriage because that's the fastest way to clear things up. If you were—unambiguously—part of the Clan, there'd be fewer grounds to worry about you."

"About *me*?" Miriam managed to control her voice. "What do you think—"

"Hush, it's not what *I* think that's the problem!"

Miriam paused. "I'm sorry."

"I accept your apology, dear friend. No, it's—the problem is, you've been too successful too fast. On your own. Think about Roland, think about what *he* tried to do years ago. Bluntly, they're afraid that a lot of young tearaways will look at your example and think, 'I could do that,' and, well, copy everything except the way you came home to face a council hearing and explain what you were doing."

Miriam looked blank for a moment. "You mean, they're afraid youngsters would use me as an object lesson and strike out on their own. Defect. Leave the Clan."

"Yes, Helge. I think that's what they're afraid of. You've handed them a huge opportunity on a plate, but it's also a threat to their survival as an institution. And there's already a crisis in train for them to worry about. Frightened people act harshly . . . your mother has every reason to be scared witless, on your behalf. Do you see?"

"That's hard to believe." Eyes downcast, Helge slowly began to walk back along the path. "Bastards," she muttered quietly under her breath. "Lying bastards."

Olga trotted to catch up. "Come along to the garden party tonight," she suggested. "Try to enjoy it? You'll meet lots of eligible gentles there, I'm sure." A quiet giggle: "If they're not overawed by your reputation!"

"Enjoy it?" Helge stopped dead, a pained expression on her face. "Last time I attended one of those events Matthias tried to blackmail me, his majesty insisted on introducing me to his idiot younger son, and two different factions tried to assassinate me! I'm just hoping that his majesty's too drunk to recognize me, otherwise—"

"This time will be different," Olga said confidently, offering her hand. "You'll see!"

TRANSLATED TRANSCRIPT BEGINS

"A most excellent evening, your grace."

"Any evening at court is a most excellent one, Otto. Blessed by the presence of our royal sun, as it were. Ah, you—a glass for the baron, here!"

(Pause.)

"That's very fine, the, ah, Sudten new grape? This year's, fresh from the cask?"

"Absolutely. His majesty's vintners are conscientious as always. I understand we can expect this crop to arrive in our own cellars presently, in perhaps a few weeks—as the ships work their way into port, weather permitting."

"As the—oh. How *do* they do it?"

"Witchcraft of some description, no doubt, though the how of it hardly matters as much as the *why*, Otto." (Pause.) "Are you still having problems with your new neighbor?"

"Why that—one-legged whore's son of a bloated tick! I'm sorry, your grace. Sky Father rot his eyes in his head, yes! It continues. As the circuit assizes will attest this high summer. And he's got the sworn men to compurge his case before the justiciars, claiming with their lying hands on the altar that every inch of the forest he's cleared has been in his family since time immemorial. Which it has *not*, on account of his family being jumped-up peddlers—"

"Not so loudly if you please, Otto. Another glass?"

"My—discreetly! Discreetly does it indeed, sir, I must apologize; it is just that the subject causes me no little inflammation of the senses. My grief is not at the ennoblement of the line, which it must be admitted happened in my grandfather's day, but his attitude is insufferable! To raze the choicest forest is bad enough, but to sow it with weeds, and then to erect fences and bar his fields to the hunt in breach of ancient right is a personal affront. And his claim to be under the instruction of his liege is . . ."

"Quite true, Otto."

"I most humbly beg your pardon, your grace, but I find that hard to credit."

(Pause.)

"It is entirely true, Otto. The merchants own considerable estates, and fully a tenth of them were turned over to this crop last spring. With considerable hardship to their tenants, I might add; an unseemly lack of care will see many of them starving. Evidently red and purple flowers mean more to them than the health of their peasants, unless by some more of their magic they can transform poppies into bread by midwinter's eve."

"Idiots." (Inarticulate muttering.) "It wouldn't be the *first* idiocy they've been guilty of, of course, but to damage the yeomanry adds an insult to the blow."

"Exactly his thought."

"He—" (Pause.) "The rising sun is of this thought?"

"Indeed. Even while our father sips his new wine, imported by tinker trickery, and raises them in his esteem without questioning their custody of the lands he's granted them, our future king asks hard questions. He's a born leader, and we are lucky to have his like."

"I'll drink to that. Long live the king!"

"Long live . . . and long live the prince!"

"Indeed, long live the prince!"

"And may we live to see the day when he succeeds his father to the throne."

"May we—" (Coughing.) (Pause.) "Indeed, my lord. Absolutely, unquestionably. Neither too early nor too late nor—ahem. Yes, I shall treasure your confidence."

"These are dangerous times, Otto."

"You can—count on me. Sir. *Should* it come to that—"

"I hope that it will not. We *all* hope that it will not, do you understand? But youth grows impatient with corruption, as dusk grows impatient with dawn and as you grow impatient with your jumped-up peddler of a neighbor. There have been vile rumors about the succession, even as to the disposition of the young prince, and the suitability of the lion of the nation for the role of shepherd . . ."

(Spluttering.) "Insupportable!"

"Yes. I merely mention it to you so that you understand how the land lies. As one of my most trusted clients . . . Well, Otto, I must be moving on. People to see, favors to bestow. But if I may leave you with one observation, it is that it might be to your advantage and my pleasure for you to present yourself to his grace of Innsford before the evening is old. In his capacity as secretary to the prince, you understand, he is most interested in collecting accounts of insults presented to the old blood by the new. Against the reckoning of future years, gods willing."

"Why, thank you, your grace! Gods willing."

"My pleasure."

TRANSCRIPT ENDS

2

RUMORS OF WAR

❦

Meanwhile, a transfinite distance and a split second away, the king-emperor of New Britain was having a bad day.

"Damn your eyes, Farnsworth." He hunched over his work-glass, tweezers in hand, one intricate gear wheel clasped delicately between its jaws. "Didn't I tell you not to disturb me at the bench?"

The unfortunate Farnsworth cleared his throat apologetically. A skinny fellow in the first graying of middle age, clad in the knee breeches and tailcoat of a royal equerry, his position as companion of the king's bedchamber made him the first point of contact for anyone who wanted some of the king's time—and also the lightning conductor for his majesty's occasional pique. "Indeed you did, your majesty." He stood on the threshold of the royal workshop, flanked on either side by the two soldiers of the Horse Guards who held the door, his attention focused on the royal watchmaker. King John the Fourth of New Britain was clearly annoyed, his plump cheeks florid and his blond curls damp with perspiration from hours of focus directed toward the tiny mechanism clamped to his workbench.

"Then what have you got to say for yourself?" demanded the monarch, moderating his tone very slightly. Farnsworth suppressed a sigh of relief: John Frederick was not his father, blessed with decisiveness but cursed with a whim of steel. Still, he wasn't out of the woods yet. "I see it is"—the king's eyes swiveled toward a mantel covered from edge to edge in whirring clocks, every one of which he had built with his own hands—"another thirty-seven minutes before I must withdraw to the Green Room and prepare for the grand opening."

"I deeply regret the necessity of encroaching upon your majesty's precious time, but"—Farnsworth took a deep breath—"it's the Ministry for Special Affairs. They've hatched some sort of alarm or excursion, and Sir Roderick says it cannot possibly wait, and the prime minister himself heard Sir Roderick out in private and sent me straight to you forthwith. He apologizes for intruding upon your majesty's business, but says he agrees the news is extremely grave and demands your most urgent attention in your capacity as commander in chief."

"*News?*" The king snorted. "*Urgent?* It's probably just some jumped-up border fort commander complaining that Milton's been squeezing their bully and biscuit again." But he carefully lowered the tiny camshaft assembly, placing it back on the velvet cloth beside the rectangular gear mill he was building, and lowered a second cloth atop the work in progress. "Where's he waiting?"

"In the Gold Office, your Majesty."

Two footmen of the royal household scurried forward to secure the items on the royal workbench. A third servant bowed deeply, then bent to untie the royal apron, while a fourth approached bearing the king's topcoat. The king slid down off his high stool and stretched. At thirty-six years old he was in good health, although his waistline showed the effect of too many state banquets, and his complexion betrayed the choleric blood pressure that so worried his physiopaths and apothecaries. He extended his arms for the coat, of conservative black broadcloth embroidered with gold frogging in the style of the earlier century. "Take me to Sir Roderick and the prime minister. Let us hear this news that is important enough to drag the royal gearsman away from his analytical engine."

Farnsworth glanced over his shoulder. "Make it so," he snapped. And it was done. The King of New Britain, Emperor of Terra Australis, by grace of God Protector-Regent of the Chrysanthemum Throne, pretender to the Throne of England, and Presider of the Grand Assembly of American States, could go nowhere without an escort of Horse Guards to protect the royal person, majors-domo to announce his presence in advance lest some hapless courtier fail to be alerted and take their cue to pay their respects, household servants to open the doors before him and close them behind him and brush the carpets before his feet fell upon them . . . but John Frederick the man had scant patience when kept waiting, and Farnsworth took considerable pride in ensuring that his lord and master's progress was as frictionless as one of the royal artificer's own jeweled gear trains.

The royal procession paced smoothly through the west wing of the Brunswick Palace, traversing wood-paneled and richly plastered corridors illuminated by the cold, clear brilliance of the electrical illuminants the technocrat-emperor favored. Courtiers and servants scattered before his progress as Farnsworth marched, stony-faced, ahead of the king, aware of the royal eyes drilling speculatively into the back of his high-collared coat. He turned into the North Hall, then through the Hall of Monsters (walled with display cabinets by the king's grandfather, who had taken his antediluvian cryptozoological studies as seriously as the present incumbent took his watchmaker's bench), and then into the New Hall. From there he turned left and paused in a small vestibule before the polished oak doors of the Gold Office.

"Open all and rise for his majesty!" called one of the guards. An answering announcement, muffled by the thickness of wood, reached Farnsworth. He nodded at the nearest footman, who moved smartly to one side and opened the door. Farnsworth stepped forward.

"His Majesty the King bids you good afternoon, and graces you with his presence to enquire of the running of his domains," he announced. Then he took two steps back, to stand beside the door, as invisible to the powerful occupants as the tape-telegraph on its pillar to one side of the enormous desk or the gigantic map of the world that covered the wall opposite the door.

John Frederick stepped inside, then glanced over his shoulder. "Shut it. Everyone who isn't cleared, get out," he said. Two men, one tall and cadaverous in his black suit, the other wizened and stooped with age, waited beside his desk as he strode toward it and threw himself down in the wide-armed chair behind it with a grunt of irritation. The stooped man watched impassively, but the tall fellow looked slightly apprehensive, like an errant pupil called into the principal's office. "Sir Roderick, Lord Douglass. We assume you would not have lightly called us away from our one private hour of the day without good reason. So if you would be good enough to be seated, perhaps you could explain to us what that reason was? You, fetch chairs for my guests."

Servants cleared for the highest discussions brought chairs for the two ministers. Lord Douglass sat first, creakily lowering himself into his seat. "Roderick, I believe this is your story," he said in a thin voice that betrayed no weakness of mind, merely the frailty of extreme old age.

"Yes, your lordship. Majesty. I have the grave duty to report to you that our intelligence confirms that two days ago the Farmers General detonated a corpuscular dissociation petard on their military test range in Northumbria."

"Shit." John Frederick closed his eyes and rubbed them with the back of one regal wrist. "And which of our agents have reported this? Roderick, they were at least six months away from that last week, what-what?"

Sir Roderick cleared his throat. "I am afraid our intelligence estimates were incorrect, your majesty." He took a deep breath. "Our initial information comes from a communicant in Lancaster who has heard eyewitness reports of the flash from villagers in the Lake District, southwest of the test range. Subsequently a weather ballonet over Iceland detected a radiant plume of corpuscular fragments indicative of a petard of the gun type, using enriched light-kernel cronosium. We've had detailed reports of the progress of the Farmers' Jenny-works in Bohemia, which has been taking in shipments of Pitchblende from the Cape. If they've got enough highly enriched cronosium to hoist a petard, and if they've also commissioned the crucible complex that was building near Kiev, then according to the revised estimates that my department has prepared we can expect the Frogs to have as many as twelve corpses in service by the end of the year, and production running at two per month through next year, rising to ten per month thereafter."

The king sighed. "We cannot afford to ignore this affront. Our credibility will be deeply weakened if we are seen to ignore such a clear challenge by an agency of the French crown. And the insult of using our former territory as a *test range*"—his voice crackled with indignation—"cannot be other than intentional." John Frederick straightened up in his chair. "Lord Douglass. This matter must be addressed by the Imperial Security Council. A new policy is required to deal with the affront. And a public position, lest panic ensue when the Frogs announce their new capability." He drummed the fingers of his left hand on the intricately lacquered desktop. "Well. What else to keep us from our workshop?"

Farnsworth focused on the prime minister. Douglass might be old and withered, but there was still a sharp mind behind the wispy white hair and liver-spotted wattles. Moreover, to the extent Farnsworth could claim to know the prime minister at all, he struck the equerry as looking shifty—and Sir Roderick was visibly sweating. *This is going to be very bad indeed*, Farnsworth realized. *They're using the French corpuscular test to soften him up. What on God's earth could be* worse *than Louis XXII with corpuscular weapons?*

"Sire." It was Douglass. Farnsworth focused on him. "This, ah, led me to question the diligence with which the Ministry for Special Affairs has been discharging its duties abroad. And indeed, Sir Roderick has instigated certain investigations without prompting, investigations which are revealing a very frightening deficit in our understanding of continental machinations against the security of your domain."

"We . . . see." The king sounded perplexed and mildly irritated. "Would you get to the point, please? If the situation is as bad as you say, it would be expedient to draw no attention to our knowledge of it, and to reassure those who know something of it but not the substance—therefore one should depart to dress for the opening as one's progression dictates on time and without sign of turmoil, at least until after the next scheduled ISC meeting. So what exactly are you talking about?"

"Sir Roderick," Douglass prompted.

Sir Roderick looked like a man about to be hanged. "Sire, it pains me to lay this before you, but in the wake of the disturbances in Boston three weeks ago I instigated certain investigations. To draw a long story short, it appears that certain of our paid agents at large have been in actual fact accepting the coin of a second paymaster, whose livres and francs have added color to their reportage—to say nothing of delaying vital intelligence. We are now trying to ascertain the extent of the damage, but it appears that there has been for some time a French spy ring operating in our very halls, and this ring has suborned at least one network of our agents overseas. My men are now trying to isolate the spies, and discover how far the rot has spread.

"I believe that in addition to perverting the course of incoming intelligence—which they were unable to do with the petard, it would seem, because weather ballonets with scintillation tubes accept no bribes—these enemy agents have been arranging for numerous shipments of gold to arrive in this country. Certainly more gold than usual has been seized on the black market in the past six months, and it appears that certain troublemakers and rabble-rousers have been living high on the hog."

"The usual?" John Frederick asked coldly.

"Levelers and Ranters," Douglass said quietly. He looked sad. "They never learn, although this treason is, I think, unprecedented in recent years. If true."

The king stood up. "We do not tolerate slander and libel and anarchism, much less as a front for that *bastard* pretender's machinations!" His cheeks shone; for a moment Farnsworth half-expected him to burst into a denunciation, but after a while the monarch regained control. "Bring forward the next ISC meeting, as soon as possible," he ordered. "Sir Roderick. We expect a daily briefing on the fruits of your investigation. We realize you have had barely nine months to get to grips with your office, but we must insist on holding you responsible for the progress of the ministry. Should you succeed in leeching it back to health you will find us a forgiving ruler, and we appreciate your candor in bringing the disease to our notice—but if this pot boils over, it will not be the Crown who is scalded." He glanced round. "Farnsworth, attend to our wardrobe. Lord Douglass, thank you for bringing the situation to our attention. We shall now proceed to appear our regal best for the state opening tonight. If you should care to seek audience with us after the recession of parliament, we would value your advice."

"I am at your majesty's service, as always," murmured the prime minister. He stood, slowly. The minister of Special Affairs rose too, as Farnsworth moved smoothly to ensure the king's progress back to his dressing room.

That evening, after the state opening and the royal progress from Brunswick Palace to the Houses of Parliament at the far end of Manhattan island, Farnsworth pulled on a heavy overcoat and slipped out through a side door of the palace, to visit an old acquaintance in a public house just off Gloriana Street.

Wooden paneling and a brown, stained ceiling testified to the Dutch origins of the Arend's Nest: the pub's front windows looked out toward the high-rise tenements crowding the inner wall of the bastion that had protected New York from continental aggression as far back as the late eighteenth century. Now a favorite haunt by day of city stock merchants and the upper crust of businessmen who filled the new office blocks behind the administrative complex, by night the Nest was mostly empty. Farnsworth slipped past the bar and stood next to a booth at the back with his coat collar turned up against the chill from the sea and his hat pulled down close to his ears. "You won't fool nay-one like that," said a familiar voice. "You look like you're trying to hide and they'll pay attendance on ye when the police come asking. And now what time have you?"

Farnsworth shook himself. "I'm sorry, but my pocket oyster's broken," he said in a robotic tone of voice.

"Then ye'll just have to tell me what time it says?"

He hauled out his watch and flipped it open. "Ten to nine."

"Jolly good." With a sigh and a rustle his welcomer moved aside to let him into the cubicle. Farnsworth sat down gratefully. "I've taken the liberty of ordering your pint already." He was a plump, slightly shabby man whom Farnsworth knew only as Jack. Farnsworth had studiously suppressed any instinct to dig deeper. Jack wore a dark suit, shiny at the elbows, and a red silk cravat that although clean was clearly in need of ironing. Beside him sat another fellow, unknown to Farnsworth: a long-faced man in early middle age, but with a consumptive pallor about him and a face that seemed to chronicle more insults than any one life should bear. Farnsworth removed his hat and scarf and placed them fastidiously on one of the hooks screwed to the upper rail of the booth. "Have you anything to report?"

"For whose ears?" Farnsworth picked up his glass. A full one sat untouched before Mr. Long-Face, which seemed an unconscionable waste of a good pint of porter to him. "No offense."

"This is, um, Rudolf," said Jack. "He's from Head Office. You remember what we spoke about earlier."

"Ah, yes." Farnsworth shuffled uneasily in his seat. *Head Office* covered a multitude of sins, most of them capital offenses in the eyes of the Homeland Security Bureau. Far more subversive than any bomb-throwing wild-eyed democrat or fly-by-night unlicensed desktop publisher spreading lies and slanders about her royal highness's enthusiasm for tight-breeched household cavalry officers . . . but the exchange of passwords had gone smoothly. Jack hadn't used the *bail out* challenge. Which meant this was official.

"Nothing new. His majesty is trying to keep a placid face but is mightily exercised over the continental despotism. They've exploded a corpuscular weapon months ahead of what our spies said was possible. Sir Roderick is dusting under chairs and tables in search of a mouse hole, as if his head depends upon it—and indeed it might, if Douglass is of a mind to hold him responsible. There is the usual ongoing crisis over precedence in the royal bedchamber, and My Lady Frazier is vexed to speak of creating a new post of— well, perhaps this is of no interest? In any case, Douglass is exercised, too. He seems much gloomier than normal, and muttered something about fearing war was making virtue of necessity, and we must ensure the French use of the new weapons—corpses, he calls them, a vile contraction—is subjected to prior restraint by a mutual terror of annihilation." With this, Farnsworth reached into an inner pocket of his jacket and produced a small envelope. He slid it across the table. "Usual drill."

Jack passed it to the stranger. It vanished immediately, and at once Farnsworth felt a load off his shoulders. He sighed and drained half his pint. Jack smiled sardonically. "Pass the noose is what we called this game in Camp Frederick."

The stranger, Rudolf, blinked his rheumy eyes, expressionless. "We require more detailed economic information," he said, in an unexpectedly educated accent. "The V1 and V2 treasury indicators, any information you can obtain about the prevalence of adulterants in the royal mint's stock, confiscations of bullion, the rate of default of debt secured against closed bodies corporate, the proposed repayment terms on the next issue of war bonds, and everything you can discover about the next budget."

Farnsworth leaned back. "That's the Exchequer," he said slowly. "I don't work there or know anything. Or know anyone who does."

Rudolf nodded. "We understand. And we don't expect miracles. All we ask is that you be aware of our needs. Douglass is a not infrequent visitor to the palace, and should he by mistake leave his brief unattended for a few minutes— well." The hint of a smile came to Rudolf's face. "Have you ever seen one of these before?" He slid a device barely larger than a box of matches onto the table.

Farnsworth stared at it. "What is it?"

"It's a camera."

"Don't be silly"—Farnsworth bent over it—"nobody could build a camera that small! Could they? And what's it made of, lacquered cardboard?"

"No." Rudolf pushed it toward him. "It's made of a material like foramin or cellulate, or a phenolic resin—even the lens. It's waterproof and small enough to conceal in a boot heel. It will take eight pictures, then you must return it to us so that we can remove the sketchplate and downlo—ah, develop it. You aim it with this viewfinder, like so, and take a picture by pressing this button—thus. Yes, it will work without daylight—this is adequate for it. Keep it—no, not that one, this one"—he produced a second camera and handed it to Farnsworth—"about your person where it will not be found easily but where you can reach it in an instant. Inside your hat ribbon in circumstances like this, perhaps, or in your periwig when paying attendance upon his majesty."

"I—" Farnsworth looked at the tiny machine as if it were a live scorpion. "Did this come from the Frogs?" he heard himself asking as if from a great distance. "Because if so—"

"No." Rudolf flushed, and for the first time showed emotion. Anger. "We aren't pawns of the Bourbon tyranny, sir. We are free democrats all, patriotic Englishmen fighting in the vanguard of the worldwide struggle for the rights of man, for freedom and equality before the law—and we'll liberate France and her dominions as well, when the time comes to join in one great brotherhood of humanity and set the east afire! But we have allies you are unaware of, and hopefully will *remain* unaware of for some time to come, lest you jeopardize the cause." He fixed Farnsworth with a gimlet stare. "Do you understand?"

Farnsworth nodded. "I—yes." He pocketed the tiny device hastily, then finished his beer. "Another pint?" he asked Jack. "In the interests of looking authentic . . ."

"By all means." Jack stood. "I'll just go to the bar."

"And I must make haste to the jakes," said Rudolf, nodding affably at Farnsworth. "We won't meet again, I trust. Remember: eight, then to Jack. He will give you a replacement. Good night." He took his hat and slipped away, leaving Farnsworth to sit alone, lonely and frightened until Jack returned with a fresh glass and a grin of conviviality, to chat about the dog racing and shore up his cover by helping him spend another evening drinking beer with his friend of convenience. Jack the Lad, Jack be Nimble, Jack the Leveler . . .

The man Farnsworth knew as Rudolf was in no particular hurry. First he took his ease in the toilet. It was a cold night for the time of year, and he was old enough to have learned what a chill could do to his bladder. As he buttoned his coat and shuffled out the back door, through the yard with the wooden casks stacked shoulder high, he stifled a rattling cough. Something was moving in his chest again, foreshadowing what fate held in store for him. "All the more reason to get this over with sooner rather than later, my son," he mumbled to himself as he unlocked the gate and slid unenthusiastically into the brick-walled alleyway.

The alley was heaped with trash and hemmed in by the tumbledown sheds at the back of the buildings that presented such a fine stone front to the highway. Rudolf picked his way past a rusting fire escape and leaned on a wooden doorway next to a patch of wall streaked with dank slime from a leaky down-pipe. The door opened silently. He ducked inside, then closed and bolted it. The darkness in the cellar was broken only by a faint skylight. Now moving faster, Rudolf crossed over to another door and rapped on it thrice. A second later the inner door opened. "Ah, it's you."

"It's me," Rudolf agreed. The sullen-faced man put away his pistol, looking relieved. "Coat," Rudolf snapped, shedding his outer garment. "Hat." The new garments were of much better cut than those that he'd removed, suitable for an operagoer of modest means—a ministry clerk, perhaps, or a legal secretary—and as he pulled them on "Rudolf" forced himself to straighten up, put a spring in his step and a spark in his eye. "Time to be off, I think. See you later."

He left by way of a staircase and a dim hallway, an electrical night-light guiding his footsteps. Finally, "Rudolf" let himself out through the front door, which was itself unlocked. The coat and hat he'd arrived in would be vanishing into the belly of the furnace that heated the law firm's offices by day. In a few minutes there'd be nothing to connect him to the man from the royal household other than a tenuous chain of hearsay—not that it would stop the Homeland Security Bureau's hounds, but with every broken link the chain would become harder to follow.

The main road out front was brightly lit by fizzing gas stands; cabs rumbled up and down it, boilers hissing as their drivers trawled for trade among the late-night crowds who dotted the sidewalk outside cafes and fashionable eating houses. The music hall along the street was emptying out, and knots of men and women stood around chattering raucously or singing the latest ditties from memory—with varying degrees of success, for the bars were awash with genever and scrumpy, and the entertainment was not noted for genteel restraint. Overhead, the neon lights blinked like the promise of a new century, bright blandishments of commerce and a ticker of news running around the outside of the theater's awning. "Rudolf" stepped off the curb, avoided a cab, and made his way across to the far side of the street. The rumble of an airship's engines echoed off the roadstone paving from overhead, a reminder of the royal presence a few miles away. "Rudolf" forced himself to focus as he walked purposefully along the sidewalk, avoiding the merrymakers and occasional vagrant. *Dear friends*, he thought; *the faces of multitudes*. He glanced around, a frisson of fear running up his spine. *I hope we're in time*.

Passing a penny to a red-cheeked lad yelling the lead from tomorrow's early edition, "Rudolf" took a copy of *The Times* and scanned the headlines as he walked. *Nader Reasserts Afghan Claim*. Nothing good could ever come from that part of the world, he reflected; especially Shah Nader's thirst for black gold he could sell to the king's navy via the oiling base at Jask. *Saboteurs Apprehended in Breasil*. All part and parcel of the big picture. *Crown Prince James Visits Santa Cruz* made it sound like a grand tour of the nation rather than a desperate hope that the Pacific warmth would do something to ease the child's ailment. "Rudolf" turned a corner into a narrower street. *Prussian Ambassador Slights French Envoy at Gala Opening*: now *that* didn't sound very clever, did it? As the joke put it, when the French diplomat said "Frog" the Germanys all croaked in chorus. *Murdock Suit: Malcolm Denies Slur*. All the best barristers arguing the big libel case on a pro bono basis—a faint smile came to the thin man's face as he read the leading paragraph, squinting under the thin glare of the lamps. Then he folded the paper beneath his arm, palming something between the pages, and strode on toward the intersection with New Street. The crowds were thicker here, and as he stepped onto the pavement at the far side a fellow ran straight into him.

"I say, sir, are you all right?" the man asked, dusting himself off. "You dropped your paper." He bent and handed a folded broadsheet to "Rudolf."

"If you'd been looking where you were going, I wouldn't have." "Rudolf" snorted, jammed the paper beneath his arm, and hurried off determinedly. Only when he'd passed the outrageously expensive plate glass windows of the Store Romanova did he slow, cough once or twice into his handkerchief, and verify with a sidelong glance that the paper clenched in his left hand was a copy of *The Clarion*.

Queen's Counselor Denies Everything, Threatens Libel Suit! screamed the headline. "Rudolf" smiled to himself. *And so he should*, he thought, *and so he should*. If *Farnsworth* said there was no substance to the rumors then he was almost certainly telling the truth—not that his loyalty was above and beyond question, for nobody was beyond question, but his dislike for her majesty was such that if there had been any substance to the rumors, the dispatches he sent via Jack would almost certainly have confirmed them. "Rudolf" took a deep, slow, breath, trying not to irritate his chest, and forced himself to relax, slowing to an old man's ambling pace. Every second that passed now meant that the incriminating letter was that much further from its origin and that much closer to the intelligence cell that would analyze it before making their conclusions known to the Continental Congress.

At the corner with Bread Street, "Rudolf" paused beside the tram stop for a minute, then waved down a cab. "Hogarth Villas," he said tersely. "On Stepford High Street."

"Sure, and it's a fine night fir it, sor." The cabbie grinned broadly in his mirror as he bled steam into the cylinder and accelerated away from the roadside. His passenger nodded, thoughtfully, but made no attempt to reply.

Hogarth Villas was a broad-fronted stretch of town houses, fronted with iron rails and a gaudy display of lanterns. It stretched for half a block along the high street, between shuttered shop fronts that slept while the villas' residents worked (and vice versa). One of the larger and better-known licensed brothels at the south end of Manhattan island, it was anything but quiet at this time of night. "Rudolf" paid off the cabbie with a generous tip, then approached the open vestibule and the two sturdy gentlemen who stood to either side of the glass inner door. "Name's Rudolf," he said quietly. "Ma'am Bishop is expecting me."

"Aye, sir, if you'd just step this way, please." The shorter of the two, built like a battleship and with a face bearing the unmistakable spoor of smallpox, opened the door for him and stepped inside. The carpet was red, the lights electric-bright, shining from the gilt-framed mirrors. In the next room, someone was playing a saucy nautical air on the piano; girlish voices chattered and laughed with the gruff undertone of the clientele. This was by no means a lower-class dive. The doorman led "Rudolf" along the hallway then through a side door into understairs quarters, where the carpet was replaced with bare teak floorboards and the expensive silk wallpaper with simple sky-blue paint. The building creaked and chattered around them, sounds of partying and other sport carrying through the lath and plaster. They climbed a narrow spiral staircase before arriving on a landing fronted by three doors. The bouncer rapped on one of them. "Here's where I leave you," he said, as it began to swing open, and he headed back toward the front of the building.

"Come in, Erasmus."

She sounded amused. Erasmus—Rudolf no more—set his shoulders determinedly and stepped forward. *No avoiding it now*, he told himself, feeling a curious sinking feeling as he met the opening door and the presence behind it.

"Ma'am." Most of the girls downstairs bared their shoulders and wore their fishtail skirts slit in front to reveal their knees, in an exaggerated burlesque of the latest mode from Nouveau Paris. The woman in the doorway was no girl, and she wore a black crêpe mourning dress. After all, she *was* in mourning. With black hair turning to steel gray at the temples, blue eyes and a face lined with worries, she might have been a well-preserved sixty or a hard-done-by thirty. The truth, like much else about her, lay in between.

"Come in. Sit down. Would you care for a sip of brandy?"

"Don't mind if I do." The room was furnished with a couple of overstuffed and slightly threadbare chairs, surplus to requirements downstairs: a bed in the corner, too narrow by far to suit the purposes of the house, and a writing desk, completed the room. The window opened onto a tiny enclosed square, barely six feet from the side of the next building.

Erasmus waited while his hostess carefully filled two glasses from a brandy decanter sitting atop the bureau, next to a conveniently burning candle—the better to dispose of the desk's contents, should they be disturbed—and handed one to him. Then she sat down. "How did it go?" she asked tensely.

He took a cautious sip from his glass. "I made the delivery. And the pickup. I have no reason to believe I was under surveillance and every reason not to."

"Not that, silly." She was fairly humming with impatience. "What word from the palace?"

"Ah." He smiled. "They seem to be most obsessed with matters of diplomatic significance." His smile slipped. "Like the way the French have pulled the wool over their eyes lately. There's a witch hunt brewing in the foreign service, and an arms race in the Ministry of War. The grand strategy of encirclement has not only crumbled, it appears to have backfired. The situation does not sound good, Margaret."

"A war would suit their purposes." She nodded to herself, her gaze unfocused. "A distraction always serves the rascals in charge." She glanced at the side door to the room. "And the . . . device? Did you give it to our source?"

"I gave it to him and showed him how to use it. All he knows is that it is a very small camera. And he needs to return it to us to have the, ah, film developed. Or downloaded, as Miss Beckstein's representative calls it."

Margaret, Lady Bishop, frowned. "I wish I trusted these alien allies of yours, Erasmus. I wish I understood their motives."

"What's to understand?" Erasmus shrugged. "Listen, I'd be dead if not for them and the alibi they supplied. Their gold is pure and their words—" It was his turn to frown. "I don't know about the aliens, but I trust *Miriam*. Miss Beckstein is a bit like you, milady. There's a sincerity to her that I find more than a little refreshing, although she can be alarmingly open at times. There are strange knots in her thinking—she looks at everything a little oddly. Still, if she doesn't trust her companions, the manner of her mistrust tells me a lot. They're in it for money, pure and simple, Margaret. There's no motive purer than the pig in search of the truffle, is there? And these pigs are very canny indeed, hence the bounteous treasury they've opened to us. They're *our* pigs, at least until it comes time to pay the butcher's bill. As Miss Beckstein says, money talks—bullshit walks."

She nodded. "The mint, and the ability to debase the currency, has always been the criminal-in-chief's best weapon, Erasmus. He could buy out the bourgeoisie from under our banner in a split second, did he but recognize their importance. It's time *we* recognized that, and acted accordingly."

"Well." Erasmus took a sip of brandy. It was fine stuff, liquid fire that warmed his old bag of bones from the inside out. "Judging from what your 'intimate source' told me, even if he recognized its importance he probably wouldn't act on it until it was too late. Indecisive doesn't begin to describe this one, milady. Stranded in a well-stocked kitchen John Frederick could starve himself to death between two cookbooks. He looks solid with the machinery of state behind him, but if he's forced to make tough choices he'll dither and haver until he's half past hanging."

"Well, that's his look out," she said tartly. "Was there anything else we can *use*?"

"Yes. If you don't mind risking the source—at least, this week. It's so big that it will leak sooner rather than later; the French have exploded a corpuscular petard. Caught the navy napping, too; they weren't supposed to have that high a command of the new physics. The flash was visible from Blackpool, apparently, and the toadstool cloud from Lancaster."

"Oh." Her eyes widened. "And with wars, and rumors of wars—"

"Yes, milady. I think something is going to have to happen, sooner or later. The situation in Persia if nothing else is a source of friction, and the temptation to *send a message* to the court of the Sun King—I wouldn't place money on it starting this year, but I can't see him lasting out the decade without strife. John Frederick wants to leave his mark on the history books, lest his son is followed rapidly by a nephew or cousin in the line of succession."

"Then let's start making plans, shall we?" She smiled. It was not a pleasant expression. "If the leviathan is determined to drink the blood of the people, there's going to be plenty to spare for the ticks."

Erasmus shivered. "Indeed, milady."

"Well then." She put her glass down. "Which brings me to another matter I have in mind." Her smile vanished. "I think it's past time you arranged for me to meet this Miss Beckstein, who you say is so like me. I have many questions for her; I'm sure we can trade more than toys once we understand each other better."

3

SPOOK SUMMIT

Twelve weeks earlier:
Mike Fleming was on his way home from his office at the DEA branch, completely exhausted.

Sometimes, when he was extremely tired, he'd lose his sense of smell. It was as if the part of his brain that dealt with scents and stinks and stuff gave up trying to make sense of the world and went to sleep without him. At other times it would come back extra strong, and any passing scent might dredge up a slew of distracting memories. It was a weird kind of borderline synaesthesia, and it reminded him uncomfortably of a time a couple of years ago when he'd been on assignment in some scummy mosquito-ridden swamp down in Florida. The hippie asshole he was staking out had made the tail, and instead of doing the usual number with a Mac-10 or running, had spiked his drink with acid. He'd spent a quarter of an hour in the bathroom of his hotel room staring at the amazing colors in the handle of his toothbrush,

marveling at the texture of his spearmint dental gel, until
he'd thrown up. And now he was so tired it was all coming
back to him in unwelcome hallucinatory detail.

Mike worked in Cambridge, but he lived out in the sticks.
The T only took him part of the way, and as he stumbled
onto the platform he realized fuzzily that he was far too tired
to drive. *Did I really just pull a fifty-hour shift in the office?*
he wondered. *Or am I imagining an extra day?* Whatever the
facts, he was beyond tired. He was at the point where his
eyelids were closing on him, randomly trying to fool him
into falling asleep on his feet. So he phoned for a taxi, nearly
zoning out against a concrete pillar just inside the station
lobby while he waited. The cab was stuffy and hot and
smelled of anonymous cheap sex and furtive medicinal
transactions. It was probably his imagination but he could
almost feel the driver watching him in the mirror, the itchy,
prickly touch of the guy's eyeballs on his face. It was a relief
to get out and slowly climb the steps to his apartment.
"Hello, strange place," he muttered to himself as he unlocked the door. "When was I last here?"

Mike knew he was tired, but it was only when he mis-
entered the code to switch off his intruder alarm twice in a
row that he got a visceral sense of how totally out of it he
was. *Whoa, hold on!* He leaned against the wall and yawned,
forced himself to focus, and deliberately held off from fumbling at the manically bleeping control panel until he'd
blinked back the fuzz enough to see the numbers. *Two days?*
he wondered vaguely as he slouched upstairs, the door banging shut behind him. *Yeah, two days.* A night and most of a
day with the SOC team picking over the bones of the buried
fortress, then a night and most of the next morning debriefing the paranoid defector in a safe house. Then more meetings all afternoon, trying to get it through Tony Vecchio's
head that yes, the source was crazy—in fact, the source was
bug-fuck crazy with brass knobs on—but he was an *interesting* crazy, whose every lead had turned over a stone with
something nasty scuttling for cover from underneath it, and
even the crazy bits were internally consistent.

Mike stumbled past the coat rail and shed his jacket and tie, then fumbled with his shoelaces for a minute. While he was busy unraveling the sacred mysteries of knot theory, Oscar slid out of the living room door, stretching stiffly and casting him a where-have-you-been glare. "I'll get to you in a minute," Mike mumbled. He was used to working irregular hours; Helen the cleaner had instructions for keeping the cat fed and watered when he wasn't about, though she drew the line at the litter tray. It turned out that unlacing the shoes took the last of his energy. He meant to check Oscar's food and water, but instead he staggered into the bedroom and collapsed on the unmade bed. Sleep came slamming down like a guillotine blade.

A couple of hours later, Oscar dragged Mike back to semi-wakefulness. "Aagh." Mike opened his eyes. "Damn. What time is it?" The elderly tom lowered his head and butted his shoulder for attention, purring quietly. *I was dreaming, wasn't I?* Mike remembered. *Something about being in a fancy restaurant with—her.* The ex-girlfriend, the journalist. Miriam. She'd dumped him when he'd explained about The Job. It'd been back during one of his self-hating patches, otherwise he probably wouldn't have been that brutal with the truth, but experience had taught him—"Damn." Oscar purred louder and leaned against his stomach. *Why was I naked from the waist down? What the hell is my subconscious trying to tell me?*

It was only about six o'clock in the evening, far too early to turn over and go back to sleep if he wanted to be ready for the office tomorrow. Mike shook his head, trying to dislodge the cobwebs. Then he sat up, gently pushed Oscar out of the way, and began to undress. After ten minutes in the shower with the heat turned right up he felt almost human, although the taste in his mouth and the stubble itching on his jaw felt like curious reminders of a forgotten binge. *Virtual bar-hopping, all the aftereffects with none of the fun.* He shook his head disgustedly, toweled himself dry, dragged on sweat pants and tee, then took stock.

The flat was remarkably tidy, considering how little time he'd had to spend on chores in the past week—thank Helen for that. She'd left him a note on the kitchen table, scribbled in her big, childish handwriting: MILK STAIL, BOUT MORE. He smiled at that. Oscar's bowls were half-full, so he ignored the cat's special pleading and went through into what had been a cramped storeroom when he moved in. Now it was an even more cramped gym, or as much of one as there was space for in the bachelor apartment. He flipped the radio on as he climbed wearily onto the exercise bike: *Maybe I should have held the shower?* he wondered as he turned the friction up a notch and began pedaling.

Fifteen minutes on the bike then a round of push-ups and he began to feel a bit looser. It was almost time to start on the punch bag, but as he came up on fifty sit-ups the phone in the living room rang. Swearing, he abandoned the exercise and made a dash for the handset before the answering machine could cut in. "Yes?" he demanded.

"Mike Fleming? Can you quote your badge number?"

"I—who *is* this?" he demanded, shivering slightly as the sweat began to evaporate.

"Mike Fleming. Badge number. This is an unsecured line." The man at the other end of the phone sounded impatient.

"Oh, okay." *More fallout from work. Head office, maybe?* Mike paused for a moment, then recited his number. "Now. What's this about?"

"Can you confirm that you were in a meeting with Tony Vecchio and Pete Garfinkle this afternoon?"

"I—" Mike's head spun. "Look, I'm not supposed to discuss this on an open line. If you want to talk about it at the office then you need to schedule an appointment—"

"Listen, Fleming. I'm not cleared for the content of the meeting. Question is, were you in it? Think before you answer, because if you answer wrong you're in deep shit."

"I—yes." Mike found himself staring at the wall opposite. "Now. Who exactly am I talking to?" The CLID display on his phone just said NUMBER WITHHELD. Which was pretty remarkable, on the face of it, because this wasn't an ordinary caller-ID box. And this wasn't an ordinary caller: his line was ex-directory, for starters.

"A minibus will pick you up in fifteen minutes, Fleming. Pack for overnight." The line went dead, leaving him staring at the phone as if it had just grown fangs.

"What the hell?" Oscar walked past his ankle, leaning heavily. "Shit." He tapped the hook then dialed the office. "Tony Vecchio's line, please, it's Mike Fleming. Oh—okay. He's in a meeting? Can you—yeah, is Pete Garfinkle in? What, he's in a meeting too? Okay, I'll try later. No, no message." He put the phone down and frowned. "Fifteen minutes?"

Once upon a time, when he was younger, Mike had believed all the myths.

He'd believed that one syringe full of heroin was enough to turn a fine, upstanding family man into a slavering junkie. He'd believed that marijuana caused lung cancer, dementia, and short-term memory loss, that freebase cocaine—crack—could trigger fits of unpredictable rage, and that the gangs of organized criminals who had a lock on the distribution and sale of illegal narcotics in the United States were about the greatest internal threat that the country faced.

When he was even younger he'd also believed in Santa Claus and the tooth fairy.

Now . . . he still believed in the gangs. Ten years of stalking grade-A scumbags and seeing just what they did to the people around them left precious little room for illusions about his fellow humanity. Some dealers were just ethically impaired entrepreneurs working in a shady high-risk field, attracted by the potential for high profits. But you had to have a ruthless streak to take that level of risk, or be oblivious to the suffering around you, and the dangers of the field seemed to repel sane people after a while. The whole business of illegal drugs was a magnet for seekers of the only *real* drug, the one that was addictive at first exposure, the one that drove people mad and kept them coming back for more until it killed them: easy money. The promise of quick cash money drew scumbags like flies to a fresh dog turd.

Anyone who was in the area inevitably started to smell of shit sooner or later, even if they'd started out clean. Even the cops, and they were supposed to be the good guys.

Ten years ago when he was a fresh-faced graduate with a degree in police science—and still believed in the tooth fairy, so to speak—he'd have arrested his own parents without a second thought if he'd seen them smoking a joint, because it was the right thing to do. But these days, Mike had learned that sometimes it made sense to turn a blind eye to human failings. About six years in, he'd gone through the not-unusual burnout period that afflicted most officers, sooner or later, if they had any imagination or empathy for their fellow citizens. Afterward, he'd clawed his way back to a precarious moral sense, an idea of what was wrong with the world that gave him something to work toward. And now there was only one type of drug addict that he could get worked up over—the kind of enemy that he wanted to lay his hands on so bad he could taste it. He wanted the money addicts; the ones who needed it so bad they'd kill, maim, and wreck numberless other lives to get their fix.

Which was why, a decade after joining up, he was still a dedicated DEA Special Agent—rather than a burned-out GS-12 desk jockey with his third nervous breakdown and his second divorce ahead of him, freewheeling past road marks on the long run down to retirement and the end of days.

When the doorbell chimed exactly twenty-two minutes after the phone rang, the Mike who answered it was dressed again and had even managed to put a comb through his lank blond hair and run an electric razor over his chin. The effect was patchy, though, and he still felt in need of a good night's sleep. He glanced at the entry phone, then relaxed. It was Pete, his partner on the current case, looking tired but not much worse for wear. Mike picked up his briefcase and opened the door. "What's the story?"

"C'mon. You think they've bothered to tell me anything?" Mike revised his opinion. Pete didn't simply look tired and overworked, he looked apprehensive. Which was kind of worrying, in view of Pete's usual supreme self-confidence.

"Okay." Mike armed the burglar alarm and locked his front door. Then he followed Pete toward a big Dodge mini-van, waiting at the curb with its engine idling. A woman and two guys were waiting in it, beside the driver, who made a big deal of checking his agency ID. He didn't know any of them except one of the men, who vaguely rang a bell. *FBI office*, Mike realized as he climbed in and sat down next to Pete. "Where are we going?" he asked as the door closed.

"Questions later," said the woman sitting next to the driver. She was a no-nonsense type in a gray suit, the kind Mike associated with internal audits and inter-agency joint committees. Mike was about to ask again, when he noticed Pete shake his head very slightly. *Oh*, he thought, and shut up as the van headed for the freeway. *I can take a hint.*

When he realized they were heading for the airport after about twenty minutes, Mike sat up and began to take notice. And when they pulled out of the main traffic stream into the public terminals at Logan and headed toward a gate with a checkpoint and barrier, the sleep seemed to fall away. "What *is* this?" he hissed at Pete.

The van barely stopped moving as whatever magic charm the driver had got him waved straight through a series of checkpoints and onto the air side of the terminal. "Look, I don't know either," Pete whispered. "Tony said to go with these guys." He sounded worried.

"Not long now," the woman in the front passenger seat said apologetically.

They drove past a row of parked executive jets, then pulled in next to a big Gulfstream, painted Air Force gray. "Okay, change of transport," called their shepherd. "Every-body out!"

"Wow." Mike looked up at the jet. "They're serious."

"Whoever they are," Pete said apprehensively. "Somehow I don't think we're in Kansas any more, Toto."

A blue-suiter checked their ID cards again at the foot of the stairs and double-checked them using a sheet of photos.

Mike climbed aboard warily. The government executive jet wasn't anything like as luxuriously fitted as the ones you saw in the movies, but that was hardly a surprise—it was a working plane, used for shifting small teams about. Mike strapped himself into a window seat and lay back as the attendant closed the door, checked to see that everyone was strapped in, and ducked inside the cockpit for a quiet conference. The plane began to taxi, louder than any airliner he'd been on in years. Minutes later they were airborne, climbing steeply into the evening sky. In all, just over an hour had elapsed since he answered the phone.

The seat belt lights barely had time to blink out before the woman was on her feet, her back to the cockpit door, facing Mike and Pete. (A couple of the other guys had to crane their heads round to see her.) "Okay, you're wondering where you're going and why," she said matter-of-factly. "We're going to a small field in Maryland. From there you're going by bus to a secure office in Fort Meade where we wait for another planeload of agents to converge from the left coast. Refreshments *will* be served," she added dryly, "although I can't tell you just why you're needed at this meeting because our hosts haven't told me."

One of the other passengers, a black man with the build of a middleweight boxer, frowned. "Can you tell us who you are?" he asked in a deep voice. "Or is that secret, too?"

"Sure. I'm Judith Herz. Boston headquarters staff, FBI, agent responsible for ANSIR coordination. If you guys want to identify yourselves, be my guest."

"I'm Bob Patterson," said the black man, after a momentary pause. "I work for DOE," he added, in tones that said *and I can't tell you any more than that.*

"Rich Wall, FBI." The thin guy with curly brown hair and a neat goatee flashed a brief grin at Herz. *Undercover?* Mike wondered. *Or specialist?* He didn't look like a special agent, that was for sure, not wearing combat pants and a nose-stud.

"Mike Fleming and Pete Garfinkle, Drug Enforcement Agency, Boston SpecOps division," Mike volunteered.

They all turned to face the last passenger, a portly

middle-aged guy with a bushy beard and a florid complexion who wore a pin-striped suit. "Hey, don't all look at
me!" he protested. "Name's Frank Milford, County Surveyor's Office." A worried frown crossed his face. "Just
what *is* this, anyway? There's got to be some mistake, here.
I don't belong—"

"We'll see," said Herz. Mike looked at her sharply. *Five
assorted cops and spooks, and a guy from the* County Surveyor's Office? *What in hell's name is going on here?* "I'm
sure all will be revealed when we arrive."

A minivan with a close-lipped driver met them at the airport.
At first it had looked as if he was heading for Baltimore, but
then they turned off the parkway, taking an unmarked feeder
road that twisted behind a wooded berm and around a slalom
course of huge stone blocks, razor-wire fences, and a gauntlet of surveillance cameras on masts. They came to a halt in
front of a gatehouse set in a high fence surrounding a complex so vast that Mike couldn't take it in. Members of a mu-
nicipal police force he'd never heard of carefully checked
everyone's ID against a prepared list, then issued red-
bordered ID badges with the letters *PV* emblazoned on
them. Then the van drove on. The compound was so big
there were road signs inside it—and three more checkpoints
to stop and present ID at before they finally drew up outside
an enormous black glass tower block. "Follow me, and do
exactly as I say," their driver told them. The entrance was a
separate building, with secured turnstiles and guards who
watched inscrutably as Mike followed his temporary companions along a passageway and then out into a huge atrium,
dominated by a black marble slab bearing a coat of arms in
a golden triangle.

"I've read about this place," Pete muttered in a slightly
overawed tone.

"So when do you think they bring out the dancing girls?"
Mike replied.

"When—" Lift doors opened and closed. Pete caught
Herz watching him and clammed up.

"Rule one: no questions," Herz told him, when she was sure she'd got his attention. She glanced at Mike as well. "Yes?"

"Rule two: no turf wars." Mike crossed his arms, trying to look self-confident. You worked for the DOJ for years, mucking out the public stables, then suddenly someone sent a car for you and drove you round to the grand palace entrance . . .

"No turf wars." Herz nodded at him with weary irony. Suddenly he got the picture.

"Whose rules are we playing by?" he asked.

"Probably these guys, NSA. At least for now." Her eyes flickered at one corner of the ceiling as the elevator came to a halt on the eighth floor. "I assure you, this is as new to me as it is to you."

Their escort led them along a carpeted, sound-deadening corridor, through fire doors and then into a reception room. "Wait here," he said, and left them under the gaze of a secretary and a security guard. Mike blinked at the huge framed photographs on the walls. *What are they doing, trying to grow the world's biggest puffball mushroom?* All the buildings seemed to have razor-wire fences around them and gigantic white domes sprouting from their roofs.

A head popped out from around a corner. "This way, please." Herz led the group as they filed through the door, informatively labeled ROOM 2B8020. Behind the door, Mike blinked with a moment of déjà vu, a flashback to the movie *Dr. Strangelove*. A doughnut-shaped conference table surrounded by rose-colored chairs filled the floor at the near end of the room, but at the other end a series of raised platforms supported a small lecture theater of seats for an audience. Large multimedia screens filled the wall opposite. "If you'd all take seats in the auditorium, please?" called their guide.

"The film you're about to see is classified. You're not to make notes, or talk about it outside your group. After it's been screened, an officer will brief you in person then take you through a team setup exercise so that you know why you're all here and what's expected of you."

Pete stuck his hand in the air.

"Yes?" asked the staffer.

"Should I understand that I'm being seconded to some kind of joint operation?" Pete asked quietly. "Because if so, this is one hell of an odd way to go about it. My superior officer either didn't know or didn't tell. What's going on?"

"He wasn't cleared," said the staffer—and without saying anything else, he left the room.

"What *is* this?" Frank demanded, looking upset. "I mean, what is this place?"

The lights dimmed. "Your attention, please." The voice came from speakers around the room, slightly breathy as its owner leaned too close to the microphone. "The following videotape was shot by a closed-circuit surveillance camera yesterday, at a jail in upstate New York."

Grainy gray-on-white video footage filled the front wall of the theater. It was shot from a camera concealed high up in one corner of the ceiling, with a fish-eye lens staring down at a cell maybe six feet by ten in size.

Mike leaned forward. He could almost smell the disinfectant. This wasn't your ordinary drunk tank. It was a separate cell, with whitewashed cinderblock walls and no window—furnished with a bunk bolted to the floor, a metal toilet and sink bolted to the wall, and not a lot else. Single occupant, high security. *This is important enough to drag me out of bed and fly me six hundred miles?* he wondered.

There was a man in the cell. He was wearing dark pinstriped trousers and a dress shirt, no tie or jacket: he looked like a stockbroker or Wall Street lawyer who'd been picked up for brawling, hair mussed, expression wild. He kept looking at the door.

"This man was arrested yesterday at two-fifteen, stepping off the Acela from Boston with a suitcase that contained some rather interesting items. Agents Fleming and Garfinkle will be pleased to know that information they passed on from the preliminary debriefing of source Greensleeves directly contributed to the bust. Mr. Morgan here was charged with possession of five kilograms of better than ninety-five percent pure cocaine hydrochloride, which goes some way to explain his agitation. There were, ah, other items in the

suitcase. I'll get to them later. For now, let's just say that
while none of them were contraband they are, if anything,
much more worrying than the cocaine."

Mike focused on the screen. The guy in the cell was
clearly uneasy about something—but what? *In solitary.*
Knowing he was under surveillance. After a while he stood
up and paced back and forth, from the door to the far end of
the cell. Occasionally he'd pause halfway, as if trying to remember something.

"Our target here has no previous police record, no convic-
tions, no fingerprints, nothing to draw him to our attention.
He hasn't even registered to vote. He has a driving license
and credit cards but, and here's the interesting bit, some
careful digging shows that the name belongs to a child who
died thirty-one years ago, aged eleven months. He appears
to be the product of a very successful identity theft that established him with a record going back at least a decade.
This James Morgan, as opposed to the one who's buried in a
family plot near Buffalo, went to college in Minnesota and
obtained average grades, majoring in business studies and
economics before moving to New York, where he acquired a
job with a small import-export company, Livingston and
Marks, for whom he has worked for nine years and six
months. According to our friends at the IRS, his entry-level
salary was $39,605 a year, he takes exactly three days of
sick leave every twelve months, and he hasn't had a pay
raise, a vacation, or a sabbatical since joining the firm."

The man on the screen seemed to make up his mind about
something. He ceased pacing and, rolling up his sleeve,
thrust his left wrist under the hot water faucet on the sink.
He seemed to be scrubbing at something—a patch or plaster,
perhaps.

"James Morgan lives in an apartment that appears to be
owned by a letting agency wholly owned by a subsidiary of
Livingston and Marks," the unseen commentator recited
dryly, as if reading from a dossier. "He pays rent of $630 a
month—and you guessed it, he hasn't had a rent rise in nine
years. And that's not the only thing that's missing. He isn't a
member of a gym or health club or a dating agency or a

church or an HMO. He doesn't own an automobile or a pet dog or a television, or subscribe to any newspapers or magazines. He uses his credit card to shop for groceries at the local Safeway twice a week, and here he screwed up—he has a loyalty card for the discounts. It turns out that he never buys toilet paper or light bulbs. However he *does* buy new movie releases on DVD, which is kind of odd for someone who doesn't own a DVD player or a TV or a computer. Once a month, every month, as regular as clockwork, he makes an overnight out of state trip, flying Delta to Dallas–Fort Worth, and while he's away he stays in the Hilton and makes a side trip to buy a Glock 20C, four spare magazines, and four two-hundred-round boxes of ammunition— although he never brings them home. Luckily for him, because he doesn't have a firearms license valid for New York State."

On the screen, something peeled off Morgan's wrist. He rubbed it some more, then turned the faucet off, raised his arm, and peered at whatever the plaster was concealing.

"Checking our records, it appears that Mr. Morgan has purchased over sixty handguns this way, spending rather more on them than he pays in rent. That's in addition to his other duties, which appear to include smuggling industrial quantities of pharmaceutical-grade narcotics. Now, this is where it gets interesting. Watch the screen."

Mike blinked. One moment Morgan was standing in front of the washbasin, peering at the inside of his wrist. The next moment, he was nowhere to be seen. The cell was empty.

Off to one side, Frank from the Surveyor's Office started to complain. "What *is* this? I don't see what this has got to do with me. So you've got a guard taking kickbacks to fool with the videotape in the county jail—"

The lights came up and the door opened. "Nope." The man standing in the doorway was slightly built, in his early forties, with receding brown hair cropped short. He smiled easily as he stepped into the room and stood in front of the screen. *It's him*, Mike realized with interest. The commentator with the dry sense of humor. "That wasn't something we pulled off a tape, that was a live feed. And I assure you, once those data packets arrived here *nobody* tampered with them."

Mike licked his lips. "This links in with what Greensleeves was saying, doesn't it?" he heard himself ask, as if from a distance.

"It does indeed." The man at the front of the auditorium looked pleased. "And that's why you're here. All of you, you've been exposed in some way to this business." He nodded at Mike. "Some of you more than others—if it wasn't for your quick thinking and the way you escalated it via Boston Special Operations, it might have been another couple of days before we realized what kind of intelligence asset you were sitting on."

"Greensleeves?" Pete asked, raising a skeptical eyebrow. "You mean the kook?"

Mike shook his head. *Source Greensleeves*, who called himself Matthias, and who kept yammering on about hidden conspiracies and other worlds in between blowing wholesale rings like they were street-corner crack houses—

"Yes, and I'm afraid he isn't a kook. Let me introduce myself. I'm Lieutenant Colonel Eric Smith, Air Force, on secondment to NSA/CSS, Office of Unconventional Programs. I work for the deputy director of technology. As of an hour ago, you guys are all on secondment from your usual assignments to a shiny new committee that doesn't have a name yet, but that reports to the director of the National Security Council directly, via whoever he puts on top of me— hence all the melted stovepipes and joint action stuff. We've got to break across the usual departmental boundaries if we're going to make this work. One reason you're here is that you've all been vetted and had the security background checks in the course of your ordinary work. In fact, all but one of you are already federal employees working in the national security or crime prevention sectors. The letters have gone out to your managers and you should get independent confirmation when you get back home to Massachusetts and New York after this briefing round and tomorrow's meetings and orientation lectures." Smith leaned against the wall at the front of the room. "Any questions?"

The guy from the DOE, Bob, looked up. "What am *I* doing here?" he rumbled. "Is NIRT a stakeholder?"

Smith looked straight at him. "Yes," he said softly. "The Nuclear Incident Response Teams are a stakeholder."

There was a hissing intake of breath: Mike glanced round in time to see Judith Herz look shocked.

"We have reason to believe that fissionable materials are involved."

4

FERTILE DISCUSSIONS

The Countess Helge and her attendants traveled in convoy with other residents of Thorold Palace that evening, to the Östhalle at the east end of the royal run that formed the artery linking the great houses at the center of Niejwein. Niejwein was the royal capital of the kingdom of Gruinmarkt, which occupied most of the territory of Massachusetts and chunks of New Jersey and New York, over here. As near as Miriam had been able to work out, the first Norse settlements on the eastern seaboard had died out in the eleventh or twelfth centuries, but their replacements—painstakingly carved out by the landless sons of the northern European nobility around the start of the sixteenth century—had flourished, albeit far less so than in her own world. They had no skyscrapers, spacecraft, or steam engines; no United States of America, no Declaration of Independence, no church or Reformation. Rome had fallen on schedule but the dark ages had been darker than in her world. With no Christianity, no Judaism, no Islam, and with no centers of scholarship to preserve the classics, the climb back up had been correspondingly more painful and protracted.

This was the world the Clan came from, descended from an itinerant tinker who had by accident discovered the ability to walk between worlds—to her own New England, land of dour puritan settlers, to the north of the iron triangle of the sugar and slave trade. *He was lucky not to be hanged as a witch*, Helge thought morosely as she stared out of her carriage window, shielding her face behind a lacquered fan as the contraption jolted along the cobblestone street. *Or institutionalized, like a Kaspar Hauser*. Strange things happened to disoriented adults who appeared as if out of thin air, speaking no known language, bewildered and lost. It had nearly happened to Miriam, the first time she accidentally world-walked. *But at least now I understand what I'm doing*, she thought.

World-walking was a recessive gene–linked trait, one whose carriers far outnumbered those who had the ability. To have the ability in full both parents must at least be carriers: the three-generation long braids knotted the Clan's six inner families together, keeping the bloodlines strong, while the outer families occasionally threw up a cluster of world-walking siblings. In the past hundred and fifty years—since the world Helge had grown up in as Miriam had industrialized—the Clan had used their ability to claw their way up from poor merchants to the second seat of power in the kingdom. The ability to send messages from one side of the continent to another within a day gave their traders a decisive edge, as did the weapons and luxury goods they were able to import from America.

The maids squeezed into the bench seat opposite Helge giggled as one wheel clattered off a pothole. She glanced at them irritably from behind her fan, unsure what the joke was, her hochsprache inadequate to follow the conversation. The carriage stank of leather and a faint aroma of stale sweat beneath the cloying toilet waters of the ladies. Helge used no such scents (it was Miriam's habit to bathe daily and wear as

little makeup as possible), but Kara was sometimes overenthusiastic, the young Lady Souterne who traveled with them
this evening seemed to think that smelling like a brothel
would guarantee her a supply of suitors, and as for the last
Clan notables to borrow this coach from the livery stable attached to the palace . . .

The four horses harnessed to the coach—not to mention
the outriders and the carriages in front—kicked up a fine
brown dust, dried out by the hot summer afternoon. It bil-
lowed so high that the occupants were forced to keep the
windows of the carriage closed. They were thick slabs of
rippled green glass, expensive as silver salvers but useful
only insofar as they let beams of dusty evening sunlight into
the oppressively hot interior. Helge could barely make out
the buildings opposite behind their high stone walls, the
shacks and lean-tos of the porters and costermongers and
pamphleteers thronging the boulevard in front of them.

With a shout from the coachmen up top, the carriage
turned off the boulevard and entered the drive up to the
front of the Östhalle, passing cottages occupied by royal
pensioners, galleries and temporary marquees for holding
exhibitions of paintings and tapestries, the wooden fence of
a bear pit, and the stone-built walls around the barracks of
the Royal Life Guards. People thronged all around, the servants and soldiers and guards and bond-slaves of the noble
visitors mingling with the royal household in residence and
with hawkers and beggars and dipsters and chancers of
every kind. A royal party could not but transpire without a
penumbra of leaky festivities trickling down to the grounds
outside.

The carriage stopped. A clatter of steps and the door
opened: four brass horns cut through the racket. "Milady?"
Kara asked. Helge rose first and clambered out onto the top
step, blinking at the slanting orange sunlight coming over
the trees. For a moment she was sure she'd caught her dress
on something—a hinge, a protruding nail—and that
presently it would tear; then she worried that a gust of wind
would render her ridiculous on this exposed platform, until

finally she recognized one of the faces looking up at her from below: "Sieur Huw?" she asked hopefully.

"Milady? If it would please you to take my hand—" he answered in English, accented but comprehensible.

She made it down the steps without embarrassing herself. "Sieur Huw, how kind of you." She managed to smile. Huw was another of those interchangeable youngbloods who infested Clan security, hot-headed adolescent duelists who would have been quite intolerable had Angbard not the means to tame them. When they grew up sufficiently to stop seeking any excuse for a brawl they could be useful: those who had two brain cells to rub together, doubly so. Huw was one of the latter, but Helge had only met him in passing and barely had his measure. Beanpole thin and tall, with brown hair falling freely below his shoulders and a receding chin to spoil what might otherwise have been rugged good looks, Huw moved with a dangerous economy of motion that suggested to those in his path that they had best find business elsewhere. But he wore neither sword nor gun at his belt today. Bearing arms in the presence of the king was a privilege reserved for the royal household and its guards. "Where's everything happening?" she asked him out of the side of her mouth.

"Around the garden at the back. Most notables have arrived already but you are by no means late. We can go through the north wing, if you want to give the impression you've been here discreetly all along," he offered.

"I suppose you were looking for me," she said, half-jokingly.

"As a matter of fact"—his gaze slid across the footmen holding the huge doors open for them—"I was." He nodded, a minute gesture toward a bow, as he crossed the threshold, then paused to bow fully before the coat of arms displayed above the floor. Miriam—remembering her manners as Helge— dropped a brief curtsey. *Are we being watched?* she wondered. Then, sharply, *Who told Huw to wait for me?* Huw waited for her politely, then offered his arm. She took it, and they walked together into the central hall of the north wing of the Östhalle.

The hall was a hollow cube, the walls supporting a wide staircase that meandered upward past three more floors beneath a ceiling glazed with a duke's fortune in lead crystal. Other rooms barely smaller than aircraft hangars opened off to either side, their windows open to admit the last of the evening sunlight. Discreet servants were already moving around the edges, lighting lamps and chandeliers. Others, bearing platters loaded with finger food, moved among the guests. More youngbloods, looking slightly anxious without their swords. Clusters of women in silks and furs, glittering with jewelry, enthusiastic girls shepherded by cynical matrons, higher orders attended by their ladies-in-waiting. Countess Helge paid barely any attention to her own retinue beyond a quick check that Lady Kara and Lady Souterne and Kara's maid Jenny and Souterne's maid whoever-she-was were following. "I'm sure there are more interesting people for you to wait upon," she said quietly, pitching her voice so that only Huw might hear it over the chatter of conversations around them. "I'm just a boring dried-up old countess with poor manners and a sideline in business journalism."

"Ha-ha. I don't think so. Your ladyship is modest beyond reproach. Would your ladyship care for an aperient?" He snapped his fingers at a servant bearing a salver laden with glasses.

"Obviously my company is so boring that it's driving you to drink already," she said with a smile.

"Milady?" He held a glass out for her.

"Thank you." Helge accepted the offered glass and sniffed. *Sherry*, or something not unlike it. A slight undertone of honeysuckle. Would they serve fortified wines here? "You were looking for me," she said, gently steering him back toward the far side of the hall and the garden party beyond. "Are you going to keep me on tenterhooks, wondering why?"

Huw sniffed, his nostrils flaring. "I do confess that you would have to ask her grace the duchess for an explanation," he said blandly. "It was at her urging that I made myself available. I'm sure she has her reasons." He smiled, trying for urbanity and coming dangerously close to a smirk. "Perhaps she thought that a, ah, 'boring dried-up old countess with poor manners and a sideline in business journalism' might need a young beau on whose arm she might lean, thereby inducing paroxysms of jealousy among the young-sters who feel themselves snubbed, or among those pullets who would imagine her a rival for their roosters?"

He repeated me word-perfect, she thought, so astonished that she forgot herself and half-drained her glass instead of sipping from it. (It was a dry sherry, or something very sim-ilar. Too dry for her taste.) *He looks like a chinless wonder with a line of witty patter but he's got a memory like a com-puter.* She raised one eyebrow at him. "I'm not in the mar-ket," she said, slowly and clearly.

"I beg your pardon?" He sounded genuinely confused, so that for a moment Helge almost relented. But the setup was too perfect.

"I said, I'm not in the marriage market," she repeated. "So I'm no threat to anyone." With some satisfaction she noticed his cheeks flush. "Nice wine. Fancy another one?" *If I'm go-ing to be a boring dried-up old countess with poor manners I might as well make the most of it,* she resolved. Otherwise the evening promised to drag.

"I think I will," he said hesitantly. "I beg your pardon, I in-tended no disrespect."

"None taken." She finished her glass. *Better drink the next one more slowly.*

"Her grace observed that you were looking for gentles with an interest in the sciences," Huw commented, half-turning to snag a fresh glass so that she had to strain to hear him. "Is that so?"

Oh. The penny dropped and Miriam felt like kicking Helge for a moment. Trying to be two people at once was so confusing! "Maybe," she said guardedly. "I'm thinking about trying to get a discussion group going. Just people talking to each other. Why do you ask?"

He shrugged. "I was hoping—well. I'm going stale here. You know about the heightened security state, I believe? I don't know much about your background—I was forced to interrupt my studies and return here." He grimaced. "It's summer recess on the other side, so I'm not losing much ground—except access to the labs and to the college facilities—but if it goes on much longer I'm going to have to take a year out. And you're right in one supposition, my father's been pressing me to complete my studies and settle down, take a wife, and accept a postal rank. It's only the generosity of the debatable society that's allowed me to keep working on my thesis this far."

"Uh-huh." Miriam, wearing the Helge identity like a formal dress, steered her interviewee around a small knot of talkative beaux and through a wide-open doorway, through a state dining room where a table set for fifty waited beneath a chandelier loaded with a hundred candles. "Well, I don't know that I could say anything on your behalf that would help you—but if it's any consolation, I know the feeling. We're cut off and isolated here. For all that we're a social elite, the intellectual climate isn't the most stimulating. I was hoping to find people who'd be interested in helping organize a series of monthly lectures and weekly study group meetings. What were—are—you studying?"

"I'm midway through a master's in media arts and sciences," Huw admitted, sounding slightly bashful about it. "Working on fabrication design templates."

"Oh." It sounded deathly boring. Miriam switched off as they threaded their way around a gaggle of female courtiers attending on some great lady. "What does that involve? What college did you say you were studying at?"

"The MIT Media Lab. We're working on a self-contained tool kit for making modern electronic devices in the field—I say! Are you all right?"

Miriam wordlessly passed him her glass then fumbled with a silk handkerchief for a few seconds. "I'm. Okay. I think." *Apart from the aftereffects of wine inhalation.* She dabbed at her sleeve, but the worst seemed to have missed it. "Tell me more . . ."

"Sure. I'm doing a dissertation project on the fab lab—it's a workbench and tool kit that's designed to do for electronics what a blacksmith's forge or a woodworking shop does for ironmongery or carpentry. You'll be able to make a radio, or an oscilloscope, or a protocol analyzer or computer, all in the field. Initially it'll be able to make all of its own principal modules from readily available components like FPGAs and PCB stock—we're working with the printable circuitry team who're trying to use semiconductor inks in bubble-jet printers to print on paper, for example. I was looking into some design modularity issues—to be blunt, I want to be able to take one home with me. But there's a long way to go—"

By the time they fetched up in the huge marquee at the rear of the palace, two drinks and forty-something invitations later, Miriam was feeling more than a little light-headed. But her imagination was running full tilt; Huw had taken to the idea of monthly seminars like a duck to water and suggested half a dozen names of likely participants along the way, all of them young inner family intellects, frustrated and stifled by the culture of conservativism that infused the Clan's structures. Most of them were actively pursuing higher education in America, but had been blocked off from their studies by the ongoing security alert. Most of them were names she'd never heard of, second sons or third daughters of unexceptional lineage—not the best and the brightest whose dossiers Kara was familiarizing her with. Huw knew them by way of something he called the debating society, which seemed to be a group of old drinking buddies who occasionally clubbed together to sponsor a gifted but impecunious student. It was, Miriam reflected, absolutely typical of the Clan that the sons and daughters with an interest in changing the way their society worked were the ones who were furthest from the levers of power, their education left to the grace and charity of dilettantes.

Most of the introductions were not Clan-related in any way, however. As the evening continued, both her smile and her ability to stay in character as the demure blue-blooded Countess Helge became increasingly strained. Huw had other obligations of a social nature to fulfill and took his leave sooner than she'd have liked, leaving her to face the crowds with only occasional support from Kara. Sieur Hyvert of this and Countess Irina of that bowed and curtseyed respectively and addressed her in hochsprache (and once, in the case of a rural backwoods laird, in loewsprache, confusing her completely), and as the evening wore on she was gripped with a worrying conviction that she was increasingly being greeted with the kindly condescension due an idiot, a mental defective—by those who were willing to speak to her at all. There were political currents here that she was not competent to navigate unaided. English was not the language of the upper class but the tongue the Clan families used among themselves, and her lack of fluency in hochsprache marked her out as odd, or stupid, or (worst of all) alien. Some of the older established nobility seemed to take the ascendancy of the Clan families as a personal affront. After one particularly pained introduction, she stifled a wince and turned round to hunt for her lady-in-waiting.

"Kara? Where are—" she began, sticking to hochsprache, that particular phrase coming more easily than most, when she realized that a knot of courtiers standing nearby was coming her way. They were mostly young, and all male, and their loud chatter and raucous laughter caught Miriam's attention in a way that was at once naggingly familiar and unwelcome. *Shit, Kara, you pick your time to go missing beautifully.* She glanced round, ready to retreat, but there was no easy way out of the path of the gaggle of jocks—

One of whom was speaking to her. "What?" she said blankly, all vestiges of hochsprache vanishing from her memory like the morning dew.

He glanced over his shoulder and said something: more laughter, with an unfriendly edge to it. "You are—wrong, the wrong, place," he said, staring down his nose at her. "Go home, grovel, bitch." Someone behind him said something in hochsprache.

Miriam glared at him. Rudeness needed no translation. And backing down wouldn't guarantee safety. Her heart hammering, she fumbled for words: "What dog, are, belong you, do you belong to? I am offense—"

Almost too late she saw his hand tightening on the hilt of his sword. *A sword?* Surprise almost drowned her fear—swords were forbidden in the royal presence, except by the bodyguard. But this wasn't the king's party. The arrogant young asshole began to turn to one side and she realized hazily that he wasn't about to draw on her—not in public—as she got a glimpse past his shoulder of a bored, half-amused golden-boy profile she'd seen once before, saying something to her assailant. *Oh shit, it's him. Egon.* The crown prince, handsome and perfect in form and a spoiled hothead by upbringing. The bottom threatened to drop out of her world: this perfect jock could literally get away with murder, if he was so inclined.

"He says, you bed him, maybe he not kill you when he king, bitch." Two other bravos, brilliantly dressed, managed to interpose themselves between the self-appointed transla- tor and his pack leader. "With the others."

A black fury threatened to cut off Miriam's vision. "Tell him to get lost," she said sharply, in English, dropping all pretense of politeness. *If you surrender they'll own you,* she thought bleakly, forcing her momentarily treacherous knees to hold her upright. *And if you won't surrender they'll try to break you.* "I'm not his—"

"You are the Countess Helge voh Thorold d'Hjorth?" someone behind her shoulder asked in stilted English. She glanced round, her heart hammering in barely suppressed anger. While the jocks made sport she'd completely missed the other group that appeared to want something of her: two gentlemen with the bearing of bodyguards, shepherding four maids who clustered around a stooped figure, moving with exaggerated caution.

"I—" Trapped between the two factions she summoned up Helge, who racked her brain for the correct form of re- sponse. "I am that one," she managed, flustered.

"Good. You are—" Then she lost him. The guard spoke too fast for her to track his words, syllables sliding into one another.

She forced a smile, tense and ugly, then stole a glance back over her shoulder, lest one of Egon's thugs was about to stick a knife in her back. But they were talking and joking about something else, their attention no longer focused on her like hunting dogs. "I beg your pardon. Please to repeat this?"

The guard stepped around her. "I'll take care of the boys," he said quietly. Louder: "This is her royal highness, the Queen Mother. She would have words with you."

"I, ah—" *hope she's not as rude as her eldest grandson.* Numb with surprise, Helge managed a curtsey. "Am it pleased by your presence, your royal high! Highness," she managed before she completely lost her ability to stay in character.

The stooped figure reached out a hand to her. "Rise."

Shit, she swore to herself. *How much worse can it get? The* one *situation where I need backup—a royal audience—comes up* twice, *and what's Kara doing?* "Your majesty," she said, bending to kiss the offered hand.

The Queen Mother resembled Mother Teresa of Calcutta—if the latter had ever sported a huge Louis Quinze hairdo and about a hundred yards of black silk taffeta held together with large ruby- and sapphire-encrusted lumps of gold. Her eyes were sunken and watery with rheum, and her face was gaunt, the skin drawn tight over her beak of a nose. She looked to be eighty years old, but having been presented before her son, Miriam reckoned she couldn't be much over sixty. "Rise, I said," the Queen Mother croaked in hochsprache. Then in English: "You shall call me Angelin. And I shall call you Helge."

"I—" Miriam blanked for a moment. It was just one shock too many. "Yes, Angelin." *You're the king's mother—you can call me anything you like and I'm not going to talk back.* She took a deep breath. (As Roland had put it, his majesty Alexis Nicholau III of the Kingdom of Gruinmerkt liked to collect jokes about his family—he had two dungeons full of them.) "What can I—I'm at your service—I mean—"

The Queen Mother's face wrinkled. After a moment Miriam realized she was smiling. *At least she isn't howling, "Off with her head!"* "What you're wondering is, why do I speak this language?" Miriam nodded mutely, still numb and shaken by the confrontation with Egon's bravos. "It's a long story." The older woman sighed breathily. "Walk with me, please."

Angelin was stooped, her back so bent that she had to crane her neck back to see the ground ahead of her. And she walked at a painful shuffle. Miriam matched her speed, feeling knuckles like walnuts in an empty leather glove clutch at her arm. *I'm being honored*, she realized. Royalty didn't stoop to using just anyone as a walking frame. After a moment a long-dormant part of her memory kicked into life: *Ankylosing spondylitis?* she wondered. If so, it was a miracle Angelin was out of bed without painkillers and antiinflammatory drugs.

"I knew your mother when she was a little girl," said the queen. Shuffle, pant. "Delightful girl, very strong-willed." *She said "I." That means she's talking personally, doesn't it? Or is it only the reigning monarch who says "we"? If that applies here?* Miriam puzzled as the queen continued: "Glad to see they haven't drowned it out of her. Have they?"

That seemed to demand a reply. "I don't think so, your royal highness." Shuffle.

"Oh, they'll try," Angelin added unreassuringly. "Just like last time."

Like what? Miriam bit her tongue. Her head was spinning with questions, fear and anger demanding attention, and the small of her back was slippery-cold with sweat. Angelin was steering her toward a side door in the palace, and her ladies-in-waiting and guards were screening her most effectively. If Kara had noticed anything—but Kara wasn't in sight and Miriam didn't dare create a scene by looking for her. "Is there anything I can do for you?" Miriam asked, desperately looking for a tactful formula, something to help her steer the conversation toward waters she was competent to navigate.

"Perhaps." The door opened before them as if by magic, to reveal a small vestibule. Four more guards waited on either side of a thronelike chair. A padded stool sat before it. "Please be seated in our presence." Two of the guards stepped forward to cradle the old queen's shoulders, while a third positioned the stool beneath her. "Take the chair; I cannot use it."

Definitely some kind of autoimmune—Miriam forced herself to stop thinking. She sat down carefully, grateful for the support.

"Leave us." Angelin's gimlet stare sent all but two of the guards packing. The last two stood in front of the door, their faces turned to the woodwork but their hands on the hilts of their swords. The Queen Mother looked back at Miriam. "It is seven years since Eloise died," said Angelin. "And Alexis is not inclined to remarry. He's got his heir, and for all his faults, lack of devotion to his wife's memory is not one of them."

"Ah." Miriam realized her fingers were digging into her knees, and she forced herself to let go.

"You can relax. This is not a job interview; nobody is going to offer you the throne," Angelin added, so abruptly that Miriam almost choked.

"But I didn't want—" She brought herself up fast. "I'm sorry. You, uh, speak English very well. The vernacular—"

"I grew up over there," said Angelin, then was silent for almost a minute.

She grew up *there?* The statement was wholly outrageous, even though the individual words made sense.

Eventually, Angelin began to speak again. "The six families have aspired to become seven for almost a century now. I was only eighteen, you know. Back in 1942. Last time the council tried to capture the throne. They didn't want me siding with my braid lineage, so they had me brought up in secrecy, in America; it wouldn't be the first time, or the last. They brought me back and civilized me then farmed me out to the third son when I came of age. Both his elder brothers subsequently died, in a hunting accident and of a fever, respectively. The council of landholders—the laandsknee— screamed blue murder and threatened to annul the marriage: but then the six started tearing each other's guts out in civil war, and that was an end to the matter, for a generation."

The lamplight flickered and Miriam felt an icy certainty

clutching at her guts. "You mean, the Clan?" she asked. "You're a world-walker?"

"I *was*." Angelin's eyes were dark hollows in the dim light. "Pregnancy changes you, you know. And I doubt I'd survive if I tried it, today. My old bones are not what they were. And I gather the other world has changed, too. But enough about me." A withered flicker of a smile: "I know your grandmother. She swears by you, you know. Well, she swears about you, but that's much the same: it means you're in her thoughts. She's pigheaded, too."

"I don't see eye to eye with her," Helge said tightly. The Duchess Hildegarde had once sent agents to kill or dishonor her, thinking her an imposter; since proven wrong, she had subsided into a resentful sulk broken only by expressions of disdain or contempt. *What a loving family we aren't.*

"She told me that herself," the Queen Mother said dismissively. Her eyes gleamed as she looked directly at Helge. "I wanted to see you myself before I made my mind up," she said.

"Made your mind up?" Miriam could hear her voice rising unpleasantly, even though everything she'd learned as Helge told her she must stick to a cultivated awe in the royal personage. "About *what*? I've just been threatened by your grandson—"

"Don't you worry about that." Angelin sounded almost amused. "I'll deal with Egon later. You may leave now. I won't stand on ceremony. Thurman, show the lady out—"

"What *is* this?" Miriam demanded plaintively.

"Later," said the Queen Mother, as one of the guards—Thurman—urged Helge toward the door. "The trait is recessive," she added, slightly louder. "That means—"

"I know what it means," Miriam replied sharply.

"We'll talk later. Go now." The Queen Mother looked away dismissively. The door closed behind Helge, stranding the younger woman at one side of a sprung dance floor where couples paced in circles around each other in complex patterns that defied interpretation. Miriam—at this moment she felt herself to be entirely Miriam, not even an echo of the social veneer that formed her alter ego Helge remaining

to cover the yawning depths—took a ragged breath. She felt
stifled by layers of artifice, suffocated by the social expectations of having to live as a noble lady: and now she had to
put up with threats, innuendo, and hints from the royal family? She felt hot and cold at once, and her stomach hurt.

The trait is recessive. The king was a carrier. That meant
that each of his sons had a one in four chance of being a carrier. *Have you thought about marriage?* Obviously not from
the right angle, because *You've been too successful, too fast.*
Wasn't Prince Egon—golden boy with a thousand-yard
stare, watching her with something ugly in his eyes—
already engaged to some foreign princess? *Raised in secrecy.* Might *he* be a carrier? *I know your grandmother.*

"Lady Helge!" It was Kara, two maids in tow, looking angry and relieved simultaneously. "Where have you been? We
were so worried!"

"Hold this," said Miriam, thrusting the empty glass at her.
Then she darted outside as fast as she could, in search of a
bush to throw up behind.

TRANSLATED TRANSCRIPT BEGINS

"Has the old goose been drinking too much, do you suppose?"

"Hist, now! She'll hear you!"

"Oh don't worry. She only understands one word in ten.
It can't be helped, I suppose. She grew up in fairyland,
wearing trousers and chopping up dead men to understand
how they work. They didn't have time to teach her how to
speak as well."

"What, you mean—" (*shocked giggle*) "—to the Crone?"

"No, I don't suppose she's *that* stupid. But she's one of the
kind such as have a thoughtful temper. You don't want to get
on the wrong side of her, you know. Wait, here she comes—"
(*English*) "—would you like another glass, ma'am?"

(*Click.*)

"Phew, there she goes again, bouncing after some
stuffed-pants longhair. This one looks like he swallowed a
ferret, look at the way he's twitching."

"Raw with lust for the old goose."

"Hist! Is that your third glass?"

"Who's counting, madam? Listen, *you* have that one. Oh, over there! Don't look, don't be so obvious. Himself with the brown hair and the, um, isn't *he* something?"

"He—"

(*Click.*)

"Not as if my lady is stupid, but she is *strange*. Witchy-weird like any of the Six, but more so, if you follow me. Wears breeches and talks the Anglaische all the time except when she's trying to learn. But she does it so badly! Look at the way she carries herself. Wagging tongues have it that she seduced Sieur Roland, but if something like that could seduce anything then *I'm* Queen of Summer Angels. What do you say, Nicky? Dried-up bluestocking or—"

"Don't underestimate her, she's not stupid, even if she doesn't understand much. She may not look like a lizard but she's descended from a long lineage of snakes. Sieur Roland is dead, isn't he, so I'm led to believe? Do you think she had something to do with that? Suck the man dry and cast aside his bones like a spider."

"Nicky! That's disgusting!"

"Not as disgusting as what that spotty lad wanted with you in the bedchamber when she was away."

"*Don't* you go talking like that about me—"

"Then don't you go calling me disgusting, *miss*."

(*Sigh.*) "I'm not calling you disgusting."

"Then it's a good thing I didn't call you a whore, isn't it? People might misunderstand."

"Here, have another—drink while she's not looking. Who *is* that longshanks oddboy, anyway?"

"Him? He's one of the hangers-on on at court. Some fancy-boy or other to the king's bedchamber. Dresser-on-of-codpieces or some such."

"You don't know, do you? She doesn't know!"

"Rubbish, he's Sieur Villem du Praha and he's married to Lady Jain of Cours, and he rides with the king's hunt. And look, there's our missy Kara going all gushy over him."

"Kara? She's—"

"You just look, whenever she gets within six feet of him

she has to tie her knees together with her stay laces to stop them falling apart. Silly little bitch, she hasn't seen the way he looks at his wife."

"Milady Kara's not one to turn her nose up at a lost cause. But what's with milady the honorable Old Goose? What's *she* doing with him?"

"Who the—knows, pardon my loewsprache, she's being a witch again. Shamelessly talking to strange men."

"What's shameless about it? She's got her *chaperone*—"

(*Laughter*.) "Red-Minge Kara is a chaperone? What color is the sky in your county, and do the fish have feathers to match the birds' scales?"

"I'd like to know what she's talking about, though."

"I've got an idea. Wait here."

(*Click*.)

"So? What's the story?"

"Give me that."

"Must be a long story to wet your throat like that."

"Long? You haven't heard the first of it—"

"Is she trying to fix Kara up with a paramour?"

"Is she—bah! Even Old Witchy-Goose isn't *that* stupid, what would people say if her lady-in-waiting got pregnant? I'm sorry I asked. I thought it would be something like that. And the promises I had to make!"

"Promises?"

"Yes, I said I'd ask you to meet Oswelt—him with the belly—behind the marquee in half an hour for a midnight promenade."

"Bitch!"

"Now now, mind your language! Remember I said you weren't a whore? I didn't *promise* you'd be there, just said I'd ask."

"You did . . ."

"So if you want . . ."

"What about her ladyship? What did you find out?"

"Well, it's as well I asked because something tells me we'll be dragged hither and back in the next months, or I'm not a household hand."

"Really? Why? What's she want from him?"

"He's not with the king's wardrobe, he's with the prince's. And you know what that means."

"Oh!"

"Yes."

"The slut!"

"Absolutely wanton."

"We'll be back here three times a night before the month is out."

"Indeed."

"Hmm. So what else did you tell master Oswelt about me . . . ?"

(*Click.*)

TRANSCRIPT ENDS

5

INCORRECT ASSUMPTIONS

T welve weeks ago (continued):
   Mike Fleming leaned back in his chair and tried desperately to stifle a yawn. *This is crazy,* he told himself. *How can you be tired at a time like* this?

The air conditioner in the conference room wheezed, losing the battle to keep the heat of the summer evening at bay. He desperately needed another coffee. Despite the couple of hours' nap he'd caught back home before the spooks from NSA sucked him in, his eyes kept half-closing, threatening him with a sleep-deprivation shutdown.

"Agent Fleming?"

"Oh. Yeah? Sorry, what was the question?"

"How long have you been awake?" It was Smith, his expression unreadable.

Mike shook himself. "About fifty hours. Got about an hour's sleep before your guys picked me up."

"Ah—right." Out of the corner of one eye Mike barely registered Herz from the FBI office looking sympathetic.

"Okay, I'll try not to keep you," said Smith. "We need you awake and alert for tomorrow. Meanwhile, can you give us a brief run-through on the background to Greensleeves? I've read Tony's write-up of your report, but everyone else here needs to be put in the frame, and it's probably better if they get it from the horse's mouth first before they get the folder. How do you take your coffee?"

Mike yawned. "Milk, no sugar." He stood up. "Shall I?"

"Be my guest." Smith waved him toward the podium.

"Okay." Mike forced himself to breathe deeply, suppressing another yawn, as Colonel Smith quietly picked up a white phone and ordered a round of coffees for the meeting. "Sorry, folks, but it's been a long couple of days." Appreciative muttering. "Source Greensleeves. Don't ask me who dreams up these stupid names. A couple of weeks ago Greensleeves, whoever he was, casually dropped the hammer on a ring operating out of Cambridge. At this time it was purely a standard narcotics investigation. A low-level wholesaler, name of Ivan Pavlovsk, was handling the supply line for a neighborhood street gang who were shifting maybe a kilo of heroin every month. Greensleeves left a code word and said he'd be back in touch later. I thought at first it was the usual caped-crusader bullshit but it turned out to be solid and the DA up there is nailing down a plea bargain that should put our Ukrainian friend behind bars for the next decade." He leaned against the podium and glanced at Smith. "Are you sure you want the whole list?"

"Give us the highlights." Smith's eyebrows wrinkled. "Up until yesterday. What you told Tony Vecchio." Tony was Mike and Pete's boss in the investigation branch.

"Okay. We had two more leads from Greensleeves, at one-week intervals. Both were for intermediate wholesale links supplying cocaine in single-digit kilogram amounts to retail operations. There was no lead on Greensleeves himself. Each time, he used a paid-for-cash or stolen mobile phone, called from somewhere populous—a restroom in the Prudential, the concourse of the Back Bay station—and spent between thirty seconds and three minutes fifteen seconds on the phone before ringing off. He came straight through to my desk extension and left voice mail each time—the third time we had a tap and trace in place but couldn't get any units there in time. He used the same password with each call, and gave no indication as to why he was trying to shop these guys to us. Until yesterday Pete here was betting it was an internal turf war. My money was on an insider wanting to cash out and make a WSP run, but either way the guy was clearly a professional." Mike paused.

"If anyone wants a recap, we're having copies of the case notes prepared for you," Smith added. "Can I ask you all *not* to make any written notes of this briefing," he added pointedly in the direction of Frank the surveyor. "We'd only have to incinerate them afterward."

Like that, is it? Mike wondered. "Shall I continue?"

"When you're ready."

"Okay. We got a tip-off from Greensleeves five weeks ago, about Case Phantom's main distribution center for Boston and Cambridge. Case Phantom is Pete's specialty, a really major pipeline we've been trying to crack for months. Greensleeves used the same code word, this time in an envelope along with a sample of merchandise and—this is significant—a saliva sample, not to mention the other thing that I presume is why we're all here. Greensleeves wanted to turn himself in, which struck us as noteworthy: but what set the alarm bells going was Greensleeves wanting to turn himself in and enlist in the Witness Protection Scheme in return for knocking over Case Phantom. And helping us get it right, this time."

Pete sighed noisily.

"Yeah," said Mike. "Operation Phoenix was part of Case Phantom, too. Back before Greensleeves decided to come aboard. It was a really big bust—the wrong kind."

Now he saw Agent Herz wince. They'd taken up the tip-off and gone in like gangbusters, half the special agents posted at the Boston DEA office with heavy support from the police. But they'd hit a wall—literally. The modern-looking office building had turned out to be a fortress, doors and windows backed by steel barriers and surveillance cameras like a foreign embassy.

Worse, the defenders hadn't been the usual half-assed

Goodfellas wannabes. Someone with a Russian army-surplus sniper's rifle had taken down two of the backup SWAT team before Lieutenant Smale had pulled them back and called up reinforcements for a siege. Then, four hours into the siege—just as they'd been getting ready to look for alternative ways in—the building had collapsed. Someone had mined its foundations with demolition charges and brought it right down on top of the cellars, which were built like a cold war nuclear bunker. The SOCOs and civil engineers were still sieving the wreckage, but Mike didn't expect them to find anything.

"In retrospect, Phoenix should have been a signal that something really weird was happening," Mike continued. "It took us a long time to dig our way into the rubble and what we found was disturbing. Bomb shelters, cold stores, closed-circuit air-conditioning . . . and fifty kilograms of pharmaceutical-grade cocaine in a vault. Plus an arsenal like a National Guard depot. But there were no bodies . . ." He trailed off introspectively. *Too tired for this*, he thought dizzily.

"Okay, now fast-forward. You've had a series of tip-offs from source Greensleeves, leading up to Greensleeves turning himself in three days ago," Colonel Smith stated. "What about the saliva sample? It's definitely him?"

Mike shrugged. "PCR says so. Matthias is definitely source Greensleeves. He got us an armored fortress in downtown Cambridge with fifty kilos of pharmaceutical-grade cocaine and a *Twilight Zone* episode to explain, plus a series of crack warehouses and meth labs up and down the coast. Biggest serial bust in maybe a decade. He's—" Mike shook his head. "I've spent a couple of hours talking to him and it's funny, he doesn't sound crazy, and after watching that video—well. Matt—Greensleeves—*doesn't* sound sane at first, he sounds like a nut. Except that he's right about everything I checked. And the guy vanishing in front of the camera is just icing on the cake. He *predicted* it." Mike shook his head again. "Like I said, he sounds crazy—but I'm beginning to believe him."

"Right." Colonel Smith broke in just as a buzzer sounded, and a marine guard opened the outer door for a steward, who wheeled in a trolley laden with coffee cups and flasks. "We'll pause right here for a moment," Smith said. "No shop talk until after coffee. Then you and Pete can tell us the rest."

The debriefing room wasn't a cell. It resembled nothing so much as someone's living room, tricked out in cheap sofas, a couple of recliners, a coffee table, and a sideboard stocked with soft drinks. The holding suite where they'd stashed Greensleeves for the duration didn't look much like a jail cell, either. It had all the facilities of a rather boring hotel room—beds, desk, compact en-suite bathroom—if the federal government had been in the business of providing motel accommodation for peripatetic bureaucrats.

But the complex had two things in common with every jail ever built. First, the door to the outside world was locked on the outside. And second, the windows didn't open. In fact, if you looked at them for long enough you'd realize that they weren't really windows at all. Both the debriefing room and the holding suite were buried in a second-story basement, and to get in you'd have to either prove your identity and sign in through two checkpoints and a pat-down search, or shoot your way past the guards.

Mike and Pete had taken the friendly approach at first, when they'd first started the full debriefing protocol. After all, he was cooperating fully and voluntarily. Why risk pissing him off and making him clam up?

"Okay, let's take it from the top." Mike smiled experimentally at the thin, hatchet-faced guy on the sofa while Pete hunched over the desk, fiddling with the interview recorder. Hatchet-face—Matt—nodded back, his expression serious. As well it should be, in his situation. Matt was an odd one; mid-thirties in age, with curly black hair and a face speckled with what looked like the remnants of bad acne, but built like a tank. He wore the same leather jacket and jeans he'd had on when he walked through the DEA office door.

"We're going to start the formal debriefing now you're here. When we've got the basics of your testimony down on tape, we'll escalate it to OCDTF and get them to sign off on your WSP participation and then set up a joint liaison team with the usual—us, the FBI, possibly FINCEN, and any other organizations whose turf is directly affected by your testimony. We can't offer you a blanket amnesty for any crimes you've committed, but along the way we'll evaluate your security requirements, and when we've got the prosecutions in train we'll be able to discuss an appropriate plea bargain for you, one that takes your time in secure accommodation here into account as time served. So you should be free to leave with a new identity and a clean record as soon as everything's wrapped up." He took a breath. "If there's anything you don't understand, say so. Okay?"

Matt just sat on the sofa, shoulders set tensely, for about thirty seconds, until Mike began to wonder if there was something wrong with him. Then: "You don't understand," he said, quietly but urgently. "If you treat this as a criminal investigation we will both die. They have agents everywhere and you have no idea what they are capable of." He had an odd foreign accent, slightly German, but with markedly softened sibilants.

"We've dealt with Mafia families." Mike smiled encouragingly.

"They are not your Mafia." Matt stared at him. "You are at war. They are a government. They will not respond as criminals, but as soldiers and politicians. I am here to defect, but if you are going to insist that they are ordinary criminals, you will lose."

"Can you point to them on a map?" Mike asked, rhetorically. The informer shook his head. He looked faintly— disappointed? Amused? Annoyed? Mike felt a stab of hot anger. *Stop playing head games with me*, he thought, *or you'll be sorry*.

Pete looked up. "Are we talking terrorists here? Like Al-Qaida?" he asked.

Matt stared at him. "I said they are a government. If you do not understand what that means we are both in very deep trouble." He picked up the cigarette packet on the table and unwrapped it carefully. His fingers were long, but his nails were very short. One was cracked, Mike noticed, and his right index finger bore an odd callus: not a shooter's finger, but something similar.

"There is more than one world," Matt said carefully as he opened the packet and removed a king-size. "This world, the world you are familiar with. The world of the United States, and of Al-Qaida. The world of automobiles and airliners and computers and guns and antibiotics. But there is another world, and you know nothing of it."

He paused for a moment to pick up the table lighter, then puffed once on the cigarette and laid it carefully on the ashtray.

"The other world is superficially like this one. There is a river not far from here, for example, roughly where the Charles River flows. But there is no city. Most of Boston lies under the open sea. Cambridge is heavily forested.

"There are people in the other world. They do not speak your language, this English tongue. They do not worship your tree-slain god. They don't have automobiles or airliners or computers or guns or antibiotics. They don't have a United States. Instead, there are countries up and down this coast, ruled by kings."

Matt picked up the cigarette and took a deep lungful of smoke. Mike glanced over at Pete to make sure he was recording, and caught a raised eyebrow. When he looked back at Matt, careful to keep his expression blank, he realized that the informant's hands were shaking slightly.

"It's a nice story," he commented. "What has it got to do with the price of cocaine?"

"Everything!" Matthias snapped.

Taken aback, Mike jerked away. Matt stared at him: he stared right back, nonplussed. "What do you mean?"

After several seconds, Matthias's tension unwound. "I'm sorry. I will get to the point," he said. "The kingdom of Gruinmarkt is dominated by a consortium of six noble houses. Their names are—no, later. The point is, some members of the noble bloodline can walk between the worlds. They can cross over to this world, and cross back again, carrying . . . goods."

He paused, expectantly.

"Well?" Mike prodded, his heart sinking. *Jesus, just what*

I need. The hottest lead this year turns out to be a card-carrying tinfoil hat job.

Matthias sighed. "Kings and nobles." He took another drag at his cigarette, and Mike forced himself to stifle a cough. "Noble houses rise and fall on the basis of their wealth. These six, they are not old. They date their fortunes to the reign of—no, to the, ah, eighteen-fifties. Before then, they were unremarkable merchants—tinkers, really. *Traders.* Today they are the high merchant families, rich beyond comprehension, a law unto themselves. Because they *trade.* They come to this world bearing dispatches and gems and valuables, and ensure that they arrive back in the empire of the Outer Kingdom—in what you would call California, Mexico, and Oregon—the next day. Without risk of disaster, without delay, without theft by the bands of savages who populate the wilderness. And the trade runs on the other side, too."

"How do they do it?" Mike asked. *Humor him, he may have something useful, after all.* Mentally, he was already working out which forms to submit to request the psychiatric assessment.

"Suppose a broker in Colombia wants half a ton of heroin to arrive in upstate New York." Matthias ground his cigarette out in the ashtray, even though it was only half-finished. "He has a choice of distribution channels. He can arrange for an intermediary to buy a fast speedboat, or a light plane, and run the Coast Guard gauntlet in the Caribbean. He can try a false compartment in a truck. Once in the United States, the cargo can be split into shipments and dispatched via other channels—expendable couriers, usually. There is an approximate risk of twenty-five percent associated with this technique. That is, the goods will probably reach the wholesaler—but one time in four, they will not." His face flickered in a fleeting grin. "Alternatively, they can contact the Clan. Who will take a commission of ten percent and guarantee delivery—or return the cost in full."

Huh? Mike sat up slightly. Matthias's habit of breaking off and looking at him expectantly was grating, but he couldn't help responding. Even if this sounded like pure bullshit, there was something compelling about the way Matt clearly believed his story.

"The Clan is a trading consortium operated by the noble houses," Matt explained. "Couriers cross over into this world and collect the cargo, in whatever quantity they can lift—they can only carry whatever they can hold across the gulf between worlds. In the other world, the Clan is invincible. Cargos of heroin or cocaine travel up the coast in wagon trains guarded by the Clan's troops. Local rulers are bribed with penicillin and aluminum tableware and spices for the table. Bandits who can muster no better than crossbows and swords are no match for soldiers with night-vision goggles and automatic weapons. It takes weeks or months, but it's secure—and sooner or later the cargo arrives in a heavily guarded depot in Boston or New York without you ever knowing it's in transit or being able to track it."

There was a click from across the room. Mike looked round. "This is bullshit," complained Pete, stripping off his headphones. He glared at Matt in disgust. "You're wasting our time, do you realize that?" To Mike, "Let's just charge him with trafficking on the basis of what we've already got, then commit him for psych—"

"I don't think so—" Mike began, just as Matthias said something guttural in a foreign language the DEA agent couldn't recognize. "I'm sorry?" he asked.

"I gave you samples," Matt complained. "Why not analyze them?"

"What for?" Mike's eyes narrowed. Something about Matthias scared him, and he didn't like that one little bit. Matt wasn't your usual garden-variety dealer's agent or hit man. There was something else about him, some kind of innate sense of his own superiority, which grated. *And* that weird accent. As if—"What should we look for?"

"The sample I gave you is of heroin, diacetyl morphine, from poppies grown on an experimental farm established by order of the high Duke Angbard Lofstrom, in the estates of King Henryk of Auswjein, which would be in North Virginia of your United States. There has never been an atomic explosion in the other world. I am informed that a device called a mass spectroscope will be able to confirm to you that the sample is depleted of an iso-, um, isotope of carbon that is created by atomic explosions. This is proof that the sample originated in another world, or was prepared at exceedingly enormous expense to give such an impression, for the mixture of carbon isotopes in this world is different."

"Uh." Pete looked as taken aback as Mike felt. "What? Why haven't you been selling your own here, if you can grow it in this other world?"

"Because it would be obvious where it came from," Matt explained with exaggerated patience. "The entire policy of the Clan for the past hundred and seventy years has been to maintain a shroud of secrecy around itself. Selling drugs that were clearly harvested on another world would not, ah, contribute to this policy."

Mike nodded at Pete. "Switch the goddamn recorder on again." He turned back to Matthias. "Summary. There exists a, a parallel world to our own. This world is not industrialized? No. There is a bunch of merchant princes, a *clan*, who can travel between there and here. These guys make their money by acting as couriers for high-value assets which can be transported through the other world without risk of interception because they are not recognized as valuable there. Drugs, in short. Matthias has kindly explained that his last heroin sample contains an, um, carbon isotope balance that will demonstrate it must have been grown on another planet. Either that, or somebody is playing implausibly expensive pranks. Memo: get a mass spectroscopy report on the referenced sample. Okay, so that brings me to the next question." He leaned toward Matthias. "Who *are* you, and how come you know all this?"

Matt extracted another cigarette from the packet and lit it. "I am of the outer families—I cannot world-walk, but must be carried whensoever I should go. I am—was—private secretary to the head of the Clan's security, Duke Lofstrom. I am here because"—he paused for a deep drag on the cigarette—"if I was *not* here they would execute me. For treason. Is that clear enough?"

"I, uh, think so." Pete had walked round behind Matt and was frantically gesturing at Mike, but Mike ignored him. "Do you have anything else to add?"

"Yes, two things. Firstly, you will find a regular Clan courier on the 14:30 Acela service from Boston to New York. I don't know who they are, so I can't give you a personal description, but standard procedure is that the designated courier arrives at the station no more than five minutes prior to departure. He sits in a reserved seat in carriage B, and he travels with an aluminum Zero-Halliburton roll-on case, model ZR-31. He will be conservatively dressed—the idea is to be mistaken for a lawyer or stockbroker, not a gangster—and will be armed with a Glock G20 pistol. You will know you have arrested a courier if he vanishes when confined in a maximum security cell." He barked a humorless laugh. "Make sure to videotape it."

"You said two things?"

"Yes. Here is the second." Matt reached into his pocket and pulled out a small, silvery metallic cylinder. Mike blinked: on first sight he almost mistook it for a pistol cartridge, but it was solid, with no sign of a percussion cap. And from the way Matt dropped it on the tabletop it looked dense.

"May I?" Mike asked.

Matt waved at it. "Of course."

Mike tried to pick it up—and almost dropped it. The slug was *heavy*. It felt slightly oily and was pleasantly warm to the touch. "Jesus! What is it?"

"Plutonium. From the Duke's private stockpile." Matt's expression was unreadable as Mike flinched away from the ingot. "Do not take my word for it; analyze it, then come back here to talk to me." He crossed his arms. "I *said* they were a government. And I can tell you everything you need to know about their nuclear weapons program . . ."

A lightning discharge always seeks the shortest path to ground. Two days after she discovered Duke Angbard's location to be so secret that nobody would even tell her how to send him a letter, Miriam's wrath ran to ground through the person of Baron Henryk, her mother's favorite uncle and the nearest body to Angbard in age, position, and temperament that she could find.

Later on, it was clear to all concerned that something like this had been bound to happen sooner or later. The dowager Hildegarde was already presumed guilty without benefit of trial, the Queen Mother was out of reach, and Patricia voh Hjorth d'Wu ab Thorold—her mother—was above question. But the consequences of Miriam's anger were something else again. And the trigger that set it off was so seemingly trivial that after the event, nobody could even recall the cause of the quarrel: a torn envelope.

At mid-morning Miriam, fresh from yet another fit of obsessive GANTT-chart filing, emerged from her bedroom to find Kara scolding one of the maidservants. The poor girl was almost in tears. "What's going on here?" Miriam demanded.

"Milady!" Kara turned, eyes wide. "She's been deliberately slow, is all. If you'd have Bernaard take a switch to her—"

"No." Miriam was blunt. "You: go lose yourself for a few minutes. Kara, let's talk."

The maid scurried away defensively, eager to be gone before the mistress changed her mind. Kara sniffed, offended, but followed Miriam over toward the chairs positioned in a circle around the cold fireplace. "What troubles you, milady?" asked Kara, apprehensively.

"What day is it?" Miriam leaned casually on the back of a priceless antique.

"Why, it's, I'd need to check a calendar. Milady?"

"It's the fourteenth." Miriam glanced out the window. "I'm sick, Kara."

"Sick?" Her eyes widened. "Shall I call an apothecary—"

"I'm sick, as in *pissed off*, not sick as in ill." Miriam's smile didn't reach her eyes. "I'm being given the runaround. Look." She held up an envelope bearing the crest of the Clan post. Its wax seal was broken. "They're returning my letters. 'Addressee unknown.'"

"Well, maybe they don't know who—"

"Letters to *Duke Angbard*, Kara."

"Oh." For a moment the teenager looked guilty.

"Know anything about it?" Miriam asked sweetly.

"Oh, but nobody writes to the duke! You write to his secretary." Kara looked confused for a moment. "Then he arranges an appointment," she added hesitantly.

"The duke's last secretary, in case you've forgotten, was Matthias. He isn't answering his correspondence any more, funnily enough."

"Oh." A look of profound puzzlement crept over Kara's face.

"I can't get *anywhere*!" Miriam burst out. "Ma—Patricia—holds formal audiences. Olga's away on urgent business most of the time and on the firing range the rest. I haven't even seen Brill since the—the accident. And Angbard won't answer his mail. What the hell am I meant to do?"

Kara looked faintly guilty. "Weren't you supposed to be going riding this afternoon?" she asked.

"I want to talk to someone," Miriam said grimly. "Who, of the Clan council, is in town? Who can I get to?"

"There's Baron Henryk, he stays at the Royal Exchange when he's working, but he—"

"He's my great-uncle, he'll have to listen to me. Excellent. He'll do."

"But, mistress! You can't just—"

Miriam smiled. There was no humor in her expression. "It has been three weeks since anyone even deigned to tell me how my company is doing, much less answered my queries about when I can go back over and resume managing it. I've been stuck in this oh-so-efficiently doppelgangered suite—secured against world-walking by a couple of hundred tons of concrete piled on the other side—for two months, cooling my heels. If Angbard doesn't want to talk to me, he'll sure as hell listen to Henryk. Right?"

Kara was clearly agitated, bouncing up and down and flapping her hands like a bird. In her green-and-brown camouflage-pattern minidress—like many of the Clan youngsters, she liked to wear imported western fashions at home—she resembled a thrush with one foot caught in a snare. "But mistress! I can arrange a meeting, if you give me time, but you can't just go barging in—"

"Want to bet?" Miriam stood up. "Get a carriage sorted, Kara. One hour. We're going round to the Royal Exchange and I'm not leaving until I've spoken to him, and that's an end to the matter."

Kara protested some more, but Miriam wasn't having it. If Lady Brill had been around she'd have been able to set Miriam straight, but Kara was too young, inexperienced, and unsure of herself to naysay her mistress. Therefore, an hour later, Miriam—with an apprehensive Kara sucked along in her undertow, not to mention a couple of maids and a gaggle of guards—boarded a closed carriage for the journey to the exchange buildings. Miriam had changed for the meeting, putting on her black interview suit and a cream blouse. She looked like an attorney or a serious business journalist, sniffing after blood in the corporate watercooler. Kara, ineffectual and lightweight, drifted along passively in the undertow, like the armed guards on the carriage roof.

The Royal Exchange was a forbidding stone pile fronted by Romanesque columns, half a mile up the road from Thorold Palace. Built a century ago to house the lumber exchange (and the tax inspectors who took the royal cut of every consignment making its way down the coast), it had long since passed into the hands of the government and now housed a number of offices. The Gruinmarkt was not long on bureaucracy—it was still very much a marcher kingdom, its focus on the wilderness beyond the mountains to the west—but even a small, primitive country had desks for scores or hundreds of secretaries of this and superintendents of that. Miriam wasn't entirely clear on why the elderly baron might live there, but she was clear on one thing: he'd talk to her.

"Which way?" Miriam asked briskly as she strode across the polished wooden floor of the main entrance.

"I think his offices are in the west wing, mistress, but *please*—"

Miriam found a uniformed footman in her way. "You. Which way to Baron Henryk's office?" she demanded.

"Er, ah, your business, milady?"

"None of yours." Miriam stared at him until he wilted. "Where do I find the baron?"

"On the second floor, west wing, Winter Passage, if it pleases you—"

"Come on." She turned and marched briskly toward the stairs, scattering a gaggle of robed clerks who stared at her in perplexity. "Come on, Kara! I haven't got all day."

"But mistress—"

The second-floor landing featured *wallpaper*—an expensive luxury, printed on linen—and portraits of dignitaries to either side. Corridors diverged in the pattern of an H. "West wing," Miriam muttered. "Right." One arm of the H featured tapestries depicting a white, snowbound landscape and scenes of industry and revelry. Miriam nearly walked right into another robed clerk. "Baron Henryk's office. Which way?" she snapped.

The frightened clerk pointed one ink-blackened fingertip. "Yonder," he quavered, then ducked and ran for cover.

Kara hurried to catch up. "Mistress, if you go shoving in you will upset the order of things."

"Then it's about time someone upset them," Miriam retorted, pausing outside a substantial door. "They've been giving me the runaround, I'm going to give them the bull in a china shop. This the place?"

"What's a Chinese shop?" Kara was even more confused than usual.

"Never mind. He's in here, isn't he?" Not waiting for a reply, Miriam rapped hard on the door.

A twenty-something fellow in knee breeches and an elaborate shirt opened it. "Yes?"

"I'm here to see Baron Henryk, at his earliest convenience," Miriam said firmly. "I assume he's in?"

"Do you have an appointment?"

The youngster didn't get it. Miriam took a deep breath. "I have, *now*. At his earliest convenience, do you hear?"

"Ah-ahem. Whom should I say . . . ?"

"His great-niece Helge." Miriam resisted for a moment the urge to tap her toe impatiently, then gave in.

The lad vanished into a large and hideously overdecorated room, and she heard a mutter of conversation. Then: "Show her in! Show her in by all means, Walther, then make yourself scarce."

The door opened wider. "Please come in, the baron will be with you momentarily." The young secretary stood aside as Miriam walked in, Kara tiptoeing at her heels, then vanished into the corridor. The door closed behind him, and for the first moment Miriam began to wonder if she'd made a mistake.

The room was built to the same vast proportions as most imperial dwellings hereabouts, so that the enormous desk in the middle of it looked dwarfishly short, like a gilded black-topped coffee table covered in red leather boxes. Bookcases lined one wall, filled with dusty ledgers, while the other walls—paneled in oak—were occupied by age-blackened oil paintings or a high window casement looking out over the high street. The plasterwork hanging from the ceiling resembled a cubist grotto, cluttered with gilded cherubim and inedible fruit. Baron Henryk hunched behind the desk, his head bent slightly to one side. His long white hair glowed in the early afternoon light from the window and his face was in shadow; he wore local court dress, hand-embroidered with gold thread, but his fingertips were dark with ink from the array of pens that fronted his desk in carved stone inkwells. "Ah, great-niece Helge! How charming to see you at such short notice." He rose slowly and gestured toward a seat. "This would be your lady-in-waiting, Lady . . . ?"

"Kara," Miriam supplied.

Kara cringed slightly and smiled ingratiatingly at the baron. "I tried to explain—"

"Hush, it's perfectly all right, child." The baron smiled at her. "Why don't you join Walther outside? Keep the servants out, why don't you. Perhaps you should take tea together in the long hall, I gather that's the custom these days among the young people."

"But I—" Kara swallowed, dipped a quick curtsey, and fled.

Henryk waited until the door closed behind her, then turned to Miriam with a faint smile on his face. "Well, well, well. To what emergency do I owe the honor of your presence?"

Miriam pulled the envelope out of her shoulder bag. "This. Addressee unknown. I was hoping you might be able to explain what's going on." She took a deep breath. "I am being given the runaround—nobody's talking to me! I'm sorry I had to barge in on you like this, at short notice. But it's reached the point where any attempt I make to go through channels and find out what's going on is being thrown back in my face."

"I see." Henryk gestured vaguely at a chair. "Please, have a seat. White or red?"

"I'm sorry?"

"Wine?" He walked over to a sideboard that Miriam had barely noticed, beside one of the bookcases. "An early-afternoon digestif, perhaps."

"White, if you don't mind. Just a little." It was one of the things that had taken Miriam by surprise when she first stumbled into the Clan's affairs, the way people hereabouts drank like fishes. Not just the hard liquor, but wine and beer—tea and coffee were expensive imports, she supposed, and the water sanitation was straight out of the dark ages. Diluting it with alcohol killed most parasites.

Henryk fiddled with a decanter, then carried two lead crystal glasses over to his desk. "Here. Make free with the bottle, you are my guest."

Miriam raised her glass. "Your health."

"Ah." Henryk sat back down with a sigh. "Now, where were we?"

"I was trying to reach people."

"Yes, I can see that." Henryk nodded to himself. "Not having much luck," he suggested.

"Right. Angbard isn't answering his mail. In fact, I can't even get a letter through to him. Same goes for everyone I know in his security operation. Which isn't to say that stuff doesn't come in the other direction, but . . . I've got a company to run, in New Britain, haven't I? They pulled me out two months ago, saying it wasn't safe, and I've been cooling my heels ever since. When *is* it going to be safe? They don't seem to realize business doesn't stop just because they're worried about Matthias having left some surprises behind, or the Lees are still thinking about signing the papers. I could be going bankrupt over there!"

"Absolutely true." Henryk took a sip of wine. "It's incontrovertible. Yes, I think I see what the problem is. You were absolutely right to come to me." He put his glass down. "Although next time I would appreciate a little bit more notice."

"Um, I'm sorry about that." For the first time Miriam noticed that the top of the desk wasn't leather, it was a black velvet cloth, hastily laid over whatever papers Henryk didn't want her intruding upon. "I'd exhausted all the regular channels."

"Yes, well, I'll be having words with Walther." A brief flicker of smile: "He needs to learn to be firmer."

"But you were free to see me at short notice."

"Not completely free, as you can see." His languid wave took in the cluttered desk. "Never mind. If in future you need to see me, have your secretary make an appointment and flag it for my eyes—it will make everything run much more smoothly. In particular, if you attach an agenda it will be dealt with before things reach this state. Your secretary should—"

"You keep saying, have your secretary do this. I don't *have* a secretary, uncle!"

Henryk raised an eyebrow. "Then who was the young lady who came with you?"

"That's Kara, she's—*oh*. You mean she's supposed to be able to handle appointments?" Miriam covered her mouth.

Baron Henryk frowned. "No, not her. You were supposed to be assigned an assistant. Who was, ahem, ah—oh yes." He jerked his chin in an abrupt nod. "That would be the Lady Brilliana, would it not? And I presume you haven't seen her for some weeks?"

"She's meant to be a secretary?" Miriam boggled at the thought. "Well, yes, but . . ." Brill probably *would* make a decent administrative assistant, now that she thought about it. Anyone who didn't take her bullet points seriously would find themselves facing real ones, sure enough. Brill was mature, competent, sensible—in the way that Kara was not—

and missing, unlike Kara. "I haven't seen her since I arrived here."

"That will almost certainly be because of the security flap," Henryk agreed. "I'll try to do something about that. Lady Brilliana is your right hand, Helge. Perhaps her earlier duties—yes, you need her watching your back while you're here more than Angbard needs another sergeant at arms."

"Another what—oh. Okay." Miriam nodded. That Angbard had planted Brill in her household as a spy (and bodyguard) wasn't exactly a secret anymore, but it hadn't occurred to her that it was meant to be permanent, or that Brilliana had other duties, as Henryk put it. *Sergeant at arms! Well.* "That would help."

"She knows what strings to pull," Henryk said. "She can teach you what to do when she's not there to pull them for you. But as a matter of general guidance, it's usually best to tug gently. You never know what might be on the other end," he added.

Miriam's ears flushed. "I didn't mean to kick the anthill over," she said defensively, "but my business wasn't de-signed to run on autopilot. I've been given the cold shoulder so comprehensively that it feels like I'm being cut out of things deliberately."

"How do you know you aren't?" asked Henryk.

"But, if I'm—" She stopped. "Okay, back to basics. *Why* would anyone cut me out of running the New Britain opera-tion, when it won't run without me? I'm not doing any good here, I mean, apart from learning to ride a horse and not look a complete idiot on a dance floor. And basic grammar. All I'm asking for is an occasional update. Why is nobody answering?"

"Because they don't trust you," Henryk replied. He put his glass down and stared at her. "Why do you think they should let you out where they can't keep an eye on you?"

"I—" Miriam stopped dead. "They *don't* trust me?" she asked, and even to herself she sounded slightly stupid. "Well, no shit. They've got my *mother* as a hostage, there's no way I can go back home until we know if Matt's blown my original identity, Angbard knows just where I live on the New Britain side—what do they think I'm going to do? Walk into a Royal Constabulary office and say, 'Look, there's a conspiracy of subversives from another world trying to invade you' or something? Ask the DEA to stick me in a witness protection program?" She realized she was getting agitated and tried to control her gestures. "I'm on side, Henryk! I *had* this argument with Angbard last year. I chewed it over with, with Roland. Think we didn't discuss the possibility of quietly disappearing on you? Guess what: we didn't! Because in the final analysis, you're family. And I've got no reason good enough to make me run away. It's not like the old days when Patricia had to put up with an abusive husband for the good of the Clan, is it? So yes, they should be able to trust me. About the only way they can expect me to be untrustworthy is if they treat me like this."

She ran down, breathing heavily. Somewhere in the middle of things, she realized, she'd spilled a couple of drops of wine on the polished walnut top of Henryk's desk. She leaned forward and blotted them up with the cuff of her jacket.

"You make a persuasive case," Henryk said thoughtfully.

Yes, but do you buy it? Miriam froze inside. *What have I put my foot in here?*

"Personally, I believe you. But I hope you can see, I have met you. I can see that you are a lady of considerable personal integrity and completely honorable in all your dealings. But the Clan is *at this moment* battling for its very survival, and the people who make such decisions—*not* Angbard, he directs, his perch is very high up the tree indeed—don't know you from, from your lady-in-waiting out there. All they see is a dossier that says 'feral infant, raised by runaway on other side, tendency toward erratic entrepreneurial behavior, feminist, unproven reliability.' They *know* you came back to the fold once, of your own accord, and that is marked down in your favor already, isn't it? You're living in the lap of luxury, taking in the social season and pursuing the remedial studies you need in order to learn how to live among us. Expecting anything more, in the middle of a crisis, is pushing things a little hard."

"You're telling me I'm a prisoner," Miriam said evenly.

"No!" Henryk looked shocked. "You're *not* a prisoner! You're—" He paused. "A probationer. Promising but unproven. If you keep to your studies, cultivate the right people, go through channels, and show the right signs of trustworthiness, then sooner rather than later you'll get exactly what you want. All you need to do is convince the security adjutants charged with your safety that you are loyal and moderately predictable—that you will at least notify them *before* you engage in potentially dangerous endeavors—and they will bow down before you." He frowned, then sniffed. "Your glass is empty, my dear. A refill, perhaps?"

"Yes, please." Miriam sat very still while Henryk paced over to the sideboard and refilled both glasses, her mind whirling. *They see me as a probationer. Right.* It wasn't a nice idea, but it explained a lot of things that had been happening lately. "If I'm on probation, then what about my mother? What about Patricia?"

"Oh, she's in terrible trouble," Henryk said reassuringly. "Absolutely *terrible*! Ghastly beyond belief!" He said it with relish as he passed her the glass. "Go on, ask me why, you know you're dying to."

"Um. Is it relevant?"

"Absolutely." Henryk nodded. "You know how we normally deal with defectors around here."

"I—" Miriam stopped. Defection was one of the unforgivable crimes. The Clan's ability to function as an organization devoted to trade between worlds scaled as a function of the number of couriers it could mobilize. Leaving, running away, didn't merely remove the defector from the Clan's control; it reduced the ability of the Clan as a whole to function. Below a certain size, networks of world-walkers were vulnerable and weak, as the Lee family (stranded unknowingly in New Britain two centuries ago) had discovered. "Go on."

"Your mother has unusual extenuating circumstances to thank for her predicament," Henryk stated coolly. "If not for which, she would probably be dead. Angbard swears blind that her disappearance was planned, intended, to draw the

faction of murderers out, and that she remained in contact
with him at all times. A sleeper agent, in other words." Henryk's cheek twitched. "Nobody is going to tell the duke that
he's lying to his face. Besides which, if Patricia *hadn't* disappeared when she did, the killing would have continued.
When she returned to the fold"—a minute shrug—"she
brought you with her. A life for a life, if you like. Even her
mother can see the value of not asking too many pointed
questions at this time, of letting sleeping secrets lie. And besides, the story might even be true. Stranger things happened
during the war."

Henryk paused for a sip of wine. "But as you can see, your
background does not inspire trust."

"Oh." Miriam frowned. "But that's not my fault!"

"Of course not." Henryk put his glass down. "But you
can't escape it. We're a young aristocracy, Helge, rough-cut
and uncivilized. This is a marcher kingdom, second sons
hunting their fortune on the edges of the great forest. The
entire population of this kingdom is perhaps five million, did
you know that? You could drop the entire population of
Niejwein into Boston and lose them. The Boston you grew
up in, that is. Without us, without the Clan, Gruinmarkt culture and high society would make England in the fifteenth
century look cosmopolitan and sophisticated. It's true that
there are enormous riches on display in the palaces and castles of the aristocracy, but it's superficial—what you see on
display is everything there is. Not like America, where
wealth is so overwhelming that the truly rich store their assets in enormous bank vaults and amuse themselves by ap-
ing the dress and manners of the poor. You're a fish out of
water, and you're understandably disoriented. The more so
because you had no inkling of your place in the great chain
of existence until perhaps six months ago. But you must realize, people here do not labor under your misconceptions.
They know you for a child of your parents, your thuggish
dead father and your unreliable tearaway mother, and they
don't expect any better of you because they *know* that blood
will out."

Miriam stared at her white-haired, hollow-cheeked great-uncle. "That's all I am, is it?" she asked in a thin voice. "An ornament on the family tree? And an untrustworthy one, at that?"

"By no means." Henryk leaned back in his chair. "But behavior like this, this display of indecorous—" He paused. "It doesn't help your case," he said tensely. "*I* understand. Others would not. It's them you have to convince. But you've chosen the middle of a crisis to do it in—not the best of timing! Some would consider it evidence of guile, to make a bid for independence when all hands are at the breach. I don't for a minute believe you would act in such a manner, but again: it is not me who you must convince. You need to learn to act within the constraints of your position, not against them. Then you'll have something to work with."

"Um. I should be going, then." She rubbed the palm of one hand nervously on her thigh. "I guess I should apologize to you for taking up your time." She paused for a moment and forced herself to swallow her pride. "Do you have any specific advice for me, about how to proceed?"

"Hmm." Baron Henryk stood and slowly walked over to the window casement. "That's an interesting question." He turned, so that his face was shadowed against the bright daylight outside. "What do you want to achieve?"

"What do I—" Miriam's mouth snapped shut. Her eyes narrowed against the glare. "I think I made myself clear enough at the extraordinary meeting three months ago," she said slowly.

"That's not what I asked." It was hard to tell, but Henryk seemed to be smiling. "Why don't you go and think about that question? When you have a better idea, we should talk again. If you'd like to join me for dinner, in a couple of weeks? Have your *confidante* write to my secretary to arrange things. Meanwhile, I'll try to find out what has happened to your assistant, and I'll ask someone in the security directorate to look into your affairs in New Britain so that you can go back to them as soon as possible. But if you'll excuse me, I have other matters to deal with right now."

Miriam rose. "Thank you for finding some time for me," she said stiffly. Halfway to the door she paused. "By the way, what is it you do exactly?"

Henryk stood. "Oh, this and that," he said lightly. "Remember to write."

Outside in the corridor, Miriam found a nervous Kara shifting from foot to foot impatiently. "Oh, milady! Can we go now?"

"Sure." Miriam walked toward the staircase, her expression pensive. "Kara, do you know what Baron Henryk does here?"

"Milady!" Kara stared at Miriam, her eyes wide. "I thought you knew!"

"Knew? Knew what?" Miriam shook her head.

Kara scurried closer before whispering loudly. "The baron is his majesty's master of spies! He collects intelligence for the crown, from countries far and wide, even from across the eastern ocean! I thought you knew . . ."

Miriam stopped dead, halfway down the first flight of stairs. *I just barged in on the Director of Central Intelligence*, she thought sickly. *And he told me I'm under house arrest.* Then: "Hang on, you mean he's the *king's* spymaster? Not the Clan's?"

"Well, yes! He's a sworn baron, milady, sworn to his majesty, or hadn't you noticed?" Kara's attempt at sarcasm fell flat, undermined by her frightened expression. "We're all his majesty's loyal subjects, here, aren't we? *Aren't* we?"

TRANSLATED TRANSCRIPT BEGINS

(*Click.*)

"Ah, your lordship, how good to see you!"

"On the contrary, the honor is mine, your grace." (Wheezing.) "Here. Walther, a chair for his grace, damnit. And a port for each of us, then make yourself scarce. Yes, the special reserve. I'm sure you've been even busier than I, your grace, this being a tedious little backwater most of the time, but if there's anything I can do for you—"

"Nonsense, Henryk, you never sleep! The boot is on the other foot and the prisoner shrieking his plea as you heat it. You won't get me with that nonsense—ah, thank you Walther."

"That will be all."

(Sound of door closing.)

"Sky Father's eye! That's good stuff. Please tell me it's not the last bottle?"

"Indeed not, your grace, and I have it on good authority that there is *at least* a case left in the Thorold Palace cellars." (Pause.) "Six?" (Pause.) "Five? Damn your eyes, four and that's my lowest!"

"I'll have them sent over forthwith. Now, what brings you round here in a screaming hurry, nephew, when I'm sure there are plenty of other fires for you to be pissing on? Would I be right in thinking it's something to do with woman trouble? And if so, which one?"

(Clink of glassware.)

"You know perfectly well *which one* could get me out of the office, pills or no pills. It's the old bitches, Henryk, they are meddling in that of which they know not, and they are going to blow the entire powder keg sky-high if I don't find a way to stop them. And I can't just bang them up in a garret like the young pullet—"

"The shrew?"

"She's not a shrew, she's just overenthusiastic. A New Woman. They've got lots of them on the other side, I hear. But the old one, her manners may be good but her poison is of a fine vintage and she is getting much too close to our corporate insurance policy. Even if she doesn't know it yet."

"Your sister—"

"Crone's pawn, uncle, Crone's pawn. Do you think it was coincidence that it was Helge who came calling on you, and not Patricia? Patricia is in a cleft stick and dare not even hiss or rattle her tail, lest the old bitches lop it off. If we could move her back to the other side things would be different, but it's all I can do to keep the situation over there from coming apart on us completely—we've lost more couriers in the past month than in the preceding decade, and if I can't stop the leakage I fear we will have to shut the network down completely. Sending Patricia back simply isn't an option, and now that she's here she's less effective than we expected. It's that blasted wasting disease. The old bitches and their quackery have her mewed up like a kitten in a sack. Meanwhile, Helge isn't much use to us here, either. I've sent her Lady B to take her in hand, which might begin to repair the damage to her high esteem among her relatives, in a year or three—or at least stop her from dancing blind in the minefield—but you can see how isolated she is. A real disappointment. I had such high hopes that those two might tackle the bitches, but the cultural barrier is just too high."

"Come now, Angbard, there's no need to be so pessimistic! The best-laid plans, et cetera. So what do you think the old she-devil is up to?"

"Well, I can't be certain, but she's certainly done *something* to shut Patricia up. And I find it somewhat fascinating to see Helge outmaneuvered so thoroughly without even knowing who she's up against."

"Do you think Patricia hasn't told her?"

"Do I—" (Pause.) "Henryk, you sly fellow! And here I was thinking *I* was asking *you* for information!"

"The rack cares not who sleeps on it, and—"

"Indeed, yes, all very well and apposite and all that. Henryk, the old bitches are turbulent and the she-devil-in-chief is plotting something, I feel it in my bowels. *I have more important things to worry about right now.* I do not have time to be looking over my shoulder for daggers. I do not have time to dance the reel to the old bitch's hurdy-gurdy, when I can't sleep at night for fear of conspirators. *What do I need to know?*"

"I say—steady on, your grace! Here, let me remedy your glass . . . my agents at court opine that the she-devil has carried off a coup. Her stroking of the royal ego has come to something, it seems, and sparked a passing fancy with the revenant."

"The—*what*? What's *she* got to do with anything?"

"The royal succession—Oh dear! Here, use my kerchief." (Bell rings.)

"Walther! Walther, I say!"

(Sound of door opening.)

"A towel for his grace! Your grace, if you would care to make use of my wardrobe—"

"No need, thank you, uncle, I am sure a little wine stain will hurt only my dignity."

"Yes, but—"

(Sound of door closing.)

"That's better." (Pause.) "The royal succession! Curse me for an imbecile, which one is it, the Pervert or the Idiot? Don't tell me, it's the Idiot. More tractable, and the Pervert's already promised to the Nordmarkt."

"That, and the Pervert's bad habits are becoming increasingly difficult to cover for. Royal privilege is all very well, but if Egon were anyone other than his father's eldest son he'd be learning wisdom from the Tree Father by now. A nastier piece of work hasn't graced the royal court in my memory. If his father is forced to notice his habits . . . remember our ruling dynasty's turbulent origins? Nobody wants to see another civil war, not with Petermann feeling his oats just across our northern border and the backwoods peers staring daggers at our Clan families' new earned wealth. I believe the old bitches think that the Pervert will go too far one of these days, in which case owning the Idiot would throttle two rabbits with one snare, nailing down Helge and securing the royal bloodline. They're not stupid, they probably think Helge is smart enough to see the advantages, to take what's being offered her, and to play along. One more generation and we—*they*—would be able to splice the monarchy into the Clan for good. Helge's a bit old, but it wouldn't be a first pregnancy—don't look so shocked, we've got her medical records—and she's in good health. Pray for an accident for the Pervert, a single pregnancy, and her payoff is, well, you know how they work."

"They're crazy!"

"What? You think she'd *refuse*?"

"*Think*? Blue mother, Henryk, did you listen to her *at all*? She is, to all intents and purposes, a modern American woman. They do *not* marry for duty. It was all I could do to stop her eloping with that waste of money, brains, and time, Roland! The old bitches had better hope they've got their claws into her deep, or she will kick back *so* hard—"

"Patricia."

"Oh. What? That? Hmm, I suppose you're right. She's rather fond of her mother, that's true. But I'm not sure it'll be enough to hold her down in the long run. It raises an interesting question of priorities, doesn't it?"

"You mean, the insurance policy versus the throne? Or . . . ?"

"Yes. I think—hmm. Helge, wearing her Miriam head, would understand the insurance policy. But not the old bitches. Whereas Patricia, for all her modernity and skeptical ways, probably wouldn't buy it. She was raised by the she-devil, after all. And, ah, Miriam is very *creatively* unreliable. Yes. What do you think?"

"You're hatching one of your plans, your grace, but you forget that I am not a mind reader."

"Oh, I apologize. Given: we do not want the old bitches to get their hands on the levers of temporal power, are we agreed? They've got too much already. They seem to have decided—well, it's a bit early to be sure, but marrying Helge to the Idiot would simultaneously tie her down and put a spoke in the wheel the reformers are trying to spin, while also tying down Patricia. That debating society . . . Luckily for us, Helge is unreliable in exactly the right sort of way. Right now they've tied her up like a turkey and she hasn't even realized what's going on. That's not very useful to us, is it? I say we should give her enough rope—no reason to tie the noose so tightly she can't escape it, what—and then a little push, and see which way she runs. Yes? Do you think that could work?"

"Angbard—your grace—that verges on criminal irresponsibility! If she *does* hang herself—"

"She'll have only herself to blame. And she'll not be a dagger for her grandmother to hold to our throat."

"She hates her grandmother! With a passion."

"I believe you overestimate her vindictiveness; at present it is merely disdain on both sides. The dowager is more than happy to use any weapon that comes to hand without worrying about hurting its feelings. Helge doesn't know enough to turn in her hand, yet. Perhaps if Helge has real reason to hate her grandmother . . ."

"Tell me you wouldn't harm your own sister."

"Mm, no. I wouldn't need to go that far, Henryk. Dowager Hildegarde is quite capable of making Helge hate her without any help from me, although admittedly a few choice whispers might fan the flames of misunderstanding. What I need from *you*, uncle, is nothing more than that you play the bad cop to my good, and perhaps the use of your ears at court. We're all loyal subjects of the Crown after all, yes? And it would hardly be in the Crown's best interests to fall into the hands of the old bitches. Or the Pervert, for that matter."

"I shall pretend I did not hear that last, as a loyal servant of the Crown. Although, come to think of it, perhaps it would be in everyone's best interests if nobody looked too hard for plots against Prince Egon, who is clearly loved by all. The resources can be better used looking for real threats, if you follow my drift. What kind of push do you intend to give Helge?"

(Glassware on tabletop.)

"Oh, a perfectly appropriate one, Henryk! A solution of poetic, even beautiful, proportions suggests itself to me. One that meshes perfectly with Helge's background and upbringing, a bait she'll be unable to resist."

"Bait? What kind of bait?"

"Put your glass down, I don't want you to lose such a fine vintage."

(Pause.)

"I'm going to let her discover the insurance policy."

TRANSCRIPT ENDS

6

INSURANCE

Two days after Miriam visited Baron Henryk, the weather broke. Torrential rain streamed across the stone front of Thorold Palace, gurgling through the carved gargoyle waterspouts and down past the windows under the eaves. Miriam, still in a state of mild shock from her meeting with her great-uncle, stayed in her rooms and brooded. A couple of times she hauled out her laptop, plugged it into the solitary electrical outlet in her suite, and tried to write a letter to her mother. After the third attempt she gave up in despair. Patricia was a nut best cracked by Helge, but Miriam wanted nothing to do with her alter-ego, the highborn lady. Trying to be Helge had gotten her into a world of hurt, and trying to measure up to their expectations of her was only going to make things worse. Besides, she had an uneasy feeling that her mother was not going to thank her for muddying the waters with Henryk.

Shortly after lunch (a tray of cold cuts delivered by two

servants from the great hall below), there came a knock on her dressing-room door. "Who is it?" she called.

"Me, Miriam! Are you decent?" The door opened. "What's the matter?" Brilliana d'Ost stepped inside and glanced around. "Are you hiding from someone? The servants speak of you as if you're a forest troll, lurking in the shadows to bite the next passing trapper's head off."

"I'm not that bad, surely." Miriam smiled. "Welcome back, anyway—it's good to see someone around here who's happy to see me. What have you been up to?" She stood up to embrace the younger woman.

"I could tell you, but then I'd have to kill you," Brill said lightly, hugging her back. Then her smile faded. "Don't assume I'm exaggerating. I've been very busy lately. Some things I can't talk about." She shed her bulky shoulder-bag and pushed the door shut behind her. "Miriam. What do you mean, happy to see you? What on earth has been going on here? I got word by way of the duke's office—"

"Am I in *that* much trouble, already?" Miriam asked, sitting down again. She saw that Brill had cut her black hair shorter than last time they'd met and was using foundation powder to cover the row of smallpox craters on the underside of her jaw. In her trouser-suit she could have been just another office intern on the streets of New York—Miriam's New York.

"Trouble?" Brill shrugged dismissively. "Trouble is for *little* people. But I hear word, 'Brilliana, your mistress needs you, go and look to her side,' and I am thinking that perhaps not all is well—and here you are, hiding like a bear with a headache!" She sat down on one of the upholstered stools that served as informal seating. "Oh, his excellency says, 'Tell her to stop making waves and we'll sort everything out.' "

"Um. Right." Miriam closed the lid on her laptop. "Can I get you anything?" she asked. "A glass of wine? Coffee?"

"Coffee would be precious, should you but have any." Brill looked wistful as Miriam tugged the bell rope. "The weather is as impoverished on the other side. Homeful for the ducks, but not enchanting lest your feet be webbed."

"Nobody told me that Henryk was a palace ogre," Miriam complained. The door opened: "Two coffees, cream, no sugar," she directed. As it closed, she continued. "I've been stuck here, all isolated, for weeks. It's not easy to fit in. Kara's done her best to help me, but that isn't much—she just isn't perceptive enough to warn me *before* I put my foot in it. Andragh"—the head of her detachment of bodyguards—"is the strong silent type, not a political advisor. Mom's busy and has her own problems, Olga's in and out but mostly out, and I'm"—she took a deep breath—"lonely and bored."

"Yes, well, that's what the boss said." Brill brooded for a moment, then burst out, "Miriam, I'm *sorry!*"

"Hey, wait a moment—"

"I mean it! I blame myself. I was supposed to stick to you like glue, but while you were in the hospital I had other tasks to attend to and my—I can't tell you who—needed me elsewhere. High priority jobs, lots of them—I've been run ragged. Our networks are in rags, new safe houses must be bought, identities created, safe procedures developed, contacts sanitized and renewed. An underground railroad which took us decades to build has to be scrapped and rebuilt from scratch, and his grace badly needs eyes and ears he can trust. I thought that you'd be all right here on your own, that not much could happen, but I didn't realize—if I had I'd have made a fuss, demanded to be released back to you!"

Brill was upset and Miriam, who hadn't expected any of this, was taken aback. "Whoa! It's all right. Seriously, we've been in the middle of a real mess and if you had to go fight security fires for Angbard—or whatever—then obviously, there were higher priorities than acting nursemaid for me. And you're here now, which is the main thing, isn't it?"

"Yes, but I *should* have been here earlier." Brill frowned. "Not letting you run amok." For a moment her flashing grin returned. "So what else have you been up to?"

Miriam sighed. "Etiquette lessons. Basic hochsprache." She began ticking points off on her fingers: "Learning to ride, memorizing long lists of who's related to who, learning to dance—court dances, over here, that is—endless appointments with the dressmaker. Oh, and getting pissed off about being given the runaround. About when I can get back to my business, that kind of thing." She pulled a face. "What's missing from this picture?" *Besides brooding over*— She stopped that line of thought dead. Brill hadn't concealed her opinion of Roland very effectively, but she knew better than to pick a fight with Miriam over his memory, especially when Miriam very definitely wasn't over him.

"Let us see. Long lists of who is who—did Kara think to instruct you in their scandals or holdings? Or worse?" Brill raised an eyebrow. "No? Methought it unlikely. The rest is not unexpected. The travel restrictions . . ." She frowned again. "I think if it was solely the decision of your uncle you should be able to return from whence you were summoned immediately. He instructed me to tell you to pay your corvée regularly. I think he wishes to shine your loyalty, to demonstrate you are reliable enough as a courier to trust with world-walking. One week or two, he says, and you should be assigned a regular courier duty to the new outposts, with permission to overnight there when not needed here. This would be unofficial, but should anyone ask they can be told you're running errands simple, not looking to your faction. Discretion is the watchword."

"Uh." Miriam blinked, taken aback. "That's—well. That's far too easy. After yesterday, I was expecting the third degree . . ."

"Henryk convinced you that you were under arrest?" Brill tossed her head as the door opened. "I'll take that." The maid closed the door and Brill transferred the silver tray to the top of a chest of drawers. "The baron is jealous of the demands upon his time, whosoever makes them," she said. "He wished you subdued for the while. Either that, else there's a discord over how to handle you. Here, this is yours."

Miriam took the mug. "I'm confused. Or he *was* trying to lower my expectations. Wasn't he?"

"In all probability." Brill sat down again. "I can't believe you bearded the lion in his den, without appointment," she added with a curious grin.

"I'm not sure I can, either," Miriam admitted. "Understand, I'm not going to blame Kara—but if she was up to managing my affairs herself I'd have known better than to go barging in. The whole issue just wouldn't have arisen in the first place. I'm not an idiot, Brill, just—"

"I would never say you were an idiot!"

"—inadequately informed. And I never said you thought I was, but you *know* what I mean, right? I don't like looking stupid, Brill."

"Well." Brilliana took a deep breath: "Be it so little consolation to you, I am supposed to be your *confidante*, and your honor is mine. It dishonors *me*—directly—should you look stupid. I plead purely out of self-interest, you understand, not at all speaking as your friend who wishes to return the favor you did me in Boston." She smiled briefly and continued, "So if you tell me what you want to achieve, I shall try to find a way to make it happen, if not instantly then certainly as rapidly as possible. How should that go?"

"Okay." Miriam screwed her eyes shut. "That's what Baron Henryk told me, you know: to work out what I want, then tell him. Over dinner, maybe next week." She opened her eyes and focused on Brilliana as if seeing her for the first time. Perhaps she was, for Helge's ghost was prompting her, *Take your allies where you find them*, and Brill was surely the nearest thing to an ally Miriam had within the Clan. "So. How about it? First, we should arrange for me to dine with the good baron next week—and yourself, I think. Secondly, I want to get back out to see how my company is running, as soon as possible. Thirdly, Ma has been dropping scarily vague hints about marriage, and this crazy old—" She caught herself. "Sorry. The king's mother. Angelin. She's dropping broad hints. *I need to know what she wants.* Never mind that creepy Prince Egon. And what's got into Ma—Patricia. Can you find out?"

Brill's eyes went very wide at the last confessions. She clenched her hands between her knees and leaned back on her stool: "The *Queen Mother* bespoke you? About *Egon*?"

"No, Egon threatened me—the Queen Mother just wanted a chat—"

"He *threatened* you? Miriam, that is completely beyond my conscience! Does Duke Angbard know?"

"Why wouldn't he?" It was Miriam's turn to look startled. "He's head of the Clan's intelligence apparatus! Isn't it his *job* to know things like that?"

"Only if people tell him!" Brill stood up, agitatedly. "I imagine I can do something toward your first two desires, but this—this is new to me. I think I had better write to the duke, by your leave. Miriam, you must steer clear of Prince Egon! He's not—he's—"

"Whoa. I got the message, very clearly, that he doesn't like me, or my relatives. Is that it? Or is there something more?"

Brill nodded, vigorously. "You know their nicknames? The two princes?"

"The . . ." Miriam's forehead creased.

"The Idiot and the Pervert," Brill said tightly. "The Idiot is clear enough. The Pervert—there are rumors. Pray you don't come to his attention."

"Huh?" Miriam stared at her. "What are you trying to tell me? He's a rapist? Wouldn't there be some kind of . . ." She trailed off, a sick realization stealing over her.

"He's the *heir* to the *throne*," Brill said, clearly and slowly, as if talking to a young and rather stupid child. "He has, as a duke in his own right, the right of summary justice. The only lord with the authority to hear a case against him is his own father. Such a case would depend upon the plaintiffs and the witnesses living long enough to bring suit. This is not America, Miriam. There, if the rich and powerful want to get away with murder, they must pay lawyers and judges. Here, they *are* the judges." Her expression brightened. "Having said that, if the crown prince tried to use such as you or I for sport, he could expect the full weight of the Clan to oppose him. Likely, even his father would disown him. You are not some peasant."

Miriam shuddered. "And if he comes to power?"

"He won't move against us." There was a hard edge to Brilliana's voice. "He may be wicked, but he isn't stupid. We are like your America in some ways: our king rules by the will of the people—at least, the people who count. The succession has to be ratified by the landsknee, the dukes and barons. If he offends too many of them, he risks his coronation." Her expression softened. "But please, make sure someone knows if he menaces you again. Otherwise . . ."

"I get the picture." Miriam nodded jerkily. *Jesus, is Egon some kind of serial killer? Or am I misunderstanding something, and it's just hardball politics?* Somehow the idea that her encounter with Egon was simply political business as usual didn't make sense. "What about the Queen Mother?"

"Oh, she's safe," Brill said dismissively. "She's family, after a fashion." She paused, looking thoughtful. "And she noticed you? Ha. It can't be about Egon, he's already carmarked for an alliance with the Nordmarkt, which means—Creon? She aims to put him into play?" She looked distant for a moment. "A royal match would seem fantastical, upon its face, but—"

"Not a hope," Miriam said, tight-lipped. "I mean that."

"But are you . . . ?" Brilliana paused, taking in Miriam's expression. "You would reject it?" she asked, wondering aloud. "You would reject a match, uncountenanced, to such a high estate?" For a moment she was starry-eyed, before practicality reasserted itself. "It would hamper your plans, true—"

"In spades," Miriam said grimly. "And in case you'd forgotten, we're not talking a prize catch, here, we're talking sloppy seconds. The one everybody calls the Idiot, to his face." She clenched her hands between her knees. "Not enough that Roland had to get himself killed, but *this*—"

"I'm sorry, my lady!"

"I don't blame you," Miriam said, startled out of her gloomy introspection. "Don't ever think I blame you!" Brilliana had been there when Roland was killed, in that terrible minute in the duke's outer office with Matthias's psychotic bondsman. If Brill had gotten there faster, or if Roland hadn't tried to play the hero, if *she* hadn't been there, a lure for him— "This is not about you," she said. Roland she might have married, giving her tacit consent to being bound into the Clan's claustrophobic family structures. "I'm not

planning on marrying anyone, ever again," Miriam added
bleakly. Anything else would be too much like an admission
that she was absolutely part of the Clan. Miriam had read
about Stockholm syndrome once, the tendency of hostages
to come to identify with their abductors. It was a concept uncomfortably close to home: sometimes her new life felt like
a perpetual struggle not to succumb to it.

Brilliana adroitly changed the subject. "Would it please
you to volunteer for an additional corvée? I can whisper to
the duke that it would do you well to walk outside this pit of
vipers."

"If you think he'd go for that," said Miriam.

"He will, if he believes you are being schemed around."
She frowned. "One other thing I would suggest."

"Oh? What's that?"

"That you invite your mother to dine with you in private.
As soon as possible." Brill paused. "If she refuses, that will
tell you everything you need to know."

"If she refuses—" Miriam stopped dead. "That's ridiculous!" she burst out. "I know she's been grumpy since being
forced out of isolation, but she already said she didn't blame
me. I haven't done anything to offend her, she's my mother!
Why wouldn't she come to visit me?"

"She might not, if she is being blackmailed." Brill stood
up. "Which would fit the other facts of your situation, milady. There's enough of it about." Her tone was crisp.
"Meanwhile, shall we retire to the morning room? You must
tell me all about your encounter with her majesty."

Letters were written and invitations issued. But as events
turned, Miriam did not get the chance to talk to her mother
in private—or to dine with the baron—over the next few
days. The evening of Brill's arrival, two summonses arrived
for her: an invitation to a private entertainment at the royal
court, hand-scribed in gold ink on vellum by a second secretary of the honorable lord registrar of nobles, and a formal
request for her services, signed by the lord high second
chamberlain of the Clan Trade Committee.

Of the two, the court summons was more perplexing. "This is a dinner invitation," Brill explained, holding the parchment at arm's length between two fingertips. "The closed company. It is open to the royal household and their closest hangers-on and friends, only about sixty people, and there will be a private performance by, oh, some entertainers." A theatrical troupe, or a chamber orchestra, or, if the royal family were feeling particularly avant garde, a diesel generator, a VCR, and a movie.

"Will the Crown Prince be there?" Miriam asked tensely.

"I don't know. Possibly not; he hunts a lot in summer. But you need to attend this. To decline the invitation would require a most serious indisposition." Brill looked nervous. "It does not wait upon your disposition, thus attendance is mandatory. I can come along, should you require me."

"I'd be scared to attend without you," Miriam admitted. "How large a retinue can I take?"

"Oh, to escort you there, as many as you like—but inside? One or two, at the most. And"—Brill glanced askance at the doorway—"Kara would be delighted to go, but might prove less than reliable." Kara was running some errand or other, arranging an evening meal or scaring up some more servants or perhaps simply taking time by herself.

"Uh-huh. And this other?" Miriam held up the other invitation.

"I was not expecting it so promptly." Brill's brow wrinkled. "You would, perhaps, like to return to Boston from time to time?" She smiled: "I believe it is probably the baron's little joke on you, to ensure that you see as much of it as you want, with a sore head, in a borrowed cellar."

"Uh. Right." Miriam grimaced. "But the royal—"

"*She* wants to see you," Brill said firmly. "What else could it be? You don't ignore the Queen Mother's whim, milady, not unless you are willing to risk the next one being delivered by a company of dragonards."

"Ah. I see." Miriam peered at the letter. "When is it for?"

"Next Sun's Day Eve . . . good. There will be plenty of time to attire you appropriately and prepare you for the company." Brill frowned minutely. "But the second chamberlain desires you to present yourself before him tomorrow. Perhaps I should look to your preparations for the royal court while you attend to your corvée?"

Miriam took a deep breath then nodded. "Do that. Mistress Tanzig has held custody of my wardrobe in your absence, Kara managed to sort me out with the use of one of the livery coaches, and if I'm away you can prepare written notes for me while I'm gone." She looked at the window pensively. "I wonder where he wants me to go?"

I should have known better, Miriam thought ruefully, as she watched smoke belch across the railway station platform from the shunting locomotive. The breeze blowing under the open cast-iron arches picked up the smuts and dragged them across the early afternoon sky. She held her hat on with one hand and her heavy carpetbag with another as she looked along the platform, hunting for her carriage.

"It's—harrumph! A postal problem we have, indeed," Lord Brunvig had said, clearing his throat, a trifle embarrassed. "Every route is in chaos and every identity must be vetted. We have *lost couriers*," the old buffer had said, in tones of horror. (As well he might, for if a Clan courier went missing in Massachusetts he or she should very well be able to make their own way home eventually unless the worst had happened.) "So. We need a fallback," he had added, quietly dignified. "Would you mind awfully . . . ?"

The Clan had plenty of quiet, disciplined men (and some women) who knew the Amtrak timetable inside out and had clean driving licenses, but precious few who had spent time in New Britain—and they weren't about to trust the hidden family with the crown jewels of their shipping service. It took time to acculturate new couriers to the point where they could be turned loose in a strange country with a high-value cargo and expected to reliably deliver it to a destination that might change from day to day, reflecting the realities of where it was safe to make a delivery on the other side of the wall of worlds. Which was why Miriam—a high lady of the Clan, a duchess's eldest child—found herself standing on a suburban railway platform on the outskirts of New London in a gray shalwar suit and shoulder cape, her broad-brimmed hat clasped to her head, tapping her heels as the small shunting engine huffed and panted, shoving a string of three carriages up to the platform. *And all because I already knew to read a gazetteer*, she thought whimsically.

Not that there was much to be whimsical about, she reflected as she waited for the first-class carriage to screech to a halt in front of her. New Britain was in the grip of a spy fever as intense as the paranoia about terrorism currently gripping the United States, aggravated by the existence of genuine sub rosa revolutionary organizations, some of whom would deal with the devil himself if it would advance their agenda. Things were, in some ways, much simpler here. The machinery of government was autocratic, and the world was polarized between two great superpowers much as it had been during the Cold War. But political simplicity and the absence of sophisticated surveillance technology didn't mean Miriam was safe. What the Constabulary (the special security police, not the common or garden-variety thief-takers) lacked in bugging devices they more than made up for in informers and spies. Her papers were as good as the Clan's fish-eyed forgers could make them, and she was confident she knew her way. But if a nosy thief-taker or weasel-eyed constable decided to finger her, they'd be straight through her bag, and while she wasn't sure what it contained she was certain that it would prove incriminating. If that happened she'd have to world-walk at the drop of a hat—and hope she could make her own way home from wherever she came out. The quid pro quo was itself trivial: a chance to spend some time in New Britain, a chance to replace the paranoia of court life in Niejwein with a different source of stress.

The shunting engine wheezed and clanked, backing off from the carriages. Somewhere down the platform a conductor blew his whistle and waved a green flag, signaling that the train was ready for boarding. Miriam stepped forward, grabbed a door handle, and pulled herself into one of the small, smoke-smelling sleeper compartments in the ladies' first-class carriage. *Alone, I hope*, she told herself. *Let me be alone . . . ?* She pulled the door shut behind her and, grunting quietly, heaved the heavy bag onto the overhead luggage net. With any luck it would stay there undisturbed until Dunedin—near to Joliet, in the United States, there being no such city as Chicago in this timeline. All she had to do was ferry it to a certain suburban address and exchange it for an identical bag, then return to New London. But Dunedin was over a thousand miles from New London. One good thing you could say about the New British railways was that the overnight express service rattled along at seventy miles an hour. But if the train was full she might end up with company, and being kept awake by genteel snoring was not Miriam's idea of fun.

Clank. The carriage bounced, almost throwing her out of her seat. A shrill whistle from the platform, and a distant asthmatic chuffing, followed by a jerk as the newly coupled locomotive began to pull. Miriam relaxed enough to unbutton her cape. *It's going to be all right*, she decided. *No snoring!*

The corridor door opened: "Carnets, please, ma'am." The inspector tugged his hat as he scratched her name off on a chalkboard. "Ah, very good. Bed make-up will be at eight bells, ma'am, and the dining car opens from seven. If you have any requests for breakfast, the cook will be glad to accommodate you." Miriam smiled faintly as he backed out through the door. First class definitely had some advantages.

Once he'd gone she pulled the slatted wooden shutters across the corridor window, and shot the bolt on the door. *Alone!* It was positively liberating, after weeks spent in the hothouse atmosphere of the Niejwein aristocracy. Her cape went up on the overhead rack first, then she bent down to unbutton her ankle boots. First-class sleeper compartments had carpet and kerosene heaters, not that she'd be needing the latter on this hot, dusty journey. Once the rows of gray, hunchbacked workers apartments petered out into open countryside, she pulled her PDA out of her belt-purse. With four hours to go until dinner—and fifteen or sixteen until the train pulled into Dunedin station—she'd have plenty of time for note taking and reading.

Precisely half an hour later, the machine emitted a strangled squawking noise and switched itself off.

"Bother." Miriam squeezed the power button without success, then stuck the stylus in the reset hole. *Beep.* The machine switched on again. Miriam breathed a sigh of relief, then tried to open the file she'd been working on. It wasn't there. A couple minutes of feverish poking proved that the machine had reset itself to factory condition, erasing not only the work she'd already done but all the other files she'd been meaning to read and edit. Miriam stared at it in dismay. "Fifteen *hours*?" she complained to the empty seat opposite: she hadn't even brought a newspaper. For a moment she was so angry she actually considered throwing the machine out the window. "*Fucking* computers." She glanced over her shoulder guiltily, but she was alone. Alone with nothing but the parched New Britain countryside rolling past, a faint smoke trail off to one side hinting at the arid wind that seemed to be plaguing the seaboard this summer.

If Miriam had one overwhelming personality flaw it was that she couldn't abide inactivity. After ten minutes of tapping her right toe on the floor she found herself nodding along, trying to make up a syncopated backbeat that followed the rhythm of the wheels as they clattered over the track joints. *Not even a book*, she thought. For a while she thought about leaving her compartment in search of the conductor, but it would look odd, wouldn't it? Single woman traveling alone, no reading matter: that was the sort of funny-peculiar thing that the Homeland Security Directorate might be interested in. The idea of writing on her PDA had lost all its residual charm, in the absence of any guarantee that the faulty device wouldn't consign long hours of work to an electronic limbo. But not doing anything went right against the grain. Worse, it was an invitation to daydream. And when she caught herself daydreaming these days, it tended to be about people she knew. Roland loomed heartbreakingly large in her thoughts. *I'll go out of my mind if I don't do something*, she realized. And almost without her willing it, her eyes turned upward to gaze at the carpetbag. *It can't do any harm to look. Can it?*

COMPANY CONFIDENTIAL

FROM: Director's office, Gerstein Center for Reproductive Medicine, Stony Brook

TO: Angbard Lofstrom, Director, Applied Genomics Corporation

Here's a summary of the figures for this FY. A detailed breakdown follows this synopsis; I look forward to hearing from you in due course.

Operations continued as scheduled this quarter. I can report that our projected figures are on course to make the Q2 targets in all areas. Demand for ART procedures including IVF, IUI, ICSI, and tubal reversal is up 2% over the same quarter last year, with an aggregate total of 672 clients treated in the Q1 period. Last year's Q2 figures indicate a viable outcome in 598 cases with a total of 661 neonates being delivered.

With reference to AGC subsidized operations, a total of 131 patients were admitted to the program during Q1. A preliminary estimate is that the total cost of subsidized treatment for these individuals during this quarter will incur operation expenses of approximately $397K (detailed breakdown to follow with general quarterly accounts). Confidence-based extrapolation from last year's Q2 crop is that this will result in roughly 125 +/-17 neonates coming to term in next year's Q1 period. Of last year's Q2 crop, PGD and chorionic villus sampling leads me to expect an 87% yield of viable W* heterozygotes.

We were extremely startled when routine screening revealed that one of our patients was a W* heterozygous carrier. As this patient was not an applicant for the AGC program, no follow-on issues arise in this case, although I have taken the liberty of redacting their contact details from all patient-monitoring systems accessible to FDA supervision—copy available on your request. However, I must urgently request policy guidance in dealing with future W*hz clients not referred to the program through your office.

Other than that, it's all business as usual at GCRM! Hope you're having a profitable and successful quarter, and feel free to contact me if you require further supplementary information or a face-to-face inspection of our facility.

Yours sincerely,

DR. ANDREW DARLING, D.O.

Director of Obstetrics

7

cops

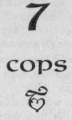

lot had happened in twelve weeks. The assorted
federal agents who had been sucked into the retreat in Maryland had acquired a name, a chain of
command, a mission statement, and a split personality. In
fact it was, thought Mike, a classic example of interdepart-
mental politics gone wrong, or of the blind men and the ele-
phant, or something. Everyone had an idea about how they
ought to work on this situation, and most of the ideas were
incompatible.

"It's not just Smith," Pete complained from the other side
of his uncluttered desk. "I am getting the runaround from
everyone. Judith says she's not allowed to use agency resources to cross-fund my research request without a directive
from the Department of Justice—she's ass-covering—Frank
says the County Surveyor's Office isn't allowed to release the
information without a FOIA, and Smith says he wants to help
but he's not allowed to because the regs say that data flows
into the NSA, never out."

Days of running around offices trying to get a consensus together were clearly taking their toll on Pete Garfinkle. Mike nodded wearily. "Have you tried public sources?"

"What? Architecture Web sites? Property developers' annual reports, that kind of thing? I could do that, but it'd take me weeks, and there's no guarantee I'd spot everything." Pete's shoulders were set, tense with frustration. "We're cops, not intelligence analysts, Mike, isn't that right? I mean, except for you, babysitting source Greensleeves. So we sit here with our thumbs up our asses while the big bad spooks run around pulling their National Security cards on everybody. I can't even requisition a goddamned report on underground parking garages in New Jersey that've been fitted with new security doors in the past six months! And this is supposed to be a goddamned joint intelligence task force?"

"Chill out." It came out more sharply than Mike had intended. "You've got me doing it too, now. Listen, let's go find a Starbucks and unwind, okay?"

"But that means—" Pete rolled his eyes.

"Yeah, I know, it means checking out of the motel. So what? It's nearly lunchtime. We've *almost certainly* got time to sign out before we have to sign back in again. Come on."

Mike and Pete cleared their cramped two-man office. It wasn't a simple process: nothing was simple, once you got the FBI and the NSA and the CIA and the DEA all trying to come up with common security standards. First, everything they were reading went into locked desk drawers. Then all the stationery supplies went into another lockable drawer. Then Mike and Pete had to cross-check each other's locked drawers before they could step outside into the corridor, lock the office door, and head for the security station by the elevator bank. FTO—the Family Trade Organization— was big on compartmentalization, big on locks, big on security—big on just about everything except internal co-operation. And big on the upper floors of skyscrapers, where prices were depressed by the post-9/11 hangover and world-walker assassins were considered a greater threat than hijacked jets.

The corridor outside was a blank stretch punctuated by locked doors, some with red lights glowing above them, the walls bare except for security-awareness posters from some weird NSA loose-lips-sink-ships propaganda committee. Mike made sure to lock his door (blue key) and spun the combination dial before he headed toward the elevator bank. The last door on the corridor was ajar. "Bill?" asked Pete.

"Pete. And Mike." Bill Swann smiled. "Got something for me?"

"Sure." Mike held out his keys, waited for Bill to take them—and Pete's—and make them disappear. "Going for lunch, probably back in an hour or so," he said.

"Okay, sign here." Swann wasn't in uniform—nobody at FTO was, because FTO didn't exist and blue or green suits on the premises might tip some civilian off—but somehow Mike didn't have any trouble seeing him as a marine sergeant. Mike examined the proffered clipboard carefully, then signed to say he'd handed in the keys to his office at 14:27 and witnessed Bill returning them to the automatic key access machine—another NSA-surplus security toy. "See you later, sirs."

"Sure thing. I hope." Pete whistled tunelessly as he scribbled his chop on the clipboard.

"Dangerous places, those Starbucks."

"You gotta watch those double-chocolate whipped cream lattes," Pete agreed as they waited at the elevator door. "They leap out at you and mug you. One mouthful and they'll be rolling you into pre-op for triple bypass surgery. Crack your rib cage *just like* the alien in, uh, *Alien.*"

"Mine's a turkey club," Mike said tersely, "and a long stand. Somewhere where . . ." The elevator arrived as he shrugged. They stood in silence on the way down. The elevator car had seen better days, its plastic trim yellowing and the carpet threadbare in patches: the poster on the back wall was yet another surplus to some super-black NSA security-awareness campaign. *We're at war and the enemy is everywhere.*

"Do you ever get a feeling you've woken up in the wrong company?" he asked Pete as they crossed the lobby.

"Frequently. Usually happens just before her husband gets home."

"Gross moral turpitude 'R' us, huh? Does Nikki know?"

"Just kidding."

Pete's marriage was solid enough that he could afford to crack jokes, Mike noted. "That's not what I meant."

"I know, I know . . ." Pete paused while they waited at the crosswalk outside. It was a hot day, and Mike wished he'd left his suit coat behind. "Let's go. Listen, it's the attitude thing that's getting to me. The whole outlook."

"Cops are from Saturn, spooks are from Uranus?"

"Something like that." Pete's eyebrows narrowed to a solid black bar when he was angry or tense. "Over there." He gestured down a side street lined with shops, in the general direction of Harvard Square. "It's a cultural thing."

"You're telling me. Different standards of evidence, different standards on sharing information, different attitudes."

"I thought it was our job to roll up this supernatural crime syndicate," Pete complained. "Collect evidence, build cases, arrange plea bargains and witness support where necessary, observe and induce cooperation, that sort of thing."

"Right." Mike nodded. A familiar Starbucks sign; there was no queue round the block, they'd made their break just in time to beat the rush. "And the management have got other ideas. Is that what you're saying?"

"We're cops. We think of legal solutions to criminal problems. Smith and the entire chain of command above us are national security. They're soldiers and intelligence agents. They work outside the law—I mean, they're governed by international law, the Geneva conventions and so on, but they work outside our domestic framework." He broke off. "I'll have a ham-and-cheese sub, large regular coffee no cream, and a danish." He glanced at Mike. "I'm buying this time."

"Okay." Mike ordered; they waited until a tray materialized, then they grabbed a pair of chairs and a table in the far corner of the shop, backs to the wall and with a good view of the other customers. "And you figure they're making it difficult because they're not geared up to share national security information with domestic police agencies, at least not without going through Homeland Security."

"Home of melted stovepipes." Pete regarded his coffee morosely. "It's frustrating, sure, but what really worries me is the policy angle. I'm not sure we're getting enough input into this. NSC grabbed the ball and the Preacher Man is too busy looking for pornographers under the bed and jailing bong dealers to have time for the turf war. Wouldn't surprise me if they've classified it so he doesn't even know we exist, or thinks we're just another drug ring roundup embedded in some sort of counterterrorist operation Wolf Boy and Daddy Warbucks are running."

Mike blew on his coffee cautiously, then took a sip. "I'm not sure they're wrong," he admitted.

"Not sure—hmm?"

"Not sure they're right, either." Mike shrugged. "I just know we're not tackling this effectively. It's the old story: if the only tool you've got is a hammer, every problem looks like a nail. Matt's former associates are a problem, okay? Only we can't get at them, can we? Which leaves policing techniques to get them the hell out of our home turf. So why the emphasis on the military stuff? I half suspect some guys who know a lot more than us figure that this *is* a situation which merits military force. It sure doesn't look like something we can do more than a holding action against from here, at any rate."

"I don't agree. We've got to track down those safe houses they're still using. What Matt said about them being short of couriers—it's got to start hurting them sooner or later! If we can capture enough of them, we can stop them."

Mike shook his head. "If we do that, it just starts up all over again a generation later," he said slowly. "Unless we can get at their home turf. Which is a military, not a policing, solution. It may look like magic, but there's got to be some kind of way to do whatever they do, hmm? Bet you that's what the Los Alamos guys are into us for. Although whether they get anywhere . . ."

"Could be." Pete sat back and scanned the shop one more

time. "It's getting a bit crowded in here. How's the home life?"

"Oh, you know." Mike got the message, put his plate down. "The cat thinks I'm a stranger, there's a layer of dust thick enough to ski on in the rec room, and my neighbors phoned the cops last time I went home because they thought I was a burglar. How 'bout you?"

"Huh. You need to get a girlfriend." Pete cracked a smile.

"Not really." Pete stirred his coffee. "The job tends to put the good ones off."

"Like, what was she called? That journalist you were seeing last year, or whenever it was."

"Drop it, Pete."

Pete stared at him. "Getting you down, huh?"

"I said, drop it." Mike looked up. "Do *you* have a life? Or is it just me?"

"Wherever I hang my hat, there's my home. That's what Nikki tells me, anyway: mostly I use the hook on the back of the office door. If I was earning overtime . . ."

"I'm saving up my vacation days." Mike finished his coffee. "When we get this under control I'm going to—I don't know. Get a life, I guess. Nine years and I could do the early retirement thing, head south and get a boat and go fishing forever. Except at this rate there won't be enough of me left to do any of that."

"You've got to stop putting everything into the job," Pete advised. "At least, take a couple of evenings a week to have a life. You about finished?"

"Nearly." Pete drained his coffee and pulled a face. "Let's take a hike. I could do with some fresh air before I go back."

They were half a block away before Pete said it. "Loose lips, Mike. I know"—he waved off Mike's answer before it began—"it's just not office politics as usual, is it?"

"No, it is not." Mike chose his next words with care. "Your data-mining hunt. Do you think they're giving you the runaround deliberately?"

"No, I—" Pete paused. "No, it's not deliberate. I think what it is is, they've got you riding herd on Greensleeves and they had to find something to keep me out of trouble as I was in on that first debrief. But they don't expect to tackle this as a civil law enforcement problem, so they're not giving me any backup. You, they can use. Intelligence, in a word." He shrugged. "It makes me mad," he added quietly.

"If they're not looking at it as a civil law enforcement problem, how do you think they're going to deal with it?"

"I don't know. And that gives me a very bad feeling."

If the altitude doesn't give you a nosebleed, the interagency catfights will do it every time, Mike reflected mordantly as he waited at the elevator bank in the Boston office. He sniffed, mildly annoyed with himself. He'd only just got back from his lunch and chat with Pete, and had just about made up his mind to do something in the evening—some propitiatory gesture in the direction of *having a life*, like phoning his sister Lois (in Boulder, safely distant) or renting a movie—when his insecure phone rang. "Mike? Deirdre here. Can you come up to the meeting room, please? Eric would like a word with you." "Eric"—Colonel Smith—was one rung above him on the embryonic org chart, and the colonel was more likely to give him a headache than offer him a Tylenol. Odds were high that the phone call meant he'd be working as late as usual tonight. *Bad cop, no life*. It was like being on a homicide case twenty-four/seven.

The twenty-first floor had once been mahogany row, back when these offices had belonged to a dot-bomb. FTO had leased them cheap, from the sixth floor up. Everything below ten was a red zone—at risk of enemy incursion. Mike's destination was the office meeting room. It bore a red security seal, but there was no combination lock—it was a meeting room, not a High Security Portal leading to an NSA-style Vault Type Room. FTO didn't have enough secrets yet to fill a bucket of warm spit, much less a multimillion-dollar bank vault in the penthouse of an office block. It was a sign, in Mike's opinion, of how badly the whole business was going. Or of how starved they were for intelligence.

Mike hit the buzzer outside the door, next to the small

CCTV lens. "Mike Fleming, as requested. You wanted to see me?"

"Come in, Mike." Smith normally tried to be friendly but sounded unusually reserved today. Taking his cue, Mike straightened up as the door opened.

Despite not being a full VTR, the meeting room was about as friendly as Dracula's crypt—no windows, air-conditioning ducts and ceiling and floor tiles made out of transparent Lexan so you could check them visually for bugs, white-noise generators glommed against every flat resonant surface to confound any bugging devices. It hummed and whistled like an asthmatic air conditioner, mumbling to itself incessantly to drown out any secrets the conferees might let slip. Meetings in the crypt always sounded like a conference of deaf folks: *Eh, what? Would you repeat that?*

Mike waited for Smith to unlock the door. Smith was in shirtsleeves, his collar undone and his tie loose. *Air conditioner must be acting up again,* Mike thought before he registered the other man sitting at the transparent table.

"What can I do for you, sir?" He glanced at the stranger, appraisingly. *Red badge, purple stripe.* In the arcane color-coded NSA hierarchy Smith had imported, that meant a visitor, but the kind of visitor who was allowed to ask pointed questions. "Good morning," Mike added, cautiously.

"Have a seat." Smith dropped back into his own chair so Mike took his cue, settled at the other side of the table. The visitor was thin-faced, in his thirties or forties, and had a receding hairline, *like Hugo Weaving in* The Matrix, Mike realized. Right down to the tie clip. That *had* to be deliberate. *An asshole, but a* high-clearance *asshole,* he thought irritably.

"Mike, this is Dr. Andrew James, from Yale by way of the Agency and the Heritage Foundation. Andrew, this is senior agent Mike Fleming, DEA, on secondment to FTO. So you know where you stand, Mike, Dr. James is our new Deputy Director of Operational Intelligence, which is to say, he's going to be running our side of the show once we achieve some organizational focus." His cheek twitched. "Any questions?"

"I'm very pleased to meet you, sir," Mike said politely, trying to keep his face impassive. *Shit, another spook.* "Spook" spelled "cowboy," as far as Mike was concerned. They tended to know nothing about law enforcement, and cared less. Which said something unpleasant about the direction in which this meeting was going to go.

"I'm sure you're pleased." James had a dry, gravelly voice. "I know what you're thinking." He didn't smile. He didn't frown. *He looks like a robot*, Mike thought. He rubbed his palms on his trousers, abruptly uneasy.

"You're dead right," James continued. "I *am* a political appointee. I'm here because certain parties in the administration want to keep a tight lock on the operational cycle of the Family Trade Organization and ensure it doesn't run wild. You're currently stovepiped into NSA and DEA, but that's got to change. We're keeping the DOJ connection, but it's been decided that the operational emphasis in the organization is going to be moved toward the military side. So my public title is Deputy Director, Political-Military Affairs, reporting to NSC. In reality, I'm going to be moving into your turf here as your DD/OI, liaising with NSC and the White House to keep them appraised of whatever you HUMINT guys can get out of our assets, and also to keep Justice in the loop. Are we clear, yet?" He cracked a wintry smile.

Mike glanced at Smith, registering his close-faced expression. *This is not good.* "Not entirely, sir," he said slowly, trying to get his thoughts in order. "I understand the oversight aspect. But am I right in saying that you see this as primarily a national security problem, rather than a domestic policing one?"

"Yes." James laid his hands flat on the tabletop, fingers spread wide across it. "We will be emphasizing national security approaches. These—this 'Clan'—is an external threat. They've got nuclear material, and the narcoterrorism angle is, in our view—that is, the strategic view received from the top down—of subsidiary importance to the question of whether a hostile power is going to start blowing up our cities."

"Am I still needed?" Mike asked bluntly, a disturbing

sense of anger and helplessness stealing over him. "Or did you call me up here to reassign me?"

James smiled again, like a shark circling wounded prey in the water. "Not exactly. Colonel Smith tells me that in the eighty-one days since this organization got off the ground, the organization has laid its hands on just one willing HUMINT asset, and he's of questionable worth. You've been tasked with interrogating him, because you were his first contact. I find that kind of hard to believe—can you summarize for me?"

Mike felt his pulse quicken. *Smith set me up.* He glanced at his boss, who narrowed his eyes and shook his head infinitesimally. *No?* Then it was James. Spook tactics. Doublecheck everyone against everyone else, trust nobody, grab the situation by the throat—*hang on.* "Can you confirm your clearances for me? No offense, but so far all I've got to go on is your word." He nodded at Smith. "Standard protocol." *Standard protocol* was *trust nobody, accept nothing*, and it was supposed to apply at all levels—which was why Swann checked Mike's ID and clearances every morning before giving him the keys to his own office. He tensed: if James wanted to make an issue of it—

But instead he nodded agreeably. "Very good, Mr. Fleming. Badge reader over there." He stood up and walked over to the machine. "Why don't you clear yourself to me, at the same time?"

"I think that would be a very good idea, sir," Mike said carefully. They both ran their badges through the scanner, and Mike noted James's list of clearances. It was about a third longer than his own. "Great, I'm allowed to tell you that you exist." He smiled, experimentally, and James nodded as he returned to his seat.

Mike took a deep breath. *Okay, so he's not a total jerk. I can live with that.* "We have a problem with intelligence assets," he began. "All we've got is one willing defector and two prisoners. The defector, as usual, is willing to tell us one hundred and fifty percent of whatever he thinks we want to hear. And the prisoners not only aren't talking, I don't think they *can* talk."

James grunted as if he'd been punched in the gut. "Explain." He held up one hand: "I've read the backgrounder and played the debrief tapes from Matt. Color me an interested ignoramus and give it to me straight, I don't have time for excuses. Pretend I'm Daddy Warbucks, if you like. That's where this buck stops."

"Uh, okay." Mike sat down again, head whirling. *The Office of the* Vice President? He's *in charge, now?* Notoriously strong-willed, the VP in this administration more than made up for any lack of experience in the Oval Office. But this was still news to Mike. *Later.*

He cleared his throat. "We got a windfall in the form of Matt. Without him, FTO wouldn't exist. We'd still be looking at eight to ten gigabucks of H and C per annum transshipping into the east coast with no clue how it was getting past the Coast Guard. We're still probably looking at half that, but for now—" He shrugged. "First thing first, Matt is probably the most valuable informer any American police or security department has acquired, ever."

He swallowed. "But we hit a concrete wall in the follow-through stage."

"Concrete." James made a steeple of his fingers, elbows braced on the transparent tabletop. "What do you mean, concrete?"

"Okay. In our first week, Pete and I holed up with Matt and milked him like crazy. Apart from the side trip to the black box down in Crypto City, of course." He nodded at Smith. "By day six on the timeline we were ready to move. Thanks to the courier snatch on day two, the other side already knew we were active, so it wasn't much of a surprise when we rolled eight empty nests in a row. The haul was pretty good but the assets had flown, money and bodies and drugs. If you've seen the details of what we found"—James nodded—"you'll know it was a very substantial operation. Disturbingly well structured. These guys are like a major espionage agency in their approach, sort of like the old-time KGB: organized in teams with secure communications and safe houses and an org chart. This isn't some street gang.

But we didn't catch anyone. There's another raid going down today, as it happens, but I expect that one to draw a blank too. These guys are way too professional."

James nodded, his expression thoughtful. "Tell me about the two prisoners."

"Well. Pete and I went back to Matt, who filled us in on the other side's security architecture. We put our heads together and took a stab, with Matt in the loop, at second-guessing how the other side's head, the Duke, would rearrange things in the light of Matt's disappearance. Matt said he'd arranged a cover that would make it look like he'd died, so we tried a few fall-backs on the working assumption that they hadn't twigged that Matt was in our pocket. We also hit another nine that we knew would be evacuated, in case they put two and two to-gether about Matt. The decoys got the same treatment as the first wave of raids, but for the special targets we pulled strings to get some special assets in for the party."

Mike leaned back. *Special assets*—the sort of people the CIA had been forbidden ever since the Church commission, the wake of Operation Phoenix, and the other deadly secrets from the sixties and early seventies. Guys with plastic-surgery fingerprints and briefcases full of very expensive custom-built toys. "We drew a blank on one site, but number two had about sixty kilos of uncut heroin, plus a bunch of documents in Code Gamma. The third site, we hit pay dirt and three couriers. One of them died in the extraction process"—killed by fentanyl fumes, brain-dead before the special assets could hook her up to a ventilator—"but the other two we bagged and tagged and shipped off to Facility Echo. Turns out there's no record of these guys anywhere—they're ghosts, they don't exist. Didn't even have any fake ID on them. I liaised with Special Agent Herz and we arranged a section 412 detention order. Because they're of no known nationality there's no one to deport them to, and once INS punches their ticket as illegal aliens we get to keep them out of the court system. Better than Camp X-ray. Shame we can't get anything useful out of them," he added apologetically.

James frowned. "Why won't they talk?"

"Well, near as we can tell, they don't speak English." Mike waited to see how James would react.

When it came, it was a minute nod. "What about Spanish?"

"Nope." Mike watched him minutely. No grasping at straws, no accusations of leg-pulling. *He's not so bad*, he thought grudgingly. *Not bad for a REMF spook.* "We know about the tattoos, so we took precautions. Courier Able had a mirror tattoo on his head, under the hairline, and Courier Bravo had one on the inside of his left wrist. We kept them hooded and blindfolded until we had time to get a security-cleared cosmetologist with a laser in to erase them. But we're pretty sure that these guys don't speak English or Spanish—or French, German, Dutch, Portuguese, Italian, Greek, Russian, Czech, Serbo-Croat, Japanese, Latin, Korean, Mandarin, or Cantonese." *And don't ask how we know*—the old fire drill trick could look very bad, very close to psychological torture, if a defense attorney dragged it up in front of a hostile jury. "They *do* speak something Germanic, we got that much, and Matt checks out as a translator. They call it hochsprache, and it sounds like it diverged from various proto-German dialects about sixteen hundred years ago—it's about as similar to German as modern Spanish is to classical Latin." He took another deep breath. "I'm trying to learn it, but there's not much to go with—I mean, neither of the detainees are willing to help, and Matthias isn't exactly a foreign-language teacher. We're working on a lexicon, and we've got a couple of research linguists coming in as soon as we get their security clearances through, but it's a big problem. I figure these guys were drafted in as mules, shuttling back and forth between buildings in the same place in both worlds—what they call doppelganger houses. To do that, they don't need to pass as Americans. But getting information out of them is difficult."

Which is an understatement and a half, Mike added mentally. Matt was becoming a headache—increasingly demanding and suspicious, paranoid about the terms of his confinement and the likelihood of his eventual release under a false identity. Sooner or later he'd stop cooperating, and then they'd be in big trouble.

"Well, we are going to have a pressing need for that expertise in the near future." James sat up abruptly, as if he'd come to some decision. "Mr. Fleming, I have some news for you which might sound negative at first, so I hope you'll listen carefully and take it positively. We have no functioning human intelligence assets at all in the place they come from. Just like the situation in Afghanistan back in 2001—and we can't afford to be flying blind. I've been reviewing your personnel file and, bluntly, you're nothing exceptional—except that you've got a three-month lead over everyone else in the field in this one area of expertise. So, with immediate effect I'm directing Colonel Smith here to reassign you from Investigations Branch to a new core team—on-location HUMINT. And your prisoner is going to be reassigned to military custody, although for the time being he'll stay where he is."

"Military custody?" Mike raised an eyebrow. "I'm not sure that's legal."

"It will be when the AG's office delivers their ruling," James said dismissively. "As I was about to say, you will continue to work on language skills and continue debriefing Matthias, and liaise with Investigations Branch as necessary—but you're also going to go back to school. Field operations school, to be precise. You're going to ride shotgun on a code word operation you haven't heard of before now, code word CLEANSWEEP, and you have BLUESKY clearance. Your primary job will be to learn who these people are and how they think, and their language and customs, and anything else that lets us get a handle on their minds. And you're going to learn them well enough to learn how to move among them undetected. Do you understand me?"

"Yes, I think I do." Mike's mouth was dry. *So they're taking this military?* "You're asking for a spy. Right?" *Can they do this? Legally?* He had a feeling that any objections he raised would be steamrolled. And raising them in the first place might be rather more serious than a career-limiting move.

"Not just a simple spy." James nodded thoughtfully. "You're going to be recruiting, training, and running other officers, in a way that we haven't really been good at since the Cold War. Over the past couple of decades we've come to rely too heavily on electronic intelligence sources—no offense," he added in Smith's direction, "and we just can't operate that way in fairyland. So you're going to go in and run our field operation. We're going in—we're going over *there*, carrying the war to the enemy. That is the mission we are tasked with, from the top down. Got that?"

"It's a lot to take in," Mike said slowly. His head was spinning. *What the hell? It sounds like he's planning an invasion!* "You mentioned some kind of special clearances, projects? Uh, CLEANSWEEP? BLUESKY?"

James nodded to Smith. "You tell him."

Smith sat up. "The, uh, Clan pose a clear and present danger to the integrity of the United States of America," he said quietly. "In fact, it's not overdramatizing things too much to say that they're the ultimate rogue state. So word is that we're to prepare, if possible, for a situation in which we can go in to, ah, impose a change of regime. BLUESKY is the intelligence enabler and CLEANSWEEP is the project to conduct espionage operations in hostile territory."

"All of this assumes we can reliably send spies into a parallel universe and bring them back again," Mike said quietly. "How would we do that?"

Dr. James glanced at Colonel Smith. "You were right about him," he murmured. To Mike: "You aren't cleared for that yet. Let's just say that we've got some long-term ideas, research projects under way. But for the time being"—he smiled at Mike, a frighteningly intense expression that revealed more teeth than a human being ought by rights to have—"we've got two enemy couriers, and they *will* work for us, whether they want to or not. We'll use them to capture more. And then we'll make those fuckers sorry they ever messed with the United States."

8

REPRODUCTIVE
POLITICS

❦

It was a shaken, thoughtful Miriam who followed the
coach attendant and the other passengers in her car up
to the dining carriage. Some of the other passengers
had dressed for dinner, but Miriam found she wasn't too out
of place once she shed the jacket: probably a good thing, because she hadn't been paying enough attention to maintaining her cover. As with the Gruinmarkt, issues of public
etiquette frequently baffled her—it was easy to get things
wrong, especially when she was worrying about other matters. *What on earth is going on with that report? What does
it mean?* she wondered as the attendant ushered her into a
seat between a ruddy-faced grandmother and her bouncing
ten-year-old charge, evidently out of some misplaced con-
cern for her solitary status. *I'm being trolled. That's the only
explanation that makes sense. Someone expected me to look
in the bag—*

"Marissa! Fold your hands and stop playing with your

fork. I'm sorry, travel makes her unmanageable," the grand-mother blasted in Miriam's ear. "Wouldn't you say so?"

Miriam smiled faintly, keeping a tight lid on her irritation at the interruption. "I don't like to speak ill of people I hardly know."

"That's all right, you know us now. Marissa, put that *down*! I'm Eleanor Crosby. You are . . . ?"

Trapped. "I'm Gillian," said Miriam, rolling out the cover identity Clan logistics had prepared for her. They'd warned her it should be used as little as possible: it wouldn't stand up to serious scrutiny. The steward was walking the length of the table with a tureen of soup balanced on one arm, ladling spoonfuls into bowls in time with the sway of the carriage. *I'm trying to think, so kindly shut up and stop bugging me.*

"Wonderful! You must be traveling to see your family? Where are you from, London or the south?"

"London," said Miriam, tensing. As soon as the waiter was past her she picked up her spoon and started on her bowl. The onion soup might have tasted good if she hadn't burned her mouth on the first sip, but it was either tuck in now or put up with Mrs. Crosby's curiosity all the way to Dunedin. As it was, she had to remain alert for the entire meal, because little Marissa's every tic and twitch seemed to attract Eleanor's loud and very vocal ire. Her place setting was a battlefield, and Mrs. Crosby seemed unable to grasp the possibility that Miriam might not want to be induced to spill her life's story before a stranger. Which was doubly frustrating because right then Miriam would have been im-mensely grateful for someone to share her conundrum with—had it not been both a secret and a matter of life and death.

After the ordeal of dinner, Miriam returned to her com-partment to discover that someone had been there while she'd been eating. One of the bench seats had been con-verted into a compact bunk bed. For a moment her pulse raced and she came close to panic: but the carpetbag was un-touched, still innocently stuffed into the luggage rack above the door. She bolted the door and carefully lifted the bag down, intending to continue her search.

When she'd opened it before dinner, carefully checking the lock first, she'd discovered the bag didn't contain the cargo she'd expected: no neatly taped bags of white powder here. Instead, there was a layer of clothing—*her* clothing, a skirt and blouse and a change of underwear from her house in the Boston of this world. *Bastards!* She'd felt faint for a moment as she stared at it. *They set me up!* Then she calmed down slightly. What if the Constabulary pulled her in for questioning and looked in her bag? What would they find? Miriam puzzled for a while. *Surely they wouldn't waste a precious cargo run just to test a cover identity?* she asked herself. Which meant—ah. *This is meant to survive a search, isn't it?*

There were more items that smacked of misdirection in the bag: a small pouch of gold coin muffled inside the newssheet wrapping of an antique vase. That would buy her a hefty fine or a month in prison if they found it (*they* being the hypothetical police agents, searching everybody as they came off the train) and it would more than suffice to explain her nervousness. *What's going on here?* Miriam puzzled. Then she'd come to the bottom of the bag and found the battered manila envelope with its puzzling contents, which she'd just had time to glance through before the cabin attendant knocked to tell her it was time for dinner.

Now she sat on the bunk, reopened the bag, and pulled out the envelope. It contained a manuscript, printed in blurry purplish ink on cheap paper in very small type, the pages torn and yellowed at the edges from too many fingers: *The Tyranny of Reason* by Jean-Paul Mavrides, whoever he was. It looked to her eyes like something smuggled out of the old Soviet Union—battered and beaten but blazingly angry, a condemnation of the divine right of kings and an assertion that only in a perfect democracy based on the common will of humanity could the common man free himself from his oppressors. "Well, I wanted something to read," she told herself mordantly, "even if I wasn't looking at a seven-year stretch for possession . . ."

She began to flick through it rapidly, pausing when she

came to the real meat, which was embedded in it in neatly laser-printed sheets interleaved every ten pages or so. *Purloined letter.* She could see the setup now, in her mind's eye, and it was less obviously a setup. They wouldn't be planning to shop her—not with a bunch of DESTROY BEFORE READING Clan security correspondence on her person. Even though it was likely that the arresting constables would simply log it as an item from the Banned List and pitch it straight into the station fireplace. So it *was* just a routine precaution, multiple layers of concealment for the letters. Which didn't help her much: with a few eye-catching exceptions they were mostly incomprehensible. She kept coming back to the letter from Dr. Darling to Angbard. *What the hell is a W* heterozygote?* she wondered. *This is significant. What is Angbard doing, messing around with a fertility clinic?* She could think of a number of explanations, none of them good—

There was a knock at the door.

Sudden panic gripped her. She shuddered and shoved the incriminating samizdat into the bag, her palms slippery with sweat. *Oh shit!* The train was moving. *If I have to try to get away—*

Another knock, this time quieter. Miriam paused, then let go of her left sleeve cuff with her right hand. The panic faded, but the adrenaline shock was still with her. She forced herself to take a deep breath and stand up, then shot the bolt back on the door. "Yes?" she demanded.

"Are you a constabule?" asked the girl Marissa, staring up at her with wide eyes. "Coz if so, I wants to know, when's you going to arrest my mam?"

"I am *not*—" Miriam stopped. "Come in here." The little girl moved as if to step back, but Miriam caught her wrist and tugged lightly. She didn't resist but came quietly, as if sleepwalking. She didn't seem to weigh anything. "Sit down," Miriam said, pointing at the bench seat opposite her bunk. She slid the door shut. "Why do you think I'm going to arrest your mam?" *Her* mother? Miriam thought, aghast: she'd taken Mrs. Crosby for sixty, but she couldn't be much older than Miriam herself. She suddenly realized she was looming over the kid. *This can't be good.* She sat down on the bunk and tried to compose her features. "I'm not going to arrest anyone, Marissa. Why, did you think I was a constable?"

Marissa nodded at her, looking slightly less frightened. "You's look like the one as nicked my nuncle? You talk all posh-like, an' dress like a rozzer. An' you got that way of looking aroun' at people, like you's sizing them for a cage."

Jesus, am I frightening the little children now? Miriam laughed nervously. "I'm not a, a rozzer, girl." *And what's her mother afraid of? Is that why she was grilling me over dinner?* "But listen, it's not safe to go asking people if they're Polis. I mean, if they aren't it's rude, and if they are, you're telling them you're afraid. If you tell them you're frightened they'll ask *why* you're frightened, understand? So you don't do that, you just ignore them. Besides, if I was with the Polis, why would I tell you the truth?"

Miriam paused, suddenly realizing she'd sawn off the logical branch her argument was sitting on: *Hope she doesn't spot it.* She stared at Marissa. Marissa had long, stringy hair lying heavy down her back and wore a smock that hadn't been laundered too recently. When she was older she'd probably have cheekbones to kill for, but right now she just looked starved and frightened. *She's about the age Rita would be—stop that.* Miriam hadn't seen Rita, her daughter, since she gave her up for adoption at the age of two days: Rita had been a minor personal disaster, an unplanned intrusion while Miriam was in med school, and the less remembered the better. "Listen. I think you should go back to your mother—you didn't tell her you were coming here, did you?" A vigorously shaken head. "Good. You don't tell her you came to see me because she'll worry. And she's got enough to worry about already, hasn't she?" *Traveling first-class, but her kid hasn't eaten much recently and her brother's been arrested?* Similarly vigorous nodding confirmed Miriam's suspicions. "What did they arrest your uncle for?"

"Sedition," Marissa said shyly.

Miriam felt light-headed with anger. "Well." She reached down into the bag and fumbled around, finding the vase and its decoy contents. She fumbled in it with clumsy fingers then brought out a small coin. "Here, do you have some-where to hide this?"

The kid looked baffled for a moment, made as if to push it away.

"What is it?" Miriam asked tensely.

"Mam said not to—"

"Ah." Miriam paused for a moment. Take, and double-take: "Marissa, what will your mam do if she finds out you've been to see me?"

The kid looked frightened. "You wouldn't!"

"Take. This." She pushed the coin into the girl's hand, folding the fingers around the buttery gleam of the royal groat—withdrawn from circulation a decade since to offset the liquidity crisis following the Persian war, now worth a hundred times its face value. "Give it to your mam. Tell her the *truth*. You came to see me, to ask. I told you, you were silly and shouldn't ask those questions. Then I gave you this." Marissa looked puzzled. "Go on. Your mam won't thump you, not if you give her this. She'll sleep better, be-cause a constable wouldn't do that." *And maybe she'll be able to buy you some more meals*, Miriam added silently.

Marissa jerked, as if she'd suddenly awakened from a bad dream. "Thank'y," she gasped, then turned and scrabbled at the door. A moment later she was gone, darting off down the corridor.

Miriam shut and bolted the door again, then rubbed her forehead. "Bastards," she muttered. There was an unhappy picture here: she could put any number of interpretations to it, a countless multitude of sad little just-so stories to explain the desperate women in the frame. A mother and her kid selling the house, selling the furniture, using their savings to get away by the first train available. The uncle on his way to a work camp—whether he was a real uncle or a live-in com-panion made no odds, such things were winked at but not ad-mitted publicly—by way of a beating and interrogation in the cells. *Sedition.* It was a movable feast. It could mean reading the wrong books (*like the one in my bag*, Miriam re-alized uncomfortably), attending the wrong meetings, even being seen in the same bars as campaigners for a universal franchise. (They campaigned for the universal *male* franchise, mostly—votes for women or nonwhites were the province of wild-eyed dreamers.) *This is a police state, after all*, Miriam reminded herself. Back home in the United States, most people had an overly romantic view of what a monarchy—not the toothless, modern constitutional monarchies of Europe, but the original *l'état c'est moi* variety—was like. In reality, a monarchy was just a fancy name for a hereditary dictatorship, Miriam decided. And that wasn't anything you wanted to get caught up in.

It was only later, lying awake in the stuffy darkness of her compartment, that Miriam's worries caught up with her. And by then it was too late to take back the coin (*what if the Clan counts the decoy cash?*) or to un-open the bag (*what if they're testing me again?*) or unread the peculiar memoranda (*what's a W* heterozygote?*) or even the samizdat tract by the executed French dissident Jean-Paul Mavrides. All because her PDA had crashed, and she hadn't bought any alternative reading matter.

The remainder of her outbound trip went uneventfully. Miriam turned out of bed at seven in the morning, forced down as much of a light breakfast as she could manage in the already oppressive heat, then alighted with her bag at Dunedin station. From there it was a brief cab ride to the safe house, an anonymous classical villa in the middle of a leafy suburb on the edge of the city center. She knocked on the door, and her contact ushered her into a basement room. Then he waited outside while she opened one of the two lockets she wore on a fine gold chain around her neck and focused on it.

The usual headache clamped around her head, making her feel breathless and sick. But she was back in the Gruinmarkt again—or rather, in an outpost in the middle of the Debatable Lands, the great interior void unclaimed by the eastern marcher states or the empire on the West Coast. Three

bored-looking men sat around a log table in the middle of
the room, one dressed to play Davy Crockett and the other
two in sharp suits and shades. It might have been a frontier
cabin, except frontier cabins didn't come with kerosene
heaters, shortwave radio sets, and a rack of Steyr assault ri-
fles by the door.

"Courier route blue four, parcel sixteen," Miriam said in
her halting hochsprache as she stepped off the taped transit
area on the floor and planted her carpetbag on the table.
Davy Crockett passed her a clipboard wordlessly, boredom
clear on his face. Miriam signed off.

Sharp Suit Number One picked up her bag. "Well, I'll be
going," he said, signing the board. Walking over to the far
side of the room he pulled a gleaming metal suitcase off the
top of a chest, then stuffed the entire carpetbag inside it.
Back on the transit area he picked up the case, nodded at
Davy Crockett, then at Miriam, and clicked his heels together. "There's no place like home," he intoned, staring
into a niche in the wall that Miriam hadn't noticed before.
Then he wasn't there anymore. *He didn't make a sound,* she
realized, massaging her forehead: not that she'd ever paid
much attention to other world-walkers in their comings and
goings, but—*doesn't teleportation imply air displacement?*

"Would you like coffee? Or wine?" asked Sharp Suit
Number Two.

"Uh, coffee is be good—" Miriam's hochsprache broke
down completely as she made it to the table. "And ibuprofen." She fanned herself with her hat. "Is it always this hot
here?"

"Stupid question." At last Davy Crockett spoke. "I've had
a requisition for a portable air conditioner and solar power
pack in for, oh, two years."

Two years? Miriam quailed at the idea of being assigned to
babysit a frontier safe house like this for any length of time.

"Still not enough hands for a game of poker," Sharp Suit
Number Two said regretfully. He blinked, slightly owlishly.

"The clock is ticking," intoned Davy Crockett. "Two
hours." He nodded at Miriam. "When's your train?"

"Um. The return leaves just after four, so allow an hour to get to the station—"

"No problem." He picked up his pack of cards, shuffled the deck, and began dealing some kind of a solitaire hand. "We'll get you there," he muttered.

"Is there anything to do here?" Miriam asked.

"Play cards." Davy Crockett's cheek twitched. "Seriously, you don't go out that door unless the roof is on fire. Wouldn't like the company hereabouts, anyways, and you've got a train to catch in five hours."

"Oh." Miriam shifted uneasily on her chair.

"I'll tell them you've arrived," said the stationmaster. He stood up heavily and shambled over to the shortwave set.

Sharp Suit Number Two fussed over the kerosene stove: presently he turned it down and returned to the table bearing a metal espresso pot. "So," he said, hunching his shoulders conspiratorially, "what's it like, then?"

Miriam looked at him blankly. "What's what like?"

"Over *there*. You know." He waved at her, a gesture that took in everything she was wearing. "Different, isn't it, to America? In Chicago you'd stand out like, oh, obvious."

"Oh, *there*." Miriam stifled a sigh: it was going to be a long wait. "Well, for starters, they don't have air-conditioning . . ."

The return journey went smoothly, with no troublesome signs of recognition. There were no unwelcome traveling companions, no desperate Marissa to spark Miriam's paranoia, and no delays. Miriam managed to keep her nimble fingers away from the courier bag, having remembered to pause in the railway station kiosk before departure and pick up a selection of newspapers and a cheap novel or two. The headlines, as always, perplexed and mystified her as she tried to make sense of them. *Comptroller-General Announces Four-Fifths per Gross Increase in Salt License Fee*—what on earth did that mean? Licensing *salt*? And there was more inside. *Sky Navy to Impress Packets* just about made sense, but when she got to the sports pages (*Chicxulub Aztecs versus Eton Barbarians: Goal Scored!*) it turned baffling. Not only did they not play football or base-ball, they didn't even play soccer or cricket: instead they had other esoteric team games—like the Aztecs versus Barbar-ians wall ball match, in which the Aztecs had apparently just scored the first goal in a major league match for fourteen years.

A day on a train gave Miriam a lot of time for thought. *I need bargaining power*, she told herself. *Otherwise they're going to keep me on a short leash forever. And sooner or later they'll get serious about marrying me off*. Serried ranks of W* heterozygote babies line-danced in her imagination when she closed her eyes and tried to sleep. *How did I get into this bind?*

Asking herself that question was pointless: if she pursued the answer far enough, she came to the uncomfortable con-clusion that it was her own fault, her own dogged tendency to dig for the truth that had gotten her into the Clan's busi-ness. (And behind that story lay Iris's shady history, her mother's attempt to escape from an unhappy Clan-decreed dynastic marriage—but some subjects were best treated with kid gloves.) *If I want some personal space I'm going to have to manufacture it for myself*, she decided. But persuading her distant relatives to back off was not easy: privacy seemed to be in scant supply outside the United States. Es-pecially if you harbored valuable genes or looked like your mere presence might upset the established order. And as to just *why* privacy was in short supply . . .

By the time she reached the safe house in the New Lon-don suburbs she was feeling tired, irritable, and increasingly itchy and dirty. She'd been in transit for three days, and the trains didn't have so much as a shower on board. *Next time I'll take an extra change of clothes*, she resolved—this kind of issue obviously didn't affect the Clan courier operations in the United States.

When she signed off the courier bag, Miriam got her first surprise: a coach was waiting for her in the courtyard of Lord Brunvig's town house, and Brill beside it, in an agony of im-patience. "Milady! It's almost two o'clock! Quick, we must get you back to your rooms immediately, there's barely time."

"Time? For what?" Miriam asked, pausing on the bottom step of the boarding platform with a sense of exquisite dread. *Oh no—*

"The royal entertainment! It's tonight! Oh, Miriam, if I had *realized* it would take you three days I would have yelled at his lordship—"

"Well, none of us thought of it, did we?" Miriam said as she climbed into the carriage. "Everything happens more slowly over there." She gritted her teeth and settled down into a corner, her nose wrinkling. *It's unavoidable*, she thought to herself. *I really* am *going to have to answer him.* Nearly six months ago the king himself had asked her a question. Brill, sitting opposite her, looked anxious. "Do I have time to clean up first?" Miriam asked. "And a bite to eat?"

"I hope so—"

"Well, then it'll all work out." Miriam managed a tired smile. "So how about telling me what's been going on while I've been away?"

Three hours later she was still hungry, even more tired, and back in the carriage with Brill. This time they were on their way to the summer palace with an escort of mounted guards, clutching scented kerchiefs to their faces to keep the worst of the smell of the open sewers at bay. *A fortune in jewelry, the most expensive luxurious clothes they can afford to impress one another with, but the drains are medieval: typical Clan priorities.* Miriam shrugged, trying to get comfortable against the hard seat back. Her maids had trussed her into the most excessive gown she'd ever set eyes on, almost as soon as she'd walked in the door. It seemed to weigh half a ton even before they'd added a tiara and a few pounds of gold and pearls. The corset was uncomfortably tight, and the layered skirts had a train that dragged along the ground behind her in a foam of lace and got in the way when she walked. *Romantic and feminine be damned, I'm going to be lucky to make it as far as the front door without tripping.* Brill had been saying something. "What was that?" she asked, distracted.

"I was saying, did you want the high points again?" Brill

sniffed pointedly. "I know you're tired, but it's important."

"I know it's important," Miriam said waspishly. Then she sighed. "Forgive me. Not your fault." *These formal events always seem to bring out the worst in me, don't they?* "This gown needs adjusting. I'm uncomfortable—and a bit tired."

"I'll arrange another session with Mistress Tanzig when we get back, milady. For tomorrow. I hope you won't hold it against her—it's hard to get the cut right when your ladyship's absent." Brill leaned forward to peer at her. "Hmm. You're being Miriam, Miriam. A word of commendation?"

"Uh, yes?"

"Let yourself be Helge. For tonight, just for tonight."

"But I—" She bit her tongue as she saw Brilliana's expression.

"You don't like being Helge," Brill said evenly. "It's not as if you go out of your way to conceal it. But just this once—" Her eyes narrowed, calculatingly, as she fanned herself. "Milady, Miriam is too *American*. Prickly about the wrong things. But this isn't a crowded garden party, this is an intimate informal household entertainment, just us and fifty or sixty family members and courtiers and ministers. If Miriam offers offense . . ."

"I . . . I'll try." Helge fanned herself weakly in the warm, clammy air and tried to relax. "I'll try to be me. For the evening."

"That's perfect!" Brilliana smiled warmly. "Now, the high points. You've met his royal highness, the princes Egon and Creon, and the Queen Mother. But this evening you're also likely to encounter his grace the Prince of Eijnmyrk and his wife, Princess Ikarie—his majesty's youngest sister—and the Duke du Tostvijk. Main thing to remember is that his grace the prince's marriage is what you would term morganatic. Then there are the high ministers and his holiness the Autonomé du Roma, high priest of Lightning Child . . ."

An intimate informal household entertainment—by the standards of the social world of the Niejwein aristocracy it was, indeed, uncomfortably small. Helge was introduced to one smiling face after another, assessed like a prize brood mare, forced to make small talk in her halting hochsprache, and stared at in mild disbelief, like a talking horse or a counting pig. At the end of it all her head was spinning with the effort of trying to remember who everybody was and how she was meant to address them. And then the moment she'd been secretly dreading arrived: "Ah, how charmed we are to see you again," said the short, portly fellow with the rosy bloom of broken blood vessels around his nose and the dauntingly heavy gold chain draped around his shoulders. He swayed slightly as if tired or slightly drunk. Helge managed to curtsey before him without saying anything. "Been what, half a year?"

Helge nodded, not trusting herself to speak. Last time they'd met he'd made her an offer which, in all probability, had been kindly meant.

"Walk with us," said his royal highness, Alexis Nicholau III, in a tone of voice that brooked no objection.

There was a state dining room beyond the doors at the end of the gallery, but Alexis drifted slowly toward a side door instead. Two lords or captains or bodyguards of rank followed discreetly, while a third slipped ahead to open the door. "Haven't seen much of you at court, these past six months," remarked the king. "Pressure of *work*, we understand." He rubbed the side of his nose morosely, then glanced at the nearest guard. "Glass of sack for the lady, Hildt." The guard vanished. "We hear a bit about you from our man Henryk. Nothing too extreme." He looked amused about something—amused, and determined.

Helge quailed inside. King Alexis might be plump, short, and drunk, but he was the *king*. "What can I do for your majesty?" she managed to ask.

"Six months." The guard returned, extended a glass of amber fortified wine for the king—and, an afterthought, a smaller fluted glass for Helge. "Just about any situation can change in six months, don't you know. Back then I said you were too old. Seems *everyone* is too old these days, or otherwise unsuitable, or married." He raised an eyebrow at her.

"Wouldn't do to marry a young maid to the Idiot—come now, do you think I don't know what my own subjects call my youngest son?"

"I've never met the . . . uh, met Creon," Helge said carefully. "At least, not to talk to. Is he, really?" She'd seen him before, at court. Prince Creon took after his father in looks, except that his father didn't drool on his collar. "My duties kept me away from court so much that I know too little—I mean to cause no offense—"

"Of course he's an idiot," Alexis said grimly. "And the worst is, he need not have been. A tragedy of birth gifted him with a condition called, by the Clan's doctors, PKU. We knew this, for our loyal subjects render their services to the crown without stint. One can live with it, we are told, without problems, if one restricts the diet carefully."

Aspartame poisoning? For a moment Helge was fully Miriam. Miriam, who had completed pre-med before switching educational tracks. She knew enough about hereditary diseases—of which phenylketonuria was quite a common one—to guess the rest of the story. "Someone in the kitchen added a sweetener to his diet while he was an infant?" she hazarded.

"Oh yes," breathed the king, and for an instant Miriam caught a flicker of the rage bottled up behind his calm face. She flinched. "By the time the plot was exposed he was . . . as you see. Ruined. And the irony of it is, *he* is the one who inherited his grandmother's trait. My wife"—for a moment the closed look returned—"never learned this. She died not long after, heartbroken. And now the doctors have discovered a way of knowing, and they say Creon is a carrier while my golden boy, my Egon—is not."

"How can they tell?" Helge asked artlessly, then concealed her expression with her glass.

"In the past year, they have developed a new blood test." Alexis was watching her expression, she realized, and felt her cheeks flush. "They can tell which children born of a world-walker and an—a, another—inherit the trait, and which do not. Creon is, the duke your uncle tells me, a carrier. His children, by a wife from the Clan, would be world-walkers. And unless the doctors conspire to make it so, they would not inherit his condition."

"I—understand," Helge managed, almost stammering with embarrassment. *How do I talk my way out of this?* she asked herself, with growing horror. *I can't tell the king to fuck off—how much does he know about me? Does he know about Ben and Rita?* Ben, her ex-husband, and Rita, her adopted-out daughter. Not to mention the other boyfriends she'd had since Ben, up to and including Roland. *Would that work? Don't royal brides have to be virgins or something, or is that only for the crown prince?* "It must be a dilemma for you."

"You have become a matter of some small interest to us," Alexis said, smiling, as he took her elbow and gently steered her, unresisting, back toward the door and the dinner party. "Pray sit at my left side and delight me with inconsequentialities over supper. You need not worry about Mother, she won't trouble you tonight with her schemes. You have plenty of time to consider how to help us with our little headache. And think," the king added quietly, as the door opened before them and everybody turned to bow or curtsey to him, "of the compensations that being a princess would bring you."

9

INTERNMENT

It had been twelve weeks, and Matt was already getting
stir-crazy.

"I'm bored," he announced from the sofa at the far
side of the room. He looked moody, as well he might. "You
keep me down here for weeks, months—no news! I hear no
things about how my case is progressing, just endless questions, 'what is this' and 'what is that.' And now this dictionary! What is a man to do?"

"I feel your pain." Mike frowned. *Has it only been twelve
weeks?* That was how long they'd been holding Matt. For the
first couple of weeks they'd kept him in a DEA safe house,
but then they'd transferred him here—to a windowless
apartment hastily assembled in the middle of an EMCON
cell occupying the top floor of a rented office block. Matt's
world had narrowed until it consisted of an efficiency filled
with blandly corporate Sears-catalog furniture, home electronics from Costco, and soft furnishings and kitchenware

from IKEA. A prison cell, in other words, but a comfortably furnished one.

Smith had been quite insistent on the prisoner's isolation; there wasn't even a television in the apartment, just a flat-screen DVD player and a library of disks. A team of decorators from spook central had wallpapered the rooms outside the apartment with fine copper mesh: there were guards on the elevator bank. The kitchenette had a microwave oven, a freezer with a dozen flavors of ready meal, and plastic cutlery in case the prisoner tried to kill himself. Nobody wanted to take any chances with losing Matthias.

Not that he was being treated like a prisoner—not like the two couriers in the deep sub-basement cell who lived like moles, seeing daylight only when Dr. James's BLUESKY spooks needed them for their experiments. But Matt wasn't a world-walker. Matt could tell Mike everything Mike wanted to know, but he couldn't take him *there*. As Pete Garfinkle had so crudely put it, it was like the difference between a pre-op transsexual and a ten-buck crack whore: Matt just didn't have the equipment to give FTO what they wanted.

"Listen, I'd like to get you somewhere better to live, a bit more freedom. A chance to get out and move about. But we're really up in the air here. We don't have closure; we need to be able to question any Clan members we get our hands on ourselves. So my boss is on me to keep pumping you until we've got a basic grammar and lexicon so if anything happens to you—say you had a heart attack tomorrow—we wouldn't be up shit creek."

"Stop bullshitting me." Matthias had been staring at the fake window in the corner of the room. (Curtains covering a sheet of glass in front of a photograph of the cityscape outside.) Now he turned back to Mike, clearly annoyed. "You do not trust me to act as interpreter, is all. Am I right?"

Mike took a deep breath, nodded. "My boss," he said, almost apologetically. And to some extent it was true; never mind Colonel Smith, the REMF—James—acted like he didn't trust his own left hand to give him the time of day. And *he* reported to Daddy Warbucks by way of the NSC—and Mike had heard all about that guy. Read about him. "Us-

ing you as an interpreter would risk exposing you to classified information. He's very security-conscious."

"As he should be." Matthias snorted exasperatedly. "All
right, I'll work on your stupid dictionary. When are we going
to start creating my new identity?"

"New identity?" Mike did a double take.

"Yah, the Witness Protection Scheme *does* try to provide
the new identity, doesn't it?"

"Oh." Mike stared at him. "The Witness Protection Program is administered by the Department of Justice. This
isn't a DOJ operation anymore, it got taken off us—I was
seconded because I was already involved. Didn't you know?"

Matthias frowned. "Who owns it?" he demanded. "The
military?" Mike forced himself not to reply. After a moment
Matt inclined his head fractionally. "I see," he murmured.

Mike licked his suddenly dry lips. *Did I just make a mistake?* he wondered. "You don't need to worry about that," he
said. "Nothing has changed."

"All right." Matt sat down again. He sent Mike a look that
clearly said, *I don't believe you.*

Mike rubbed his hands together and tried to change the subject. "What would happen if—say—you were a world-walker,
and you tried to cross over while you were up here?" he asked.

"I'd fall." Matt glanced at the floor. "How high . . . ?"

"Twenty-fourth floor." The set of Matt's shoulders relaxed
imperceptibly. Mike had no problem reading the gesture:
I'm safe from them, here.

"Would you always fall?" Mike persisted.

"Well—not if there was a mountain on the other side."
Matt nodded thoughtfully. "Might be doppelgangered with a
tower, in which case he'd get a bad headache and go
nowhere. Or the world-walker might be lying down, in contact with solid object—go nowhere then, too."

"Do you know if anyone has ever tried to world-walk
from inside an aircraft?" Mike asked.

Matt laughed raucously.

"What's so funny?" Mike demanded.

"You Americans! You're so crazy!" Matthias rubbed his
eyes. "Listen. The Clan, they *know* if you world-walk from

high up you fall down, yes? Planes are no different. Now, a parachute—you could live, true. But where would you land? In the Gruinmarkt or Nordmarkt or the Debatable Lands, hundreds of miles away! The world is a dangerous place, when you have to walk everywhere."

"Ah." Mike nodded. "Has anyone ever world-walked from inside a moving automobile?" he asked.

"That would be suicidal."

"Even if the person were wearing chain mail? Metal armor?" Mike persisted.

"Well, maybe they'd survive . . ." Matt stared at him. "So what?"

"Hmm." Mike made a mental note. Okay, that was two more of the checklist items checked off. He had a long list of queries to raise with Matt, questions about field effects and conductive boundaries and just about anything else that might be useful to the geeks who were busting their brains to figure out how world-walking worked. *Now to change the subject before he figures out what I'm looking for.* "What happens if someone world-walks while holding a hand cart?"

"Hand carts don't work," Matt said dismissively.

"Okay. So it really is down to whatever a world-walker can carry, then? How many trips per day?"

"Well." Matt paused. "The standard corvée duty owed to the Clan by adult world-walkers requires ten trips in five days, then two days off, and is repeated for a whole month, then a month off. So that would be one hundred and twenty return trips per year, carrying perhaps fifty kilograms for a woman, eighty to a hundred for a man. More trips for professional couriers, time off for pregnant women, but it averages out."

"There's an implicit 'but' there," Mike prodded.

"Yes. Women in late pregnancy with a child that will itself be a world-walker cannot world-walk at all. Or if they try, the consequences are not pretty. But I digress. The corvée is *negotiated*. To a Clan member, the act of world-walking is painful. Do it once, they suffer a headache; twice in rapid succession and a hangover with vomiting is not unusual. Thrice—they won't do it three times, unless in fear of life and limb. There are drugs they can take, to reduce the blood pressure and swaddle the pain, but they are of limited effectiveness. Four trips in eight hours, with drugs, is punishing. I have seen it myself, strong couriers reduced to cripples. If used to destruction, you might force as many as ten crossings in a period of twenty-four hours; but likely you would kill the world-walker, or put them in bed for a month."

"So." Mike doodled a note on his paper pad. "It *might* be possible for a strong male courier, with meds, to move, say, five hundred kilograms in a day. But a more reasonable upper limit is two hundred kilograms. And the load must be divided evenly into sections that one person can carry."

Matthias nodded. "That's it."

"Hmm." *An SADM demolition nuke weighs about fifty kilos, but no way has the Clan got one of them*, Mike told himself, mentally crossing his fingers. They'd all been retired years ago. If the thin white duke was going to do anything with his nuclear stockpile, it would probably be a crude bomb, one that would weigh half a ton or more and require considerable assembly on site. There was no risk of a backpack nuclear raid on 1600 Pennsylvania Avenue, then. Good. *Still, if James's mules are limited like that, we won't be able to do much more than send a couple of spies over, will we?*

"Okay, so no pregnant couriers, eh? What do the Clan's women do when they're pregnant? I gather things are a bit basic over there; if they can't world-walk, does that mean you have doctors—" Mike's pager buzzed. "Hang on a minute." He stood up. There was an access point in the EMCON insulated room. He read the pager's display, frowning. "I've got to go. Back soon."

"About the military—" Matthias was on his feet.

"I *said* I'll be back," Mike snapped, hurrying toward the vestibule. "Just got to take a call." He paused in front of the camera as the inner door slid shut, so the guard could get a good look at him. "Why don't you work on the dictionary for a bit? I'll be back soon as I can."

One of the guards outside Matt's room had a Secure Field Voice Terminal. Mike took it, ducked into the Post-Debriefing Office, plugged it into one of the red-painted wall sockets, and signed on to his voice mail. *The joy of working for spooks*, he thought gloomily. Back at DEA Boston, he'd just have picked up the phone and asked Irene, the senior receptionist, to put him through. No pissing around with encrypted Internet telephony and firewalls and paranoid INFOSEC audits in case the freakazoid hackers had figured out a way to hack in. Sometimes he wondered what he'd done to deserve being forced to work with these guys. *Obviously I must have done something* really *bad in an earlier life.* "Mike here. What is it?"

"We got the thumbs-up." No preamble: it was Colonel Smith. "BLUESKY has emplaced the cache and on that basis our NSC cutout has approved CLEANSWEEP and you are go for action."

"Whoops." Mike swallowed, his heart giving a lurch. "What now?"

"Where are you?"

"I'm on the twenty-fourth—sorry, I'm in Facility Lambda. Just been talking to Client Zero." More time-wasting code words to remember for something that was really quite straightforward.

"Well, that's nice to hear. Listen, I want you in my office soonest. We've got a lot to discuss."

"Okay, will comply. See you soon."

Smith hung up, and Mike shut down the SFVT carefully, going through the post-call sanitary checklist for practice. (A radiation-hardened pocket PC running some exotic NSA-written software, the SFVT could make secure voice calls anywhere with a broadband Internet connection—as long as you scrubbed its little brains clean afterward to make sure it didn't remember any classified gossip, a chore that made Mike wish for the days of carrier pigeons. And as long as the software didn't crash.) "Got to go," he told the guard. "If Matt asks, I got called away by my boss and I'll be back as soon as I can."

He signed out through the retinal scanners by the door,

then waited for the armed guard in front of the elevator bank. Mike gestured at one of the doors. "Get me the twenty-second." The guard nodded and pushed the call button. He'd already signed Mike in, knew his clearances, and knew what floors he was allowed to visit. A minute later the elevator car arrived and Mike went inside. It could have been the elevator in any other office block, except for the cameras in each corner, the call buttons covered by a crudely welded metal sheet, and the emergency hatch that was padlocked shut on the outside. *No escape*, that was the message it was meant to send. *No entry. High security. No alternative points of view.*

Mike found Smith in his office, a cramped cubbyhole dominated by an unfeasibly large safe. Smith looked tired and aggravated and energized all at once. "Mike! Grab a seat." He was busy with something on his Secure Data Terminal—a desktop computer by any other name—and turned the screen so that Mike couldn't see it from the visitor's chair. "Help yourself to a Diet Coke." There was a pallet-load of two-liter plastic bottles of pop just inside the door—it was Smith's major personal vice, and he swore it helped him think more clearly. "I'm just finishing . . . up . . . this!" He switched the monitor off and shoved the keyboard away from him, then grinned, frighteningly. "We've got the green light."

Mike nodded, trying to look duly appreciative. "That's a big deal." *How big?* Sometimes it was hard to be sure. Green light, red light—when the whole program was black, unaccountable, and off the books, who knew what anything meant? "Where do I come into it?" *I'm a cop, damnit, not some kind of spook.*

Smith leaned back in his chair. With one hand he picked up an odd, knobby plastic gadget; with the other he pulled a string that seemed to vanish into its guts. It began to whirr as he rotated his wrist. "You're going into fairyland."

"Fairyland."

"Where the bad guys come from. Official code name for Niejwein, as of now. The doc's little joke." *Whirr, whirr.* "How's the grammar?"

"I'm—" Mike licked his lips. "I have no idea," he admitted. "I try to talk to Matt in hochsprache, and I've got some grasp of the basics, but I have no idea how well I'll do over there until—" He shrugged. "We need more people to talk to. When can I have access to the other prisoners?"

"Later." *Whirr, whirr.* "Thing is, right now they're our only transport system. Research has got some ideas, but there's a long way to go."

"You're using them for transport? How?" Mike frowned.

Smith smiled faintly. "You're a cop. You wouldn't approve."

I'm not going to like this. "Why not?"

"The first army lawyers we tried had a nervous breakdown as soon as we got to the world-walking bit—does *posse comitatus* apply if it's geographically collocated with the continental USA?—but I figure the AG's office will get that straightened out soon enough. In the meantime, we got a temporary waiver. These guys want to act like a hostile foreign government, they can *be* one—it makes life easier all round. They're illegal combatants, and we can do what we like with them. There's even some question over whether they're *human*—being able to cross their eyes and think themselves into another universe is kind of unusual—but they're still working on that case. Meanwhile, we've found a way to make them cooperate. *Battle Royale.*"

"Tell me." Mike sat up.

Smith reached into one of his desk drawers and pulled something out. It looked like a giant padlock, big enough to go round a man's neck. "Ever seen one of these?"

"Oh *shit*." Mike stared, sick to his stomach. "Shining Path used them . . ."

"Yeah, well, it works for our purposes." Smith put the collar-bomb down. "We put one on a prisoner. Set it for three hours, give him a backpack and a camera, and tell him to bury the backpack in the other world, photograph the location, then come back so we can take the collar off. We're careful to use a location at least five miles from the nearest habitation in fairyland, to stop 'em finding a tool shop. So far they've both come back."

"That's—" Mike shook his head, at a loss for words.

Ruthless sprang to mind. *Abuse of prisoners* was another unwelcome thought. Something about it crossed the line that
divided business as usual from savagery. *Fucking spooks!*

Smith grinned at him. "Before we sent them the first time,
we showed them what happened when one of these suckers
counts down. Trust me, we've got no intention of killing
them unless they try to escape." *Whirr, whirr.* "But we can't
risk them getting loose and telling the Clan what we're doing, can we?"

"Crazy." Mike shook his head again. "So you've got two
tame couriers."

"For very limited values of tame."

"So." Mike licked his dry lips.

The thing in Smith's rapidly swiveling hand was now
making a high-pitched whine. He caught Mike staring at it.
"Gyroball exerciser. You should try it, Mike. They're really
good. I'm spending too much time with this damn mouse, if
I don't exercise my wrist seizes up."

Mike nodded jerkily. *What's going on?* Smith was
serious-minded, committed, highly professional, and just a
bit more paranoid than was good for anyone. The collar-
bomb thing had to be a need-to-know secret. "So why are
you telling me all this?"

"Because you're going to cross over piggyback on one of
our mules before the end of the month, and once there you'll
be staying for at least two weeks," Smith said, so casually
that Mike nearly started coughing.

"Jesus, Eric, don't you think you could give me some
warning when you're going to spring something like that?"
Mike paused. He'd tried to keep a sharp note out of his
voice, not entirely successfully. Since Dr. James's visit he'd
known this was coming, sooner or later—but he'd been expecting more time. "Look, the lexicon and dictionary aren't
done yet, our linguists aren't through their in-processing,
and Matt's not competent to work on it on his own. If something goes wrong while I'm on the other side and you lose
Matt's cooperation as well, it'll seriously jeopardize my successor's ability to pick up the pieces. Anyway, don't I know
too much? Last week I had a GS-12 telling me I'm not al-

lowed to leave the country on vacation, I can't even go to fricken' *Tijuana*, and now you're talking about a hostile insertion and a theater assignment? I'm a cop, not James Bond!"

"Relax, Mike, it's all in hand. We've cut orders for some army linguists, they're already cleared. You don't need to know everything about the contingency planning that's going into this. More to the point, by the time you go out into the field you'll be far enough out of the core decision loop that even if the bad guys capture you, you won't be able to give our strategic goals away." Smith's smile was unreassuring.

"That's supposed to make me feel better?" Mike stared. "Listen, this is all ass-backward. We ought to be trying to arrest more couriers on this side before we even think about going over there. We can secure our own soil without engaging in some kind of insane adventure, surely?"

Smith snorted. "You're still thinking like a cop. I'd be right with you, except we've got a big tactical security problem, son. We're not dealing with some Trashcanistan where the State Department can make the local kleptocrats shit themselves just by sneezing: we're in the dark. We have zero assets, SIGINT is useless when the other guy's infrastructure is pony express . . . We're going to need to get intelligence on the ground, not to mention establishing a network of informers. We don't even know what local political tensions we can leverage. So we've got to put someone in charge on the ground with enough of an overview to know what's important—and the hat fits you."

"You're talking about making me semi-autonomous," Mike said, then licked his suddenly dry lips. "What is this, back to the OSS?" He was referring to the almost legendary Second World War agency—the predecessor to the CIA—and the cowboy stunts that had led to its postwar shutdown.

"Not entirely." Smith looked serious. "And yes, you're right. Normally we wouldn't let someone like you loose in the field. But you're on the inside, you're one of our local language and custom experts, and you can hand Matt over to someone else—"

"But I can't! Not if we want to preserve his cooperation

and keep getting useful stuff out of him. He's a key witness—"

"He's not a witness," Smith said quietly. "You forget he's an unlawful combatant. He's just one who's chosen to co-operate with us, and we're giving him the kid-glove treatment because of that. For now."

"He's enrolled in the Witness Protection Scheme," Mike persisted. "Meaning he's on the books, unlike your two mules. There's no need to treat this like Afghanistan; we can crack the Clan over here by handling it as an enforcement problem."

"Wrong." Smith shook his head. "And if you went digging you'd find that Source Greensleeves has vanished from the DEA evidence trail and the WPS. Look, you're looking at this with your cop head on, not your national security head. The Clan are a geopolitical nightmare. All our conventional bases are insecure: they're designed to a doctrine that says security is about keeping bad guys at arm's length—except now we're facing a threat that can close the distance unde-tected. It's like a human stealth technology. Nor are our tradi-tional allies going to be worth a warm bucket of spit. Firstly, they don't know what we're up against, and if they did, they'd be up against their own private insurgencies as well. Secondly, they're positioned badly—we can't use 'em for basing, they can't use us, the normal rules don't apply. And then it gets worse. Imagine what Al-Qaida could do to us if they could hire these freaks for transport. Or North Korea?"

"Oh." Mike hunched his shoulders defensively. *The spooks have legitimate fears*, he told himself. *But how do I know they're legitimate? How do I know they're not seeing things?* Then: *But what do we really know about the Clan? What makes them tick?*

"Some of those sneaky bastards we call allies would stab us in the back as soon as look at us," said Smith, mistaking Mike's thoughtful silence for complicity. "This isn't the Cold War anymore, and we're not up against godless com-munism, we're up against drug smugglers *sans frontiers*. If you think the Dutch are going to be any use—"

Mike, who had been to Amsterdam on business a couple of times, and had a pretty good idea what the Dutch authorities would think about drug smugglers with a plutonium supply, held his silence. Smith's venting was just that—effusions born of the frustration of fighting an invisible foe with inadequate intelligence and insufficient reach. More to the point . . . *They've dragged me into their covert ops world*, he realized. *If I make a fuss, will they let me out again?*

"Phase one," Mike said when Smith ran down. "When does it kick off? What should I be doing?"

Smith scribbled a note on his yellow legal pad. "I'll e-mail you the details, securely. First briefing is Tuesday, kickoff should be week after next. You'd better keep your overnight bag by your desk, and be prepared to relocate on my word." His grin widened. "In a couple of days you're going back to school, like Dr. James said. You'll be studying Spying 101. It'll be fun . . ."

Mike had been home for barely an hour when the phone rang.

Home wasn't somewhere he saw a lot of these days: since he had joined the magical mystery tour from spook central, his personal life had been patchy at best. From working the mostly regular hours of a cop—regular insofar as they varied wildly and he could be called out at odd times of day or night, but at least got shifts off to recover—he'd found himself putting in eighty- to hundred-hour weeks in one or another of the secure offices the Family Trade Organization had established. Helen the cleaner had taken Oscar in for a couple of weeks at one point, and the tomcat still hadn't forgiven him. That hurt; he and Oscar went back a long way together. Oscar had been with him before he'd been married to his ex-wife. Oscar had watched girlfriends come and go, then mostly had the place to himself since 9/11. But everyone had to make sacrifices during wartime—even elderly tomcats.

Mike had showered and unloaded the dishwasher and stuck a meal in the microwave, and he was working on a tin of pet food for Oscar (who was encouraging him by trying to get tangled up in his ankles) when the doorbell rang. "Shit." Mike put the can down. Oscar yowled reproachfully as he fumbled the handset of the entryphone. "Yes?"

"Mike?" It was Pete Garfinkle. Pete had moved sideways into Monitoring and Surveillance lately. "Mind if I come up?"

"Sure, be my guest."

By the time Pete knocked on the apartment door, Oscar was head down in the chow bowl and Mike was well into second thoughts. The microwave oven buzzed for attention just as the door rattled. "Come on in. I was just about to eat—"

"S'okay." Pete held up a plastic bag. "I figured you wouldn't turn away a six-pack, and I hit Taco Bell on the way over." The bag clinked as he planted it on the kitchen table.

Mike grinned. "Grab a chair. Glasses in the top cupboard."

"Glasses? We don't need no steenkin' glasses!"

Mike planted his dinner on a plate, still in the plastic container, and grabbed a fork and two glasses. "Mm. Smells like . . . chicken." He pulled a face. "I've got a freezer-load of sweet 'n' sour chicken balls, can you believe it? The job lot was going cheap at Costco."

"Lovely." Pete eyed Mike's food warily, then twisted the cap off a bottle. "Sam Adams good enough?"

"It'll go down nicely." Mike started on his rice and chicken as Pete poured two bottles into their respective glasses. "What's with the Taco Bell thing? I thought Nikki liked to cook."

Pete shrugged sheepishly. "Nikki likes to cook," he said. "*Healthy* things. Y'know? Once in a while a man's got to do what a man's got to do, 'specially if it involves a barbecue and a slab of dead meat. And when it's not barbecue season, a dose of White Castle, or maybe Taco Bell . . ."

"I see." Mike ate junk food out of necessity born of eighty-hour working weeks: Pete ate junk food because he needed a furtive vice and most of the ordinary ones would cost him his job. "What's she doing?"

"It's her yoga class tonight." Pete took a long mouthful of beer. "Figured I'd come by and cheer you up. Chat about a little personal problem I've been having."

Mike looked at him sharply. "Beer first," he suggested. "Then let's take a hike." Pete didn't *do* personal problems: he had what by Mike's envious standards looked like an ideal marriage. He especially didn't drop around co-workers' apartments to wail about things, which meant . . . "Is it that thing we were talking about over lunch the other day?"

"Yeah. Yeah, I guess it is." Pete managed to look furtive and scared over his beer glass, which put the wind up Mike even more. "How's the beer?"

"Beer's fine." Mike shunted his dinner aside and stood up. "C'mon, let's go down the backyard and sit out. There's a couple of chairs down there."

Outside, the air hit him like a freshly washed towel, heavy and hot and damp enough to make breathing hard for a moment. Mike waited until Pete cleared the doorway, bag of bottles in hand. "Spill it."

"Chairs first. You'd better be sitting down for this."

Mike gestured at the tatty deck chairs on the rear stoop. "How bad is it?"

"Bad enough." Pete dropped into one of the chairs and handed Mike a bottle. "Go on, sit down."

Mike sat. "I don't think anyone's listening here."

"Indoors." It was a statement, not a question.

"They lock everything down." Mike popped the lid off the beer. "Can't blame them for being suspicious of cops—we don't have that kind of home life."

"Yeah, well." Pete glanced up at the roof suspiciously, then shrugged. The rumble of traffic and the scritching of cicadas would make life hard for any eavesdroppers. "I called Tony Vecchio up today."

Mike sat bolt upright. "Shit, man! Not from work—"

"Relax, I'm not that stupid." Pete took another swig from his bottle.

Mike peered at him. He was obviously rattled. Maybe even as badly rattled as Mike was, in the wake of his little chat with Smith. *Explosive collars. What else is going on?* "I'm not going to like this, am I?"

"I needed to ask some questions." Pete looked uncomfortable. "We've gone native, you know? Inside FTO, surrounded by the military and their national security obsession, we've stopped trying to do our jobs properly. I don't know about you, but I swore an oath to uphold the law—remember that?

Anyway, I wanted to get some perspective. Tony knew about Matt because he was there when Matt came in, so I figured he'd help."

"You wanted a priest to hear your confession."

"Exactly."

Mike sighed. "Okay, so spill it."

"Tony stonewalled!" Pete looked angry for a moment. "First he said he didn't know anything. Then he told me that he'd never heard of Matt, that nobody of that name had come in, there were no WPP admissions this year. *Then* he told me I'd been suspended on full pay, medical disability in the line of work, for the past ten weeks, and he appreciated how I must feel! I mean, what the fuck?"

"Shit." Mike tipped the last of his bottle down his throat, then leaned forward. "You want to know what I think."

"Yes?"

"Close call." He wiped his forehead. "Listen, what you did was *amazingly* stupid. If you'd asked me . . . shit. They've farmed us out to the military. We belong to Defense right now, we don't exist on personnel's books—I mean, I'll bet if you went digging you'd find that we've both been listed on medical leave ever since this thing started. And the paperwork on Matt will be a whitewash. He's a ghost, Pete, like the poor fucks in Gitmo, trapped in Daddy Warbucks's machine. Have you met Dr. James yet?"

"James? Isn't he Smith's boss? The political one?"

"Yeah, him. I take it you haven't met . . . James is a Company man, all the way through. Works for the NSC, runs covert ops, the whole lot. That's who we're working for. And you know what happens to people who go outside official channels in CIA land? You just don't *do* that. I've been doing some reading in my copious spare time. You, me, we got sucked in because we were already on the edge of something very big and very classified and very black. Eric told me some, some stuff. About how the military perceive the national security implications of what we're up against. It made my hair stand on end. I think he's wrong about some—maybe most— of this, but I couldn't tell him that to his face. Now, I happen to think we ought to be treating this more like a policing problem, ought to be enforcing the law—but doesn't that sort of presuppose that we're dealing with criminals? What I'm hearing is that like Matt, they think we're dealing with another government, a rogue state, like North Korea or Cuba or something. And right now, they've won the argument. I don't see us getting any backup from Justice, Pete. If you start going behind their backs without evidence, they will stick it to you hard. But if we don't, who knows what kind of mess they're going to get us into?"

"Shit." Pete stared at him.

"Drink." Mike reached into the bag, thrust another bottle at Pete. "Listen, we'll work on this together. Just keep an eye on what's going on, okay? Compare notes. Try to remember who we are and what kind of job we're supposed to be doing, so that if the spooks fuck up we'll be in the clear and able to carry on. Maybe talk to Judith, she's FBI, I think she'll see it our way. Form a, I guess, a Justice Department network." He found he was waving his hands around helplessly. "We're the underdogs right now. Defense grabbed the ball while our team's back was turned. But it's not going to last forever. And when we get an opportunity to make our case we need to be ready . . ."

TELEPHONY INTERCEPT TRANSCRIPT
LOGGED 18:47 04/06

"Hello, who's this?"

"Paulie?"

"Miriam—I mean, hi babe! Wow! It's been ages, I've been worrying about you—"

"Yeah, well, there's been some heavy stuff going down. I take it you heard—"

"How could I *not*? I'm, like, this side of things is completely firewalled from, you know, your uncle's *other* business interests, but I've been catching it from all sides. You were right about the shit hitting the fan, then Brill turned up with her usual calm head on and sorted most of it out, but they've been running me ragged and I haven't heard *any-*

thing from you, you could have written! So what's going on in fairyland?"

"Politics, I think. First they dragged me over there full time, then they wouldn't let me back out. I've been out of the loop so long: I mean, I'm frightened. Anyway, now I'm running some errands for them in New Britain they've eased up a bit. I get to cross over here and make phone calls, y'know, like prisoner's privileges? But that's all I can do right now, until they're sure nobody's made me. I'm officially in France, at least that's what the INS think. Anyway, I *am* going to get them to clear me so we can do lunch and start putting things back together, soon. Trust me on this, right? Tomorrow I've, well, I've managed to wangle a week in New London. I'm supposed to be moving carpetbags of confidential letters about, but I've figured out a better way. So I get to drop by the works and see who's holding it together, or not as the case may be, bang heads and kick ass, that kind of thing. Then let's do lunch, hey?"

"Sounds like a plan, babe."

"Well, that's most of the plan, anyway. There *is* something else. Two somethings, actually. Tell me no if you don't want to get involved, okay?"

"Miriam, *would* I?"

"Just saying. Look, one of them's probably not an issue. I want you to round me up a prescription for a friend. Nothing illegal but he can't get to see a doctor—he's out of the country—so if you could order it from one of those dodgy Mexican Web sites and mail it to me I'd be ever so grateful."

"Um, okay. If you say so. What's it you're wanting?"

"Um. Two packs of RIFINAH-300 antibiotic tablets, one hundred tabs per pack, not the small twenty-tablet bottles. They should only set you back a few bucks—it's dirt cheap, they use it all over the third world. As soon as you've got it, mail it to me via your, uh, contact. Family postal service should reach me soon enough."

"Okay, I think I've got that, RIFINAH-300, a hundred tablets per pack, two packs. That it?"

"Well, there's the other thing. But that's the one I think you might want to punt on."

"Hmm. Tell me, Miriam, okay? Let me make my own mind up?"

"Okay, it's this: I want all the information you can find—public stuff, company financials, profiles of directors, that sort of thing—on two companies. The first is the Gerstein Center for Reproductive Medicine, in Stony Brook. The second is an outfit called Applied Genomics Corporation. In particular I'm interested in any details you can find about financial transfers from Applied Genomics Corporation to the Gerstein Center—and especially about when they started."

"Applied Genomics, eh? Is this—is this like our old friends at Proteome?"

"Yes, Paulie. That's why I said you could say no. Just walk away from it and pretend you never heard from me."

"I couldn't do that."

"Yeah, well, *couldn't* and *should* are—look, Paulie, I'm sticking my nose into something it's not supposed to be in, and I don't want to get you burned. So the first order of the day is cover your ass. Don't do *anything* that might draw attention to yourself. Don't post the stuff to me or call me about it, that's why I'm using a pay phone. I'll come collect when we do lunch, and I don't mind if all you've got is their annual filings and disclosures."

"What are they *doing*?"

"I—I'm not sure. But, uh, sometime in the past year my relatives have come up with a genetic test for, uh, the family headache. And I was wondering *how* they did that when this other thing, the connection with this fertility clinic, crawled out of the woodwork and bit me. Paulie, there's something—stuff about some kind of W-star genetic trait—that gives me an itchy feeling. The same itch I got when we were investigating that money-laundering scam that turned out to be—well. I think it might have something to do with why they're giving me the runaround, why I'm being pressured to . . ."

"Pressured to what?"

"Never mind. One thing at a time, huh? Look, I've got to go soon. And then I'm going to be on the other side for a week. Let's do lunch, okay?"

"Okay, kid! See you around. Take care and give my best to Brill and Olga."

"Will do. You take care too. Especially around, uh, the second job. I mean that, I want you to be around so I can buy you lunch. It's been too long, okay?"

"Yeah. Nice to hear from you!"

"Bye."

"Bye."

TRANSCRIPT ENDS — DURATION 00:06:42

10

DIFFERENCES OF OPINION

W hat the *hell* do you think you're doing in my office?" Miriam asked in a dangerous voice.

The man in the swivel chair turned round slowly and stared at her with expressionless eyes. "Running it," he said slowly.

"Ah. I see."

The office was cramped, a row of high stools perched in front of the wooden angled desks that formed one wall: they were the only occupants. Miriam had just stepped through the front door, not even bothering to go check on the lab. She'd meant to hang her coat up first, then go find Roger or the rest of the lab team before chasing up the paperwork and calling on her solicitor and then on Sir Alfred Durant, her largest customer. Instead of which—

"Morgan, isn't it? Just who told you you were running the show?"

Morgan leaned back in his swivel chair. "The thin white duke." He smiled lazily. She'd met Morgan before: a strong

right hand, basically, but not the sharpest tool in the box
when it came to general management. "Angbard. He sent me
over here after the takedown in Boston. Said I was too hot to
stay over there, and he needed someone to keep an eye on
things here. Anyway, it's on autopilot, just ticking over.
Every week I get a set of instructions, and execute them."
His smile faded. "I don't recall being notified that you had
permission to be here."

"I don't recall having given Angbard permission to manage *my* company," Miriam said tensely. "Never mind the
fact that he knows as much about running a tech R&D bureau as I know about fly-fishing. Neither do you, is my
guess. What have you been up to while I was in Niejwein?"
It was a none-too-subtle jab, to tell Morgan that she had the
ear of important people. Maybe it worked: he stopped smiling and sat up.

"Expansion plans—the new works—are on hold. I had to
let two of your workmen go, they were insubordinate—"

"Workmen?" She leaned across the desk toward him.
"*Which* workmen?"

"I'd have to look their names up. Some dirty-fingered fellow from the furnace room, spent all his time playing with
rubber—"

"Jesus. Christ." Miriam stared at him with thinly concealed contempt. "You fired Roger, you mean."

"Roger? Hmm, that may have been his name."

"Well, well, well." Miriam breathed deeply, flexing her
fingertips, trying to retain control. *Give me strength!* "You
know what this company makes, don't you?"

"Brake pads?" Morgan sniffed dismissively. Like most of
the Clan's sharp young security men, he didn't have much
time for the plebeian pursuits of industrial development.

"No." Miriam took another deep breath. "We're a design
bureau. We *design* brakes—better brakes than anyone else in
New Britain, because we've got a forty- to fifty-year lead in
materials science thanks to our presence in the United
States—and sell licenses to manufacture our *designs*. So.
Did it occur to you that it might just be a *bad idea* to fire our
senior materials scientist?"

Morgan shook his head minutely, but his eyes narrowed. "That was a *scientist*?"

I'm going to strangle him, Miriam thought faintly, *so help me I am*. "Yes, Morgan, Roger is a real live scientist. They don't wear white coats here, you see, nor do they live in drafty castles in Bavaria and carry around racks of smoking test tubes. Nor do they wear placards round their necks that say SCIENTIST. They actually *work for a living*. Unlike some people I could mention. I spent five months getting Roger up to speed on some of the new materials we were introducing—I was going to get him started on productizing cyanoacrylate adhesives, next!—and you went and, and *sacked* him—"

She stopped. She was, she realized, breathing too fast. Morgan was leaning backward again, trying to get away from her. "I didn't know!" he protested. "I was just doing what Angbard told me. Angbard said no, don't buy the new works, and this artisan told me I was a fool to my face! What was I meant to do?"

Miriam came back down to earth. "You've got a point about Angbard," she admitted. "Leave him to me, I'll deal with him when I can get through to him." Morgan nodded rapidly. "Did he tell you to shut down the business? Or just put the expansion on hold?"

"The latter," Morgan admitted. "I don't think he's paying much attention to what goes on here. He's fighting fires constantly at present."

"Well, he could have avoided adding to them right here if he'd left me in charge; the one thing you can't afford to do with a business like this is ignore it. How many points are you on?"

Morgan hesitated for a moment. "Five." Five thousandths of the gross take, in mob-speak.

Ten, or I'm a monkey's aunt. "Okay, it's like this. Angbard wants a quiet life. Angbard doesn't need to hear bad news. But if you let this company drift it will be an ex-company very fast—it's a start-up, do you know what that means? It's got just *one* major product and *one* major customer, and if

Sir Alfred realizes we're drifting he'll cut us loose. He can afford to tie us up in court until we go bust or until Angbard has to bail us out, and he'll do that if we don't show signs of delivering new products he can use. I think you can see that going bust would be bad, wouldn't it? Especially for your points."

"Yes." Morgan was watching her with ill-concealed fear now. "So what do you think I should do?"

"Well—" Miriam hesitated for a moment, then pressed on. *What the hell can he do? It's my way or the highway!* "I suggest you listen to me and run things my way. No need to tell Angbard, not yet. When he sends you instructions you just say 'yes sir,' then forward them to me, and I'll tell you how to implement them, what else needs doing, and so on. If Angbard doesn't want me expanding fast, fine: I can work around that. In the short term, though, we've got to position the company so that it's less vulnerable—and so that when we're ready to expand we can just pump money in and do it. In the long term, I work on Angbard. I haven't been able to get in to see him for months, but the crisis won't last forever—you leave him to me. I can't be around as much as I want—I've got this week to myself, but they keep dragging me back to the capital and sooner or later I'm liable to be stuck there for a while—so you're going to be my general manager here. *If* you want the job, and if you follow orders until you've learned enough about the way things work not to sack our most important employee because you've mistaken him for the janitor."

"Hah." He looked sour. "What's in it for me?"

Miriam shrugged. "You've got five points. Do you want that to be five points of nothing, or five points on an outfit that's going to be turning over the equivalent of a hundred million dollars a year?"

"Ah. Okay." Morgan nodded, slowly this time. Miriam put on her best poker face. She wasn't happy; Morgan was barely up to the job and was a long way from her first choice for a general manager, but on the other hand he was *here*. And willing to be bribed, which made everything possible.

If there was one thing the Clan had taught Miriam, it was the importance of being able to hammer out a quick compromise when one was needed, to build coalitions on the fly—and to recognize when a palm crossed with gold would trump weeks of negotiations. Normally she was bad at it, as events in Niejwein had demonstrated, but here was an opportunity to do it right. "I'll take it," he said, with barely concealed ill-grace. "You didn't leave me a choice, did you?"

"Oh, you had a choice." She smiled, humorlessly. "You could have decided to wreck the company I created and screw yourself out of a fortune at the same time. Not much of a choice, is it?"

"Okay, my lady capitalist. So what *do* you suggest I do? Now that I'm running this business under your advice?" He crossed his arms.

Miriam walked around the desk. "You start by giving me back my chair," she said. "And then we go look round the shop and come up with an action plan. But I can tell you this much, the first item on it will be to track down Roger and offer him his old job back. Along with all the back pay he lost when you sacked him. Now"—she gestured at the door—"shall we go and assess the damage?"

Five days of hard work, stressful and unpleasant, passed her by like a bad dream. At the end of the first day, Miriam went home to her house on the outskirts of Cambridgetown, to find it shuttered, dark, and cold, the servants nowhere to be found. On the second day, she met with her company lawyer, Bates; on the third day, Morgan reported finding the misplaced Roger; and on the fourth day, she actually began to feel as if she was getting somewhere. The agency Bates recommended had sent her a cook, a gardener, and a maid, and the house was actually inhabitable again. (In the meantime, she'd spent two nights in the Brighton Hotel, rather than repeat the first night's fitful shivering on a dust-sheeted sofa.) A visit to Roger, cap in hand, had begun to convince him that it was all an unfortunate mistake, but she was getting *very* tired of telling everybody that she'd been hospitalized with a fever during a business trip to Derry City and had taken a month to convalesce afterward. Whether they believed the story . . . well, why hadn't she written? Never mind. Her earlier reputation for mystery and eccentricity, formerly a social handicap of the worst kind, suddenly came in handy.

On the fifth day, while Morgan was away performing his corvée duty for the Clan, a parcel arrived.

Miriam was in the office that morning, going over the accounts carefully—Morgan had left that side of things almost completely to Bates's clerk, and Miriam wanted to double-check him—when the bell outside the window rang. She stood up and slid the window back. "Yes?" she asked.

"Delivery." An eyebrow rose. "Hah! Fancy seeing you here. Sign, please." It was Sharp Suit Number Two from the verminous hole of a post office near Chicago, wearing a fetching magenta tailcoat over the oddly flared breeches that seemed to be the coming fashion for gentlemen this year.

"Thanks." Miriam signed off on his pad. "Want to come in? Or . . . ?"

"No, no, must be going," he said hastily. "Just didn't realize this was a Clan operation."

"It is." Miriam nodded. *Isn't it?* she asked herself. "Good day to you."

"Adieu." He tipped his bicorn hat at her, then turned away.

She slid the window closed and carried the parcel over to the desk. Inside it were two large plastic bottles of RIFINAH-300 tablets and a handwritten note from Paulette: *Here's your first item, the other will be ready by tomorrow.* "Good old Paulie," Miriam muttered to herself, smiling. She tucked the bottles into her shoulder-bag, went back to the accounts. They'd wait until after lunch. Then she had to go and visit a friend.

Lunch. Standing up stiffly, Miriam put the heavy ledger back in its place on the shelf, then walked through into the laboratory. John Probity was bent over a test apparatus, tightening something with a spanner. "I shall be calling on a business contact after lunch," Miriam announced to his back, "so I may not be back this afternoon. If you could shut up shop in the evening I would be obliged. Either I, or Mr. Morgan, will be in the office tomorrow if anyone calls."

"Aye, mam," Probity grunted. A fellow of grim determination and few words, the only time she'd ever seen him look happy was when she'd announced that Roger would be rejoining the company on Monday next. So rather than waiting for any further response, Miriam turned on her heel and headed out to catch a cab back home. Not only was she hungry, she needed a change of clothes: it would hardly do for her to be seen in the vicinity of Burgeson the pawnbroker while dressed for the office—that is, as a respectable moneyed widow of some independent means. Lips might flap, and flapping lips in his vicinity had an alarming tendency to draw the attention of the Royal Constabulary.

The electric streetcar rattled its way across the trestle bridge over the river, swaying slightly as it went. The air was slightly hazy, a warm, damp summer afternoon that smelled slightly of smoke. Traffic was heavy, horse-drawn carts and steam trucks rumbling and rattling past the streetcar, drivers shouting at one another—Miriam peered out of the window, watching for her stop. She'd traded her dove-gray shalwar suit and cape for the pinafore of a domestic, worn with a slightly threadbare straw hat. With the "Gillian" identity papers tucked in her shabby shoulder-bag, there was nothing to mark her out as anything other than a scullery maid on a scarce day off, except the two jars of pills in her bag—and she'd decanted them into glass bottles rather than leaving them in their original plastic wrappers. *Nothing to it*, she thought dreamily, staring out at the paddlewheel steamers on the Charles River, letting a beam of sunlight warm her face. *I could be anyone I want.* Once you took the first step and got used to the idea of living under a false identity, it was easy . . .

It was a seductive fantasy, but it was hardly practical. Not with so many strange relatives wanting to get their claws into her skin, to graft a piece of her onto the old family tree.

A year ago she'd been an only child, adopted at that, with no relatives but an elderly mother and a daughter she hadn't seen in years. Now, she found she craved nothing quite as much as placid anonymity. *I want my freedom back*, she realized. *No amount of money or power can make up for losing it.* It was something that the Clan, with their sprawling extended families and their low-tech background, didn't seem to understand about her. A flash of anger: *I'm just going to have to take it back, aren't I?*

She'd grown up in a world where she'd been led to expect that she could create her own identity, her own success story, rather than vicariously acquiring her identity from her role in a hierarchy, the way the Clan seemed to expect her to. And it was at times like this—when independence seemed a streetcar ride away—that their expectations were at their most tiresome and her natural instinct to rebel came to the fore, an instinct bolstered by the self-confidence she'd acquired from starting up her own business in this strange, subtly alien city.

Highgate High Street, tall brick-fronted houses huddling against one another as if for comfort against the winter gales. Holmes Alley, piles of uncleared refuse lining the gutters. She stepped around the worst of the filth carefully. The shop front was shuttered and dark, and her heart gave a small downward lurch. *I thought they had let him go. Or have they arrested him again?* Miriam glanced over her shoulder, then walked past the shop to the battered door with the bellpull: *E Burgeson, Esq.* When she tugged, it took almost a second for the rattle of the doorbell upstairs to reach her. She waited for the chimes to die away, waited and waited, pulled the doorbell again, waited some more. *Damn, he's not home*, she thought. She began to turn away, just as there was a click from the latch.

"Please, no deliveries—" A hideous fit of coughing doubled the man in the doorway over, racking him painfully.

Miriam stared. Burgeson the pawnbroker, her first contact in New Britain, possibly the nearest thing to a friend she had here, was coughing his lungs bloody.

"Erasmus?" she asked. "You're ill, aren't you?" *Shit, he looks awful*, she realized, abruptly worried. In the dusty sunlight filtering down between the houses he looked half dead already.

"Euh, euw—" He tried to straighten up, succeeded after another bout of rattling coughing. "Miriam? How—hah— good to see you." *Cough.* "But not in. This state."

"Let's go inside," she suggested firmly. "I want to take a look at you."

Miriam followed Burgeson's halting progress up the steeply pitched spiral staircase, up to the front door of his apartment. She'd been here before, seen the cavernous twelve-foot ceiling walled on both sides by dusty, tottering shelves of books, the perfectly circular living room with its overstuffed sofa and scratched grand piano. The genteel bachelor-pad disarray of a cultured life going slowly downhill in the grip of chronic illness. Much of his life was a mystery to her, but she'd picked up some tantalizing hints. He'd once had a family, before he'd spent seven years in one of his majesty's logging camps out in the northwestern wilderness. And he wasn't as old as he looked. But his usual gauntness had now given way to the stooped, cadaverous, sunken-cheeked look of the terminally ill. "Make yourself at home. Can I"—he paused for the coughing fit—"make you a pot of tea?" He finished on a croak.

Miriam perched tensely on the edge of the sofa. "Yes, please," she said. Remembering the pain of a childhood vaccination, she added, "It's the consumption, isn't it?" *Consumption. The white death, tuberculosis.* He'd picked it up in the camps, been in remission for a long time. *But this is as bad as I've ever seen him—*

"Yes." He shuffled toward the kitchen. "I've not so many months left in me."

He's whistling past the graveyard, she realized, appalled. "How old are you, Erasmus?" she called through the doorway.

"Thirty-nine." The closing kitchen door cut the rest off. Miriam stared after him, slightly horrified. She'd taken him for at least a decade older, well into middle age. This was a roomy apartment, top of the line for the working classes in this time and place. It had luxuries like indoor plumbing, piped town gas, batteries for electricity. But it was no place to live alone, with tuberculosis eating away at your lungs. She stood up and followed the sounds through to the kitchen.

"Erasmus—" She paused in the doorway. He had his back turned to her, washing his hands thoroughly under a stream of water piped from the coal-fired stove.

"Yes?" He half-turned, his face in shadow.

"Have you eaten in the past hour or two?" she asked.

Evidently she'd surprised him, for he shut the tap off and turned round, drying his hands on a towel. "What kind of question is that to be asking?" He cocked his head on one side, and something of the old Erasmus flickered into light.

"I'm asking if you've eaten," she said impatiently, tapping her toe.

"Not recently, no." He put the towel down and reached back into his pocket for his handkerchief.

"Okay." She dug around in her bag. "I've got something for you. You're *certain* what you've got is consumption?"

"Ahem—" He coughed, hacking repeatedly, into the handkerchief. "Yes, Miriam, it's the white death." He looked grim. "I've seen it take enough of my friends to know my number's come up."

"Okay." She tipped two tablets out into the palm of her hand, held them out toward him: "I want you to take these right now. Wash them down with tea, and make sure you don't eat anything for half an hour afterwards."

He looked at her in confusion, not taking the tablets. After a moment he smiled. "More of your utopian nonsense and magic, Miriam? Think this'll cure me and make me whole again?"

Miriam rolled her eyes. "Humor me. Please?"

"Ah, well. I suppose so." He took the two tablets and swallowed them one at a time, looking slightly disgusted. "What are they meant to do? I've got no time for quack nostrums as a rule . . ." The kettle began to whistle, and he turned back to the stove to pour water into a tarnished metal teapot.

"Remember the DVD player I showed you? The movie?" Miriam asked his turned back.

He froze.

"It's not magical," she added. "You need to take two of these tablets at the same time, on an empty stomach, every day *without fail*, for six months. That should—I hope—stop the disease from progressing. It won't make your lungs heal from the damage already done, and there's a chance, about one in ten, that it won't work, or that it'll make you feel èven more sick, in which case I'll have to find some different medicine for you. But you should lose the coughing in a couple of weeks and begin to feel better in a month. Don't stop taking them, though, until six months are up, or it may come back." She paused. "It's not a utopia I come from, and the drugs don't always work. But they're better than anything I've seen here."

"Not a utopia." He turned to face her, holding the teapot. "You've got some very strange notions, young lady."

"I'm thirty-three, *old man*. You want to put that teapot down before you spill it? And no, it's not a utopia. Thing is, the bac—germs—that cause consumption, they evolve over time to resist the drugs. If you stop taking the medicine before you're completely cured, there's a chance that you'll develop a resistant strain of infection and these drugs will stop working. Too many homeless people where I come from stopped taking them when they felt better—result is, there are still people dying of tuberculosis in New York City." He was halfway back to the living room as she followed him, lecturing his receding back. "That stuff is the cheap first-line treatment. And you'll by god finish the bloody course, because I need you alive!"

He put the teapot down. When he turned round he was smiling broadly. "Hah! Now that's a surprise, ma'am."

"What?" Miriam, stopped in midstream, was perplexed.

He exhaled through a gap between his teeth. "You've shown no sign of needing anyone ever before, if I may be blunt. A veritable force of nature, that's you."

Miriam sat down heavily. "A force of nature with family problems. And a dilemma."

"Ah. I see. And you want to tell me about it?"

"Well—" She paused. "Later. What brought the tuberculosis back? How long did they hold you for?" *How have you been?* she wanted to ask, but that might imply an intimacy in their relationship that had never been explicit in the past.

"Oh, questions, questions." He poured tea into two china cups, neither of them chipped. "Always the questions." He chuckled painfully. "The kind of questions that turn worlds upside down. One lump or two?"

"None, thank you." Miriam accepted a cup. "Did they charge you?"

"No." Burgeson looked unaccountably irritated, as if the Political Police's failure to charge him reflected negatively on his revolutionary credentials. "They just banged me up and squatted in my shop." He brightened: "Some party or parties unknown—and not related to my friends—did them an extreme mischief on the premises." He cracked his knuckles. "And I was in custody! Clearly innocent! The best alibi!" He managed not to laugh. "They still charged me with possession—went through the bookshelves, seems I'd missed a tract or two—but the beak only gave me a month in the cells. Unfortunately that's when the cough came back, so they kicked me out to die on the street."

"Bastards," Miriam said absently. Burgeson winced slightly at the unladylike language but held his tongue. "I've been seeing a lot of that." She told him about the train journey, about Marissa and her mother who was afraid Miriam was an informer or police agent. "Is something happening?"

"Oh, you should know better than to ask me that." He glanced at her speculatively. When she nodded slightly, he went on: "The economy." He raised a finger. "It's in the midden. Spinning its wheels fit to blow a boiler. We have plenty out of work, queues for broth around the street corners—bodies sleeping in the streets, dying in the gutter of starvation in some cases. Go walk around Whitechapel or Ontario if you don't believe it. There's a shortage of money, debtors are unable to pay their rack, and I am having to be very careful who I choose to give the ticket to. Nobody likes a pawnbroker, you know. And that's just the top of it: I've heard rumors that in the camps they're going through convicts' teeth in search of gold, can you believe it? Claiming it as Crown property. *Secundus*." He raised another finger. "The harvest is piss-poor. It's been getting worse for a few years, this unseasonable strange weather and peculiar storms, but this year it hit the corn. And with a potato blight rotting the spuds in the field—" He shrugged. A third finger: "Finally, there is the game of thrones. Which heats up apace, as the dauphin casts a greedy eye at our beloved royal father's dominions in the Persian Gulf. He's an ambitious little swine, the dauphin, looking to shore up his claim to the iron throne of Caesar in St. Petersburg, and a short victorious war that would leave French boots a-cooling in the Indian ocean would line his broadcloth handsomely." Erasmus smiled thinly. "Would you like me to elaborate?"

"Um, no." Miriam shook her head. "Different players, but the game's the same." She sipped her tea. *Global climate change? What* is *the world's population here, anyway?* Suddenly she had a strange vision, a billion coal-fired cooking stoves staining the sky with as bad a smog as a billion SUVs. *Convergence . . .*

"So times are bad and the Constabulary are getting heavy-handed. The Evil Empire is rattling its sabers and threatening to invade, just to add to the fun. And the economy is stuck in a liquidity trap that's been getting worse for months, with deflation setting in . . . ?" She shook her head again. "And I thought things were bad back home."

"So where have *you* been?" Erasmus asked, cocking his head to one side. There was something birdlike about his movements, but now Miriam could see that it was a side effect of the disease eating him from the inside out, leaving him gaunt and huge-eyed. "I thought you'd abandoned me." He said it in such a self-consciously histrionic tone that she almost laughed.

"Nothing so spectacular! After you were arrested, the shit hit the fan"—she ignored the wince and continued—"and— well. The people who were trying to kill me have been neutralized. But one of them defected to the police in my own . . . in the world I grew up in. He, his man, killed—"

She stopped for a moment, unable to continue. "Roland's dead. And, and." *Nothing else matters in comparison.* It was true; she couldn't care less about everything. Roland's absence still felt like a gaping hole in her life, every time she woke up, every time she noticed it.

After a few seconds she forced herself to continue. "The Clan's entire fortune there, in my world, is based on smuggling. They've been driven underground. Some of them seem to have blamed me for it; as a result, they've been keeping me on a very short leash. I'm not the family black sheep anymore, but I'm not exactly trusted, and it took me a lot of work just to be allowed out here on my own. Some of them have got a scheme to marry me off. They're big on arranged marriages," she added bitterly. "It's a good way of silencing inconveniently loud women."

"You're not so easy to silence," Erasmus noted after she'd stopped talking. He smiled. "Which is a good thing: it is our willingness to allow ourselves to be silenced easily that allows scoundrels to get away with so much, as a friend of mine put it—you might like to drop in on her next time you're in New London, incidentally. She's another loud woman who doesn't believe in being silenced. She's called Margaret, Lady Bishop, and you can find her at Hogarth Villas: I think you've got a lot in common." He cracked his knuckles again. "But you haven't told me why you wanted to see me. Much less, why you wanted to save my life."

"I didn't?" She shook herself. "Damn, I'm stupid. It's—well. Look, I managed to steal a week over here, and it's nearly over, and I've wasted most of it repairing the damage Morgan inflicted on my company through neglect—"

"I thought you said he was stupid and lazy?"

"He is. But—"

"Well then, imagine how much damage he could have done if he was stupid and *energetic.*"

She pulled a face. "I did: that's why I made him general manager. I think I've got him sufficiently house-trained to minimize the damage in future. Only time will tell."

"Ah, nepotism," Erasmus said, nodding sagaciously. "But your week is up and you have nothing to show for it?"

"Well." She looked at him speculatively. "I've been doing some thinking. And it seems to me that I've been letting them take me for granted. They have their own set of assumptions about how I should behave, and if I let them apply those assumptions to me they'll back me into a corner. So I need to do something, acquire leverage. Make them let me alone."

"That could be dangerous," Erasmus said neutrally.

"You bet it's dangerous!" Miriam rolled her teacup between her hands, fidgeting. "They've got my mother." Tight-lipped: "She's dependent on certain medicines. They think that's enough to get a handle on me. But if I can establish my autonomy, *I* can provide her meds. I just have to get them to leave me alone."

"Hmm. As I understood it, when you first told me about your turbulent family, they wouldn't leave you alone because you signify an inheritance of enormous wealth, is that not the case?" He raised an eyebrow at her.

"Yes," she said grudgingly. "Not that it makes a lot of difference to me."

"Hah. Perhaps not, but they might be reluctant to leave you alone not because they insist on controlling you for control's own sake but because they fear the disposition of such wealth in directions inimical to their own interests. In which case you will need a tool with which to express your urgency somewhat persuasively . . ."

"I was leaning toward blackmail, myself." She frowned. "Their pressure is relatively subtle, social expectations and so forth. There are lots of secrets in this kind of culture, embarrassing facts best not aired in public and so on. Given a handful of truths it's possible to suggest to people that they butt out"—her expression brightened—"and if there's one thing I'm told I'm good at, it's digging up embarrassing truths."

Erasmus tried again. "But, that is to say—you are applying your not-inconsiderable reasoning skills to this as a social paradox. Your real problem is a temporal, political one. If you try to blackmail them—"

"They're aristocrats. The personal is political," she said dismissively. "Once you get a pig by the nose, its body will follow, right?"

"Right," he said reluctantly.

"I'd better hope so," she added, "because if I'm wrong about them, well, it doesn't bear thinking about. So I'm not going to worry about it. But everything I've seen *so far* tells me that it's going to work. Matthias blackmailed Roland . . ." She stared bleakly at the thin patina of dust on top of the lid of Erasmus's piano. "Blackmail seems to be a way of life inside the Clan. So I'd better get with the program."

"Hi, Paulie!"

Miriam waved from across the station concourse, smiling when Paulette spotted her and headed straight to where she was standing.

"Hey, Miriam, that's a great coat! You're looking good. Listen, there's this new brasserie just outside the center, you up to eating or do you just want to hang out? We could go back to the office—"

"Eating would be good." Miriam rubbed her forehead. "Made two crossings this morning; I need something in my stomach so I can take the ibuprofen." She winced theatrically. "I'd rather not go near the office," she added quietly as Paulie led her toward one of the side doors of the station. "Too much chance someone's bugged it."

"Uh-huh." Paulette didn't break stride: not that Miriam had expected her to. Back when Miriam had been a senior reporter for *The Industry Weatherman* Paulette had been her research assistant—right up until one of Miriam's investigations had gotten them both escorted off the premises with extreme prejudice. Then when Miriam had gotten mixed up with the Clan she'd hired Paulie to look after her interests back home in Boston, United States timeline. Paulette knew about the Clan, had grown up in a tough neighborhood where some of the residents had mob connections. Angbard knew about Paulette, which meant there was a very real risk the office was indeed bugged, and thus Miriam had arranged to meet up with her at Penn Station.

The brasserie was crowded but not totally logjammed yet, and Paulette managed to get them a table near the back. "I need breakfast," Miriam said, frowning. "What's good?"

"The bruschetta's passable, and I was going to go for the spaghetti al polpette." Paulette shrugged. "To drink, the usual hangover juice, right?"

"Yeah, a double OJ it is." At which point the waitress caught up with them and Miriam held back until Paulette had ordered. "Now. Did you get me the stuff I asked for?"

"Sure." Miriam felt something against her leg—the plastic shopping bag Paulie had been carrying. It was surprisingly heavy—lots of paper, a box file perhaps. "It's in there."

"Okay. *All* of that is for me?" Miriam stared, perplexed.

Paulette grinned. "Give me credit."

"Yeah, I know you're good—but *that* much?"

"I have my ways," Paulie said smugly. Quieter: "Don't worry, I kept it low-key. First up are the public filings, SEC stuff, all hard copy. The downloads I did in a cybercafe, using an anonymous Hotmail account I never access from home. To pay for the searches, I got an account with a special online bank: they issue one-time credit card numbers you can use to pay for something over the Net. The idea is, you use the number once, the transaction is charged to your account at the bank, then the number goes away. Anyone wants to trace me, they're going to have to break the bank's security first, okay?"

"You've been getting very good at the anonymous stuff," Miriam said admiringly.

"Listen, knowing whose toes you might be treading on kind of incentivized me! I'm not planning on taking any risks. Look, at first sight it all looks kosher—I mean, the clinic is just a straightforward reproductive medicine outfit, specializing in fertility problems, and the company you fingered, Applied Genomics, is a respectable pharmaceutical outfit. They manufacture diagnostic instruments, specializing in lab tests for inborn errors of metabolism: simple test-tube stuff that's easy to use in the field. They've got a neat line in HIV testing kits for the developing world, that kind of thing. You were right about a connection, though. Next in the stack after the filings, well, I found this S.503(c) charity called the Humana Reproductive Assistance Foundation. Applied Genomics pays a big chunk of money to HRAF every year and none of the shareholders have ever queried it, even though it's in six or sometimes seven figures. HRAF in turn looks pretty kosher, but what I was able to tell is that for the past twenty years they've been feeding money to a whole bundle of fertility clinics. The money is earmarked for programs to help infertile couples have children—what *is* this, Miriam? If it's another of your money-laundering leads, it looks like a dead end."

"It's not a money-laundering lead. I think it really *is* a fertility clinic." The drinks arrived and Miriam paused to take a tablet and wash it down with freshly squeezed orange juice. "It's something else I ran across, okay?"

Paulette glanced away.

"I'm sorry, I didn't mean to snap. Been having a shitty time lately."

"You have?" Paulette shook her head, then looked back at Miriam. "Things haven't been so rosy here, either."

"Oh no. You go first, okay?"

"Nah, it's nothing. Man trouble, no real direction. You've heard it all before." Paulie backed off and Miriam eyed her suspiciously.

"You're tap-dancing around on account of Roland, aren't you? Well, there's no need to do that. I've—I've gotten used to it." Miriam glanced down as the waitress slid a platter of bruschetta onto the table in front of her. "It doesn't get any better, but it gets easier to deal with the, with the . . ." She gave up and picked up a piece of the bread, nibbling on it to conceal her sudden spasm of depression.

Paulette stared at her. "So call me an insensitive cow, but what else is eating you?" she asked.

"It's"—Miriam waved a hand, her mouth full—"reproductive politics. You'd think they'd figure I'm too old for it but no, you're *never* too old for the Clan to start looking for something to do with your ovaries. Fallout from the civil war they had a few decades ago: they don't have enough world-walkers, so the pressure is on those they *do* have to breed like a bunny. But I didn't have the story completely straight before. You know all the stuff about arranged marriages I told you? I should have asked who did the arranging. It turns out to be the old ladies, everyone's grandmother. There's a lot of status tied up in it, and it seems I got a whole bunch of folks ticked off at me just because I exist. To make matters worse, Ma's turned strange on me—she's gone native, even seems to be playing along with the whole business. I think she's being blackmailed, crudely, over her medication. The king, *his* mother's part of the Clan, he's trying to set up the younger son, who is a basket case into the bargain—brain damage at an early age—and he's got me in his sights. And the elder son seems to have decided to hate me for some reason. Don't know if it's connected, but there's more." Miriam took another mouthful of orange juice before she could continue.

"I ran across this secret memo, from the director of the Gerstein Center to Angbard, of all people, talking about the results of some project that Applied Genomics is funding. And I smell a rat. A great, big, dead-and-decomposing-under-the-front-stoop, reproductive politics rodent. Angbard is paying for in-vitro fertilization treatments. Meanwhile everybody keeps yammering about how few world-walkers there are and how it's every woman's duty to spawn like a rabbit, and then there's this stuff about looking for W-star heterozygotes. Carriers for some kind of gene, in other words. And I just learned of a genetic test that's become available in the past year, god knows from where, that can tell if someone's a carrier or an active world-walker. You fill in the dotted lines, Paulie—you tell me I'm not imagining things, okay?" Miriam realized her voice had risen, and she looked around hastily, but the restaurant was busy and the background racket was loud enough to cover her.

Paulette stared at her, clutching her bread knife in one fist as if it were the emergency inflation toggle on a life jacket.

"I've never heard such a . . . !" She put the knife down, very carefully. "You're serious."

"Oh yes." Miriam took another bite of bruschetta. It tasted of cardboard, despite the olive oil and chopped tomato. "What would be the point of being flippant?"

Paulette picked up her bruschetta and nibbled at it. "That is so monumentally paranoid that I don't know where to begin. You think Angbard is paying for IVF for these families and using donors from the Clan." She thought for a minute. "It wouldn't work, would it? They wouldn't be world-walkers?"

"Not as I understand it, no." Miriam finished her starter. The din and clatter of the restaurant was making her headache worse. "But they'd have a huge pool of, in effect, outer family members. Half of them female. Thousands, adding many hundreds more every year. Suppose—how long has this been going on for? How long has HRAF been going?"

"I don't know." Paulette looked uncomfortable. "Sixteen years?"

"Okay. Suppose. Imagine HRAF is about creating a pool of outer family people living in the United States who don't know what they are. In, say, another five years they start hitting age twenty-one. Six hundred . . . call it three hundred women a year. HRAF have their details. They send them all letters asking if they're willing to accept money to be surrogate mothers. What does a surrogate cost—ten, twenty thousand bucks? Maybe nine out of ten will say no, but that leaves thirty women, each of whom can provide a new world-walker every year—or walkers, you're not going to tell me that the Gerstein Center isn't going to dose them with clomiphene, to try for twins or triplets. Call it fifty new world-walkers per year. Say half of the surrogate mothers agree to continue for four years, and you've got, let's see, a hundred and twenty-five new world-walkers per annual cohort from Angbard's breeding program. Paulie, there are only about a thousand world-walkers in the Clan! In just eight years, half the world-walkers will come from this scheme—in twenty years, they'll outnumber the Clan's native-born world-walkers, even if the average Clan female produces four world-walking children." She drank the rest of her orange juice.

"It's like that movie, *The Boys from Brazil*," Paulie murmured. "Cloning up an army of bad guys and making sure they're raised loyal to the cause." She looked uncomfortable. "Miriam, I met Angbard. He isn't the type to do that."

"Um. No." Miriam stared at her plate. All of a sudden she didn't feel hungry. "Charming, ruthless, and manipulative, I'll grant you. Liable to back a conspiracy to create a test-tube master race? I'm—I don't see it either. Except, I *saw* that memo! With my own eyes! If it's real, it looks like there's something really smelly going on at that clinic. And I need to get a handle on it."

"Why?" Paulette asked pointedly. She stabbed at her bruschetta with a knife. "What *is* getting into you, Miriam? What have they got on you?"

"They—" She stared. "Blackmail is business as usual," she said bitterly. "I figure I need to get an edge of my own, before they marry me off to the Idiot. Simple as that."

"Huh." Paulette put her knife down with exaggerated care. "Miriam. I told you about what things were like when I was growing up."

"Yes." Miriam nodded. "Goodfellas. Well, I was born into the mob, I guess, so using their own tactics—blackmail seems to be the family sport—"

"Miriam!" Paulette reached across the table and took her hand. "Listen. As your agent, and as your legal adviser, I would really be a lot happier if you would drop this. You're right, the clinic shit sounds dirty. But if your uncle is involved, it means money. The tough guys, they used to cut their wives and children a lot of slack—as long as they didn't try to nose in on the business. You see what I'm saying? This is family business and they're going to take it a whole lot differently if you go digging—"

"Nuh-uh, no way." Miriam shook her head vehemently. "I know them, Paulie. They're more medieval than that. Everything is on the outside, you know? Their politics is entirely personal. So's their business. If I get the goods on this scheme, then I've got a handle on whoever's running it—"

Miriam stopped dead as the waitress sashayed in and scooped up her plate with a smile.

"I still don't like it." Paulette frowned. "I *mean* that. I think you're misreading them. Just because you're little miss heiress, it doesn't make you exempt. They've got their code: item number two on it, after 'don't talk to the cops,' is 'don't stick your nose where it doesn't belong.' And this sounds like exactly the sort of business people wake up dead for sticking their nose into."

Miriam shrugged. "Paulie, I've got status among them. I couldn't just vanish. Too many people would ask questions."

"Like they did when you appeared out of nowhere?" Paulette stared at her cynically. "Miriam. Seriously, one last time, I've got a bad feeling about this. *Please*, just for me, will you drop it?"

Miriam crossed her arms, irritated. "Who's paying your wages?"

The main course appeared, savory meatballs in a hot, sweet tomato sauce. Paulie nodded, her face frozen. "Okay, if that's how you want to do it," she said quietly. "You're the boss, you know best. Okay?"

"Oh . . . okay." *I went too far*, Miriam realized. *Shit. How do I apologize for* that*?* She glanced down at her plate. "Yeah, that's how I want to play it," she said. *Play it all the way*, then *apologize*. Paulie was a mensch, she'd come round.

"First I have to figure out if it really *is* what it seems to be. Although given that stuff about W-star heterozygotes, I can't see what else it might be. Then if I'm right, I have to figure out how to use it. At best"—she bit into a meatball—"it could give me all the leverage I need. They couldn't touch me, not even my psycho grandmother could. Hmm, great meatballs. So yeah, I think I need to go pay the clinic an anonymous visit." She flashed Paulette a tentative smile. "Know where I can buy a stethoscope around here?"

11

ARRESTED

T he auditor smiled as she walked in the door. "I've come to see Dr. Darling," she announced, parking her briefcase beside the desk. Her expression was disturbingly cheery as she raised an ID card: "FDA, clinical audit division. I don't have an appointment."

The receptionist visibly teetered on the edge of a panic attack for a few seconds. "I'm afraid Dr. Darling isn't—" She lost her thread. The auditor didn't look particularly threatening: just another office worker in a conservative suit, shoulder-length black hair, severe spectacles. But she was from the FDA. And *unannounced*! "I'll just see if I can get him? Wait right here . . ."

The auditor tapped her toe a trifle impatiently as the receptionist fielded two incoming calls and paged Dr. Darling. Glancing round, the auditor took in the waiting area, from the bleached pine curves of the desk to the powder-blue modular sofa for visitors to sit on. The walls were hung with anodyne still-life paintings of fruit baskets, alternating with certificates testifying that this HMO or that insurance company had voted the clinic an award for excellence in some obscure field. It was all very professional, nothing that could possibly offend anyone. A classic medical industry head office, all promises and no downside. Not a hint that it might be the front end for a slave factory, or dabbling in eugenics. "Excuse me?" She looked up. "Dr. Darling will be right with you."

The door opened. Dr. Andrew Darling was forty-something, excessively coiffed and sporting a thousand-dollar smile. "Good morning! You must be from the FDA, Dr., ah . . . ?"

"Anderson," said Miriam, holding up the ID card and mentally crossing her fingers. *Get me a fake ID*, she'd told Brill. *Not police or DEA or anything like that, but I want to be able to walk into any restaurant or drugstore and scare the living daylights out of the manager.* And Brill had just narrowed her eyes and looked at Miriam thoughtfully and nodded, and all of a sudden Miriam was an FDA standards compliance officer called Julie Anderson.

It was, she reflected, a bit like magic. The Clan could—of necessity—do things with false ID that beggared the imagination, far better than anything she'd had to work with on undercover investigations for *The Industry Weatherman*. It was funny what a few million dollars a year in the right pockets could buy you. As long as you had the brass neck— the sense of personal invulnerability—to make effective use of it. Miriam's wrist itched under the temporary tattoo. *Yes*, she thought.

"Ah, Dr. Anderson." Darling barely examined her card. "If you'd care to follow me?"

Darling turned and led her through a maze of cubicles and corridors lined with the usual water coolers, photocopiers, and wilting rubber plants, to an office that seemed too cluttered and compact to be that of an executive. There were files of hard-copy case notes on his desk and a subsiding heap of medical journals behind the glass front of a very used-looking bookcase. "I wasn't expecting a compliance audit this month," he said.

"I know. You should have received a preliminary e-mail

by now, though. This isn't the start of a full investigation, I
hope; more of a precautionary check, I didn't bring a full
team with me. To be frank, I'm hoping you can just clarify a
few points for me and we can leave it at that?"

"That's very irregular." Darling looked slightly puzzled.

Another false note and he'll see through me, Miriam realized edgily. But it was too late for second thoughts now. She
stared at him through the lenses of her false spectacles and
concentrated on playing her role to perfection. "We've been
asked to investigate quietly. By another government
agency." She tapped her briefcase. "You've been dealing
with Applied Genomics via a cutout trust. All perfectly
aboveboard." She smiled. "Don't tell me this is the first time
anyone's asked you about it?"

She'd struck pay dirt: Darling's face turned gray. "Who
sent you here?"

"You know I can't tell you that." Miriam did her best to look
irritated but patient. "It's the Reproductive Assistance Foundation children, the W-star heterozygotes. I've been asked some
inconvenient questions by our sister agency. What are your
postnatal follow-up protocols? What process did you subject
your study guidelines to for ethical clearance, and what facilities do you have in place to recall patients in the event that it
turns out that there are complications—if, just for the sake of
argument, the W-star trait is associated with inborn errors of
metabolism such as a hyperlipidemia or phenylketonuria? I
am—surprised—Dr. Darling, to put it mildly, that there
doesn't seem to be any mention of this trait in the approvals
filing for your clinic. And I was hoping you could offer me an
explanation that doesn't necessitate further investigation."

Darling blinked rapidly. "I—the W-star trait, where did
you *hear* about that? Nobody's supposed to—" He stood up
hastily and walked over to the office door, pushed it shut.

"I can't disclose my sources." Miriam stared at him coolly.

"Was it Homeland Security?"

"I can neither confirm nor deny that."

"Why are you here on your own?" There was a nasty edge
to his voice.

Here comes the hard sell. "Because this is best dealt with quietly." She concentrated on thinking herself into the skin of the person who was using Julie Anderson, compliance inspector, FDA, as a convenient cover identity. "I repeat, I can't tell you who I am. I wasn't here, I don't exist. We know about your relationship with Applied Genomics. Mr. Angbard is the subject of an ongoing federal investigation. I'm here to follow up a loose end and make sure nothing unravels when I pull on it, if you follow me. This is all going to be swept under the rug so tightly that it didn't happen, it never existed, nobody's going to admit anything, and there won't be any prosecutions—at least not in public. Are you with me so far? We do not need any scandals. But we need to know several things. We need to know *how many*, and *when they were born*, and *where they live*. And then we're going to make sure that when Mr. Angbard and his interesting supply of money vanishes quietly—no, don't ask—your problem goes away too. Did you ever see the Indiana Jones movies, Dr. Darling? If you like, I'm from the Federal Warehouse. I'm one of the curators. And I want your address list, in hard copy, before I walk out of this building. Do you understand me?"

Darling swallowed. "What you're asking for is unethical as hell, not to mention illegal," he said. "Doesn't medical confidentiality mean anything to you people?"

Miriam smiled humorlessly. She was really getting into this, she decided: being a spook was *fun*. "I'm sure using substituted semen for in-vitro fertilization is also unethical and illegal. Now are we going to do this quietly, or am I going to have to go away and come back with a FEMA emergency court order and an arrest warrant?"

"Shit." It was the sweet sound of surrender. "Are you going to indemnify me? Or entertain a plea bargain? If you get this stuff, I want immunity from prosecution arising from it."

"You are not the target of this investigation," Miriam stonewalled. *If he expects paperwork . . .* "And this isn't prosecution territory in any event, as I believe I already said. I was never here, you didn't give me any files, there's not going to be any fallout or any collateral damage. We don't want a paper trail. Do you follow?"

"I—oh hell." Darling shuffled. "Okay, I'll get you the files." He glanced at the door. "Will hard copy do? We don't keep this stuff on a networked server."

"Paper will be fine." Miriam nodded. "In the first instance, we're just after a contact sheet for the W-star subjects. I can come back for their full medical records later." *Not that I'm going to, because they won't be worth a three-dollar bill.*

"Okay. Wait here." Darling stood up and left the office, closing the door quietly.

Miriam shut her eyes and breathed a sigh of relief. *Okay, he's doing it*, she decided. *He's bought the story. Right?* This was always the hardest part of an investigation, getting the target's trust. But after about thirty seconds she opened her eyes again. *Am I missing something?* She rubbed her palms on her knees: they were damp. She hadn't been on this end of an investigation for more than a year, and it made her as nervous as a cat passing the back fence of a boarding kennel. She thought she'd laid the groundwork adequately, but . . . *Darling's been falsifying IVF donor records for Angbard by way of this nonprofit trust. I've just dropped the hammer on him. What could go wrong at this stage?*

Well, in the worst case scenario Darling could just pick up the phone and *call* Angbard, tell him someone from the FDA was sniffing around the operation. But that wasn't very likely, and in any case it would take time for Angbard to send Clan security round to deal with her, time in which she could simply vanish from the scene. (She resisted the urge to push back her left sleeve and glance at the temporary tattoo: if she bugged out now she'd probably end up somewhere in the wild woods, over on the other side, with a splitting headache.) Next worst scenario: Darling was going to phone the FDA, and would discover pretty quickly that there was no field inspector called Anderson. At which point she could either run away or pull the full black-helicopters tinfoil-hat spook thing. This being a deeply paranoid decade, the odds were that he'd believe her—and if not, she could still bug out. But the third worst case—

Miriam stood up as the door opened. It was Darling, and there was a security guard with him. "That's her," he said. The guard took a step forward and Miriam flicked her sleeve back to stare at the knotwork design in brown henna that writhed on the back of her wrist like a snake endlessly swallowing its own tail, inducing feelings of nausea. "Arrest her."

The guard reached out to grab Miriam as she brought the knot into focus, putting her mind into the state in which she could world-walk with the ease of long practice. Hands closed around her right arm as lightning stabbed at the base of her skull. "Ow!" She winced, vision flickering, and tried again. *Nothing*. Her stomach twisted and she began to double over, head a throbbing wall of pain. *What the hell—*

"On the ground!" said the guard. "Lie down!" Something hard shoved into the base of her skull. "Okay, I don't think she's armed, sir. If you can help me with these—"

Handcuffs. Miriam tried to move her wrists but they didn't want to respond, flopping around behind her as the guard pinioned them. *The building must be doppelgangered*, she realized through the crippling headache. *Which means the whole clinic is a Clan front—that's impossible!*

Her stomach flip-flopped. Hands were lifting her: something sharp pressed against the side of her neck. "Okay, that's ten mills of Valium. Wait two minutes, then get the cuffs off her and take her down to recovery ward B, there's a spare room off the main bay. I'll meet you down there."

"Going . . . be sick . . ." She'd spoken aloud, she thought. But there was a great empty hollow space inside her, and everything felt warm and wet, as if she were dissolving in a vast salty ocean of comfort and sleep. *Valium?* she thought. *What went wrong?* It was the last thing she thought for a long time.

It was dark, and her head hurt. Miriam tried to stretch and found she couldn't move. *That's odd*, she thought fuzzily, *I don't remember going to bed*. She tried to stretch again, but her head was spinning and her knees ached and she felt a sudden urge to urinate. She was lying on her back. *Why am I on my back?* The urge was irresistible and for some reason she couldn't fight it. But that was okay. If it wasn't for the headache and the knee thing she could fall asleep again; she felt warm and comfortable, as if a hot pillow was pressing down on her. *Drugs*, she thought vaguely, *I'm sedated.* It was so funny she felt like giggling, but laughter was too much like hard work.

"—sample bottle please, and get her a new catheter bag—" The words made no sense.

Miriam tried to ask, "What's going on?" but nothing came out. There was an unpleasant pressure between her legs and a sensation of cold, uncomfortable and intimate. *Not due for a smear test*, she thought irrelevantly, and managed to make an indignant grunt.

"She's too light, give me another five mikes," said the same voice. Then there was a prickling at her wrist and the world went away for a while.

The next time she woke up was both better and worse. She had a pounding headache and her mouth felt as if a family of small rodents had set up home on her tongue—but she was in a bed, and fully conscious, the soft Valium blanket no longer pressing down on her. Instead, she was alert—and completely aware of just how stunningly stupid she'd been.

In her careful list of what might have gone wrong, she'd overlooked option three: the entire clinic was a front for Angbard's organization, in which case it was no surprise at all that it was doppelgangered. And Darling had known she was a hoaxer as soon as she opened her mouth, because none of the IVF scheme details had been registered with the relevant FDA supervisory committees. Nobody outside the clan had ever *heard* of W* heterozygotes. So . . .

She groaned and tried to roll over, away from the too-bright sunlight that was hurting her eyelids, only to be brought up short by a metal bracelet locked around her left wrist. *Shit.* She opened her eyes to see a whitewashed concrete wall inches away from her nose. *I'm a prisoner.*

The realization was crushing, and with it came a sense of

total despair at her own stupidity. *I told Paulie to take care and not go barging in, why couldn't I listen to my own advice?* She pushed herself upright and looked around, taking stock of her situation.

She was lying on a narrow cot in a room about five feet wide and maybe eight feet long. Next to the end of the bed, a stainless-steel sink was bolted to the wall. At the foot of the bed she could see a similarly grim-looking commode next to the door. The bed had a foam pillow and a sheet, and that was it. They'd dressed her in a hospital gown, taken her clothes, and handcuffed her to a ring in the wall by a length of chain. There was a window set high up in one wall, through which the morning—or afternoon—sunlight slid, and a naked bulb recessed in the ceiling, but she couldn't see a light switch. There was no mirror over the washbasin, no handle on the inside of the door, and absolutely no sign to betray where she was. But she already knew roughly what this place had to be, and where. It was a doppelganger cell in one of the Clan's surviving safe houses. An oubliette. People could vanish in here, never be seen again. For all she knew, maybe that was the idea—there'd be a sealed room on the other side, air full of carbon monoxide or some other silent killer so that if she somehow unchained herself and tried to world-walk . . .

Miriam shook her head, desperately trying to dispel the bubbling panic. *I do not need this now*, she told herself faintly. *I mustn't go to pieces.* But telling herself didn't help much. In fact, it seemed to make things worse. She'd stuck her nose into Angbard's business, and she'd have to be a blind fool to imagine that Angbard would just slap her lightly across the wrist and say, "Don't do it again." Angbard's authority was based on the simple, drastic fact that everybody knew that you didn't cross the duke. Roland had been terrified of him, Baron Oliver and her grandmother the dowager had given Angbard a wide berth, focusing instead on weaklings among his associates—the only person she'd known to openly cross Angbard was Matthias, and he'd just *vanished*. Quite possibly she was going to find out where he'd gone. If not—she cringed. It wasn't as if she could try to bluff that it was just a stupid, sophomoric prank, an attempt to get his attention. Angbard wasn't an idiot, and more important, he didn't think *she* was. Which meant that he was bound to take her seriously. And the last thing she wanted was for Angbard to get it into his head that she was looking for—not to use any euphemisms—blackmail material. She glanced at her wrist, halfway desperate enough to try and world-walk anyway, risking the doppelganger room. Then she gave an involuntary moan of despair. Her temporary tattoo was gone.

There must have been a hidden camera or spy hole somewhere in the walls, because she didn't have to wait long. Maybe half an hour after she awakened, the door rattled and slammed open. Miriam flinched away but was brought up short by the chain. Two guys in business suits stared at her from the doorway like leashed hounds watching a rabbit. Behind them stood an older man with a dry, sallow face and an expression like a hungry ferret: "We can do this two ways, easy or hard. Easy is, you sit in this wheelchair and don't say nothing. You don't want hard."

"Do you know who I am?" asked Miriam.

One of the hounds glanced at the ferret for approval: receiving it, he stepped forward and punched her in the solar plexus. She writhed on the bed, trying to suck in enough air to scream, while the ferret watched her. "We know just who you are," he said after a minute, so quietly that she nearly missed his words beneath the noise of her own racking gasps. "Boys, get her into the chair. She'll be easy now— won't you?"

There was a wheelchair waiting in the corridor and they got her into it in short order, transferring the handcuff and discreetly tucking it under her robe. Miriam didn't pay much attention to the ride. Her chest was on fire, she'd lost bladder control when the guard punched her, and she felt too frightened and humiliated to risk meeting anyone's eyes.

They wheeled her to an elevator, then along another hallway, and she caught a brief glimpse of daylight before they pushed her up a ramp into the back of an ambulance, all stainless-steel fittings and emergency kits strapped to the walls. Ferret clambered in with her, and after they secured the chair to the floor both hounds climbed out. They shut the doors, and a short time later the ambulance moved off. Miriam stared at the ferret and licked her lips. "Can I talk now?"

"No." She flinched in anticipation but he didn't hit her. The ambulance turned a corner and accelerated, then the driver goosed the siren.

Ferret caught her looking at him. "Always talking," he said tiredly. "Do you want anything?"

Miriam stared. "Do I want anything?" She shook her head. "Got a towel?"

He reached out and grabbed a handful of tissues from a box, dumping them in her lap with an expression of mild distaste. "When we get where we're going I'm going to wheel you out in that chair and take you to a transfer station. You will use the sigil there to follow me across. You won't speak to anyone, under any circumstances. You will be given clothes, then you will follow me to a room where somebody important will give you orders. You will do exactly what they tell you to do. If you do not obey their orders I will hurt you or kill you, because that's my job. Do you understand?"

The siren cut in again. Miriam stared at him some more: then she nodded, frightened beyond words. This quiet, middle-aged man terrified her. Something about him suggested that if he thought he should kill her he wouldn't hesitate for a second—and he'd sleep soundly in his bed afterward.

The ferret looked satisfied. He shook his head, then leaned back. His suit coat fell open far enough that Miriam could see his handgun. She licked her lips: if she'd been a comic-book heroine, she supposed she would lean forward and make a grab for it. But she wasn't a superhero. Comic-book Miriam lived in the land of make-believe, and it was real-world Miriam who'd somehow have to get out of this mess intact. Comic-book Miriam wouldn't let herself get trapped, beaten, and cowed in the back of an ambulance with a fifty-something goodfella, on her way to an appointment with someone who had the power to have her killed. She wouldn't have pissed herself the first time one of the hounds punched her, or ignored Paulie and Erasmus, or gone in to see Dr. Darling without backup, or tried to get to see Baron Henryk without preparation . . . *I'm a fuckup*, she thought miserably. *I'm not safe to be allowed out on my own.*

The ambulance braked hard, turned, and slowed to a stop. "Remember what I said. And no yakking." The doors opened, revealing an underground car park and both hounds—this time one of them cradled a short-barreled Steyr AUG. *Definitely Clan Security*, Miriam registered, her knees going weak with dread. *They've got me dead to rights*, except that as far as Security were concerned, nobody had any rights: the Clan had been in a state of perpetual warfare since long before she was born, and even before that they'd taken a very medieval approach to dealing with dissent.

The garage was pretty clearly part of a Clan transshipment station, just like the others she'd seen: carefully designed to look like corporate offices from the outside, but equipped as a transdimensional fortress / post office once you got past the discreetly armored doors. The Clan had an almost Roman approach to standardizing the design of their bases. As the ferret directed her toward the stairs at the back of the vehicle park Miriam looked around, sickly certain that she wouldn't be seeing its like again—not for a long, long time. They'd taken her locket, emphasizing the point by scrubbing her temporary tattoo. Escape was not an option they had in mind for her.

As it turned out, they weren't going to leave her any options at all. The ferret and his helpers rolled her out of the ambulance, still in the chair, and wheeled her over to an elevator at the back of the garage. She glanced over her shoulder: from the inside, the garage doors looked huge and intimidating, reinforced against the risk of a police raid. They rode in silence down to a sub-basement level, then the guards wheeled her down a short dusty passage to a room walled in pigeonholes. The room was dominated by an open area marked out with yellow tape on the floor, in front of what looked like a window bay covered by a green baize curtain. "When the curtain opens, use the sigil," said the ferret, wheeling her into position. "I'll be right behind you."

"But I'm in a chair—" Miriam began to rise, but a hand pushed down on her shoulder.

"You're electrically insulated. Rubber tires."

Miriam sat down again. *Electrically insulated?* she wondered. Her office chair, the one she'd first world-walked in while sitting at home, had plastic castors for feet—

The curtain opened on stomach-churning disorder. Miriam glanced round. The hound was waiting. She looked back and let her mind go blank. A moment later she was facing a closed red curtain, her head pounding as if someone were hammering a railroad spike through it. Her already-sore guts knotted in pain. She glanced round again.

"Don't even think it," the ferret murmured as he wheeled her out of the transfer zone. "Remember what I told you."

Another corridor rolled past, this time featuring a tiled floor and wooden panels on the walls. It was narrow and gloomy, illuminated by weak electric bulbs. *A great Clan house, but which one?* She shifted in the wheelchair, wincing against the headache that was clogging her thoughts. Whoever they were, just maintaining an electrical system was a sign of wealth and influence. And they were somewhere near New York, near the capital city Niejwein, in other words. Her guts were close to cramping with dread. Clan Security had its own infrastructure, separate from the Clan Trade Committee's postal service. Whoever she was being taken to see, they weren't low down the pecking order. Baron Henryk, perhaps—or possibly the duke himself. Or—

The ferret stopped beside a door and knocked twice. Someone unseen opened it from the inside. "Consignment delivered," the ferret told the worried-looking maidservant in the entrance, as he unlocked the handcuff securing her to the wheelchair with a flourish of a key ring she hadn't even noticed him holding. "Stand up," he told Miriam. To the servant: "You've got ten minutes. Then I want her back, ready or not."

Miriam pushed herself upright, wincing as she was assailed by various aches and pains. She took a stumbling step forward and the maid caught her arm. "This way, please you," she said haltingly, her accent thick enough to cut with a knife. Miriam nodded as the ferret disappeared and another servant closed the door behind her. "We are, please you, to disrobe—"

They had clothing waiting for her, a bodice and shift. Day wear for Niejwein. Miriam let them lace her up without speaking. Her hair was a mess, but they had a plain linen cap to cover it up. *If they were just going to kill me out of hand they wouldn't bother with this*, Miriam told herself, and desperately tried to believe it.

Ten minutes later there was another rap on the door. One of the maids went to answer it. There was a whispered exchange of hochsprache, then the ferret stepped inside and looked her up and down. "She'll do," he said tersely. "You. This way."

The ferret led her up the corridor to a narrow servant's staircase, then along a landing to a thick oak door. It opened without a knock. "Go through," said the ferret. "He's waiting for you." He gave her a light shove in the small of the back; unbalanced, Miriam lurched forward into the light.

The room was large, high-ceilinged, and cold in the way that only a room in a palace heated by open fires can be cold. High windows drizzled sunlight across about an acre of handwoven, richly embroidered carpet. There was no furniture except for a writing desk and a chair against one wall, situated directly beneath a dusty oil painting of a man in a leather coat standing beside a heavily laden pony.

Miriam took a couple of steps toward the middle of the room before she realized who was sitting behind the desk, poring over a note. She stopped dead, her heart flip-flopping in panic. "Great-uncle, I—"

"Shut up." It was Baron Henryk, the head of the royal secret police, not kindly, casual Uncle Henryk, who faced Miriam from behind the desk. Uncle Henryk was amusing and friendly. Baron Henryk looked anything but friendly. "Do you know what this is?" He brandished the sheet of paper at her.

Miriam shook her head.

"It's an execution warrant," said Henryk, pushing a pair of

reading glasses up his nose. "Stand over here, where I can see you." He jotted something on the sheet of paper, then folded it once and moved it to an out-tray. "Not the full-dress public variety, more what the Americans' CIA would call a termination expedient order. Your uncle runs them past me as partly a courtesy to the Crown—as a duke he has the right of high justice, should he choose to use it—but also as a measure of prudence." Reflectively: "It's a little hard to undo afterward if it turns out you switched someone off by mistake."

"You, you approve execution warrants for the Clan?"

"Don't you tell me you didn't suspect something of the kind." Henryk stared at her for a moment, then looked at the next note on his in-tray and frowned. "Hmm." He picked up a different pen and scrawled a red slash across the page, folded it, and put it in the out-tray. "I don't think so." He put the pen down as carefully as if it were a loaded gun, then looked back at Miriam. "I'm not ready to give up on you yet."

Miriam took a deep breath. "What—who—was that?"

"It could have been you." His lips quirked. "We can't protect you forever, you know." He carefully drew a black velvet cloth across the papers and turned round to face her. "Especially if you keep putting your head through every snare you come across."

"Why am I here?" She wanted to ask, *How much do you think I know?* But right now that might be a very bad idea indeed. Possibly she knew more than Henryk realized, and if that was the case, admitting it could be a fatal mistake.

"You're here because you stuck your nose where it didn't belong. *I'm* here because I'm trying to control the damage." He took his reading glasses off and folded them carefully, then placed them on top of the black cloth. "Let's get this straight. We know you learned about something you aren't supposed to know about. That's . . . not good. Then you compounded it by getting involved—and getting involved personally! You could have been identified. The next step might have been full public disclosure, with who knows what consequences. Helge, that is not acceptable. Before,

before all this started, you came to me complaining that you were being treated as if you were under arrest. This time, make no mistake, you *are* under arrest."

She tried to stay silent, but it was too hard. "What are you going to do with me?"

Baron Henryk didn't reply at first. Instead, he looked up at the windows for a while, as if inspecting the quality of the plasterwork of the surrounds. "Interfering with the Clan post is a capital offense," he said, pushing back his chair. He stood up heavily and crossed the carpet to the far side of the room, limping slightly. Miriam stood as if rooted to the spot. "Just so that you understand how serious the situation is, I was not exaggerating when I said that execution warrant might be yours." Henryk turned and squinted at her across the room from between fingers held in a frame, like a cinematographer assessing a camera angle. "Hmm."

Miriam shivered involuntarily and took a step toward him. "Then why—"

"Because you are still useful to us," Henryk said calmly. "Stop, stand still." He walked across to the other corner of the room, looked at her from between crossed fingers. "That's good. As I was saying, you made a habit of sticking your nose into affairs where it has no business. Luckily this time we found out before it became common knowledge—otherwise I would have had to approve a great deal more death warrants in order to cover up your misbehavior, and your mother would never forgive me." He made the rectangle again.

"What are you doing?"

"I'm thinking of taking your portrait; be still." He squinted and shifted a little. "It's a hobby of mine, plate-glass daguerreotyping." He lowered his hands and limped back toward his desk. "The Queen Mother approves of you."

Miriam took another deep breath, distressed. "What's that got to do with things?"

"It suggests a way out of the dilemma." Henryk stopped, just out of arm's reach, and watched her. "Interfering with the post, Helge, isn't the only capital offense. Making the head of Clan Security look like an idiot—*that* is a capital offense, albeit a more subtle one for which the punishment is never made public. As for jeopardizing relations between the Clan and the Crown, that is *really* serious. Lèse-majesté, possibly treason. Not that you're guilty of the latter two, not yet, but I wouldn't put it past you, given how you've got the crown prince's nose out of joint already." He chuckled quietly. "We can't afford to give you any more rope to play with, Helge, or you will succeed in hanging yourself. I'm afraid this is where the buck stops." He walked back to his desk and unfolded the black cloth, swearing mildly as he spilled his spectacles. " 'Deferred pending overriding necessity,' Helge, that's all the slack I can buy you." He held up the folded paper. "So here's what is going to happen.

"You will speak to nobody about reading the post, without my permission, or that of the duke your uncle. The, ah, loose ends who might have deduced your activity have been tied off. If you do not speak of it, and we do not speak of it, it did not happen. This paper will remain on file for a few years, until we feel we can trust you. *But*." He paced back toward the other side of the room. "You will have nothing more to do with the Clan postal service ever again, Helge, ever again. This is the immediate consequence of your actions. You are to be permanently removed from the corvée, and temporarily deprived of the ability to walk between worlds." He grimaced. "Don't force us to make it permanent, there are ways and means short of execution that would achieve that end"—he picked up a pen-sized cylinder and held it for her to see, then put it down again—"do you see?"

Miriam swallowed. *That's a laser! He's talking about blinding me!* The idea of spending the rest of her life unable to see horrified her. "I understand," she managed to croak.

"Good." Baron Henryk looked slightly relieved. "I'm sure you appreciate that your position is somewhat fraught. But the Queen Mother approves of you." Pace, pace, pace: he was off again, as if he didn't want to face her. "She has requested your attendance upon her and her youngest surviving grandson at your convenience, Helge. I trust you know what this is about."

Miriam felt the blood draining from her face. "What?" she asked nervously.

"Face facts." Henryk could sound as fussily pedantic as any schoolteacher when he was upset. "You are a Clan lady of high birth, single, still of childbearing age. If you can't serve the commerce committee, how else may you serve us? There's not a lot else for you to do," he said, almost apologetically. "So you're going to go back to your residence and wait there, and work on your, what you think of as, your cover identity. Countess Helge voh Thorold d'Hjorth. You're not going to be allowed to be Miriam Beckstein again until we're sure we can trust you. We know about your dissociative tendencies, this unfortunate tendency toward imposter syndrome. It's time we gave you some help in breaking the habit. Think of it as an enforced vacation from the pressures of modern life, *hein*? Practice your hochsprache and persist with the gentle arts, and try not to overexert yourself too much. One way or the other, you're going to make yourself of use, even if only to give us another generation of world-walkers or a royal heir. It will go easier for you if you cooperate of your own free choice."

"You want to marry me off to the Idiot," she heard herself saying. "You want me to bear world-walking children who are in line for the throne. If Egon were to die—"

"That would be treason," Henryk said sharply, staring at her. "The Clan would never, *ever*, countenance treason."

The blood was roaring in Miriam's ears: *You wouldn't dabble, but you might play at it in earnest,* she thought. *Get me out of here!* A monstrous sense of claustrophobia pressed down on her, and her stomach twisted. "I feel sick," she said.

"Oh, I hope not." Henryk looked alarmed. "It's much too soon for *that*."

12

FORCED
ACCULTURATION

❦

The ferret was waiting outside with two men-at-arms. They handcuffed her wrists behind her back, then marched her back down the narrow staircase and out to a walled courtyard at the rear of the building where a carriage was waiting. The windows were shuttered, screens secured with padlocks. Miriam didn't resist as they loaded her in and bolted the door. What would be the point? Henryk was right about one thing—she'd screwed up completely, and before she tried to dig her way out of this mess it would be a good idea to think the consequences of her actions through very carefully indeed.

The carriage was small and stuffy and threw her around as it wandered interminably along. The noise of a busy street market reached her, muffled by the shutters. Then there was shouting, the clangor of hammers on metal. *Smith Alley*, she thought. Every time the carriage swayed across a rut in the cobblestone road surface it lurched from side to side, throwing her against the walls. It stank of leather, and stale sweat, and fear.

After a brief eternity the carriage lurched to a halt, and someone unlocked the door. The light was harsh: blinking, Miriam tried to stretch the kinks out of her back and legs. "This way," said the ferret.

It was another of those goddamn mansions with closed courtyards and separate servants' quarters. Miriam panted as she tried to keep up, half-dazzled by the glare of daylight. The ferret's two minions seized her by the elbows and half-dragged her to a small door. They propelled her up four flights of stairs—passing two servants who stood rigidly still, their faces turned to the wall so that they might not see her disgrace—then paused in front of a door. *At least it's not the cellar*, Miriam thought bleakly. She'd already seen what the Clan's dungeons looked like. The ferret paused and stared at her, then nodded minutely.

"These will be your quarters." He glanced at the door. "You may consider yourself under house arrest. Your belongings will be moved here, once we have searched them. Your maidservants likewise, and you may continue your activities as before, with reservations. I will pay attendance in the outer chamber. You will not leave your quarters without my approval, and I will accompany you wherever you go. Any messages you wish to send you will give to me for approval. You will not invite anyone to visit you without my approval. If you attempt to disobey these terms, then"—he shrugged—"I stand ready to do my duty."

Miriam swallowed. "Where are we?" she asked.

"Doppelgangered." The ferret's cheek twitched. Abruptly, he turned and pushed the door open. He stepped behind her and unlocked the cuffs. "Go on in."

Miriam shuffled through the door to her new home, staring at the floor. It was rough-cut stone, with an intricate handwoven carpet laid across it. Behind her, the door scraped shut: there was a rattle of bolts. She looked up, across a waiting room—perhaps a little smaller than her chambers in Thorold Palace had been—at a window casement overlooking the walled courtyard they'd brought her in through.

So I'm under house arrest. "It could have been worse," she told herself quietly. The place was furnished— expensively, by local standards—although there was no electric lighting in evidence. Doors led off to other rooms. The fireplace was about the size of her living room back in Cambridge, but right now it was unlit. "Where are the servants?" She was beginning to feel hungry: it was the stomach-stuck-to-ribs haven't-eaten-for-days kind of hunger that sometimes came on after extreme stress. She walked over to the nearest door, opened it. A housemaid jumped to her feet from a stool just inside the doorway and ducked a deep curtsey.

"Do you know who I am?" Miriam asked.

The woman looked confused. "Myn'demme?"

Of course. "I am Countess Helge," Miriam began in her halting hochsprache. "Where—what—is food here?" The woman looked even more confused. "I am—to eat—" she tried again, a sinking feeling in her heart. It was, she realized, going to be very hard to get anything done.

It took Miriam only an evening to appreciate how far her universe had shrunk. She had four rooms: a bedroom dominated by a huge curtained bed, the reception room, a waiting room that doubled as a dining area, and the outer vestibule. The ferret lived in the vestibule, so she avoided it. What lay beyond its external door, which was formidably barred, she had no idea. The only window with a view, in the reception room, overlooked the courtyard but was not high enough to see over the crenellated walls. This wasn't a show house in the style of Thorold Palace, but a converted castle from an older, grimmer age. A window with a scenic view would have been an invitation to a crossbow bolt. The sanitary facilities were, predictably, primitive.

Three maidservants came when she tugged the bellpulls in the bedroom or the reception room. None of them spoke

English, and they all seemed terrified of her. Or perhaps they were afraid of being seen talking to her by the ferret. She was forced to communicate in her halting hochsprache, but they weren't much use when it came to getting language practice.

On the evening of her first day, after she'd picked over a supper of cold cuts and boiled Jerusalem artichokes, the ferret came and ordered her into the vestibule. "Wait here," he said, and went back into the reception room, locking the door. Miriam worked her way into an anxious frenzy while he was gone, terrified that Baron Henryk had revisited his decision to leave her alive; a distant thumping on the other side of the door suggested structural changes in progress. When the ferret opened the door again and returned to his seat by the barred door, Miriam looked at him in disbelief. "Go on," he said impatiently; "I told you your possessions would be moved in, didn't I?"

There was a huge wardrobe in her bedroom now, and a dresser. Relieved, Miriam hurried to look through them— but there was nothing in the drawers or on the chest but the garments Mistress Tanzig had laboriously assembled for her. No laptop, no books, no Advil, no CD Walkman, nothing remotely reminiscent of American life. "Damn," Miriam complained. She sat on the embroidered backless bench that served for a chair. "Now what?" Obviously Henryk's security people considered anything that hinted of her original home to be suspect, and after a moment she couldn't fault them. The laptop—if she'd had a digital camera she might have loaded a picture of the Clan sigil into it, then made her escape. Or she might have slid a Polaroid between the pages of a book. They'd made a clean sweep of her possessions, taking everything except that which a noblewoman of the Gruinmarkt might have owned—even her battered reporter's notebook and automatic pencil were gone. Which left her with a wardrobe full of native costumes and a jewel box with enough ropes of pearls to hang herself with, but nothing that might facilitate her flight. *Henryk really does expect me to revert to being Helge*, she thought. She looked around in mild desperation. There was a strange book on the dresser. She reached for it, opened the leather cover: *Notes towards a Hochsprache-Anglaische Grammarion* it said, printed in an old-fashioned type. "Shit." Succumbing to the inevitable, Miriam started reading her homework.

The next morning she wore a local outfit. *Better get used to it*, she thought resignedly. *No more jeans and tees for slobbing about in.* She was sitting on the bench by the window casement, staring out at the courtyard to relieve her eyes from studying the grammarion, when the door to the vestibule opened without warning. It was the ferret, with two unfamiliar maidservants standing behind him, and another man: avuncular-looking, with receding hair and spectacles and a beer gut. He was holding a large leather briefcase. "Milady voh Thorold d'Hjorth?" he said in a slightly creepy way that made Miriam take an instant dislike to him.

"Yes?" She frowned at the ferret.

"If you will permit me to introduce myself? I am Dr. Robard ven Hjalmar. Your great-uncle the baron asked me to pay a house call."

"What kind of doctor are you?"

"The medical kind." He managed a smile that was halfway between a simper and a smirk.

"A medical—" Miriam paused. "I don't need a doctor," she said automatically. "I'm fine." Which wasn't strictly true—her ribs ached from the punch, and she was feeling unnaturally torpid and depressed—but something about ven Hjalmar made her mistrust him instinctively.

"You don't need a doctor *now*," he said fussily, and planted his case on the floor. "However, I have been asked to take you on as one of my patients."

The ferret cleared his throat. "Dr. ven Hjalmar ministers to the royal family."

"Oh, I see." Miriam put the book down, carefully positioning the bookmark. "What does that entail?" *Why me?*

"I am required to testify to your health and fitness." Ven Hjalmar's gaze slid around the room nervously, avoiding her. "You are, I am sure you are aware, of a certain age—not too old for a first confinement, but certainly in need of care and attention. And I understand you may have other medical needs. If you would be so good as to retire to your bedchamber, your maids will relieve you of your outerwear so that I may prepare my report. You need not be afraid, you will be chaperoned and your guardian will be right outside the door."

Miriam glared at the ferret. "Do I get an opportunity to say no?"

The ferret was stony-faced. "Remember your instructions." The two unfamiliar maids stepped forward and took Miriam by the arms. She tensed, on the edge of panic: but the ferret was watching her.

What happened next was one of the most unintrusive but oddly unpleasant medical examinations Miriam had ever undergone. The servants led her into the bedroom; then, with the door closed, one of them (a beefy blond woman with rosy cheeks and the look of an amateur boxer to her) held Miriam's wrists together while the other unlaced her bodice. Neither of them spoke. "Let me—go," Miriam tried, but boxer-woman just stared at her dumbly.

"Stand still, please." It was ven Hjalmar. Boxer-woman refused to let go, holding her pinioned. "Open your mouth. Ah—hah. Very good." He stepped around her and she felt a stethoscope through her chemise. "Breathe in—and out. Ah, good." He worked fast, giving her a basic examination. Then: "I gather you were given a pap smear on the other side. I'll have the results of that back in a day or so. Meanwhile, I'd like to ask you some questions about your medical history."

Pap smear? Miriam blinked. "Make them let me go," she said stubbornly, flexing her wrists.

"Not yet." Ven Hjalmar looked down his nose at her, standing there in her underwear with her wrists immobilized by boxer-woman. "When, exactly, did you lose your maidenhood?"

"None of your business." She tried not to snarl. *If you do not obey their orders I will hurt you*, the ferret had said: she didn't dare forget.

"I assure you, it is very much my business." Ven Hjalmar

shrugged. "And it will be the worse for you if you don't answer."

"Why do you want to know?" she demanded. Boxer-woman tugged on her left wrist, hard enough to make her wince. "What *is* this?"

"I am attempting to compile a report for the Crown," Ven Hjalmar said primly. "You are thirty-three years old, I understand? You are in good health and disease-free, and I am informed already that you are not a virgin, but this is old for a first pregnancy, such as you will be attempting within the next year. I need to know everything about your reproductive history. If you will not tell me, I will have to examine you intimately, and then guess as to the rest. Which would you prefer?"

"It won't be a first pregnancy," Miriam admitted through gritted teeth. *Damn, why couldn't I have gotten my tubes tied?* She knew why: she'd never gotten around to it. She even knew why she'd never gotten around to it—the sneaking suspicion that one day there might be a right time and a right man to start a family with. The huge irony being that as a direct result she was now being lined up to start a family with absolutely the wrong man at the wrong time. "I was twenty-one." She tried to pull away again. "Make her let go of me."

"Keep talking," said ven Hjalmar.

Miriam tensed, but boxer-woman was developing an evil Nurse Ratched glare. "One child. Girl, the father was my ex-husband, I was still studying—a contraceptive accident. I didn't want an abortion but we couldn't afford to bring her up so Mom suggested we adopt out—"

Scribble scribble. Ven Hjalmar's pen was busy. Miriam kept talking, her mind blank; she managed one barefaced lie (that she didn't know anything about the adopters), but that was it. Abject surrender. She felt dirty. What business was it of this quack to pick over her sexual history? He wanted to know everything: had she suffered from morning sickness, what medicines had they prescribed, had she ever had bladder problems—*only when your hired thugs punch me in the gut*—and more. He went on for hours. Miriam made another stab at resistance when he started asking for names of every man she'd slept with, but at that point he dropped the matter and switched to asking about her hearing. But the interrogation left her feeling unaccountably dirty, like shop-soiled linen on display for all to see.

Finally, ven Hjalmar muttered something to Nurse Ratched, who let go of Miriam. Miriam took a step back, then sat down on the padded bench. "Yes?" she asked wearily.

"You have something of an attitude problem, young lady."

"No shit." Miriam drew her knees up beneath her shift and crossed her arms defensively around them. "You're the one giving me the third degree in front of an audience."

"They won't say anything." Ven Hjalmar smiled and said something to the other servant woman. She made a gabbling noise, incoherent and liquid, and turned to face Miriam. "As you can see."

Miriam looked away the moment she saw the tongueless ruin inside the woman's mouth. *Oh shit, I'm going to have bad dreams tonight.* "I see," she said weakly, trying to recover what was left of her shredded dignity. "What did she do to deserve that?"

"She discussed her mistress's intimate details." Ven Hjalmar shook his head lugubriously. "The royal family takes medical confidentiality *very* seriously."

Unaccountably, Miriam felt slightly less disheartened. *So even you're afraid, huh? We'll see what we can do with that.* "So what happens next?"

"I think we can skip the virginity test. It isn't as if you are being considered for the crown prince, after all." Ven Hjalmar stood up. "I believe you are a perfectly fit young woman, of sound body, perhaps a little disturbed by your circumstances but that will pass. If you would like something to help your mood, I am sure we can do something about that—have you considered Prozac? Guaranteed to cure all black humors, so I'm assured by the manufacturer. I shall take my leave now, and your own maidservants will help return you to your usual peak of feminine beauty." He produced the odd, simpering smile once again. "Incidentally," he added sotto voce, "I understand and commiserate with the difficult circumstances of your marriage. If it's any consolation, you may not have to lie with the, ah, afflicted one if you do not wish to. A sample can be obtained and a douche prepared, if you prefer."

"What if I don't want to become pregnant?"

Ven Hjalmar paused with his hand on the door handle. "I really don't think you ought to trouble yourself with such unrealistic fantasies," he said.

"But, what if?" Miriam called to him. Her fingernails bit into her palms hard enough to draw blood.

"Prozac," said ven Hjalmar, as he opened the door.

Three days after Dr. ven Hjalmar's humiliating interrogation, Miriam was beginning to wish she'd taken him up on the offer of antidepressants when the ferret knocked on the door.

"What is it?" she asked, looking up from her book.

"You have an invitation," he said in hochsprache. He'd taken to using it almost all the time, except when she was obviously floundering. As ever, her jailer's expression was unreadable. "The baron says you may accept it if you wish." He repeated himself in English, just in case she hadn't got the message.

"An invitation." *Where to?* Her imagination whirled like a hamster on a wheel: *Not the royal court, obviously, or it would be compulsory . . .*

"From the honorable Duchess Patricia voh Hjorth d'Wu ab Thorold. Your mother. She begs your forgiveness for not writing and invites the honorable Countess Helge voh Thorold d'Hjorth to visit with her for lunch tomorrow."

"Tell her I'd, I'd—" Miriam licked her lips. "Of course I'll go."

"I shall tell her." The ferret began to withdraw. "I shall make arrangements. You will be ready to travel by eleven and you will be back here no later than five of the afternoon."

"Wait!" Miriam stood up. "Can I see Olga Thorold Arnesen?"

"No." He began to close the door.

"Or Lady Brilliana d'Ost?"

The ferret stopped and stared at her. "If you continue to pester me I will hurt you." Then he shut the door.

Miriam paced back and forth across the reception room in a blind panic, stir-crazy from confinement but apprehensive about whatever Iris would say to her. *Of course Henryk will have told her,* she thought. But blood was thicker than water, and surely Iris wouldn't side with him against her—or would she? *She's been so distant and cold since she rejoined the Clan.* The change in her mood had been like a safety curtain dropping across the stage at the end of a play, locking in the warmth and the light. *Mom's got her own problems. She said so.* Like her own mother, the poisonous dowager Hildegarde. *The old women's plot.* She crossed her arms. *Henryk must have told her, or she wouldn't have known where to send the invitation,* she thought. *If I can persuade her to give me a locket I could make a clean break for it—*

But a cold, cynical thought still nagged at her. *What if Mom wants me to marry Prince Stupid? She wouldn't do that . . . would she?*

The ruthless reproductive realpolitik within the Clan had made an early victim of Patricia voh Hjorth: her own mother had forced her into marriage to a violent sociopath. The scars had taken a long time to scab over, even after Patricia had made her run to the other world and settled down to life as Iris Beckstein for nearly a third of a century. Iris wouldn't have dreamed of forcing her own daughter into a loveless marriage of convenience. But now she was back in the suffocating bosom of the Clan, which way would Patricia jump—especially if her own skin was at stake?

Back home in Cambridge, Miriam's mother had never made a big thing about wanting grandchildren. But that was then.

They took Miriam to visit her mother for lunch in a sealed sedan chair carried by two strapping porters. It was a hot day, but there were no windows, just a wooden grille behind her head. It was impossible to see out of. She protested when she saw it, but the ferret just stared at her. "Do you want to attend the duchess, or not?" he asked. Miriam gave in, willing to accept one more indignity if it gave her a chance to talk to Iris. *Maybe she'll be able to get me out of this*, she told herself grimly.

The box swayed like a ship on choppy water. It seemed to take forever to make its way across town. By the time the porters planted it with a bone-jarring thump, Miriam had gone from being off her appetite to the first green-cheeked anticipation of full-blown nausea: she welcomed the rattle of chains and the opening of the door like a galley slave released from belowdecks, blinking and gasping. "Are we there?"

"Momentarily." The ferret was as imperturbable as ever. "This way." Another closed courtyard with barred windows. Miriam's spirit fell. *They're just shuffling me between prisons*, she realized. *I'm surprised he didn't handcuff me to the chair.*

Now the nerves took over. "Where is—she isn't under arrest too, is she?"

Unexpectedly, the ferret chuckled. "No, not exactly."

"Oh." Miriam followed him, two paces ahead of the guards he'd brought along. She glanced at the walls to either side, half-wishing she could make a break for freedom. A couple of gulls squawked raucous abuse from the roofline. She envied them their insolent disdain for terrestrial boundaries.

They came to a solid door in one wall, where a liveried servant exchanged words with the ferret, then produced a key. The door opened on a walled garden. There was a gazebo against the far wall, glass windows—expensively imported, a hallmark of a Clan property—propped open to allow the breeze in. "Go right in," said the ferret. "I believe you are expected. I will collect you later."

"What? Aren't you coming in with me? I thought you were supposed to be watching me at all times?"

The ferret snorted. "Not here." Then he stepped back through the gate and closed it with a solid click.

Wow. Miriam narrowed her eyes as she looked at the gazebo. *Mom's got clout, then?* She marched up to the door. "Hello?" she asked.

"Come right in, dear."

Her mother watched her from a nest of cushions piled on top of a broad-winged armchair. She looked more frail than ever, wearing a black velvet gown with more ruffles and bows than a lace factory. "Has someone died?" Miriam asked, stepping into the shadow of the gazebo.

"Sit down, make yourself comfortable. No one's died yet, but I'm told it was a close-run thing."

Miriam sat in the only other chair, next to the circular cast-iron table. Iris watched her: she returned her mother's gaze nervously. After a while she cleared her throat. "How much has Henryk told you?"

"Enough."

Another silence.

"I know I shouldn't have done it," Miriam said, when she couldn't take it anymore. "But I was being deliberately cut out of my own affairs. And they've been trying to set me up—"

"It's too late for excuses, kid." Miriam stared. Her mother didn't look angry. She didn't look sad, but she didn't look pleased to see her, either. The silence stretched out until finally Iris sighed and shuffled against her cushions, sitting up. "I wanted to look at you."

"What?"

"I wanted to look at you again," said Iris. "One last time. You know they're going to try to break you?"

"I don't break easily." Miriam knew it was false bravado even as the words left her mouth. The great hollow fear congealing inside her gave the lie away. But what else could she say?

Her mother glanced away evasively. "We don't bend." She shook her head. "None of us does—not me, not you, not even your grandmother. But sooner or later we break. Thirty-three years is what it took, kid, but look at me now. One of the old bitches already."

"What do you mean?" Miriam tensed.

"I mean I'm about to sell you down the river." Iris looked at her sharply. "At least, that's how it's going to seem at first. I'm not going to lie to you: I don't see any alternatives.

We're stuck playing the long game, kid, and I'm still learning the rules."

"Suppose you explain what you just said." There was an acid taste in her mouth. Miriam forced herself to unclench her fingers from the arms of her chair. "About selling me down the river."

Iris coughed, wheezing. Miriam waited her out. Presently her mother regained control. "I don't like this any more than you do. It's just the way things work around here. I don't have any alternatives, I'm locked up here and you managed to get caught breaking the unwritten rules." She sighed. "I thought you had more sense than to do that—to get caught, I mean. Anyway, we're both out of alternatives. If *I* don't play the game, neither of us is going to live very long."

"I don't need this!" Miriam finally let go of her tightly controlled frustration. "I have been locked up and policed and poked and pried at and subjected to humiliating medical examinations, and it's all just some game you're playing for status points? What did you do, promise the Queen Mother you'd marry me off to her grandson if she beat you at poker?"

Iris reached out and grabbed her wrist. Startled, Miriam froze. Her mother's hand felt hot, bony, as weak as a sparrow: "No, never that! But if you knew what it was like to grow up here, fifty years ago . . ."

Miriam surprised herself: "Suppose you tell me?" *Go on, justify yourself*, she willed. There were butterflies in her stomach. Whatever was coming, it was bound to be bad.

Her mother nodded thoughtfully. Then her lips quirked in the first sign of a smile Miriam had seen since she'd arrived.

"You know how the Clan braids its families, one arranged marriage after another to keep the bloodline strong." Miriam nodded. "And you know what this means: the meddling old grannies."

"But Mom, Henryk and Angbard—"

"Hush. I know about the breeding program." Miriam's jaw dropped. "Angbard told me about it. He's not stupid enough to think he can push it through without . . . without allies. In another ten years the first of the babies will be coming up for adoption. He needs to convince the meddling old grannies to accept them, or we'll be finished as a trading network within another couple of generations. So he asked me for advice. I'm his consultant, I guess. I don't think most of the families realize just how close to the edge we are, how badly the civil war damaged us. Small gene pool, insufficient numbers—it's not good. I've seen the numbers. If we don't do something about it, the Clan could be extinct within two centuries." Her voice hardened. "But then you barged right in, doing what you do—snooping. Yes, I know it's what you did for a living for all those years, but you've got to understand, you can't do that right now. Not here, it's much too dangerous. People here who *really* want to keep secrets tend to react violently to intrusion. And there's a flip side to the coin. I know you and the-bitch-my-mother don't get on well"—a twinkle in her eye as she said this: Miriam bit her tongue—"but Hildegarde is just doing what she's always done, playing the long game, defending her status. Which is tenuous here because we are, let's face it, women. Here in the Gruinmarkt—hell, everywhere in the whole wide world—power comes from a big swinging dick. We, you and me, we're the badly adjusted misfits here: you've got the illusion that you're anybody's social equal and I, I've been outside . . ."

She fell silent. Miriam shook her head. "This isn't like you, Mom."

"This *place* isn't like me, kid. No, listen: what happens to the Clan if Angbard, or his successor, starts introducing farmed baby world-walkers in, oh, ten years' time? Without tying them in to the existing great families, without getting the old bitches to take them in and adopt them as their own? And what happens a generation down the line when they become adults?"

Miriam frowned. "Um. We have lots more world-walkers?"

"Nuts. You're not thinking like a politician: it shifts the balance of power, kid, that's what happens. And it shifts it away from the braids, away from the meddling old grannies—away from *us*. It's ugly out there, Miriam, I don't think you've seen enough of the Gruinmarkt to realize just how nasty this world is if you're a woman. We're insulated

by wealth and privilege, we have a role in the society of the
Clan. But if you take that all away we are, well . . . it's not as
bad as Afghanistan under those Taliban maniacs, but it's not
far off. This is what I'm getting at when I talk about the long
game. It's the game the old women of the Clan have been
playing for a century and a half now, and the name of the
game is preserving the status of their granddaughters. Do
you want a measure of control over your own life? Because
if so, you've got to match the old bitches at their own game.
And that's"—Iris's voice wavered—"difficult. I've been trying to help you, but then you kicked the foundations out
from underneath my position . . ."

"I—" Miriam paused. "What *is* your position? Is it the
medicines?"

"I take it you've met Dr. ven Hjalmar?"

"Yes." Miriam tensed.

"Who do you think he works for? And who do you think I
get my meds from? Copaxone and prednisone, by the grace
of Hildegarde. If there's an accident in the supply chain, a
courier gets caught out and I go short—well, that's all she
wrote." Iris made a sharp cutting gesture.

"Mom!" Miriam stared, aghast.

"Blackmail is just business as usual," Iris said with heavy
irony. "I've been trying to tell you it's not pretty, but would
you get the message?"

"But—" Miriam was half out of her chair with anger.
"Can't you get Angbard to help you out? Surely they can't
stop you crossing over and visiting a doctor—"

"Shush, Miriam. Sit down, you're making me itch."
Miriam forced herself to untense: she sat down again on the
edge of her chair, leaning forward. "If I bring Angbard into
this, I lose. Because then I owe him, and I've dragged him
into the game, do you see? Look, the rules are really very
simple. You grow up hating and fearing your grandmother.
Then she marries you off to some near-stranger. A generation later, you have your own grandchildren and you realize
you've got to hurt them just the way your own great-aunts
and grandmother hurt you, or you'll be doing them an even
worse disservice; if you don't, then instead of a legacy of

some degree of power all they'll inherit is the status of elderly has-been chattel. *That* is what the braid system means, Miriam. You're—you're old enough and mature enough to understand this. I wasn't, I was about sixteen when my great-aunt—my grandmother was dead by then—leaned on the-bitch-my-mother and twisted her arm and made her give me reason to hate her."

"Um. It sounds like—" Miriam winced and rubbed her forehead. "There's something about this in game theory, isn't there?"

"Yes." Iris looked distant. "I told Morris about it, years ago. He called it an iterated cross-generational prisoner's dilemma. That haunted me, you know. Your father was a very smart man. And kind."

Miriam nodded; she missed him. Not that he was her real father. Her real father had been killed in an ambush by assassins shortly after Miriam's birth, the incident that had prompted Iris to run away and go to ground in Boston, where she'd met and lived with Morris and brought Miriam up in ignorance of her background. But Morris had died years ago, and now . . .

"When I gave you the locket I didn't expect you to jump straight in and get caught up in the Clan so rapidly. I was going to warn you off. But once you got picked up, there wasn't much else I could do. So I called up Angbard and came back in. I figure I'm not good for many more years, even with the drugs, but while I'm around I can watch your back. Do you see?"

"That was a mistake, it would seem."

"Oh yes." Iris was silent for almost a minute. "Because there are no grandchildren, and in the terms of the game that means I'm not a full player. I thought for a while your business plans on the other side would serve instead, but there's the glass ceiling again: you're a woman. You've set yourself up to do something that just isn't in the rules, so lots of people want to take you down. They want to make you play the game, to conform to expectations, because that reinforces their own role. If you don't conform, you threaten them, so they'll use that as an excuse to destroy you. And now they've got me as a hostage to use against you."

"Oh. Oh shit."

"You can say that again." Iris reached out and tugged a bellpull. There was a distant chime. "Do you want some lunch? I wouldn't blame you if all this has put you off your appetite . . ."

Miriam succumbed to depression on the way back to her prison. The sedan chair felt like a microcosm for her life right now, boxed in and darkly claustrophobic, the walls pressing tighter on every side, forcing her into a coerced and unwilling conformity. When she was very young she'd sometimes fantasized about having a long-lost family, played the *I'm really a princess but I was swapped at birth for a commoner* make-believe game. Somehow it had never involved being locked inside a swaying leather-lined box that smelled of old sweat and potpourri, her freedom restricted and her independence denied. The idea that once people decided you were going to be a princess, or a countess, your life stopped being your own, your *body* stopped being private, had never occurred to her back when she was a kid. *I need to talk to someone*, Miriam realized. Someone other than Iris, who right now was in as much of a mess as she was. *Otherwise I am going to go crazy.*

It had not escaped her attention that there were no sharp-edged implements in any of the rooms she had access to.

When they let her out in the walled courtyard, Miriam looked up at the sky above the gatehouse. The air was close and humid, and the clouds had a distinct yellowish tinge: the threat of thunder hung like a blanket across the city. "You'd better go in," said the ferret, in a rare sign of solicitude. Or maybe he just wanted to get her under cover and call a guard so that he could catch some rest.

"Right." Miriam climbed the staircase back to her rooms tiredly, drained of both energy and optimism.

"Milady!" Miriam looked up as the doors closed behind her with a thud. "Oh! You look sad! Are you unwell? What's wrong?"

It was Kara, her young, naive lady-in-waiting. Miriam

managed a tired smile. "It's a long story," she said. Gradually she realized there was something odd about Kara. "Hey, what happened to your hair?" Kara had worn it long, down her back: now it was bundled up in an intricate coil atop her head. And she was wearing traditional dress. Kara loved to try imported American fashions.

"Do you like it? It's for a wedding."

"Oh? Whose?"

"Mine. I'm to be married tomorrow." Kara began to cry—not happily, but the quiet sobbing of desperation.

"What!" The next thing Miriam knew, she was hugging Kara while the younger woman shuddered, sniffling, her face pressed against Miriam's shoulder. "Come on, relax, you can let it all out. Tell me about it." She gently steered Kara toward the bench seat under the window. Glancing around, she realized that the servants had made themselves scarce. "You're going to have to tell me how you convinced them to let you in here. Hell, you're going to have to tell me how you *found* me. But not right now. Calm down. What's this about a wedding?"

That set Kara off again. Miriam gritted her teeth. *Why me? Why now?* The first was easy: Miriam had unwittingly designated herself as adult role model when she first met Kara. The second question, though—

"My father—after you disappeared last week—he summoned me urgently. I know the match was not his idea, for last we spoke he said I should perhaps wait another summer, but now he said his mind was made up and that a week hence I should be married into a braid alliance. He seemed quite pleased until I protested, but he said you had written that you no longer wanted me and that I should best find a new home for myself! I, I could not believe that! Tell me, milady, it isn't true, is it?"

"It's not true," Miriam confirmed, stroking her hair. "Be still. I didn't write to your father." *I'll bet someone else did, though.* "Isn't this a bit sudden? I mean, don't these things take time to arrange? Who's the lucky man, anyway?" *You haven't been sneaking a boyfriend, have you?* she wanted to ask, but that seemed a little blunt given Kara's delicate state of mind.

"It's sudden." Kara sniffled against her shoulder for a while. "I've never *met* the man," she wailed quietly.

"What, never?"

"Ouch! No, never!" Miriam forced herself to relax her grip as Kara continued. "He's called Raph ven Wu, second son of Paulus ven Wu, and he's ten years older than me and I've never met him and what if I hate him? It's all about money. Granma says not to worry and it will all work out—"

"Your grandmother talked to you?"

"Yes, Granma Elise is really kind and she says he's a well-mannered knight who she has known since he was a babe and who is honorable and will see to my welfare—but he's terribly old! He's almost thirty. And I'm afraid, I'm afraid—" Her lower lip was quivering again. "Granma says it will be all right but I just don't know. And the wedding's to be tomorrow, in the Halle Temple of Our Lady of the Dead, and I want you to come. Will you be there?" She held on to Miriam like a drowning woman clutching at a life raft.

"You didn't say how you found me," Miriam prodded gently.

"Oh, I petitioned Baron Henryk! He said you were staying here and I could see you if I wanted. He even said I should invite you to witness at my wedding. Will you come? Please?"

Oh, so that's *what it's about.* To Miriam the message couldn't have been clearer. And she had no doubt at all that it *was* a message, and that she was the intended recipient. She looked out of the window, turning her head so that Kara wouldn't see her expression. "I'll come if they let me," she said, surprising herself with the mildness of her tone.

"Of course they'll let you!" Kara said fiercely. "Why wouldn't they? Are you in trouble, milady?"

"You could say that." Miriam thought about it for a moment. "But probably no worse than yours."

Afterward, Erasmus Burgeson always wondered why he hadn't seen it coming.

It was a humid evening, and he'd sat on the open top deck

of the streetcar as it rattled toward the hotel downtown where he was to meet his contact. He breathed deeply, relishing the faint smoky tang of the air now that his sore old lungs had stopped troubling him: *I wonder where Miriam is?* he idly thought, opening and refolding his morning news sheet. She'd changed his life with that last visit and those jars of wonder pills. *Probably off somewhere engaging in strange new ventures in exotic worlds far more advanced than this one*, he told himself. Democracies, places ruled by the will of the people rather than the whim of a nearsighted tyrant. He sighed and focused on the foreign affairs pages.

Nader Demands Rights to Peshawar Province. The Persian situation was clearly deteriorating, with the Shah's greedy eyes fastened on the southern provinces of French Indoostan. Of course, the idiot in New London wouldn't be able to let something like that slip past him: *Government Offers to Intercede with Court of St. Peter*. As if the French would listen to British representations on behalf of a megalomaniac widely seen as one of John Frederick's cat's-paws . . . *Prussian Ambassador Wins Duel*. Well, yes—diplomatic immunity meant never having to back out of a fight if you could portray it as an affair of honor. Burgeson sniffed. *Bloody-handed aristocrats*. The streetcar bell dinged as it rattled across a set of points and turned a wide corner.

Erasmus folded the paper neatly and stood up. *Nothing to do with the price of bread*, he thought cynically as he descended the tight circular staircase at the rear of the car. The price of bread was up almost four-twelfths over its price at this time last year, and there had been food riots in Texico when the corn flour handed out by the poor boards had proven to be moldy. Fourteen dead, nearly sixty injured when the cavalry went in after the magistrates read the riot act. The streetcar stopped and Erasmus followed a couple of hopeful hedonists out onto the crowded pavement outside. The place was normally busy, but tonight it was positively fizzing. There was something unusual in the air. He took another deep breath. Not having his chest rattle painfully was like being young again: he felt lively and full of energy. And the night was also young.

The Cardiff Hotel—named for Lord Cardiff of Virginia, not the French provincial capital of Wales—was brightly lit with electricals, broad float-glass doors open to the world. A green-and-white-striped canopy overhung the pavement, and a pianist was busy banging both keyboards on his upright instrument for all he was worth, the brass-capped hammers setting up a pounding military beat. Burgeson stepped inside and made his way to the back of the bar, searching for the right booth. A hand waved, just visible above the crowd: he nodded and joined his fellow conspirator.

"Nice evening," Farnsworth said nervously.

"Indeed." Erasmus eyed the other man's mug: clearly he was in need of the Dutch courage. "Can I get you something?"

"I'm sure—ah." A table-runner appeared. "Have you any of the hemp porter?" Farnsworth enquired. "And a drop of laudanum."

"I'll have the house ale," said Erasmus, trying not to raise an eyebrow. *Surely it's a bit early for laudanum?* Unless Farnsworth really *was* upset about something.

When the table-runner had left, Farnsworth raised his tankard and drained it. "That's better. I'm sorry, Rudolf."

Burgeson leaned forward, tensely. "What for?"

"The news—" Farnsworth waved his hand helplessly. "I have no images, you understand."

Burgeson tried to calm his racing heart. He felt lightheaded, slightly breathless: "Is that all? There's no reason to apologize for that, my friend."

Farnsworth shook his head. "Bad news," he croaked.

The table-runner returned with their drinks. Farnsworth buried his snout in his mug. Erasmus, trying to rein in his impatience, scanned the throng. It was loud, too loud for even their neighbors in the next booth to overhear them, and there were no obvious signs of informers. "What is it, then?"

"Prince James is—it's not good."

"Ah." Erasmus relaxed a little. Not that he was pleased by news of the crown prince's suffering—no matter that the

eight-year-old was due to grow up to be tyrant of New
Britain, he was still just a bairn and could not be held responsible for his parents' misdeeds—but if it was just more
trivial court gossip it meant the sky hadn't fallen in yet. "So
how is he?"

"The announcement will be made in about two hours'
time. I have to be back at the palace by midnight to plan his
majesty's wardrobe for the funeral."

"The—" Erasmus stopped. *"What?"*

"Oh yes." Farnsworth nodded lugubriously. "It will mean
war, you mark my words."

War? Erasmus blinked rapidly. "What are you talking
about?"

"Don't you know?" Farnsworth seemed startled.

"I've been on a train all afternoon," said Erasmus. "Has
something happened?" *Something more than a sick little boy
dying?*

"They caught one of the assassins," Farnsworth said
tensely. "An Ottoman subject." He peered blearily at Burgeson's uncomprehending face. "Prince James was murdered
just after lunchtime today; shot in the chest from a building
overlooking the Franciscan palace. It was a conspiracy!
Bomb-throwing foreigners on our soil, spreading terror and
fomenting fear. Naval intelligence says it's a message for his
majesty. The crisis in the Persian Gulf. Sir Roderick is rec-
ommending a bill of attainder to his majesty that will seize
all Ottoman assets held by institutions here until they back
down."

Burgeson stared at him. "You. Have got to be kidding."

Farnsworth shook his head. "All hell's broken loose, the
seventh seal has sounded, and I very much fear that we are
about to be bathed in the blood of ten million lambs—
conscripted into a war started as a distraction from the
empty larders of the provinces, a matter which has most exercised the prime minister these past weeks." He grabbed
Burgeson's hand. "You've got to do something! Make your
friends listen! It's the outside threat to distract and befuddle
us, the oldest trick in the library. A brief successful war to
wrap themselves in the glory of the flag and justify calls for

austerity and belt-tightening, and to distract attention from the empty coffers and supply a pretext to issue war bonds. Only this time, we know the Frogs have got corpses. And so have we. So it's going to be an unusually violent war. And of course they'll clamp down on dissenters and Ranters. They'll implement French rule here, if you give them the chance." French rule—summary justice, the martial law of the Duc du Muscovy. *The Stolypin necktie* as an answer to all arguments, as that strange otherworld history book Miriam had given him had put it. Erasmus felt cold sweat spring out at the back of his neck.

"I'll tell them immediately," he said, rising.

"Your drink—"

"You finish it. You look as if you need it more than I do. I've got a job to do."

"Good luck."

Erasmus dived into the throng of agitated, wildly speculating men filling the bar and worked his way outside. A street hawker was selling the last of the evening edition: he snagged a copy and stared at the headlines. ARAB TERROR screamed the masthead in dripping red letters above an engravature of the boy prince lying on the ground, his eyes open. "Shit." Erasmus looked around, searching for a cab. *I'll have to notify Lady Bishop,* he thought, *and Iron John. Find out what the Central Committees want to do about the situation.* Another thought struck him. *I must talk to Miriam; she knows of other worlds more advanced than this. They're ruled by republics, they must have corpuscular weapons—I wonder what she knows about them?* A cab pulled up and he climbed in. *Perhaps we could achieve a better negotiating position if the movement had some . . .*

13

BREAKOUT

ike realized something was wrong the moment he passed the checkpoint on the fourteenth floor and found Pete Garfinkle and Colonel Smith waiting for him, with a blue-suiter behind them. The guard was carrying a gun and trying to look in six different directions simultaneously. This worried Mike. Armed guards were a normal fact of life in the FTO, but nervous ones were something new.

"What's up?" he asked.

"We have a problem," said Smith.

"Matt went for a walk about two hours ago," said Pete, nervously fingering his document folder.

"Went for a—"

"Down the express elevator from the twenty-third floor, or so it would appear judging from the elevator logs," Smith added. "Although there's no evidence he was actually in the elevator car except for the RFID tags concealed in his underwear. Which he is no longer wearing. And there's a missing window on the twenty-third floor. Shall we talk about it?"

They went up to the newly installed Vault Type Room on the nineteenth floor and Smith signed them in. Then they authenticated each other and locked the door. The blue-suiter waited outside, which was a relief to Mike—but only a temporary one. "Do we know where he went?" he asked as soon as they were seated around the transparent conference table.

"Not a clue." Smith inclined his head toward Pete. "Dr. James is going to shit a brick the size of the World Trade Center as soon as he finds out, which is"—he glanced at his wrist-watch—"going to happen in about thirty minutes, so it is *important* that we are singing from the same hymn book before he drops in. Unless we can find our runaway first." The colonel grinned humorlessly. "So. From the top. How would you characterize Client Zero's state of mind last time you spoke to him?"

I'm not on the spot, Mike realized with an enormous sense of guilt-tinged relief—because it meant someone else was going to catch it in the neck. "He seemed perfectly fine, to be honest. A bit stir-crazy, but that's not unexpected. He wasn't depressed or suicidal or excessively edgy, if that's what you're looking for. Why? What happened?"

Colonel Smith shook his head and shoved his voice recorder closer to Mike's side of the table. "Summarize first. Then we'll go round the circle. Treat this as a legal deposition. Afterward I'll fill you in."

"Okay." Mike recounted his last meeting with Matthias. "He was asking about his Witness Protection Program status, but—" Mike stopped dead. "You said he took a lift down from the twenty-third-floor window. He was on the twenty-*fourth* floor. With no direct elevator between them. How'd he get downstairs?" *Through two security checkpoints and four locked doors and then downstairs in an elevator car with a webcam and a security guard?*

"Later," Smith said firmly.

"Uh, I'd like to register a note of caution here. Did anyone *see* Client Zero move between floors twenty-four and twenty-three? And was there any evidence that he left the building by one of the ground-level doors?"

There was a pregnant pause.

"I'd have to say that we don't know that," said Smith. His eyes tracked, almost imperceptibly, toward the door outside which the blue-suiter with the gun would be standing guard.

"Oh." *Oh shit*, thought Mike.

"I'm betting he got riled up and broke out," said Smith, his voice even. "How he managed that is a troubling question, as is why he chose to do it right at this moment. But he's a smart cookie, is Client Zero. Just in case he had outside help, we're going to full Case Red lockdown. Nobody goes below the tenth floor without an armed escort until we've clarified the situation."

"He can't have evaded our monitoring completely, even if he managed to bypass the guards."

Smith's pager beeped for attention. He glanced at it, then stood up: "I'm going to deposit this, then take a call. Back in ten minutes." He disappeared through the door, taking the voice recorder and leaving Mike and Pete alone in the windowless room with the glass furniture and the vault fittings.

"He got stir-crazy," said Mike.

Pete looked at him.

"What am I not hearing?" asked Mike.

Pete coughed. "After your last meeting I dropped in on him. He was pissed—you said you'd been called away—"

"By Eric, he can confirm it—"

"Well sure, but Matt didn't see it that way, he thought you were bullshitting. He was worried. So to get him calmed down I tried to draw him out a bit about why he came over to us. I mean, you've been doing all those grammar sessions and he was getting bored, you know?"

"Okay." Mike leaned back to listen.

Pete got into the flow of things. "He had this crazy paranoid-sounding rant about how he was a second-class citizen as far as the bad guys are concerned, on account of how he can't do the magic disappearing trick—well, I'll buy that. And then something about a long-lost cousin turning up and destabilizing some plans of his. Seems she grew up on our side of the fence, worked in Cambridge as some kind of tech journalist. They rediscovered her by accident and she made the wheels fall off Matt's little red wagon by snooping around and stirring up shit. So Matt tried to persuade this Helga woman to get off his case and she—she's called Miriam something here, something Jewish-sounding—"

Can't be, thought Mike. *She can't be the same woman.* The idea was too preposterous for words.

Pete stopped. "What is it?" he asked.

"Nothing. So what happened? What went wrong with Matt's plans?"

"She wouldn't blackmail—he said she wouldn't play ball, but that's my reading—and there's some stuff about her discovering a whole other world where the Clan guys have got a bunch of relatives who don't like them and who were paying Matt to look after their interests—he's always been a bit of a moonlighter—and the upshot is, he had to cut and run. He's still pissed at her. He came to us because he figured we'd protect him from his former associates."

"Uh-huh." Mike nodded. *Miriam—what was her other name?* "What's this got to do with the time of day?"

"Well." Pete looked embarrassed. "I asked him how he thought it had worked, and that was when he got agitated. Said you'd told him something about him being in military custody now? So I tried to get him calmed down, told him it wasn't what it sounded like. But he wasn't having it. And at about five in the morning he went missing. Do I have to draw you a diagram?"

"No," said Mike. He sighed. "I knew this military thing was a bad idea."

"Yeah, well. Which of us is going to tell Smith?"

They found the colonel at the security checkpoint by elevator bank B, talking to one of the guards. He didn't look terribly happy. "What are you doing here?" he demanded.

"I've got a hypothesis I'd like to test, sir. I think Matt may still be in the building. Did we catch him leaving?"

"That's what I was just ascertaining," said Smith. He

glanced around irritably. "Get me . . ." He snapped his fingers, searching for a name—"Sergeant Scoville, mister."

"Sir." The guard pulled out his walkie-talkie and began talking to someone.

"So." Smith pointed a bony finger at Mike. "Explain."

"Client Zero is no dummy. He knows he's upstairs. He decided he wants to take a walk. We can be fairly sure he can move between floors but he's not on camera, so either he's been holding out on us—and I don't believe he's got what it takes to hack our sensors—or he's gone to ground. My bet is either under the false floor or over the suspended ceiling, probably on the twenty-third but possibly on the twenty-fourth or twenty-fifth floor. He probably ran into the security zone on the twenty-second and bounced. Now he'll be waiting for an opportunity to go elevator surfing or a chance to slip outside while we're distracted."

"Okay. Now tell me why he's doing this. Where's he likely to go?"

Mike glanced at Pete. "I think he's breaking out because he thought he was looking at a comfortable relax-a-thon in the Witness Protection Program, and a new identity afterward, with us to protect him from his former associates. Unfortunately, once Dr. James switched him to military custody we lost track of the WP program and his new identity, and he finally twigged that he was one step away from being given the whole unlawful-combatant treatment. As for where he's going—I bet he's got his own spare identity stashed away, from before he decided to come in. It won't be as good as what we could have given him *if* we'd kept him in witness protection, but it beats being a ghost detainee."

"Right." The guard offered Smith his handset. "Jack? Our current best guess is that the target's still in the building, above the security zone on ten. My top priority is, I want you to secure the entry zone and the lobby. Nobody leaves the building even if a Boeing flies into the top floor: our target may try to provoke an evacuation so he can escape in the crowd. I want a security detail to start on floor ten and work their way upstairs, one level at a time, until they get to the roof. They will need torches, floor-tile lifters, and ladders

because they're going to check the crawlways and over-
heads, and they need to be armed because our target is dangerous. How soon can you get that started? How many
bodies have we got up here anyway?" He listened for a few
seconds. "Damn, I'd hoped for more. Okay, assemble them.
Smith out." He glanced back at the two DEA agents. "Right.
Any other suggestions?"

Mike took a deep breath. "Is he still valuable to us, if we
can get him back?"

"Possibly." Smith stared at him. "Your call, son."

Time stood still. "I need to work on my grammar," Mike
said slowly. "But of course, after CLEANSWEEP we'll have
more subjects to work with."

Smith held out his hand for the walkie-talkie, watching
Mike's face as he spoke: "Sergeant? Change of plan. Hold
the floor sweep, I don't think we've got enough people to
risk it, if the target manages to arm himself . . . Instead I
want you to stand by to execute code BLUEBEARD. That's
BLUEBEARD. I'm going to make an announcement in a
couple of minutes. If the fugitive doesn't give himself up,
we'll execute BLUEBEARD, then ventilate and search the
place afterward."

Pete looked shocked. Mike elbowed the younger agent in
the ribs to get his attention. "Go get us all respirators," he
said. Smith nodded at him. "You really going to do it, sir?"

Smith nodded again. "We need to test the security system,
anyway."

"Ri-ight." The desk guard was watching nervously, as if
the colonel had sprouted a second head. Mike grimaced. "I
love the smell of nerve gas in the morning." Pete reappeared
and handed over a sealed polythene pack containing a respirator mask and a preloaded antidote syringe.

"It's not nerve gas, it's fentanyl," Smith corrected him.
"Where's the PA mike on this level?" he asked the desk
guard.

"Fentanyl is a controlled substance," said Pete, a condi-
tioned reflex kicking in.

Mike looked round edgily. BLUEBEARD was a last-ditch
antiterrorist defense; on command, compressed gas cylin-

ders plugged into the air-conditioning on each floor would pump a narcotic mist throughout the building. Sure, there was an antidote, and the ventilator masks ought to stop it dead, but the only time it had ever been used for this purpose—in Russia, when a bunch of Chechen terrorists had taken a theater crowd hostage—more than a fifth of the by-standers had been killed. Gas and confined spaces did not mix well.

"Relax, boys." Smith looked bored, if anything. "If you're thinking about that Russian thing, forget it—they didn't have respirator masks there. You're perfectly safe." He pulled the gooseneck PA mike toward his mouth and hit the red button. "Is this thing—yes, it's live." His voice rumbled through the corridors and floor, amplified through hidden speakers. "Matt, I know you're in here. You've got five minutes to sur-render. If you want to live, come out from wherever you're hiding, and go to the nearest elevator bank. Hit the button for the tenth floor, then lie down on the floor of the elevator car with your hands on your head. This is your only warning."

He killed the PA and turned to the walkie-talkie: "Okay, you heard me, Sergeant. Fifteen minutes from my mark, I want you to execute BLUEBEARD on all floors above ten. You've got ten minutes from right *now* to do a cross-check on all person-nel and make sure they're ready. Antidote kits out, boys. Over."

Smith unsealed his respirator kit. "What are you waiting for?"

"The broken window on the twenty-third," Mike said slowly. "Has it been repaired? And has anyone secured the window-cleaning system?" He opened the packaging around his respirator as he spoke, peeling the polythene wrapper away and yanking the red seal tab to activate the filter cartridge.

"The—" Pete's eyes narrowed.

"We've agreed Matt's not stupid. He probably guessed we'd have something like BLUEBEARD. Maybe he broke the window because he wanted fresh air to breathe?" Mike pointed toward the nearest outside wall. "That got me think-ing. Someone's got to clean the windows, haven't they? That means a motorized basket, right? Maybe he figured he could ride it down past the security zone while we're busy trying not to choke ourselves?"

"Point." Smith began to reach for the walkie-talkie again.

"How about Pete and I check out floor twenty-three?" Mike asked, pulling the mask over his head. "We've got respirators, we're armed, we can take a walkie-talkie. More to the point, maybe we can talk him down. Is that okay by you?"

Smith thought for a moment. Finally he nodded. "Okay, you have my approval. Stick together, don't take any risks, and remember—I'm not going to cancel BLUEBEARD if he gets the drop on you. Especially not if he takes one of you hostage. Understood?"

"Yes." Mike glanced at Pete, who nodded.

Smith gestured at the charging station by the security desk: "Take one of these, they're fully charged." He picked up his own walkie-talkie. "Sergeant, I want you to check out the janitorial facilities, find out how they clean the windows above the tenth floor. If there's an outside winch, I want it secured."

Mike headed for the central service core, opening his holster. "Come on," he told Pete, his voice muffled by the mask.

"What's the plan?"

"I want to check out the floor tiles where he smashed the window. Where is it?"

"Twenty-third floor. You turn left at the checkpoint, then take the first transverse corridor past the service core. You want to follow me?"

"He's not armed, is he?"

"I don't *think* so." Pete sounded uncertain.

"Well, then." Mike held his gun at his side and gestured at the door onto the fire stairs with his free hand. "Let's go."

They took the steps fast. Mike rapidly discovered that breathing through a gas mask was hard work. He paused, gasping for air, on the twenty-second-floor landing, leaning against a brace of drab green pipes running up and down. Pete seemed to be doing fine: *There's no justice*, he thought. "Shit. I can't run in this thing." *I'm too old for this SWAT-team game. I'm not thirty-six yet, and I can't run up flights of stairs in a gas mask anymore. What's wrong with me?* He pulled his mask off and shoved it into the inside pocket of his jacket.

"You sure it's safe to do that?" asked Pete. Mike noticed that he wasn't wearing his mask, either.

"I'll hear when Smith trips the gas tanks," he said with a confidence he didn't feel. "Anyway, make sure you've got yours, right? Okay, here's how we'll do it when we come out of the stairwell. I'll go first, covering the floor. You follow me, covering the ceiling and my back. We head for the window, and if he's not there, we head for the security station and the PA mike for this floor and I try talking to him. What's wrong with this picture?"

Pete shook his head. "Nothing obvious to me."

"Okay, let's go." Mike shoved himself back onto the stairs and took the last two flights, paused to catch his breath just inside the door, then pushed through.

The twenty-third floor was eerily deserted, a high-altitude *Mary Celeste*. Beige carpet tiles, slightly scuffed and in need of cleaning, floored corridors where doors stood open on unfurnished office suites. The black bubbles of surveillance cameras sprouted from ceiling tiles, some of them discolored by water seepage. One of the reasons floor twenty-three had been left vacant was that it had needed more refitting than the rest of the building, thanks to a burst pipe the previous winter. Some of the lighting panels flickered erratically. Mike headed up the corridor, cautiously checking side doors opening off it for any sign of human presence. *Just because we don't think he's armed doesn't mean he isn't*, he told himself, whenever he felt self-conscious.

He turned the corner onto the last stretch of passageway. There was no door at the end, just a wide open-plan office space, almost a thousand square feet of it, walled in windows. Abandoned desks and shelving units clustered in forlorn huddles around the floor. He could hear something now, the whistle of wind blowing past an empty gap in the glass side of the building. It was slightly chilly, even though it was a hot day down below. Mike paused just outside the door and glanced over his shoulder at Pete, who was staring tensely at the ceiling behind them. "Going in."

"Okay."

Mike ducked through the entrance and spun round. Anti-climax: nobody was lurking in the corners behind him. *But what about the desks*—he crouched, casting his gaze around at ankle level. No, there were no giveaway legs visible under the furniture. Nothing, no sign that anybody had visited the place.

"He's not here?"

"Hush." Mike backed toward the wall beside the door. "Keep me covered from right there." He slid along the wall, around the edge of the room. *Three minutes left*, he thought. *What if—*

There was nobody behind any of the furniture. None of the ceiling or floor tiles had been disturbed. The room looked abandoned, except for the missing window unit. Those double-glazed cells didn't break easily; they were toughened glass, held in place by plastic gaskets and screws. Someone had removed the thing, probably unscrewed it, and then shoved it right out of the frame. The breeze was rustling playfully around him, tugging at his jacket, pinching his trouser cuffs. Mike crouched down below the level of the windows and looked up, and out, letting his eyes grow accustomed to the bright daylight above him.

There. Outside the glass, barely visible—it ran behind one of the concrete pillars framing the stretch of glazing—a wire. It was quite a thick wire, but it was almost invisible against the bright daylight. Only a slight vibration gave it away. Mike looked back at Pete, raised a finger to his lips, then beckoned urgently. He cast his gaze along the wall. Another wire stood out on the far side of the missing window pane. *Gotcha.*

Pete hunkered down next to him. "What is it?" he whispered.

"There's a window-cleaning car somewhere below us, right outside the open cell. I figure he's waiting while we run BLUEBEARD. Then he's going to try to break back in while everyone's expecting him to be down and out."

"You say that as if you think there are other options."

"I can think of several, but Matt's not stupid—he knows

the more elaborate the scheme, the more likely it is to go wrong. I mean, he might have just done this as a distraction, but then what if we didn't notice it at all? Whatever, I think he's down there, below us."

"In which case, all we have to do is get him to come back in."

"Yeah. But he obviously wants out, and—listen, these cars are self-propelled. He's probably as low as he can go, waiting for everyone to clear out before he breaks another window."

"Right." Pete straightened up, holding his pistol. "I'll reel him in." And before Mike could move to stop him he leaned out of the window, shoulders set, aiming straight down. "Hey—"

A gray shadow dropped across the window, accompanied by a grating of metal on metal. Pete vanished beneath it, tumbling out of the window.

"Fuck!" Mike jumped up in time to register two more wires and the basketwork cage of a window-cleaning lift wobbling behind the glass with someone inside it: then Matt swung the improvised club he was holding at the window cell Mike was standing next to, and to Mike's enormous surprise it leapt out of its frame and fell on him. He stumbled backward, away from the wall, his arm going numb. *How did he get above us?* he thought, dazed and confused. Then he registered that he'd dropped his pistol. *That's bad*, he thought, his stomach heaving.

Someone kicked it away from him. *Not fair*. He felt dizzy and sick. Things grayed out for a moment. When they came back into focus he was sitting down, his back to a desk. There was something wrong with his face—it was hard to breathe. *The mask*. He looked up.

Matthias squatted on his heels opposite him, holding the gun, looking bored. "Ah, you're with me again. I was beginning to worry."

Those window cells had to weigh thirty or forty pounds each—thick slabs of double-glazed laminate clamped between aluminum frames. Matt must have unscrewed it first, then dropped decoy lines below the window-cleaning car before retreating up top to wait like a spider above his trap. The damn thing had hit his head when Matt shoved it at him. A flash of anger: "Like you worried about Pete when you pulled that stunt? We could have worked something out—"

"I doubt it." Something about Matt's tone sent a chill down Mike's spine.

"Why are you doing this?"

"Because your organization has failed to protect me. It was worth a try—if you'd gone after the Clan as a police operation, that would have given the thin white duke something more urgent to worry about than a missing secretary, no? But the military—that was a bad idea. I'm not going to Camp X-ray, Michael."

"Nobody said you were." Mike tried to push himself up against the desk, but a growing sensation of nausea stopped him.

"And now I will leave. On your feet."

Mike took a deep breath, trying to ignore his butterfly diaphragm. "What do you want from me?"

Matt smiled humorlessly. "I want you to take me downstairs. And then we will get into a car and drive somewhere where I will contrive to make you lose me."

"You know that's not possible."

Matt shrugged. "I don't care whether it is possible or not, it is what will happen. Seeking your government's help was a mistake. I'm going underground."

Mike took another deep breath. His stomach clenched: he waited the spasm out, trying to will the blurring in his vision and the pounding at his temples away. "No. I mean. Why? What do you hope to achieve?"

"Revenge. Against the bitch."

"Who?"

Mike must have looked puzzled, because Matt threw back his head and laughed, a rich belly-chuckle that would have given Mike an opening if he'd been in any condition to move. "The queen in shadow." Matt stopped laughing. "Anyway, we're leaving."

"They won't let you," Mike said tiredly.

"Want to bet? Remember the sample of metal I gave you, from the duke's private stockpile?"

The plutonium ingot. Mike could see it coming, like a driver stalled on a level crossing at night staring into the lights of an oncoming freight train. He blinked tiredly, trying to focus his double vision. "What, the, the—"

"There are gadgets," Matthias explained. "An explosive device made with this magic metal of yours. The current duke's father stole several of them three decades ago . . . anyway. I have the keys to the stockpile. They are held in storage areas in cities across the United States. It is the Clan's ultimate deterrent, if you like: they were much more paranoid during the, the seventies when the civil war was being fought. The active one is on a timer, a very long timer, but if the battery runs down, it will explode. The battery is good for a year. I thought, when I came to you months ago, you would let me out in time and I would reset it and that would be all, an insurance policy against your good intentions, nothing more. But now"—he looked irritated—"you leave me no alternative."

"Oh Jesus." Mike stared at him. "Tell me you didn't."

Matt shook his head. "But I did. Or at least, you cannot prove that I *didn't*. So, you see, as soon as you are ready to stand, we will go down and talk to your boss, yes? And you will explain that you have to drive me somewhere. And you and I, we will go and I will get lost. But before I go, I will take you to the lockup and you will wait with the device, of course, until it can be defused, and we will all be happy and nobody will be hurt. Yes?"

"You'll tell me where it is?" Mike demanded.

"Of course." Matt smiled like a shark. "I know where the others are, too. They aren't active yet—if you do not follow me, I will not need to use them, no?"

Three images of a satanically smirking Matt hovered in front of Mike's nose: the back of his neck prickled in a cold sweat. *I'm going to be sick*, he realized. *I'm probably concussed*. The idea that the Clan had planted atomic bombs in

storage lockers across the United States was like something
out of a bad thriller—like the idea Islamic terrorists would
crash hijacked airliners into the World Trade Center, before
9/11. *Oh Jesus, I've got to tell someone!* "I feel sick."

"I know." Matt peered at him. "Your eyes, the pupils are
different sizes. Stand up now. It is very important you do not
go to sleep." Matt straightened up and took a step back.
Mike pushed against the panel behind him and shoved himself upright, wobbling drunkenly. "To the elevators," said
Matt, gesturing with Mike's own stolen gun.

What have I forgotten? Mike wondered dizzily. He stumbled and lurched toward the doorway. *Feel sick . . .*

"Elevator first. There is a telephone there, no?"

"Mmph." His stomach heaved: he tried desperately not to
throw up.

"Go on."

Mike stumbled on down the corridor. He was certain he'd
forgotten something, something important that had been on
his mind before he got distracted, before the slab of window
landed on him and Matt made his outrageous claim about the
nuclear time bomb. Matt closed the door on the room with
the damaged windows behind him, an unconscious slave to
habit. Mike leaned against the wall, head down.

"What is it?" Matt demanded, pausing.

"I don't feel so well—" *What's going to happen?* Mike
had a nagging sense that it was right on the tip of his tongue.
Then his stomach gave a lurch. "Ugh."

Matt took a step back, standing between Mike and the elevator core. He blinked, disgustedly. "Get it over with."

"Going to be—" Mike never finished the sentence. A giant's fist grabbed him under the ribs and twisted, turning his
throat into a fire hose. He doubled over, emptying his guts
across the carpet and halfway up the wall opposite.

Matt's face twisted in disgust. "You're no use to me like
that. Wait here." The next door along was a restroom. "I'll
get you some towels—"

There was a ringing in Mike's ears, and a hissing. His guts
stopped heaving, but he felt unaccountably tired. *What have*

I forgotten? he asked himself, as he sat down and leaned against the wall. He felt his eyes closing. Something hard-edged was digging into his ribs. *Oh, that. Must be time, then.* He could put the mask on again in a few minutes, couldn't he? *Just a quick nap . . .* Almost without willing it he felt his hand fumbling for the respirator, dragging it out of his inside pocket. His hands felt incredibly hot, but not in a painful way—it was like the best, most wonderful warm bath he'd ever had, all concentrated in his extremities. He never wanted it to stop. But that was all right: he managed to raise the mask to his face, doubling over to get his head low enough to reach, and inhaled through the filter. *I wonder if Matt heard Eric's announcement?* he thought dizzily. *If he was outside the building, at the time . . .*

He was still breathing through the respirator when they found him twenty minutes later, put him on a stretcher, and hauled him off to hospital in an ambulance with blaring siren and flashing lights. But it took them another ten minutes to find Matthias—and by then it was five minutes too late to ask him whether he'd been bluffing.

14

ULTIMATUM

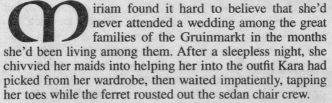

Miriam found it hard to believe that she'd
never attended a wedding among the great
families of the Gruinmarkt in the months
she'd been living among them. After a sleepless night, she
chivvied her maids into helping her into the outfit Kara had
picked from her wardrobe, then waited impatiently, tapping
her toes while the ferret rousted out the sedan chair crew.

Another tedious, uneven magical mystery tour: another
bland mansion with walled grounds, somewhere else in the
city. Miriam straightened her back as the ferret and his
guards waited. "This way," he indicated, nodding toward a
narrow passageway. "You will wait at the back, behind the
wooden screen. You will say nothing during the ceremony.
Observe, do not interfere or it will be the worse for you. I
will fetch you from the reception afterward."

"Worse?" she asked—rhetorically, for she had a very
good idea what he meant. "All right." She stuck her nose in
the air and marched down the corridor as though her guards

didn't exist, as if she were attending this function of her own accord, and the occasion were a happy one.

The passage led to a small chapel, located near the back of the building in the oldest construction. The walls were of un-dressed stone, woodwork blackened with age. Her first sur-prise was that it was tiny, barely larger than her reception room. Her second surprise was the altar, and the brightly painted statues behind it. She'd have taken them for saints, but the iconography was wrong—no trinity here, but a confusing family tree of bickering authorities, a heavenly bureaucracy with responsibility for everything from births, marriages, and deaths to law enforcement, tax returns, and the afterlife. The post-migration Norse-descended tribes who had eventually settled the eastern seaboard of North America in this world had adopted the Church of Rome, but the Church of Rome hadn't adopted Christianity, or Judaism, or anything remotely monotheistic. The Church here was a formalization and out-growth of the older Roman pantheon, echoes of which had survived in the Catholic hierarchy of saints, the names and roles of the gods updated for more recent usage with a smat-tering of Norse add-ons. *But no blood-eagles*, Miriam thought, as she walked past the pews of menfolk to take her place behind the wooden latticework screen at the back, be-hind the women of the two households.

There were only about ten women present, and about twice that number of men; they were mostly servants and bodyguards, as far as Miriam could tell. A couple of heads turned as she walked in, including one formidable-looking lady. "Wer ind'she?"

"Excuse me, I am Helge. Kara asks me to, to come," she managed in her halting hochsprache.

"Ah." The woman frowned. She wasn't much older than Miriam, but her attitude and the deference the others showed her suggested she was important. And there was a family re-semblance. *Mother? Aunt?* Miriam dipped her head. The frown vanished. "I am . . . please? You are here," she said in heavily accented English. "I am Countess Frea. My daugh-ter . . ." She shrugged, reaching the limits of her linguistic ability, and muttered something apologetic-sounding in hochsprache, too fast for Miriam to catch.

Miriam smiled and nodded. Some of the younger women were whispering, but then one of them moved aside and gestured to her. A seat at the back. *Yes, well.* Miriam accepted it silently, annoyed that her grasp of the language was insufficient to tell whether she was being snubbed or honored. *I've been depending on Kara too much. And Brill,* she told herself. *Wherever she's gotten to.* Brilliana's other duties made guessing at her whereabouts much less easy than dealing with Kara.

Another knot of women arrived, with much bowing and nodding and kissing of cheeks on both sides: an old lady with her daughters—both older than Kara's mother, Frea—and their attendants. A brief introduction: Miriam bobbed her head and was happy enough to be ignored. At the front a couple of priests in odd vestments had begun chanting something in what might have been a mutant dialect of Latin, filtered through many generations of hochsprache-speaking colonials. A young lad swung an incense censer, spilling fumes across the altar as they continued. To Miriam's uneducated eye (she'd been raised by her mother and her agnostic Jewish foster-father, and churchgoing hadn't been on the agenda) it looked vaguely Catholic—until a third priest emerged from the not-a-vestry at the back, clutching an indignant white chicken and a silver knife. At which point Miriam was grateful for her place at the rear, which meant nobody was in a position to notice the way she closed her eyes until the squawking and gurgling stopped. It wasn't that she was particularly squeamish herself, but she found the idea of killing an animal in cold blood as part of a religious ritual rather disturbing. *I got the impression from Olga that they didn't do that anymore,* she pondered. *What else did I get wrong?*

Things speeded up after the sacrifice, which the priests dedicated to the Lady of Domestic Harmony, the Lord of the Household, and sundry other parties of the hearth who were contractually obliged to bless familial alliances, as far as

Miriam could tell, or who at least had to be bought off in order for the whole enterprise not to end in a messy annulment some hours later. Two men walked up to the altar, neither of them particularly young: Frea's eyes lingered on the older one, making Miriam suspect he might be a relative. *Kara's father?* The priests asked him a whole bunch of questions, the answers to which seemed to boil down to "Yes, she's my daughter to give away." The other man waited patiently. Miriam couldn't see him clearly because of the screen, but she had an impression that he was in his thirties, balding, and stockily built. And there was a sword at his belt. *A sword? In church? I don't understand these people . . .* Now it was his turn to answer questions. They sounded a lot like "How much are you willing to pay for this guy's daughter?" to Miriam, but she was barely catching one word in four. It could have been anything from "Will you take her as your wife and love her and cherish her?" to "That'll be three pounds of silver and sixteen goats, and make sure you keep her away from the wine." The questioning went on and on, until Miriam's eyes began to glaze over with a curious mixture of boredom and anxiety.

Some sort of resolution seemed to be reached. One of the priests turned and marched into the back room. A few seconds later he reappeared, followed by a subdued-looking Kara. They didn't go in for frothy white wedding dresses and veils, it seemed. Kara was wearing a rich gown, but nothing significantly different from what she might have worn for any other public event. The bald guy with the sword asked her something, and she nodded: and a moment later the other priest offered them both a cup containing some kind of fluid. *I hope that's wine*, Miriam thought with a sinking feeling as they sipped from it. She couldn't see the chicken anymore. *Somehow I don't think these guys hold with abstractions like transubstantiation.*

Conversation started up on the bench ahead of her almost immediately. "It's done," or "That's that," if she understood it correctly. Two of the younger maids (daughters? nieces? servants?) stood up, and one of them giggled quietly. Up front, the men were already rising and filing out of the side door. "You will with us, come?" asked the old woman in front of Miriam, and it took her a moment to realize she was being spoken to.

"Yes," she said uncertainly.

"Good." The old lady reached out and grabbed Miriam's wrist, leaning on it as she levered herself up off the wooden bench. "You've got strong bones," she said, and cackled quietly.

"I have?"

"Your babies will need that." She let go of Miriam's arm, oblivious to her expression. "Come."

There didn't seem to be any alternative. They filed upstairs, into a chilly ballroom where servants with trays circulated, keeping everyone sufficiently lubricated with wine to ensure a smooth occasion. Miriam ended up with her back to a wall, observing the knots of chattering women, the puff-chested clump of young men, the elders circulating and talking to one another. The menfolk mostly had swords, which took her aback slightly. It wasn't something she'd seen in a social setting before—but then, too many of her social encounters had been in the royal court, or with other senior members of the nobility present. Carrying ironwork in the presence of the monarch was a faux pas of the kind that could get you executed. *I've been sheltered*, she decided. *Or I just had too small and too skewed a sample to see much of how things* really *work here.*

Kara and the bald guy had been installed on two stools on a raised platform, and had much larger cups than anyone else. Miriam tried to establish eye contact, but the bride was so focused on the floorboards that it would probably take a two-by-four to get her attention. *A happy occasion indeed*, she thought ironically, and drained her glass. *How long until I can get away from this?*

A hand clutching a bottle appeared in front of her and tilted it over her glass. "A drop more, perhaps?"

"Um." Startled, Miriam looked sideways. "Yes, please." He was in his late twenties, as far as she could tell, and he looked as if he had southeast Asian ancestry, which made him stand out in this crowd as effectively as if he'd had green skin and eyes on stalks. He was dressed like most of the men hereabouts, in loose-cut trousers and a tunic, but unlike the others he didn't have a sword, or even a dagger, on his belt. "Do I know you?"

"I think not." His English was oddly accented, but it wasn't a hochsprache accent—there was something familiar about it. "Allow me to introduce myself? I am James, second son of Ang, of family Lee." He looked slightly amused at her reaction. "I see you have heard of me."

"I met your brother," she said before she could stop herself. "Do you know who *I* am?"

He nodded, and she tensed, scanning the room for the ferret, his guards, anyone—because the circumstances under which she'd met his brother were anything but friendly. *Damn, where are they? Why now?* Her pulse roared in her ears, and she took a deep breath, ready to yell for help: but then he chuckled and slopped a bolus of wine into her glass. "You convinced the thin white duke to send him back to us alive," said Lee. He raised his own glass to her. "I would thank you for that."

Miriam felt her knees go weak with relief. "It was the sensible thing to do," she said. The roaring subsided. She took a sip of wine to cover her confusion, and after a moment she felt calm enough to ask, "Why are you here?"

"Here? At this happy occasion in particular, or this primitive city in general?" He seemed amused by her question. "I have the honor of being a hostage against my brother's safe return and the blood treaty between our families." Was it really amusement, or was it ironic detachment? Miriam blinked: she was finding James Lee remarkably difficult to read, but at least now she could place his accent. Lee's family had struck out for the west coast two centuries ago. In the process they'd gotten lost, detached from the Clan, worldwalking to the alien timeline of New Britain rather than the United States. His accent was New British—a form of American English, surely, but one that had evolved differently from the vernacular of her own home. "I cannot travel far." He nodded toward a couple of unexceptional fellows

standing near the door. "But they let me out to mingle with
society. I know Leon." Another nod at the balding middle-
aged groom, now chatting animatedly to Kara's father from
his throne at the far end of the room. "We play cards regularly, whist and black knave and other games." He raised his
glass. "And so, to your very good health!"

Miriam raised her own glass: "And to yours." She eyed
him speculatively. He was, she began to realize, a bit of a
hunk—and with brains, too. What that implied was interesting: he was a hostage, sure, but might he also be something
more? *A spy, perhaps?*

"Are you here because of, of her?" asked Lee, glancing at
the platform.

"Yes." Miriam nodded. "She was my lady-in-waiting. Before this happened."

"Hmph." He studied her face closely. "You say that as if it
came as a surprise to you, milady."

"It did." *Damn, I shouldn't be giving this much away!* "I
wasn't asked my opinion, shall we say." It was probably the
wine, on an empty stomach, she realized. She was feeling
wobbly enough as it was, and the sense of isolation was
creeping up on her again.

"I'd heard a rumor that you were out of favor."

He was fishing, but he sounded almost sympathetic.
Miriam looked at him sharply. *Handsome is as handsome
does*, she reminded herself. "A rumor?"

"There's a, a grapevine." He shrugged. "I'm not the only
guest of the families who is gathered to their bosom with all
the kind solicitude due an asp"—he snorted—"and people
will talk, after all! One rumor made play of a scandal between
you and a youngblood of the duke's faction who, regrettably,
died some months ago in an incident nobody will discuss: according to others, you kicked up a fuss sufficient to wake the
dead, rattling skeletons in their closets until other parties felt
the need to remove you from the game board to the toy box, if
you will pardon the mixed metaphor." He raised an eyebrow.
"I'm sure the truth is both less scandalous and more sympathetic than any of the rumors would have it."

"Really." She smiled tightly and took a full mouthful of wine. "As a matter of fact *both* the rumors are more or less true, in outline at least. I'm pleased you're polite enough not to raise the third one: it would be interesting to compare notes on the climate in New Britain some day, but right now I suspect we'd only upset our minders."

Now it was Lee's turn to look unhappy. "I want you to know that I did not approve of the attempts on your life," he said rapidly. "It was unnecessary and stupid and—"

"Purely traditional." Miriam finished her wine and pushed her glass at him. "Right. And you're young and sensible and know how your hidebound grandparents ought to be running the family if they weren't stuck in the past?"

He gave her an ironic smile as he refilled both their glasses. "Exactly. Oh dear, this bottle appears to be empty, I wonder how that happened?" He made a minute gesture and a servant came sidling up to replace it: *How does he do that?* Miriam wondered.

"Let me guess." Her nose was beginning to prickle, a sure sign that she'd had enough and that she needed to be watching her tongue, but right now she didn't care about discretion. Right now she felt like letting her hair down, and damn the consequences for another day. Besides, Lee was handsome and smart and a good listener, a rare combination in this benighted backwater. "You'd been kicking shins a little too hard, so the honorable head of the family sent you here when he needed a hostage to exchange with Angbard. Right?"

James Lee sighed. "You have such an interesting idiom—and so forthright. To the bone. Yes, that is exactly it. And yourself . . . ?"

Miriam frowned. "I don't fit in here," she said quietly. "They want to shut me in a box. Y'know, where I come from, women don't take that. Not second-class citizens, not at all. I grew up in Boston, the Boston of the United States. Able to look after myself. It's different to the world you know: women have the vote, can own property, have legal equality, run businesses—" She took a deep breath, feeling the bleak depression poised, ready to come crashing down on her again. "You can guess how well I fit in here."

"Hmm." His glass was empty. Miriam watched as he re-filled it. "It occurs to me that we shall both be drunk before this is over."

"I can think of less appropriate company to get drunk in." She shrugged, slightly unbalanced by everything. A discordance of strings sought their tune from a balcony set back above the doorway, musicians with acoustic instruments preparing to play something not unlike a baroque chamber piece. "And in the morning we'll both be sober and Kara will still be married to some fellow she hadn't even met yesterday." She glanced around, wishing there was somewhere she could spit to get the nasty taste out of her mouth.

"This is a problem for you?"

"It's not so much a problem as a warning." She took a step backward and leaned against the wall. She felt tired. "The bastards are going to marry me off," she heard herself explaining. "This is so embarrassing. Where I grew up you just don't *do* that to people. Especially not to your daughter. But Mom's got her—reasons—and I suppose the duke thinks he's got his, and I, I made a couple of mistakes." *Fucking stupid ones*, she thought despairingly. *It could be worse; if I wasn't lucky enough to be a privileged rich bitch and the duke's niece to boot, they'd probably have killed me, but instead they're just going to nail me down and use me as a pawn in their political chess game. Oops.* She put a hand to her mouth. *Did I say any of that aloud?* Lee was watching her sympathetically.

"We could elope together," he offered, his expression hinting that this suggestion was not intended to be taken entirely seriously.

"I don't think so." She forced a grin. *You're cute but you're no Roland. Roland I'd have eloped with in a split second. Damn him for getting himself killed . . .* "But thanks for the offer."

"Oh, it was nothing. If there's anything I can do, all you need is to ask."

"Oh, a copy of the family knotwork would do fine," she said, and hiccoughed.

"Is that all?" He shook his head. "They'd chase you down if you went anywhere in the three known worlds."

"Three *known* worlds?" Her glass was empty again. Couples were whirling in slow stately circles around the dance floor, and she had a vague idea that she might be able to join them if she was just a bit more sober: her lessons had covered this one—

"Vary the knotwork, vary the destination." James shrugged. "Once that much became clear, two of our youngsters tried it. The first couple of times, they got headaches and stayed where they were. On the second attempt one of them vanished, then came back a few hours later with a story about a desert of ice. On the third attempt, they both vanished, and stayed missing."

Miriam's eyes widened. "You're kidding!"

He took her glass and placed it on the floor, alongside his own, by the skirting board. Then he straightened up again. "No."

"What did they find?"

He offered her his hand. "Will you dance? People will gossip less . . ."

"Sure." She took it. He led her onto the floor. In deference to the oldsters the tempo was slow, and she managed to follow him without too much stumbling. "I'm crap at this. Not enough practice when drunk."

"I shouldn't worry." The room spun around her. "In answer to your question, we don't know. Nobody knows. The elders forbade further experiments when they failed to return."

"Oh." She leaned her weight against him, feeling deflated, the elephantine weight of depression returning to her shoulders. For a moment she'd been able to smell the fresh air drifting through the bars of her cell—and then it turned out to be prison air-conditioning. The music spiraled to an end, leaving her washed up on the floor by the doorway. The ferret was waiting, looking bored. "I think this is my cue to say good-bye," she told Lee.

"I'm sure we'll meet again," he said, smiling a lazy grin of intrigue.

As several days turned into a week and the evenings grew long and humid, Miriam grew resigned to her confinement. As prisons went, it was luxurious—multiple rooms, anxious servants, no shortage of basic amenities, even a walled courtyard she could go and walk in by prior arrangement—but it lacked two essentials that she'd taken for granted her entire life: freedom and the social contact of her equals.

After Kara's marriage, she was left with only the carefully vetted maids and the ferret for company. The servants didn't have a word of English between them, and the ferret had a very low tolerance for chitchat. After a while Miriam gritted her teeth and tried to speak hochsprache exclusively. While a couple of the servants regarded her as crack-brained, an imbecile to be humored, a couple of the younger maids responded, albeit cautiously. A noblewoman's wrath was subject to few constraints: they would clam up rather than risk provoking her. And it didn't take long for Miriam to discover another unwelcome truth: her servants had been chosen, it seemed, on the basis of their ignorance and tractability. They were all terrified of the ferret, frightened of her, and strangers to the city (or overgrown town) of Niejwein. They'd been brought in from villages and towns outside, knew nobody here outside the great house, and weren't even able to go outside on their own.

About a week into the confinement, the boredom reached an excruciating peak. "I need something to read, or something to write," she told the ferret. "I'll go out of my head with boredom if I don't have something to do!"

"Go practice your tapestry stitch, then."

Miriam put her foot down. "I'm crap at sewing. I want a notepad and mechanical pencil. Why can't I have a notepad? Are you afraid I'll keep a diary, or something?"

The ferret looked at her. He'd been cleaning his fingernails with a wickedly sharp knife. "You can't have a notepad," he said calmly. "Stop pestering me or I'll beat you."

"Why not?"

Something in her expression gave him pause for thought: "You might try to draw an escape knot from memory," he said.

"Ri-ight." She scowled furiously. "And how likely do you think that is? Isn't this place doppelgangered in New York?"

"You might get the knot wrong," he pointed out.

"And kill myself by accident." She shook her head. "Listen, do you really want me depressed to the point of suicide? Because this, this—" The phrase *sensory deprivation* sprung to mind, but that wasn't quite right. "This *emptiness* is driving me crazy. I don't know whose idea keeping me here was, but I'm not used to inactivity. And I'm rubbish at tapestry or needlepoint. And the staff aren't exactly good for practicing conversational hochsprache."

He stood up. "I will see what I can do," he said. "Now go away." And she did.

Two days later a leather-bound notebook and a pen materialized on her dresser. There was a note in the book: *Remember you are thirty feet up*, it said. The ferret insisted on holding it whenever she went downstairs to walk in the garden. But at least it was progress. Miriam drew a viciously complicated three-loop Möbius strip on the first page, just to deter the ferret from snooping inside, then found herself blocked, unable to write anything. *I should have studied shorthand*, she thought bitterly. Privacy, it seemed, was a phenomenon dependent on trust—and if there was one thing she didn't have these days, it was the confidence of her relatives.

One foggy morning, almost two weeks after Kara's arranged wedding, there was a knock at the door to her reception room. Miriam looked up: this usually meant the ferret wanted to see her. Today, though, the ferret tiptoed in and stood to one side as two tough-looking men in business suits and dark glasses—Secret Service chic—entered and rapidly searched the apartment. "What's going on?" she asked, but the ferret ignored her.

One of the guards stepped outside. A moment later, the door opened again. It was Henryk, leaning heavily on a walking stick. The ferret scurried to fetch a padded stool for the baron, positioning it in front of Miriam's seat in the window bay. Miriam stared at Henryk. Her heart pounded and she felt slightly sick, but she stayed seated. *I'm not going to beg*, she told herself uncertainly. *What does the old bastard want?*

"Good morning, my dear Helge. I hope you are keeping well?" He spoke in hochsprache, but the phrases were stock.

"I am well. I thank you," she said haltingly, frowning. *I'm not going to let him show me up—*

"Good." He turned to the ferret: "Clear the room. Now."

Thirty seconds later they were alone. "What require—do you *want*?" she asked.

"Hmm." He tilted his head thoughtfully. "Your accent is atrocious." She must have looked blank: he repeated himself in English. "We can continue in this tongue if you'd rather."

"Okay." She nodded reluctantly.

"Tonight there will be another private family reception at the summer palace," Henryk said without preamble. "A dinner, to be followed by dancing. Let me explain your role in it. Your mother will be there, as will her half-brother, the duke. His majesty, and the Queen Mother, and his youngest son, will also be there. There will be a number of other notables present as guests, but you are being given a signal honor as a personal guest of his majesty. You will be seated with them at the high table, and you will behave with the utmost circumspection. This means, basically, *think* before you open your mouth." He smiled thinly. "And don't talk out of turn."

"Huh." Miriam frowned. "What about the crown prince? Is he going to be there?"

"Egon?" Henryk looked bemused. "No, why should he be? He's off on a hunting trip somewhere, I think."

"Oh." *One less thing to worry about*, Miriam thought. "Is that all?"

"Not quite." Henryk paused, as if uncertain how to continue. "You know what our plans for you are," he said slowly. "There are some facts you need to understand. The younger prince—you have met him." Miriam nodded, suppressing a shudder. The prince belonged in a hospital ward with nursing attendants and a special restricted diet. *Brain damage.* "He's a little slow, but he is not a vegetable, Helge. You should respect him. If he had not been poisoned—" A shadow crossed his face.

"What do you expect me to do?"

"I expect you to marry him and bear his children." Henryk looked pained at being made to spell it out. "Nothing more and nothing less, and it is not just what *I* expect of you—the Clan proposes and the Clan disposes. But you can do this the easy way, if you like. Go through the ceremony, then Dr. ven Hjalmar will sort you out. You don't need to worry about bedding the imbecile, if that thought upsets you: the doctor has made a sufficient study of artificial insemination. You'll be pregnant, but you'll have the best antenatal care we can provide, and in an emergency the doctor will get you to a hospital on the other side within half an hour. The well-being of your child will be a matter of state security. Once you are mother to a child in the line of succession, a certain piece of paper can be discreetly buried. Two or more children would be better, but I shall leave that as a matter for you and your doctor to decide upon—your age, after all, is an issue."

"Um." Miriam swallowed her distaste. *Spitting would send entirely the wrong message*, she thought, her head spinning. And besides, she'd been angry about this for weeks already, to the point where the indignation and fury had lost their immediate edge. It wasn't simply the thought of pregnancy—although she hadn't enjoyed her one and only experience of it more than ten years ago—but the idea of compulsion. The idea that you could be compelled to bear a child was deeply repugnant. She'd never been one for getting too exercised over the abortion debate, but Henryk's bald-faced orders brought it into tight focus. *You* will *be pregnant. Huh. And how'd you like it if I told* you *that you were going to be anally probed by aliens?* "And what's your position on this?" she asked, hoping to distract herself.

"My position?" Henryk seemed puzzled. "I don't *have* a position, my dear. I just want you to have a happy and fruitful marriage to the second heir to the throne—and to keep out of trouble. Which, thankfully, won't be a problem for a while once you're pregnant, and afterwards . . ." He looked at her penetratingly. "I think you'd make a very good mother," he said, "once you come to terms with your situation."

Not if you and everybody blackmail me into it, she

thought. *I don't take well to being forced.* "Is that the only option you see for me?"

"Truthfully, yes. It's that or, well, we're not unreasonable. You'd just go to sleep one night in your bed and not wake up in the morning. Case completed."

Miriam stared at him despite the roaring in her ears. Everything was gray for a while; finally some atavistic reflex buried deep in her spine remembered she needed to breathe, and she inhaled explosively. "Okay," she said. "I just want to make sure that I've got it straight. I go through with this—marry the imbecile, get pregnant, bear at least one child. Or I tell you to fuck off, and you kill me. Is that the whole picture?"

"No." Henryk regarded her thoughtfully for a while. "I wish it were. Unfortunately, your history suggests that you don't take well to being coerced. So additional pressure is needed. Either you go through with this, or we withdraw your mother's medication. If you don't cooperate, you will be responsible for *her* death. Because we need an heir to the royal blood who is one of us much more badly than we need you, or her, or indeed anyone else. Do you understand *now*?"

Miriam was halfway out of her chair before she knew it, and Henryk's hands were raised protectively across his face. She managed to regain her control a split second short of striking him. *That would be a mistake*, she realized coldly, through a haze of outrage. She wanted to hurt him, so badly that it was almost a physical need. "You fucking *bastard*," she spat in hochsprache. Henryk turned white. Olga had taught her those words: *bastard* was worse than *cunt* in English, much worse.

"If you were a man I'd demand satisfaction for that." Henryk backhanded her across the face almost contemptuously. Miriam staggered backward until she fell across the window seat. Henryk leaned over her: "You are an adult—it's time you behaved like one, not a spoiled brat," he spat at her, quivering with rage. She licked her lips, tasting blood. "You have a family. You have responsibilities! This foolish pursuit of independence will hurt them—worse, it may *kill* them—if you continue to indulge it. You disgust me!"

He was breathing deeply, his hands twisted around the head of his cane. Miriam felt sticky dampness on her lip: her nose was bleeding. After a moment Henryk took a step back, breathing heavily.

"I hate you," she said quietly. "I'm not going to forget this."

"I don't expect you to." He straightened up, adjusting his short cape. "I'd be disappointed in you if you did. But I'm doing this for everyone's good. Once the Queen Mother placed her youngest grandson in play . . . well, one day you'll know enough to admit I was right, although I don't ever expect you to thank me for it." He glanced at the window. "You have enough time to get ready. A coach will be waiting for you at nine. It's up to you whether you go willingly, or in leg irons."

"Did Angbard approve this scheme?" she demanded. *Would he really sacrifice Mom?* His half-sister?

Henryk nodded. His cheek twitched. "It wasn't his idea, and he doesn't like it, but he believes it is essential to bring you to heel. And he agreed that this was the one threat that you would take seriously. Good day." He turned and strode toward the door, leaving her to gape after him, slack-jawed with helpless fury.

TRANSLATED TRANSCRIPT BEGINS

CONSPIRATOR #1: "I am most unhappy about this latest development, Sudtmann."

CONSPIRATOR #2: "As am I, your royal highness, as am I." (Metallic clink.)

CONSPIRATOR #3: (Unintelligible.) "—deeply worrying?"

CONSPIRATOR #1: "Not really. *More wine, now.*" (Pause.) "That's better."

(Pause.)

CONSPIRATOR #2: "Your highness?"

CONSPIRATOR #1: (Sighs.) "It may be better to be feared than to be loved, but there is a price attached to maintaining a bloody reputation. And it seems the bill must still be honored whether the debtor be prince or pauper."

CONSPIRATOR #3: "Sir? I don't, do not—"

CONSPIRATOR #1: "He's *weak.* To be backed into the

stocks like a goat! This is the plan of the tinkers, mark my word: the poison she-snake in our bosom intends to get an heir to the throne in her grasp soon enough. And he cannot gainsay her!"

CONSPIRATOR #2: "Sir? Your brother, surely he is unsuitable—"

CONSPIRATOR #1: "Yes, but any whelp of his would be another matter! And the libels continue apace."

CONSPIRATOR #4: "The libels play into our hands, sire. For the bloodier they be, the more feared you become. And fear is currency to the wise prince."

CONSPIRATOR #1: "Yes, but it wins me nothing should my accession not meet with the approval of the court of landholders. And the court of landholders is increasingly in the grip of the tinkers. A tithe of their rent would repay a quarter of the promissory notes my father and his father before him took from the west, but does he—"

(Pause.)

(Noises.)

(Unintelligible.) "—regularity of bowels."

CONSPIRATOR #2: "I'll see to it, sir."

CONSPIRATOR #3: "A pessary of rowan. There are other subtleties to consider."

CONSPIRATOR #4: "It will be suspicious. And remember, two may keep a secret—if one of them is dead."

CONSPIRATOR #1: "Enough skulking!"

CONSPIRATOR #2: "Sir?"

CONSPIRATOR #1: "It is clearly treasonable intent that we confront in this instance. They've addled whatever is left of my father's wits, turned him against me, and once they are sure of a succession I'll doubtless meet with a convenient hunting accident. I cannot—*will* not—permit this. But once it becomes clear that the tinkers are not the force they once were, I'll be seen as the savior of the realm. *And* feared without scruple of libel: honestly, as a prince should be."

CONSPIRATOR #4: "There is a reinforced company of the Life Guards stationed across the river. We shall have to move fast."

CONSPIRATOR #1: "On the contrary, they will do as I tell

them—whose life did you think they were supposed to guard? Hah! But I am concerned about your alchemists and their expensive mud pie. Have they succeeded in killing themselves yet?"

CONSPIRATOR #4: "On the contrary. And they have enough fine powder stockpiled to blow down the wolf's lair. Not much use for the artillery, but . . ."

CONSPIRATOR #1: "We have a use for it on the stage. Arrange to have a roundup of plotters, marked for dispatch afterward—I'm sure you can arrange some witnesses, Sudtmann, guards who will swear to our instructions at the question? More in sorrow than in anger, I shall dispatch the traitors in the name of the Crown. And the kingdom will be secure against the blasted tinkers for another generation, at least."

CONSPIRATOR #3: "But your father—"

CONSPIRATOR #1: "He'll fall in with me of necessity." (Metallic noise.) "He may be weak, but he's not stupid. Once the tinkers realize the dice are cast, they will declare blood feud against the Crown. He'll have to do it. I stress, this is not a coup *against* the Crown, it is a coup *for* the Crown, to defend it from the enemies within."

CONSPIRATOR #3: "And none shall call it by any other name."

CONSPIRATOR #2: "And if the blast should fail to live up to expectations?"

CONSPIRATOR #1: "Then I shall lead the guards in an heroic attempt to rescue the palace from the rebels who appear to have seized it. Long live the king!"

CONSPIRATOR #4: "I should give the alchemists their final reward then, sir."

CONSPIRATOR #1: "Make it so, and may Sky Father have mercy on them in the afterlife, for their services to the Crown."

TRANSLATED TRANSCRIPT ENDS

15

GOING IN

Recovery from fentanyl poisoning was relatively rapid: the pain came later. They kept asking *questions*, even when he was on a drip and hallucinating. "What happened? What did he say?" All Mike could do was shake his head and mutter incoherently. Later, he made a full statement. And another. A whole goddamn committee camped by his hospital bed for an afternoon, trying to come up with an agreed timeline for the fuckup. Mike was expecting to be suspended pending investigation, but from the noises they were making it sounded like they wanted to sweep everything under the rug, pretend Matt had never existed. Maybe that was how the DOD dealt with unwelcome problems: or maybe they just didn't want to admit that they'd destabilized a willing defector. Later another committee came by to grill him about Matt's nuclear threat, but when he asked what action they were taking on it they told him he had no need to know—from which he deduced that they were taking it very seriously indeed.

It didn't matter to Mike. He was out of the loop, officially injured in the line of duty. He lay in bed for two days, numb with apathy and guilt, mind constantly circling back to worry at the same unwelcome realization. *I fucked up.* On the second day a card arrived from Nikki, an invitation to Pete's funeral. And then, just as he was graduating from depression to self-loathing, Smith dropped in.

"How are you feeling?"

"Better." Which was a lie. "Not sleeping too good."

"Yeah, well." Smith mustered a sympathetic expression that looked horribly artificial to Mike. "We need you back on duty."

"Huh?"

The colonel dragged the nearest chair over and sat down next to Mike's bed. Mike peered at him, noticing the bags under his eyes for the first time, the two-day stubble. "I'd like to be able to give you a month off, refer you for counseling, and let you recover at your own pace. Unfortunately, I can't. You were due into in-processing today and you're on the critical path for CLEANSWEEP. And your immediate backup was Pete."

"Oh." Mike was silent for a moment. "I was expecting an enquiry, you know?"

"There's *been* a board of enquiry." Smith leaned forward. "We don't have time to piss around, Mike. We had a video take on you when Source Greensleeves offed Pete and took you hostage, it turned up yesterday. Left hand didn't know what the right hand was doing, excessive compartmentalization in our security architecture, et cetera. Nobody's blaming you for what happened; if anyone gets blamed it's going to be me for sending you guys in in the first place. *But.* We're moving too fast to play the blame game right now—"

Mike gestured at the table on the other side of the bed: "Pete's funeral is tomorrow. I was planning on being there."

Smith looked worried. "Shit, our schedule puts you on a ranch in Maryland—wait, hang on, it's not like that. I'll get you to the funeral, even if I have to bend a few rules. But I really *do* need you back on duty."

Mike stared at him. "Spill it."

Smith stared right back. "Spill what?"

"*It.*" Mike crossed his arms. "This setup *stinks*. Whatever happened to your professional assets? I thought you guys majored in infiltrating hostile territory. You're the military, you go to exotic places and meet interesting people and kill them. I'm just a cop. Why do you need me so badly?"

"Hold onto that thought." Smith paused for a moment. "Look, I think you habitually overestimate what we can do. We're very good at blowing shit up, that's true. And NSA can tap every phone call on the planet, break almost any code," he added, with a trace of pride. "But . . . we're *not* good at human intelligence anymore. Not since the end of the Cold War, when most of the old HUMINT programs were shut down. You don't get promoted in Langley by learning Pashtun and going to freeze your butt off in a cave in central Asia for six years, among people who'll torture you to death in an eyeblink if they figure out who you are. The best and the brightest go into administration or electronic intelligence; the people who volunteer for spying missions and get through the training are often, bluntly speaking, nutjobs. A couple of years ago we had to fire the CIA station chief in Bonn, did you know that? One of our top guys in Germany. He'd been invoicing for a ring of informers but it turned out he was a member of an evangelical church, and what he was really doing was bankrolling a church mission. Anyway, you've got a three-month lead on anyone we could train up to do the job, and whatever your own opinion of your abilities, you are not *bad*. You've done police undercover work and stakeouts and run informers—that's about ninety percent of the skill set of a field agent. So rather than pulling one of our few competent field agents out of whatever very important job they're already doing, and *trying* to teach them hochsprache, we figured we'd take you and give you the additional ten percent of the skill set that you'll need."

A long pause. "Bullshit. What *else*?"

"What do you mean?"

"You know damn well I'm unreliable. I'm not acculturated, I still *think like a cop*, even if you're right and the job overlap is significant. I'm unreliable from a departmental point of view: I've got the wrong instincts. And this isn't a Hollywood movie where delicate operations get handed to maverick outsiders. So. What aren't you telling me?"

Smith shrugged. "I told them you'd see through it," he said, glancing at the door. Then he reached into his vest pocket and pulled out a photograph. "When did you last see this woman?"

"Who—oh. Her. What's she got to do with this?" Mike's mouth went dry.

Smith glared at him, clearly irritated. "Now *you're* the one who's playing games. You've been through the clearance process, we know what color underpants you wear, we interviewed your ex-wife, we grabbed your home phone records." He waved the photograph. "Confession is good for the soul, Mike. Level with me and I'll level with you. How well do you know this woman?"

Shit. Should have guessed they'd figure it out. "There's not much to tell." Mike struggled to drag his scattered thoughts back together. "I met her a few years ago. She's a journalist, she was doing a story about drug testing for the glossy she worked for. It worked out really well at first. Did a couple of dates, began to get serious." *How much do they want to know?* It was still a sore point for him. "Yes, we did sleep together."

"Mike. Mike." Smith shook his head. "That's not what this is about, not really, we're not the East German Stasi."

"Well, what *did* you want to know?" Mike glared at him. "She's a *journalist*, Colonel. She wasn't faking it. I picked her up at the office a couple of times. I didn't have a fucking clue she was anything else! Let me remind you that I didn't know the Clan existed, back then. None of us did. I don't think she did, either."

"I'm not—I wasn't—" For a moment Smith looked embarrassed. "Carry on. Tell me in your own words."

"It didn't work out," Mike said slowly. "We were talking about taking a vacation together. Maybe even moving in. But then something spooked her. We had a couple of rows— she's a liberal, we got bickering over some stupid shit. And then—" He shook his head. "It didn't work out."

"How long have you known she was involved with the Clan?" asked Smith.

Mike shook his head. "Not known. Wasn't sure." *But Pete was*, he realized. And what Matthias said— "Listen, it's over between us. Two, three years ago. I didn't put two and two together about the woman who Source Greensleeves kept ranting about until he waved it in my face, and even then— how many journalists called Miriam are there?"

Smith put the photograph away. Then he nodded at Mike. "How would you characterize your relationship with her?" he asked.

"Turbulent. And over." Mike reached over to the bedside stand and picked up a glass of water. "If you're thinking what I think you're thinking, it won't work."

"And maybe I'm not thinking what you think I'm thinking." Smith suddenly grinned. "Honey traps were an old Stasi trick, and they didn't work consistently—in this situation, the collateral damage from blowback if it goes wrong is too high. But can you confirm that you do—*did*—know Miriam Beckstein, journalist, last employed by *The Industry Weatherman*?"

Mike nodded.

"Well, there's your explanation! Now do you see why you're needed?"

Mike nodded warily. "What do you want me to do?"

"Well, like Dr. James told you two weeks ago, we want you to set up a spy ring in Niejwein. That hasn't changed. What *has* changed is that we now have a list of starting points for you. It's a very short list, and she's right at the top of it. If we're right—if she's a recent recruit, dragged in by her long-lost family—she may be a potential asset. As long as she's inside the Clan, that is: she's not a lot of use to us over here, except as another mule."

Mike shivered momentarily, visualizing a collar bomb around a throat he'd buried his face in. "When?" he asked.

"We know roughly where the royal palace is, in Niejwein: it overlaps with Queens. Niejwein isn't a big city, it won't be hard for you to get there with the right disguise and cover story. Which, by the way, is that you're a Clan member from the west coast. It won't stand up to scrutiny, but from what we know about Niejwein it won't come in for much unless you try and play it for real. They're pretty primitive over there. And we've got an extra edge I haven't mentioned. We captured a courier last week."

"You did?" Mike sat up.

"And his dispatches." Smith frowned at Mike. "You don't need to know the details. Anyway, it seems your girlfriend is going up in the world. She's due to be the guest of honor at a royal reception in two weeks' time, and the document taken from the courier includes what appears to be an invitation to a country cousin." Smith looked smug for a moment. "One of the things the Clan are good at is postal security—which works against them at times like this. As long as they don't know we've got couriers working for us, you're in the clear."

"Hey, are you telling me . . ."

"Yes. You're going to crash a royal garden party and make her an offer she can't refuse."

A week of twelve-hour days in a training camp on the edge of a sprawling army base couldn't prepare Mike Fleming for the experience of his first world-walk. On the contrary: he'd been led to expect a glossy high-tech send-off, and instead what he was getting looked very much like a ringside seat at an execution.

It was nearly noon. His personal trainer, who he knew only as John, had woken him at six o'clock and rushed him through breakfast. John had a halting grasp of hochsprache, but insisted Mike speak nothing else to him, playing dumb whenever Mike lapsed into English out of frustration or in search of some unmapped concept. Then he'd been taken on a tour of Facilities. A quiet woman who looked like she worked weekends in Macy's kitted him out in what they figured would pass for local costume—no cod-medieval "men in tights" nonsense, but rough woolen fabric, leggings, and an overtunic and leather boots.

Next on his itinerary was the armory. A hatchet-faced

warrant officer checked him out and told him what was what in English. "This is your sword. Nearest we've got to it is a cutlass, note the curve in the blade—forget point work. If you ever did any fencing at school, forget that too. This is strictly for edge work, German-style. Oh, and if you have to use it you're probably dead. We don't have a couple of months to work you up to competent. Luckily for you, you're also allowed one of these." He held up a nylon holster, already laden with a black automatic pistol. "Glock 20C, fifteen-round magazine, ten mill." Just like the handguns "James Morgan" had been buying and, presumptively, a standard Clan issue. "You have two spare magazines. I take it you've checked out on one." In answer to Mike's mute head shake, he swore and glared at John: "What *is* it with you folks? Are you *trying* to get him killed?"

Half an hour on the range upstairs from the armory reassured Mike marginally and seemed to mollify the armorer. He could hit things with it, strip it down, and could reload and clean it. "Next trip," said John. "We have a, a thing that flies—"

Thing that flies turned out to be John's best attempt at saying *helicopter* in hochsprache. It gave Mike a splitting headache as it thudded along in the direction of Long Island. When it landed at the Downtown Manhattan Heliport, John handed him a trenchcoat and a broad-brimmed hat. "Very funny," he snarled, still half-deafened by the rotor noise.

"Wear it." A minivan with blacked-out windows was waiting in the parking lot: funnily enough, there were no other cars present.

"Huh." Mike clambered down from the chopper and trudged across the barge to the minivan. The side door opened. Inside it, Colonel Smith was waiting for him.

"Sorry 'bout the cloak-and-dagger nonsense," Smith said unapologetically as their driver pulled out into the approach road behind another minivan. Mike glanced over his shoulder as a third van discreetly joined the convoy. "Can't take any chances."

"What? Where are we going?"

"Nearest geographical cognate we could figure." Smith

pulled back his sleeve. He was wearing something that looked like a digital watch that had swallowed a mobile phone—after a moment Mike recognized it as a GPS receiver. Smith frowned. "Doesn't work too well—too many skyscrapers."

The minivan slid through the New York traffic in fits and starts, bumper to bumper with a yellow cab that had somehow intercalated itself in the convoy. Mike lost track of where they were going after a couple of minutes and a baroque detour around some roadwork. "What's the setup?"

Smith opened a folder with red and yellow stripes along its cover. "Pay attention, you don't get to take this with you. A courier is ready to take you across to Zone Blue. You go over piggyback. In Zone Blue, we currently have a forward support team of three—Sergeant Hastert, PFC O'Neil, and PFC Icke. They'll look after you, also give the courier a bunch of crap to bring back over to us. You do *exactly* what the sergeant tells you. After you leave Zone Blue, they'll exfiltrate. Let me emphasize, there won't be anybody there. What there *will* be is a buried radio transmitter, like this." Smith pulled an egg-shaped device with a stubby aerial out of his pocket. "You dig it up, push the button, and the backup team will be alerted to come check you out for shadows. If you've got unwelcome company, they will kill it or take it prisoner—at their discretion—or leave you the fuck alone. They will not be more than an hour away from you at any time, so if they don't show up within an hour, someone's in trouble. Procedure is to revisit the zone at daily intervals for one week, then back off to once a week for a month. You also need to memorize *this*. Directions to Zone Green, which is your fallback site. There's no equipment or personnel there, so if you're captured and tortured you can't give anyone away, but if you go there you'll be observed and contacted."

Mike studied the sheet of typed directions, feeling a bead of sweat trickle down his forehead. *It's real*, he realized. *It's not some kind of elaborate joke. It's really going to happen*. Nervous dread made a hollow nest in his stomach. "The palace—" He'd seen maps of that already, a big stone pile near a small town, at one end of a road lined with slightly smaller stone piles.

"Over the page." A basic sketch map showed Zone Blue in relation to the palace. "There are complications to do with the transport protocol for this run."

"What do you mean?" Mike looked up.

"It's in the center of town. The courier may try to escape." Smith stared at him. "You're going piggyback. Hold out your hand."

"What—"

Smith snapped a bracelet shut around Mike's wrist. "Transmitter. *Very* short range. Here's the key." He handed Mike a key. "Turn clockwise to release the transmitter. Two twists anticlockwise and it will send the detonate command. If Three tries to attack you—"

"Okay." Mike stared at the thing, repelled and fascinated. "What do I do with it?"

Smith shrugged. "If it goes according to plan and Team X-ray meets you in, they hold Courier Three while you take the bracelet off and hand it to him. Then you send him back over to us and we take the necklace off and put him back in his box. If he tries to run, or attacks you, kill him." He stared at Mike. "I'm serious. If he does either of those things, he'll try to kill *you*. Wouldn't you, in his situation?"

In his situation—Mike tried to get a handle on it, but his mind kept slipping up unwelcome channels, looking into irrelevances. "Courier Three—I thought you only had two?"

"Need to know." Smith shook his head. "Look, we're there."

Manhattan wasn't just skyscrapers; old brownstones still thrived in the shadow of the tall towers. Smith waited for the other minivans to draw up, then opened the door and led Mike up the front steps of an ordinary-looking house while half a dozen men and a couple of women in the sort of business attire that yelled "cop" stood discreet guard.

The house looked ordinary enough from inside—but Smith headed straight for an unobtrusive door and into what had probably been a living room before someone ripped out the furniture, boarded up the windows, installed antiblast paneling and floodlights, and spray-painted a big *X* in the middle of the floor. Now there was something sinister about it, a cramped, dark terminus that needed only a trapdoor and a dangling rope to turn it into a place of execution. "Wait here."

Mike waited while Smith and two of his underlings bustled back out again. A minute later they returned, half-supporting and half-dragging a third man between them. He was unshaven and looked tired, bent forward with his hands cuffed tightly behind his back: his scalp had been shaved and there was a big dressing taped to one temple. As he looked around and saw Mike his eyes widened with fear. Then another of the anonymous guards stepped forward and swiftly clamped a metal collar around his throat.

"Shizz . . ." His knees sagged.

"Wait," Mike said, trying his hochsprache. "You—carry—me. Yes?" He saw the other man's eyes. The expression of terror began to fade. "Come—go—back here." Mike paused. "Does he know what the collar is?" he asked Smith, lapsing into English.

Smith nodded.

"They take"—gesture at throat—"undress, off. You run"—tap at wrist, at the bracelet Smith had put there, then finger across throat. "Understand?"

"Yes," said the prisoner. Then a gabble of words jumbled together too fast for Mike to parse.

"Slower."

Courier Three fell silent. "Not kill."

"No. You carry me."

"I carry, yes, I carry!"

The courier's head bobbed as if his neck had been replaced by loose springs. Mike tasted stomach acid, swallowed. *This isn't right. I'm supposed to capture more people, so we can use them like* this? Even a prison cell had to be better than being led to a dingy room and having a bomb clamped to your neck.

"Ready?" asked Smith.

"Yeah." Mike pointed to the *X* on the floor. "Stand here." Courier Three crouched down on the spot, legs and arms braced. Mike looked at him, momentarily perplexed. "What do I do now?" he asked.

"You sit on him," said Smith. He was holding something. "Go on."

"Okay." With some trepidation, Mike lowered himself onto Courier Three's back. The man grunted. Mike could feel his spine, the warmth of his ribs through the seat of his pants. *This is weird*, he began to think, just as Smith held something under Three's nose. Then the world changed.

Mike blinked at the darkness. Someone tapped him on the back of the head with something hard. "Say your name."

"Mike Fleming." His seat groaned and began to collapse, and he fell over sideways. "What the fuck—"

A thud was followed by a muffled groan. "Okay, wiseass, cut that out!" Light appeared, and Mike rolled over onto his back and tried to sit up.

Someone else was groaning—*Courier Three?* he wondered. "What's going on?"

"All under control, sir," drawled the man with the gun. "You just sort yourself out while we keep watch."

Mike nodded, taking stock of the situation. He was in some kind of room with no windows, a door, a dirt floor, three armed strangers, and a captured Clan courier wearing a bomb around his neck. The good news was that the desperados were pointing their guns at the courier, the door, and the ground, respectively—which left none for him. Ergo, they were friendly. "Which of you is Sergeant Hastert?" he asked.

"I am." Hastert was the one covering the ground. He grinned at Mike, an expression he'd have found deeply alarming if it wasn't for the fact that any other expression would have been infinitely worse. Courier Three groaned again. Mike realized he was clutching his head. "Dennis, keep laughing boy here covered. Mr. Fleming, you've got the remote control. If you'd care to pass it to me, we can take care of the mule until it's time for him to go home. Meanwhile, you 'n I've got some talking to do."

"Okay." Mike unlocked his bracelet with a shudder of relief and passed it to the sergeant, who leaned over Courier Three while one of the others kept his AR-15 pointed at the prisoner the whole time.

"Listen, you," said Hastert. "This here won't go off now—" He was speaking English, loudly and slowly.

"He doesn't understand," said Mike.

"Huh?"

"He doesn't speak English. He thought we were going to kill him, back in New York."

"Hmm." Hastert stared at him with pale blue eyes. "You try, then."

Mike stared at Courier Three. "You go. Soon, now, back over. Not die. Shoot if run? Yes."

The prisoner nodded slightly. Then went back to groaning quietly and clutching his head.

"Not much to look at, ain't he?" Hastert was genial.

"Let's get out of here."

Hastert opened the door and led Mike through into another bare room with a dirt floor, leaving the two other soldiers with their precious courier. There was a window in here, with wooden shutters, and Hastert switched off his flashlight. As Mike's eyes adjusted he got a good look at what the sergeant was wearing: rough woolen trousers and jerkin over another layer that bulged like a bulletproof jacket. "We stay indoors during the day," Hastert said, acknowledging his curiosity. "But this is a special occasion. Keep your voice low, by the way. It's a crowded neighborhood."

"You know where the palace is?"

"Yeah. We'll get you there. Once laughing boy has gotten over his headache and gone home."

"Huh." Mike sank down into a crouch against one wall. It was whitewashed, he noticed, but the plaster or bricks underneath it were uneven. "This the best hotel you could get?"

"You should see how they live hereabouts." Hastert shrugged. "This is the Sheraton. Let me fill you in . . ."

Mike tried to listen, but he was too tense. There were noises outside: occasional chatter, oddly slurred and almost comprehensible snatches of hochsprache. The thud of horses' hooves passed the door from time to time, followed by the creak and rattle of carts. After about an hour, the inner door opened and one of the other soldiers came out. He nodded. "All done."

Mike shifted. "What now?"

Hastert checked his watch. "One hour to go, then we move out. Jack, go dig out a couple of MREs, and you and Dennis chow down. Sir, do you know what this is?" He held up a radio transmitter, like the one Colonel Smith had shown Mike earlier.

"Yes." Mike nodded. "Radio transmitter. Right?"

"Right." Hastert looked at him thoughtfully, then reached into a shapeless-looking sack on the floor beside him and pulled out an entrenching tool. "We're going to put it in right—*here*." He buried the gadget under a thin layer of soil and tamped it down, then scattered the residue. "Think you can find it?"

Mike mentally measured the distance from the door. "Yes, I think so."

"Good. Your life depends on it." Hastert didn't smile. "Because when you get back here, we won't be around."

"I've been briefed." Mike tried not to snap. It was warm and stifling in the dirt-floored shack, and the endless waiting was getting to him.

"Yes, sir, but I didn't see you being briefed, so if you'll excuse me we'll go over it again, shall we?"

"Okay . . ." Mike swallowed. "Thanks."

The next hour passed a bit faster, which made it all the more shocking when the inner door opened and the other two men came through. "Ready when you are, boss." It was the taller one, O'Neil. Mike blinked. *Hey, all three of them are white*, he realized: a statistical anomaly, or maybe something else. *No sugar trade here means no African slave trade*. Just another logistics headache that Smith was dealing with behind his back, finding special forces troops who looked like locals.

"Let's go." Hastert stood up. "Far as the garden party, we're your bodyguard. Once you're inside, we'll split. Anything goes wrong, make for the garden gate opposite the ceremonial parade ground—I'll point it out to you."

He opened the door. It was late afternoon outside, dusty and bright and hot, but with a breeze blowing off the sea that took the edge off the heat. The shack turned out to be one of a whole row fronting a narrow dirt track: a similar row faced them. Half the doors and windows were wide open, with chickens and geese wandering in and out freely to peck in the roadside dirt. There were *people*. Ragged, skinny children, stooped women and men in colorless robes or baggy trousers. People who looked away when Hastert stared at them, hastily finding somewhere else to go, something else to do. The road was filthy, an open gutter down the middle running with sewage. "Come on," said O'Neil, behind Mike. "You're blocking the door."

Mike stepped forward, trying to project confidence. *I'm a big man*, he told himself. *I'm armed, I've got bodyguards, my clothing's new, and I'm well-fed.* He glanced up the street. Nothing on this row was straight: whoever built it hadn't heard of zoning laws, or even a straight line. A cart pulled by a couple of bored oxen, piled high with sacks, was slowly rattling toward them. Behind it, a mass of sheep bleated plaintively, spilling into doorways in a slow woolly flood. "Follow me, and try to look like you're leading," Hastert muttered.

The walk through the town seemed to take forever, although it was probably more like twenty or thirty minutes. Mike tried not to gape like a fool: sometimes it was hard. Smells and sounds assailed him. Wood smoke was alarmingly common, given that most of the houses were timbered. It almost covered up the pervasive stench of shit rising from the hot, fetid gutters. In the distance some kind of street vendor was shouting over and over again—briefly they walked past one edge of a kind of open square, cobblestoned and lined with a dizzying mess of stalls like open-walled huts. Wicker baskets full of caged chickens, scrawny and sometimes half-bald. A table covered in muddy beetroot. Rats, glimpsed out of the corner of the eye, scurrying under cover. *Is this where she's been living?* he wondered, momentarily aghast. Remembering Miriam's attitude to food hygiene and her nearly aseptic kitchen worktop, he suddenly had a moment of doubt.

Shit, who am I kidding? Mike wondered, tensed up as if he was about to go through the back door of some perp's meth lab. *This is fucking crazy! I've got barely any grasp of the language, no way out, I'm in a hostile city in a foreign country and if they get their hands on me*—a sick certainty filled him as they reached a much wider road and turned onto it—*and I'm supposed to be making contact with an ex-girlfriend who cut me dead last time I called her!* He forced himself to straighten his back and move out into the clear middle of this road (no open sewers here), then took it in. Big stone walls to either side, imposing gatehouses with solid wooden doors. No windows at ground level. Multistory piles some way behind the walls, like pocket castles. *That's what they are*, he suddenly realized. *This place is* primitive. *No police, but heaven help you if the mob catches you stealing. The rich have their own small armies. Warlords, like Afghanistan.* A moment later his earlier thought overtook the latest one, colliding in a messy train-wreck: *And Miriam's rich. She's one of the people who own these castles. What does* that *mean?*

There were more people hanging around this street, and stalls mounted on brightly colored cart wheels were selling food and (by the smell) slightly rancid beer to them. The road ended ahead, not in a junction but in a huge gate with a park beyond it. Or something that looked like a park. In the distance, a huge palace loomed above tents and crowd. Mike took a deep breath. "This it?" he asked Hastert.

"Yessir." Hastert passed him a rolled-up piece of heavy paper. "This will get you in. I'm told it's an invitation."

"And you . . . ?"

"Got to stop at the gate, sir. Turns out there's a law against bringing guards. You're allowed to bear a gentleman's arms, you're supposed to be Sieur Vincensh d'Lofstrom, but we're . . . not. See that side gate? We'll run a rotating watch on it. Any trouble, hotfoot it there and we'll provide a distraction while we guide you to Zone Green."

"Check." Mike glanced nervously at a passing bear, which watched him with oddly wise eyes until its owner jerked viciously on the chain riveted to its iron collar. "If I'm not back in four hours, you'll know I'm in trouble."

"Okay, four hours." Hastert nodded. "Good luck, sir."

"Thanks." Mike shivered. "Hope I don't need it." He took a deep breath and glanced at the guards by the gate, their bright red and yellow uniforms and eight-foot poleaxes. The other side of the gate was a confused whirl of people and sounds and smells, a Renaissance Faire with added stench and more alcohol. *Are you somewhere in there, Miriam?* he wondered. And: *What am I going to say when I find you?* Aloud: "Here goes."

16

INTERRUPTION

☙

Miriam sat alone in her bedroom for a couple of hours, thoughts spinning feverishly through her brain. *Shall I stay or shall I go?* The old Clash song held a certain resonance. *Give the bastards what they want and Iris doesn't get hurt.* The logic was sound, but the sick sense of humiliation she felt whenever she thought about it gave her a visceral urge to lash out. *Go through with it. One year, two at the most. Yes, and then what?*

They'd use artificial insemination. She'd have one or more small infants, be exhausted from the effort—it wasn't for nothing that they called it labor—and the babies would in turn be hostages to use against her. The idea of bringing up children didn't fill her with enthusiasm; she'd seen friends turned old before their days by the workload of diaper changes and late-night feedings. It was probably different for royalty: she'd have servants and wet nurses on call. But still, wasn't that a bit irresponsible? Miriam felt a twinge of conscience. She'd gotten into this mess of her own accord. It wouldn't be fair to take out her resentment on a baby who wasn't even around at the time. Or on the idiot prince. It wasn't *his* fault.

I wish I could just run away. She lay back on the bed and indulged her escape fantasies for a while, studiously not thinking about Iris. *I could go back to New Britain. I've got friends there.* But the Clan knew all about her company and her contacts. *I'd have to start from scratch. Talk to Erasmus about a new identity.* And without the Clan connection, she'd be a lot less useful to him and his friends. *What if he wanted to stay in their good books?* He could easily turn her over to Morgan. Nameless dread filled her. New Britain didn't look like a hot place to spend the rest of her days, especially starting out halfway broke in the middle of a recession while trying to hide from the Clan. Which obviously ruled out technology start-ups, businesses based on her existing know-how, anything that might draw their attention. *Iris found Morris. Who or what hope have I got?*

Her thoughts turned to Cambridge. Home. *I could go back to being a journalist*, she thought. *Yeah, right.* That would work precisely as long as it took for her to run into someone she'd interviewed at a trade conference. Or until she needed a bank account and a driving license. Post-9/11, disappearing and getting a new identity was becoming increasingly difficult—

Which leaves the feds, she thought. *I could go look up Mike. He worked for the DEA, didn't he?* Since Matthias went over the wall, something had clearly gone deeply wrong with the Clan courier networks. Matthias had blabbed to someone, and whatever he'd told them had caused the feds to start staking out safe houses. *Which means they know something about the Clan*, she told herself, with a dawning sense that she'd been far too slow on the uptake. She sat up. *I've been an idiot. If I defected, I could join the Witness Protection Program and then—*

She hit a brick wall. A series of unwelcome visions began playing themselves out in the theater of her imagination.

There went Angbard—a scheming old bastard he might be, but still her uncle—shoved into a federal penitentiary at his age. *Lock him up for life and throw away the key.* And there went Iris—*the entire family, everybody, they could arrest us all for complicity, criminal conspiracy. Right?* There went Olga. And Brill—probably for murder, in her case, come to think of it. The government would play hardball. They'd find some way to come over here and mess things up. If necessary, they'd chop up a captured world-walker's brains to figure out what made them tick, grow it in a petri dish and mount it on a bomber. Before 9/11 she wouldn't have credited it, but this was a whole different world, these were dangerous times, and the administration might do *anything* if it thought there was a serious threat to the nation.

Forget law and order: it would be all-out war. Afghanistan was a source of hard drugs and terrorism before 9/11, and look what they'd done there when the rules changed. Everybody had cheered the collapse of the Taliban—and yes, those bastards had it coming—but what about the village goatherds on the receiving end of cluster bombs, intended for sheep that looked like guerillas when viewed in infrared from thirty thousand feet? What about the women and children killed when some bastard up the road with a satellite phone decided to settle a local long-running blood feud using a B-52 bomber, by phoning the CIA and telling them that there were Al-Qaida gunmen in the next village?

I can't do that, Miriam thought despairingly. She flopped back on the bed again. *I want out, sure. But do I want out badly enough to* kill *people?* If the only person to suffer was Baron Henryk, perhaps the answer was yes—and that asshole doctor, she wouldn't mind hurting him, or at least putting him through the same level of humiliation he'd inflicted on her. But the idea of turning everyone in the Clan over to the US government cut too close to the bone. *I* am *one of them,* she realized, turning the unwelcome idea over in her mind to examine it for feel. *I don't think like them and I hate the way they work, but I can't hand my family over to the government.* Leaving aside the fact that the Clan thought *they* were a government—and had a reasonable claim to being one—that thought clarified things somewhat.

And then there's Mom.

Miriam took a deep breath. Her mood of fragile hope crashed, giving way to bleak depression. *Henryk's got me. Iris is right, I'm out of options. Unless something unexpected happens, I am stuck with this. I'll have to go through with it.* She winced. *What did they say about pregnancy? You can't worldwalk while you're expecting.* Another unwanted, hostile imposition on her freedom. *He won't need a prison cell while I'm pregnant,* she realized. *And afterward* . . . when Iris had made her escape she'd been young and healthy. By the time Miriam delivered, she'd be close to her mid-thirties.

There was a knock. Miriam pushed herself upright and stretched. The knock repeated, tentative, uncertain of itself. *Not the ferret,* she thought, walking over to the door. "Yes?" she demanded.

"Milady, we're to—" She didn't understand the rest, but she knew the tone of voice. She opened the door.

"You are, me, to dress?" Miriam managed haltingly. The two servants bobbed. "Good." She shrugged. *This is going to happen,* she realized dismally, walking toward the wardrobe as if on autopilot. *Oh well. I guess I should leave this to Helge, then. Helge?* "Now what am I to wear?" she said aloud, surprising herself with her diction.

The Clan weren't big on subtle messages. Helge let the servants lace her into an underdress, then help her into a winter gown of black silk and deep blue velvet. It had long sleeves, full skirts, and a neckline that rose to a high collar. Current fashion favored a revealing décolletage, but she was in a funereal mood. She wrapped a thick rope of pearls around her waist as a belt, and looped another around her collar. Then she checked her appearance in the mirror. Her cheek was coming up in a fine bruise where Henryk had struck her, so she picked out a black lace veil, cloak, and matching gloves from her armoire. *Let 'em wonder what kind of damaged goods they're buying,* she thought bitterly. This outfit wouldn't give much away: truthfully, it looked like Victorian mourning drag. "I'm ready to go now," she announced, entering the reception room. "Where is that, that idle—"

"Right here." The front door was open, the ferret standing beside it. "My, how mysterious."

"Is the coach ready?"

"If you would care to follow me . . ."

She managed to descend the staircase without tripping, and she clambered into the coach that was waiting. A sealed coach, with shuttered windows, she observed. *Still a prisoner, I see*, she noted ironically. *Someone doesn't trust me*.

The air was close and the evening warm. Helge fanned herself as the coach clattered and swayed out of the courtyard and across the streets. Alone in the dark, she brooded listlessly. *Is this the right thing to do?* she wondered, then felt like kicking herself: *See any alternatives, stupid?* She felt stiff and defensive, her dress constricting and hot— more like a suit of armor than a display of glamour and wealth. *I'm going to look like an idiot*, she thought, *preposterously frumpy*. A moment later: *Why should I care what they think? Bah*.

After an interminable ride—which might have been five minutes or half an hour—the roadway smoothed, wheels crunching over gravel, and the carriage halted. Someone busied themselves with the padlock outside, then a glare of setting sunlight almost blinded Helge as she squeezed through the door.

"Milady." It was—what was his name? *Some flunky of Henryk's*, she decided. He handed her down the steps to a small gaggle of guards and ladies-in-waiting and general rubberneckers. "Please allow me to welcome you to the royal household. This is Sir Rybeck, master of the royal stables. And this is—"

It was a receiving line. For *her*. Helge offered her hand as she was gently moved along it, accepting bows and courtesies and strange lips on the back of her glove, smiling fixedly and trying not to bare her teeth. Two court ladies-in-waiting picked up the train of her cloak, and four guards in the red and gold of the royal troupe walked before her with long, viciously curved axes held aloft. *This is* public, she realized with a sinking feeling. *They're saying* publicly *that I rate the respect due a member of the royal household!* Which meant there'd have to be some kind of announcement soon. Which in turn meant that they were definitely going through with it.

She'd never paid too much attention to royal etiquette in the past, and anything she'd accidentally read about in her old life was obviously inapplicable, but it was seriously intimidating. People were acting as if they were *afraid* of her. And if anyone thought her gown was unfashionable or noticed her bruised cheek under the veil, they were keeping quiet about it.

There was a huge banquet hall with several tables set up inside it, one of them on a raised platform at the back. People thronged the floor of the hall: as she entered the room there was a ripple of low-key conversation. Faces turned toward her. Butterflies flapped their wings in her stomach. "What now?" she asked her guide quietly, gripping his arm, forcing her hochsprache to perform.

"I escort you to the antechamber. You greet the king. You greet the prince. There will be drinks. Then there will be the meal." He kept his diction clear and his phrases short, speaking slowly out of deference to her poor language skills. To her surprise, Helge understood most of what he said.

"Is the duke here? Angbard? Or Baron Henryk?" she asked.

His reply was a small shrug. "Alas, matters of state keep both of them away."

"Oh." *Right.* Matters of state, it seemed, conspired to keep her from giving them a piece of her mind. She walked past the curious crowds—she smiled and nodded at enquiries, but kept her feet moving—then a door opened ahead of her. Guards grounded their axes. None of the nobles at *this* show were wearing swords. She went right ahead, then her escort stopped, a restraining hand on hers. Miriam paused, then recognized the sad-faced man in front of her. Her mind went blank. *He's wearing a crown. You're supposed to be marrying his son. What am I supposed to do now?* Helge bent her knee in a deep curtsey. "Your majesty. I am, it pleases, me to see you."

"Countess Helge. Your presence brings light to an old man's eye. Please, take our arm." He smiled hesitantly, his face wrinkling with the look of a man who'd born more cruel blows than anyone should face.

She bit her tongue and took the proffered arm gingerly. For an instant the urge to try a throw she'd learned in a self-defense class years ago taunted her. However, throwing the king over her shoulder might bear even less pleasant consequences than telling Baron Henryk to fuck off. "Yes, your majesty," she said meekly, falling back into the Helge role, and she allowed Alexis Nicholau III to lead her across the room toward the stooped figure of his mother the queen, and the equally stooped, but much huskier, figure of his son, Prince Creon.

"We understand you know why you are here?"

"I—" Helge tripped over her tongue. "I am to marry, yes?"

"That is the idea." The king frowned slightly. Then he reached up and lifted one corner of her veil. "Ah. We understand now." He let it fall. "We apologize for our curiosity. Was it serious?"

"I—" *could break Henryk's career* right now, *for good*, she realized. *But that way it wouldn't be personal, would it?* "I walk into bed-post," she said slowly. She felt a sudden stab of rage. *Let him wonder when it's going to come.* "Is nothing serious."

"Good." The frown lifted slightly. "We trust you will willingly uphold your party's side of the bargain, then?"

Bargain? What bargain? She looked at him blankly, then realized what he must be talking about. "I am the daughter of my mother."

"That is more than sufficient." He nodded. "A glass of wine for the countess," he casually dropped in the direction of a baron, who hustled away to find a waiter. "Prince Creon is a troubling responsibility," he said.

"Responsibility?" It was a new word to Helge.

"*Responsibility*," he repeated in English. "Hmm. Your tongue comes along wonderfully. Soon few will think you a half-wit like my son."

Aha. "That is the veil, the, uh, cover, for the marriage?"

"For now." The king nodded. Miriam forced herself to unkink her fingers before she burst a seam in her gloves. They were curled into claws. *They think I'm an idiot?* "It is a useful fiction."

"But your son—"

"Can speak for himself." The king smiled sadly. "Can't you, Creon?"

"Muh-marriage?" Creon lurched toward Helge curiously, stopped when he was facing her.

Helge sighed. He *wasn't* ugly, that was the bad news. If you straightened his back, wiped away the string of drool, and unwound the genetic disorder that had left him wide-open to brain damage delivered by an assassin's dose of artificial sweetener in his food when he was a child, he'd be more than presentable: he'd be a catch, like his elder brother. The thought of the older one nearly made her shudder: she caught herself in time. *Remember what they call them, the Idiot and the Pervert*, she warned herself. "Hello, Creon," she said slowly.

"Muh-marriage?" he mumbled. "I'm hungry—"

It was a miracle he was still walking. Or conscious. She pitied him. "Do you know what that means?" she asked.

"Muh, muh—" He reached out a hand and she took it. He looked at her for a moment, puzzled as if by something far beyond his understanding, and squeezed. Helge yelped. Heads turned.

"We must apologize again," said the prince's father, stepping in to detach his hand from her wrist. He did so gently, then raised an eyebrow. "You are sure this is the prize you want?" he asked quietly.

Helge licked her lips. "So my mother tells me." *And the rest of my long-lost family. At gunpoint.*

"Ah well, on your head be it, just so long as you are gentle with him. He needs protecting. It is not his fault."

"I—" *I'd like to find the assholes who did this to him and give them something in return.* "I know that." As unwilling arranged marriages went, Creon looked unlikely to be a demanding husband. *I just hope Doctor ven Hjalmar knows what he's doing*, she thought. *If he doesn't, if they expect me to* sleep *with Creon . . .* all of a sudden, test tubes and turkey basters held a remarkable allure. A glass of sparkling wine appeared in her hand and she drank it down in one mouthful, then held out her glass for a refill. "I will look after him," she promised, and was surprised to find that it came easily. *It's not his fault he's damaged goods*, she thought, then did a double take. *Is that what Henryk thinks I am?*

The king nodded. "We must circulate," he said. "At dinner, you will be seated to our left." Then he disappeared, leaving her with Creon and his discreet minders, and the Queen Mother. Which latter worthy grimaced at her horribly—or perhaps it was intended as an impish grin—and hobbled over.

"It will go well," she insisted, gripping Helge's wrist. "You are a modest young woman, I see. Good for you, Helge. You have good hips, too." She winked. "You will enjoy the fruits, if not the planting."

"Uh. Thank you," Helge said carefully, and detached herself as soon as she could, which turned out to be when Angelin's glass ran dry. She glanced around, wondering if she could find somewhere to hide. Her disguise wasn't exactly helping make her inconspicuous. Then she spotted a familiar face across the room. She slid along the wall toward his corner. His eyes slid past her at first: *What's wrong?* she wondered. Then she realized. *Oh, he doesn't recognize me.* She pushed back the veil and nodded at him, and James Lee started. "Hi," she said, reverting to English.

"Hi yourself." He eyed her up and down. "How—modest?"

"I'm supposed to be saving myself for my husband." She pulled a face. "Not that he'd notice."

"Hah. I didn't know you were married."

"I'm not. Yet. Are you?"

"Oh, absolutely not. So where's the lucky man?" He looked mildly irritated. *So, have I got your interest?* Miriam wondered idly.

"Over there." She tilted her head, then spotted the Queen Mother looking round. " 'Scuse me." She dropped her veil.

"You're not—" He looked aghast. "You're going to marry the Idiot?"

She sighed. "I wish people wouldn't call him that."

"But you—" He stopped. "You *are*. You're going to do it."

"Yes," she said tightly. "I have a shortage of alternative offers, in case you'd forgotten. A woman of my age and status needs to be grateful for what she can get"—and for her relatives refraining from poisoning her mother—"and all that."

"Ha. I'd marry you, if you asked," said Lee. There was a dangerous gleam in his eye.

"If—" She took a deep breath, constrained by the armor of her role. "I am *required* to produce royal offspring," she said bitterly.

Lee glanced away. "The traditional penalty for indiscretions with the wives of royalty is rather drastic," he murmured.

She snorted quietly. "I wasn't offering." *Yet.* "I'm not in the market." *But get back to me after I've been married to Creon for a year or two. By then, even the goats will be looking attractive.* "Listen, did you remember what I asked for?"

"Oh, this?" A twist of his hand, and a gleam of silver: a small locket on a chain slid into his palm.

Helge's breath caught. Freedom in a capsule. It was almost painful. If she took it she could desert all her responsibilities, her duty to Patricia, her impending marriage to the damaged cadet branch of the monarchy—"What do you want for it?" she asked quietly.

"From you?" Lee stared at her for a long second. "One kiss, my lady."

The spell broke. She reached out and folded his fingers around the chain. "Not now," she said gently. "You've no idea what it costs me to say that. But—"

He laid a finger on the back of her hand. "Take it now."

"Really?"

"Just say you will let me petition for my fee later, that's all I ask."

She breathed out slowly. Her knees suddenly felt like jelly. *Wow, you're a sweet-talker.* "You know you're asking for something dangerous."

"For you, no risk is too great." He smiled, challenging her to deny it.

She took another deep breath. "Yes, then."

He tilted his hand upside-down and she felt the locket and its chain pour into her gloved hand. She fumbled hastily with the buttons at her wrist, then slid the family treasure inside and refastened the sleeve. "Have you any idea what this means to me?" she asked.

"It's the key to a prison cell." He raised his wineglass. "I've been in that cell too. If I wanted to leave badly enough—"

"Oh. Oh. I see." The hell of it was, he was telling the truth: he could violate his status as a hostage anytime he felt like it—anytime he felt like restarting a war that his own family could only lose. She felt a sudden stab of empathy for him. *That's dangerous*, part of her realized. Another part of her remembered Roland, and felt betrayed. But Roland was dead, and she was still alive, and seemingly destined for a loveless marriage: why shouldn't she enjoy a discreet fling on the side? *But not now*, she rationalized. Not right under the eyes of the royal dynasty, not with half the Clan waiting outside for a grand dinner at which a betrothal would be announced. Not until after the royal wedding, and the pregnancy—her mind shied away from thinking of it as *her* pregnancy—and the birth of the heir. The heir to the throne who'd be a W* heterozygote and on whose behalf Henryk wouldn't, bless him, even *dream* of treason. After all, as the old epigram put it, *Treason doth never prosper: what's the reason? Why if it prosper, none dare call it treason.*

A bell rang, breaking through the quiet conversation. "That means dinner," said Lee, bowing slightly, then turning to slip away. "I'll see you later."

They filed out through the door, Helge on the king's arm, before an audience of hundreds of faces. She felt her knees knock. For a moment she half-panicked: then she realized nobody could see her face. "Put back your veil, my dear," the king murmured. "Your seat."

Hypnotized, she sat down on something extremely hard and unforgiving, like a slab of solid wood. *A throne*. A brassy cacophony of trumpetlike horns blatted from the sidelines as other notables stepped forward and sat down to either side of—then opposite—her. She moved her veil out of the way, then recoiled. A wizened old woman—a crone in spirit as well as age—sat across the table from her. "*You*," she accused.

"Is that any way to address your grandmother?" The old dowager looked down her nose at her. "I beg your pardon, your majesty, one needs must teach the young flower that those who stand tallest are the first to be cut down to size."

"This is *your* doing," Helge accused.

"Hardly. It's traditional." Hildegarde snorted. "Eat your sweetbreads. It's long past time you and I had a talk and cleared the air between us."

"We'd listen to her, if we were you," the king told Helge. Then he turned to speak to the elderly courtier on his right, effectively locking her out of his sphere of conversation.

"There's nothing to talk about," Helge said sullenly. She toyed with her food, some sort of meat in a glazed sugar sauce.

"Your traditional demeanor does you credit, my dear, but it doesn't deceive me. You're still looking for a way out. Let me tell you, there isn't one."

"Uh-huh." Helge took a mouthful of appetizer. It was disgustingly rich, implausible as an appetizer. Oily, too.

"Every woman in our lineage goes through this sooner or later," explained the dowager. She stabbed a piece of meat with her knife, held it to her mouth, and nibbled delicately at it with her yellowing teeth. "You're nothing special, child."

Helge stared at her, speechless with rage.

"Go on, hate me," Hildegarde said indulgently. "It goes with the territory." She'd switched to English, in deference to her granddaughter's trouble with the vernacular, but now Miriam was having trouble staying in character as Helge. "It'll go easier for you if you hate me. Go on."

"I thought you didn't believe in me." Miriam bit into the sweetbread. *Sheep's pancreas*, a part of her remembered. "Last time we met you called me a fraud."

"Allow me to concede that your mother vouched for you satisfactorily. And I will admit she is who she claims to be. Even after a third of a century of blessed peace and quiet she's hard to deny, the minx."

"She's no—"

"Yes she *is*. Don't you see that? She even fooled you."

"No she didn't."

"Yes she did." The dowager put her fork down. "She's always been the devious viper in my bosom. She brought you up to be loyal to her and her only. When she decided to come in from the cold, she sent you on ahead to test the waters. Now she's making a play for the royal succession. And she's got you thinking she's a poor, harmless victim and you're doing this to protect her, hasn't she?"

Miriam stared at Hildegarde, aghast. "That's not how it is," she said hesitantly.

Her grandmother looked at her disdainfully. "As you grow older you'll see things more clearly. You won't feel yourself changing on the inside, but the outside—ah, that's different. You've got to learn to look beneath the skin, child. The war of mother against daughters continues, and you can't simply opt out of it by imagining there to be some special truce between your mother and yourself." Servants were circulating with silver goblets of pale wine. "Ah, it's time."

"What?"

"Don't drink that yet," the dowager snapped. "It's mead," she added, "not that I'd expect you to know what that is, considering how Patricia neglected your upbringing."

Miriam flushed.

There was another blast of trumpets. Everyone downed eating-knives and looked at the raised platform expectantly.

"A toast," announced the king, raising his voice. "This evening, we have the honor to announce that our son Creon offers his hand to this lady, the Countess Helge voh Thorold d'Hjorth, in alliance of marriage. Her guardian, the Dowager Duchess Hildegarde voh Hjorth d'Hjalmar, is present this evening. My lady, what say you?"

He's not talking to me, Miriam realized, as the dowager shuffled to her feet. "Your majesty, my lord. On behalf of my family I thank you from the bottom of my heart for this offer, and I assure you that she would be delighted to accept."

Miriam stared, rosy-cheeked with embarrassment and anger, at her ancient grandmother.

"Thank you," the king said formally. "May the alliance of our lines be peaceful and fruitful." He raised his silver goblet. "To the happy couple!"

Several hundred silver goblets flashed in the light from the huge chandelier that dominated the ceiling of the room. A rumble of approval echoed like thunder across the room. Miriam looked around, her head twitching like a trapped bird.

"You can drink now," the dowager murmured, casting her voice over the racket. "You look like you need it."

"But I—do I get a chance to say anything?"

"No, for what would you say? In a decade you'll be glad you didn't speak. Just remember you owe me this opportunity to better yourself! I've worked hard for it, and if you let me down, girl—"

Incandescent with anger, Miriam glared across the table at her grandmother. "You told Henryk to threaten Mom. Didn't you?"

"What if I did?" The dowager stared at her. "Your mother's misled you quite enough already. It's time you learned how the world works. You'll understand in your time, even if you don't like it now. And one day you'll be a player yourself."

"I wouldn't cross the road to piss on you if you were on fire," Miriam retorted half-heartedly. She took a deep mouthful of the mead. It tasted of honey and broken hearts. Her cheeks itched. Overtaken by an obscure emotion, she pulled her veil down again. Tears of sorrow, tears of rage—who could tell the difference? Not her. *I'll get you*, she thought. *I* will *be different! And nothing like this will ever happen to any daughter of mine!*

The thunder of applause didn't seem to be dying down. To her left, an elderly count was looking around in puzzlement. "Eh, what-what?" The applause had a rhythmic note, almost thunderous, as if a huge crowd outside was stamping their feet in synchrony.

"That's enough," called the king. "You can stop now!" He sounded in good spirits.

People were looking around. *That's odd*, thought Miriam, puzzled. *That's not applause. If I didn't know better I'd say it was—*

There was an angry bang, with a harsh, flat note to it, then a sound, like a trillion angry bees. The windows overhead blew in, scattering shards of glass across the diners. Amidst the screams Miriam heard a harsh banging sound from outside, the noise of wheel-lock guns firing. The king turned to her. "Get under the table," he said quietly: *"Now."*

What? Miriam shuddered. Fragments of glass fell across the dining table. A jagged piece landed on the back of her hand, sticking into her glove. There was no pain at first. "What—"

Abruptly the king wasn't there anymore. The dowager was gone, too. There was another deep thud that jarred her teeth and made her ears hurt. The main door to the hall was open, and smoke came billowing in through it.

Suddenly Miriam was very afraid. She tried to slide down under the table but her voluminous skirts got in the way, trapping her in a twisted mound of fabric. There was shouting, and more banging, gunfire. From off to one side she heard the flat crackle of an automatic weapon, firing in controlled bursts. People were running around the hall, trying to get out. She tugged and managed to get untangled. *What the hell is going on?* She ducked round the back of the throne, dropping to the floor behind the raised platform. Half a dozen servants and diners cowered there, including James Lee: he opened his mouth to ask her something.

A body fell from the platform in a spray of blood. Miriam crouched, arms covering her head. There was another bang from the room at the back where the royal party had assembled for dinner, an eternity ago. Men in black—black combat fatigues, torsos bulky with flak jackets, heads weirdly misshapen with gas masks—ran past the back of the dais, two of them staying to train guns behind. "Get down!" screamed one of the men in black. Then he saw her. "Milady? This way, *now.*" *Shit, Clan security, Angbard's men,* Miriam thought, dizzy with the need for oxygen: *What's happening?*

"This way."

Miriam flinched. "Who's attacking us?"

"I don't *know*, milady—move!" She rose to a crouch, began to duck-walk along the back of the platform. "You, sir! On your feet, have you a gun?"

There was a noise behind her, so loud that she didn't hear it so much as feel it in her abdomen. Someone thumped her hard in the small of her back and she went down, trying to curl up, her spine a red-hot column of agony. She was dimly aware of Clan guards rushing past. Blood on the floor, plaster and debris pattering down from the ceiling. There was more gunfire, some shouting.

As Miriam caught her breath she began to realize that the gunfire was continuing. And the Clan guards—*there's only a handful of them*, she realized. *They may have modern weapons, but that's a* lot *of muskets out there. And cannon, by the sound of it.* Sick fear gripped her. *What's going on?*

Miriam felt sick to her stomach. The pain in her back was easing. It was bad, but not crippling: the boning of her corset had spread the force of the blow. She risked pushing herself to her knees and nothing happened. Then she looked round.

King Alexis Nicholau III sat with his legs sprawled apart, leaning against an ornamental pillar with an expression of ironic amusement on what was left of his face. About half of his brains were spread across the pillar, forming the body of an exclamation mark of which his face was the period.

"Surrender in the name of his majesty!" The hoarse voice sounded slightly desperate, as if he knew that if they didn't surrender his head was going to end up gracing the top of a pike. "Yield in the name of his majesty, King Egon!"

Miriam kilted up her dress and began to crawl rapidly across the floor, past bodies and a howling, weeping old woman she didn't recognize. She passed a servant lying on his back with blood pooling around him: evidently he hadn't understood enough English. There was more smoke now, and it smelled of wood. *I've got to get out of here*, she realized. *Fucking Egon!* His accession to the throne depended on the support of the nobility, of course. *He'll have to kill everyone here*, she realized coldly. If he thought his father had decided to sideline him in favor of his younger brother, how better to assure himself of the support of the old nobility than to liquidate the one group of noble houses who were the greatest threat to them?

She turned and crawled toward the door to the reception chamber. A bullet cracked off the tiled floor in front of her, spraying chips of marble, and she pulled back hastily.

It was twilight outside, and the chandelier was down. The soldiers outside seemed determined to bottle a couple of hundred people up inside a burning building with no fire extinguishers. People who'd come here to celebrate her betrothal. She felt a rising sense of nausea. Not that she'd wanted it herself, but this wasn't her idea of how to extract herself from the situation—

There was a side door, discreet and undecorated, behind one of the pillars. She eyed the bullet holes high up it warily, then glanced round at the dais. It was partly shielded. She crawled forward again, her shoulder blades twitching. People were screaming now, cries of alarm mingling with the awful panting gasps of the wounded.

The door opened onto darkness. Miriam stood up as she ducked inside. *Isn't this the passage they brought me through to see the queen, the first time?* she wondered. *If so, there should be another door here—*

She pushed the door carefully and it opened into another room, largely obscured by the pillar and drapes positioned to hide it from genteel attention. She froze in place, trying to look like another ornate swag of curtain. Half a dozen soldiers in what looked like stained leather overalls worn under chain-mesh surcoats were standing guard. Some held swords, but a couple were armed with modern-looking pistols. Two of them were covering a group of captives who lay facedown on the floor. "You will guard these tinkers in the rear," one of them told his companion. "If there is any risk of escape, kill them." He continued in rapid hochsprache, too fast for Miriam's ear.

Two of the guards were yanking the captives to their feet. They seemed slow to move, disoriented. The guards were brutally efficient, dragging them forward toward the main door. The talkative one bent over a lump on the floor and did something. "Hurry!" Then he followed the others out hastily.

Shit. That's got to be a bomb. As soon as he was out, Miriam scurried forward. It was green, it had shoulder straps, and there was some kind of timer on top of it. *One of Matthias's leftover toys. Why am I not surprised? If I move it*—She froze, indecisive. *What if there's a trembler switch?* She glanced at the door they'd left through. *I've got to get out of here!*

Miriam ducked into the next servant's passage, darting along it. She reached the outer receiving chamber with the floor-to-ceiling glass doors, worth a fortune in this place, just about the time the men in black were leaving it. Creeping forward, she looked out across a scene of devastation. Beyond the shattered windows lay what seemed to be half the palace guard. They lay in windrows, many of them still clutching their broken pikestaffs. Another gout of thunder and a lick of flame told her why: across the ha-ha at the end of the terrace, a group of figures moved urgently about their business, manhandling an archaic-looking cannon back into position to bear on the west wing of the palace. More isolated gunfire banged across the garden, the flat bursts of the black powder weapons sounding like a Fourth of July party.

Jesus, it's a full-scale coup, she thought, just as another distinctive figure stumbled around the front of the building.

"Creon!" she called out, forgetting that she was trying to hide. He was out in front, while she was at the back of the reception room, in near-darkness. He probably couldn't hear her anyway. Her heart lurched. *What's he doing? Who the hell knows what he thinks he's doing?* Right now he was silhouetted against the twilight outside, but in a moment—

Creon loped away from the front of the palace, toward the gun crew. He seemed to be waving his arms

"Creon! No!" she yelled. Too late. One of the pikemen beside the cannon saw him, pointed: another soldier raised an ominously modern weapon, a rifle. *They're protecting their artillery*, she realized blankly. *Probably realize there'll be no more modern ammunition when*—Creon dropped like a stone.

Miriam shook herself, like a dog awakening from a deep sleep. Appalled, she took a step forward.

Someone grabbed at her from behind. He missed her, snagging her veil instead. She spun round and lashed out hard with her left fist, all the anger and frustration of the past days boiling up inside her. Then she doubled over in pain as her assailant punched her in the stomach.

"Aushlaant' bisch—"

She gasped for air, looking up. He had a dagger in his hand, and an expression on his face that made her elbows and knees turn to jelly. *He's going to—*

The back of the man's head vanished in a red spray, and he dropped like a stone.

"*Fuck!*" she screamed, finally getting her breath back.

"Miriam?" Hesitantly. *I know that voice*, she thought dizzily. "Are you all right?"

"No," she managed to choke. Putting one arm out she tried to lever herself up.

"Let me help—"

"No." She managed to half sit up, then discovered her corset wouldn't let her. "Yes." *What the fuck are* you *doing here?* she wondered.

A hand under her left armpit gave her the support she needed. Her right hip hurt and her back and stomach felt bruised. She stood gasping for a minute, then turned and stared, too tired and bewildered to feel any surprise. He was wearing hiking gear and what looked like an army-surplus camo jacket under a merchant's robe, obviously picked up on his way here. It was simply the final ironic joke to cap a whole day of petty horrors. "Tell me what you're doing here," she said, trying to keep her tone level. *Think of the devil and he'll drop by to say hello . . .*

"I don't know," he said shakily. "It wasn't meant to go like this. I was just sent here to have a quiet chat with you, gunfights weren't on the agenda." He stared at the body and swallowed.

"The agenda," she said tartly, forcing herself to ignore it. "Are you still working for the DEA? Would this happen to be their idea?"

He cleared his throat. "I'm still a DEA agent, yes. In a manner of speaking. But there are chain-of-command issues." He shook his head. "Any idea why that guy was trying to kill you?"

She felt an inane giggle trying to work its way up her

throat, stifled it ruthlessly. *Three years older, three years wiser.* The last time she'd seen Mike she'd told him to scratch her name out of his address book. She'd been half-convinced he was a psychopath. Now she'd met some real psychopaths and she wasn't so sure. "People just sort of keep trying to kill me around here. It seems to be the national sport."

"Poor Miriam." His tone was mock-sympathetic, but when she looked at him sharply his expression was anything but light. "I was sent here to have a little talk with you. Our intelligence was that this was a royal garden party: do they always blow the place up for kicks?"

"No. But the king was supposed to be announcing a royal wedding." She glanced over her shoulder again. "The groom's brother seems to have taken exception."

"If this is their idea of a wedding party, I'd hate to see a divorce. Who're the happy couple?"

"That's the groom, over here." She nodded at the window, at the darkness and flames beyond. "This was meant to be my engagement." *That's right, oversimplify the situation for him,* she mocked herself. "Only it seems to have turned into the excuse for a coup. I reckon this bastard was one of Egon's thugs."

"I'm sorry."

"No, that's all right," she said numbly. "It was an arranged marriage. They like to deal with uppity women by marrying them off." She stared at him fixedly. *I can't believe I'm standing in a burning palace talking to Mike Fleming!* "So this is DEA business, right? I guess Matthias spilled his guts in return for protection?"

"DEA—Matthias—" He stared at her tensely. A thought struck Miriam: hoping he wouldn't notice, she clasped her hands together in front of her, trying to unobtrusively unfasten one cuff.

"How well did you know Matt?" Mike asked.

"He tried to kill me, and murdered my—" She bit her tongue. "It's a long story."

"I'll bet."

The sleeve was coming loose. She looked him in the eye. "Well?"

"Are you happy here?" he asked cautiously. "Because you don't look it . . ."

"Am I—" The laugh from hell was back, trying to get out again. "The fuck I am! If you can get me away from here—" Her voice broke. "Please, Mike! Can you?" She hated the tremor of desperation but she couldn't stop it. "I'm going mad!"

"I—I—oh shit."

Her heart fell. "What is it?"

"I." His voice was small. "I don't think I can."

"Why not?"

"We're moving in over here," he said, in a voice that sounded like he was trying to figure out how to give her some bad news. "We need world-walkers."

"You've come to the right place. Except the folks outside want them all dead; I think this could be a civil war breaking out, you know?"

"We need world-walkers." He looked troubled. "But what the organization is doing with them—I'm sorry, but I've got to ask—"

"Yes, I'm a goddamn world-walker!" Miriam vented. "That's my mother you want to blame—she ran away decades ago, then they came and fetched her back and found me. Why do you want to know?"

He seemed to relax, as if coming to a decision. "I've got to go now," he said.

"Can you put me in the Witness Protection Program?" she asked.

"I'd love to—I'd like nothing better than to get you into a safe house and a debriefing program. But listen, I'd also say—and I'm not supposed to—you should wait a bit. They're using world-walkers as mules, Miriam. I mean, the folks I work for now, big-hat federal spooks. I was supposed to try and convince you to work as an informer for us, if that's possible, but I guess this shit means it's not . . ."

"It wouldn't have worked anyway," she said heavily. "They don't trust me."

He paused. "I can't say I'm surprised. But at least I can report that. Identify you as a sympathizer, I mean. That'll make things easier later on." A longer pause. "If you can get over to Boston, do you still have my home number?"

"Damn," she said bleakly, staring at him. The old Mike would *never* have given a smuggler an even break. "It's that bad, is it?"

He nodded minutely. "There's a turf war inside the bureaucracy. Cops like me are on the down side at present. Things are really bad. Matt created quite a mess."

"I can imagine." Miriam certainly could. She'd brainstormed a lot of things a determined world-walker could do; like reach the places other terrorists couldn't reach, and escape to do it over again. If the government thought they were dealing with more than just a ring of supernatural drug smugglers . . . "Listen, this wasn't my idea." She thought about the locket. "Do you need a lift out of here?"

"No." He turned, his back to the window. "This was *supposed* to be a quick in and out, with maybe a friendly chat in the middle. I've got my own way out of this. Take my advice, Miriam: get the hell away from these people. They're pure poison. Go to ground, then phone me in a week or so and I'll see if there's a way to get you into the program without the spooks shutting you down."

"Easier said than done," she said bitterly, her shoulders shaking. *They've got me over a barrel, they've got Mom—* and this seemed to be her night for meeting unexorcised ghosts. "They've got my mom."

"Oh." He paused. "That makes things difficult, doesn't it?" He took a deep breath. "I've got to go now." He glanced at the locket she was dangling openly. "On foot, through the shit going down outside. Look, you get the hell out of here. Use your magic whatever. Call me. I won't be back for a week or so, but I'll see what I can do."

"I'll remember that."

"Right." He began to back toward the window. "Oh, and stay down until you world-walk. I don't want you getting shot by accident."

"Okay." She held her hands up.

Some impulse made her ask, "Do you still have the hots for me, Mike?"

"In your dreams."

Then he was gone. Miriam began to notice the screams and moans from the building, the pops and crackling and quiet roar of fire. And found she could smell smoke on the nighttime breeze.

I am in a burning building, she thought madly. *The king's just been shot. The man I was supposed to marry is dead, there's a bomb behind me, the crown prince is holding a coup and shooting world-walkers.* She tittered in disbelief. *And not only did James Lee make a pass, but I just ran into an ex-boyfriend who's working for the DEA.*

She raised a fist to her mouth, the locket clenched tightly inside it. *If I run away, they'll think Egon's men got me*, she thought slowly, trying to gather her scattered wits. *That means Mom's off the hook! And—*

If she could remember Mike's phone number, she could defect. There was something happening there, okay. It had already started, so it wouldn't be *her* fault if she sought sanctuary, the feds were already able to reach the Clan at home. "I could do it," she told herself. "All I have to do is world-walk away from here. Then pick up the telephone."

She glanced at the locket. "Hang on. It was James's. Is it a Lee locket, or a Clan locket?" There was a big difference: a Lee locket would take her to New Britain, where a Clan locket would dump her somewhere in downtown New York. Which would be a pain, but if she could make it overnight, get some cash, she could phone Mike in the morning. Whereas if she ended up in New London . . . "Only one way to find out."

Miriam turned round and stared at the corpse. He wore a soldier's greatcoat. She'd need that: her current outfit wasn't exactly inconspicuous anywhere. Swallowing bile, she stooped and rolled the body over. It was surprisingly heavy, but the coat wasn't fastened and she managed to keep it out of the puddle. She pulled it over her shoulders: the pockets were heavy. Mentally she flipped a die, tensing. *New York or New London*. Please *let it be New York . . .*

She stared at the knotwork by the light of a blazing palace. It was hard to concentrate on world-walking, to find the right state of mind. The sky lit up behind her for a moment, as a pulse of sound slammed through her, then cut off suddenly. She stumbled, a dull ache digging into her temples, and her stomach flipped. The rich sweetbreads came up in a rush, leaving her bent over the stone gutter. The *stone* gutter. She straightened up slowly, taking in the narrow street, the loaf-shaped paving bricks, the shuttered houses leaning over her. The piles of stinking refuse and fish guts, the broken cartwheel at one corner.

"Fuck, I don't believe this," she said, and kicked at the curbstone. "Ouch." It was New London, and her dream of easy defection shattered on the rock of reality. Frustrated, she looked around. "I could go back," she told herself faintly. "Or not . . ." She'd run into the Clan again, and she might not be able to get away. With Creon dead, and the US military able to invade the Gruinmarkt, Henryk might do anything: going back was far too dangerous to contemplate. *It'd be much harder to steal a Clan locket and run for New York, wouldn't it? Damn, I've got to find Erasmus . . .*

There was a chink of metal on stone, from about twenty yards up the alleyway.

A chuckle.

"Well, lookee here! And what's a fine girl like her doing in a place like this?"

Miriam's stomach lurched again. *Not only am I in New London instead of New York*, she realized, *I'm in the bad part of town.*

There was another chuckle. "Let's ask her, why don't we?" And the bad part of town had noticed her.

Turn the page for a preview of
BOOK FOUR OF THE MERCHANT PRINCES

THE
MERCHANT'S
WAR

(0-7653-1671-4)

CHARLES STROSS

Available now from Tor

AFTER THE WEDDING PARTY

The wreckage still smoldered in the wan dawn light, sending a column of grayish-white smoke spiraling into the misty sky above Niejwein. Two mounted men surveyed it from a vantage point beside the palace gatehouse.

"What a mess."

"Unavoidable, I think. The best laid plans . . . have they found his majesty yet, your grace?"

The first speaker shrugged. His horse shuffled, blowing out noisily: the smell of smoke, or possibly the bodies, was making it nervous. "If he was inside the great hall we might never find identifiable remains. That could be a problem: I believe the blast must have far exceeded the plotters' intent. The soldiers found the Idiot, though—what was left of him. Near chopped in half by the rebels' guns."

It was not a cold morning, and the second speaker wore a

heavy riding coat: nevertheless he shivered. "If these are the spells the witch families play with, then I think we may conclude that his presumptive majesty struck not a moment too soon. The tinkers have become too accustomed to having the Crown at their convenience. This could well be our best opportunity to break their grip before they bring damnation to us all."

The first speaker stroked his beard. "That is the direction of my thoughts." He looked pensive. "I think it behooves us to offer our condolences and our support in his hour of need to his majesty; a little bird tells me that he is of like mind. Then we should look to our own security. His Lordship of Greifhalt has a most efficient levy which I think will prove sufficient to our immediate needs, and for the honor of his grandfather he has to come to our aid. We can count on Lyssa, too, and Sudtmann. For your part . . . ?"

"Count me among your party, your grace. I think I can contribute—" he paused, thinking "—two hundred? Yes, two hundred of horse certainly, and perhaps more once I've seen to the borders."

"That will be helpful, Otto. The more you can send, the better—as long as you do not neglect the essentials. We cannot afford to feed the scavengers, of whichever kind." The first speaker shook his head again, looking at the smoking rubble. Stooped figures picked their way through it, inspecting the battlefield for identifiable bodies, their movements as jerky as carrion birds. "But first, an appropriate demonstration of our loyalty is called for."

The Duke of Innsford nudged his horse forward; his companion, Otto, Baron Neuhalle, followed, and behind him—at a discreet distance—the duke's personal company followed suit. The scale of destruction only became apparent as Innsford rode down the slope towards what had been the Summer Palace of Niejwein. "It really does appear to have been visited by a dragon," he commented, keeping Neuhalle in view. "I can see why that story is spreading. . . ."

"Oh yes. And it came to dinner with his late majesty and half the witch-families' heads of household at his table for the feast," Neuhalle agreed. "They'll draw the right conclusion. But what a mess." He gestured at the wreckage. "Rebuilding the palace will take years, once the immediate task of ensuring that his majesty's reign is long and untroubled by tinkers and demon-traffickers is completed. And I do not believe that will be easy. The old fox will move fast—"

Neuhalle broke off, composing his face in an expression of attentive politeness as he reined in his horse. "Otto Neuhalle, to pay his respects to his majesty," he called.

"Advance and be recognized." Neuhalle nudged his horse forward towards the guards officer supervising the salvage attempt. "Ah, my lord. If you would care to dismount, I will escort you to the royal party at once."

"Certainly." Neuhalle bowed his head and climbed heavily down, handing the reins to his secretary. "I have the honor of accompanying his grace, the Duke of Innsford. By your leave . . . ?"

The guards officer—a hetman, from his livery—looked past him, his eyes widening. "Your Grace! Please accept my most humble apologies for the poor state of our hospitality." He bowed as elaborately as any courtier, his expression guarded as a merchant in the company of thieves: clearly he understood the political implications of a visit from the duke. "I shall request an audience at once."

"That will be satisfactory," Innsford agreed, condescending to grace the earth with his boot heels. "I trust the work proceeds apace?"

"Indeed." A lance of royal life guards came to attention behind the hetman, at the barked order of their sergeant: "'tis a grim business, though. If you would care to follow me?"

"Yes," said Innsford.

Neuhalle followed his patron and the hetman, ignoring the soldiers who walked to either side of him as if they were ghosts. "His majesty—the former prince, I mean—I trust he is well?"

"Yes, indeed." The hetman seemed disinclined to give much away.

"And is there any announcement of the blame for this outrage?" asked Innsford.

"Oh, yes." The hetman glanced over his shoulder nervously, as if trying to judge how much he could disclose. "His majesty is most certain of their identity."

Neuhalle's pulse raced. "We came to assure his majesty of our complete loyalty to his cause." Innsford cast him a fishy glance, but did not contradict him. "He can rely on our support in the face of this atrocious treason." Although the question of whose treason had flattened the palace was an interesting one, it was nothing like as interesting to Neuhalle as the question of who the former crown prince was going to blame for it—for the explosion that had killed his father. After all, he couldn't admit to having done it himself, could he?

They rounded the walls of the west wing—still standing in the morning light, although the roof of the Queen's Ballroom had fallen in behind it—and passed a small huddle of life guards bearing imported repeating pistols at their belts. A white campaign pavilion squatted like a puffball on the lawn next to the wreckage of the west wing kitchens, and more soldiers marched around it in small groups or worked feverishly on a timber frame that was going up beside it. "Please, I beg you, wait here a while."

Innsford paused, leaning on his cane as if tired: Neuhalle moved closer to him, continuing the pretense that their escorts were as transparent as air while the hetman hurried towards the big tent, his progress punctuated interminably as he was passed from sentry to sentry. The guards were clearly taking no chances with their new monarch's life. "A bad night for the kingdom," he remarked quietly. "Long live the king."

"Indeed." Innsford looked almost amused. "And may his reign be long and peaceful." It was the right thing to say under the circumstances, indeed the only thing to say—their escort looked remarkably twitchy, in the shadow of the ruined palace—but Neuhalle had to force himself not to wince. The chances that King Egon's reign would be peaceful were slim, at best.

They didn't have long to reflect on the new order in peace. The guards hetman came loping back across the turf: "His

grace the duke of Niejwein awaits you and bids me say that
his majesty is in conference right now, but will see you
presently," he managed, a long speech by his standards.
"Come this way."

The big pavilion was set up for the prince's guests: royal
companions and master of hounds at one side, and smaller
rooms for the royal functions at the other. The middle was
given over to an open space. The duke of Niejwein sat on a
plain camp stool in the middle of the open area, surrounded
by an ever-changing swarm of attendants: a thin-faced man
of early middle years, he was, as Innsford might have remarked, *one of us*—a scion of the old nobility, the first fifty
families whose longships had cleaved the Atlantic waves
four centuries ago to stake their claims to the wild forested
hills of the western lands. He was no friend of the merchant
princes, the tinker nobles with their vast wealth and strange
fashions, who over the past century had spread across the social map of the Gruinmarkt like a fungal blight across the
bark of an ancient beech tree. Neuhalle felt a surge of optimism as he set eyes on the duke. "Your Grace." He bowed,
while his patron nodded and clasped hands with his peer.

"Be welcome, your Grace. I had hoped to see you here.
Rise, Otto. You are both welcome in this time of sorrow. I
trust you have been appraised of the situation?" Niejwein's
left eyebrow levered itself painfully upwards.

"In outline," Innsford conceded. "Otto was entertaining
me in Oestgate when the courier reached us. We came at
once." They had ridden since an hour before dawn from
thirty miles down the coast, nearly killing half a dozen
mounts with their urgency. "Gunpowder and treason." His
lips quirked. "I scarcely credited it until I saw the wreckage."

"His majesty blames the tinkers for bringing this down
upon our heads," Niejwein said bluntly.

"A falling-out among thieves, perhaps?" Otto offered
hopefully.

"Something like that." Niejwein nodded, a secretive expression on his face. "His majesty is most keen to inquire of
the surviving tinkers the reason why they slew his father us-

ing such vile tools. Indeed, he views it as a matter of over-whelming urgency to purge the body of the kingdom of their witchery."

"How many of the tinkers survived?" asked Innsford.

"Oh, most of them. Details are still emerging. But beside the death of his majesty's father and his majesty's younger brother—" Otto started at that point "—it appears that his majesty is the only surviving heir for the time being." Niejwein nodded to himself. "The queen mother is missing. Of the tinkers, the heads of three of their families were present, some eighteen nobles in total, including the bitch they planned to whelp by the Idiot—" Otto started again, then contained himself "—and sixty sundry gentles of other houses. The tinkers not being without allies."

"But the main company of those families are untouched," Innsford stated.

"For the time being." Niejwein's cheek twitched. *Has he the palsy?* Otto wondered. "As I said, his majesty—" Niejwein stopped and rose to his feet, turning to face one of the side panels. A moment later he dropped to one knee: Otto scrambled to follow suit.

"Rise, gentlemen." Otto allowed himself to look up at his new monarch. The Pervert—*no, forget you ever heard that name, on pain of your neck*, he told himself—was every inch a prince: tall, hale of limb, fair of face, with a regal bearing and a knowing gleam in his eye. Otto, Baron Neuhalle, had known Egon since he was barely crawling. And he was absolutely terrified of him.

"Sire." Innsford looked suitably grave. "I came as soon as I heard the news, to pledge myself to you anew and offer whatever aid you desire in your time of need." Not grief, Otto noted.

Prince Egon—no, King Egon—smiled. "We appreciate the thought, and we thank your grace for your thoughtfulness. Your inclination to avoid any little misunderstandings is most creditable."

"Sire." Innsford nodded, suppressing any sign of unease.

Egon turned to Niejwein. "Is there any word of that jumped-up horse thief Lofstrom?" he asked off-handedly.

Neuhalle kept his face still: to talk of Angbard, Duke Lofstrom, so crudely meant that the wind was blowing in exactly the direction Innsford had predicted. But then, it wasn't
hard to guess that the new monarch—who had hated his
grandmother and never seen eye-to-eye with his father—
would react viciously towards the single biggest threat to his
authority over the kingdom.

"No word as yet, sire." Niejwein paused. "I have sent out
couriers," he added. "As soon as he is located he will be in-
vited to present an explanation to you."

"And of my somewhat-absent chief of intelligence?"

"Nor him, sire. He was leading the party of the tinkers at
the past evening's reception, though. I believe he may still be
around here."

"Find proof of his death." Egon's tone was uncompromis-
ing. "Bring it to me, or bring *him*. And the same for the rest
of the upstarts. I want them all rounded up and brought to
the capital."

"Sire. If they resist . . . ?"

Egon glanced at Innsford. "Let us speak bluntly. The tinker vermin are as rich a target as they are a tough one, but
they are not invulnerable and I *will* cut them down to size.
Through magic and conspiracy, and by taking advantage of
the good will of my forefathers, they've grown like a canker
in my father's kingdom. But I intend to put a stop to them.
One tenth of theirs, your grace, will be yours if you serve me
well. Another tenth for our good servant Niejwein here. The
rest to be apportioned appropriately, between the Crown and
its honest servants. Who will of course want to summon
their families to attend the forthcoming coronation, and to
take advantage of the security provided for them by the
Royal Life Guards in this time of crisis."

Neuhalle shrank inwardly, aghast. *He wants hostages of
us?* He found himself nodding involuntarily. To do aught
else would be to brand himself as a rebel, and it seemed that
Egon had no intention of being the bluntest scythe in the
royal barn: but to start a reign with such an unambiguous
display of mistrust boded ill for the future.

"We are your obedient servants," Innsford assured him.

"Good!" Egon smiled broadly. "I look forward to seeing your lady wife in the next week or two, before the campaign begins."

"Campaign—" Neuhalle bit his tongue, but the prince's eyes had already turned to him. And the prince was smiling prettily, as if all the fires of Hell didn't burn in the imagination concealed by that golden boy's face.

"Why, certainly there shall be a campaign," Egon assured him, beaming widely. "There will be no room for sedition in our reign! We shall raise the nobility to its traditional status again, reasserting those values that have run thin in the blood of recent years." He winked. "And to rid the kingdom of the proliferation of witches that have corrupted it is but one part of that program." He gestured idly at the wooden framework taking place on the lawn outside the pavilion. "It'll make for a good show at the coronation, eh?"

Neuhalle stared. What he had thought to be the framework of a temporary palace was, when seen from this angle, the platform and scaffold of a gallows scaled to hang at least a dozen at a time. "I'm sure your coronation will be a great day, sire," he murmured. "Absolutely, a day to remember."